CLOUD CUCKOO LAND

CLOUD CUCKOO LAND

STEVEN SIVELL

Ziji

Published by Ziji Publishing

Distributed by Turnaround Distribution Services Ltd.
Telephone 020 8829 3000

ISBN-13: 978-0-9554051-0-5

Printed by Creative Print and Design, Wales..

For Flore, Ondine, and Anton.

CHAPTER ONE

His big hands are wrapped around a foam coffee cup, his fair hair hangs across his forehead and his round face is aimed vaguely southwards.

He looks like some kind of out-of-work Viking, in need of a break. Early afternoon light pours in through the steamed-up windows. On the other side of the glass the vague, static shapes of buildings across the street can be made out. A few soft-focus people pass, galloping and limping.

Students arrive in the canteen. They mooch and shuffle along the service counter. They pick up their hot drinks and transfer a few vouchers from Velcro trouser pockets into the tea-lady's hand. Then they settle on the orange plastic stools and light hand-rolled cigarettes. They have that air of professional fatigue about them, a fatigue brought on by stringing together the late nights. They sit there in random teams, like preoccupied athletes at rest on the bench, in between turns at the high jump or the vaulting horse.

Leonard finished his coffee, picked up his bag and left the humid warmth of the canteen. Outside, he pulled on his blue and red winter coat, which was quilted horizontally across the body and arms. It must have been a down-filled coat because a few, spidery white feathers inched their way out of its worn seams. It was a bulky coat, the sort someone who worked outdoors would wear, someone like a baggage handler at an arctic airport.

He walked a few blocks to the city centre, following signs that pointed to the 'Administration District'. He walked in the middle of the road as there was hardly any traffic and because the pavements were cluttered with litter. Queuing in amongst the stacked rubbish, were long, orderly lines of people. They carried sacks and buckets, and when Leonard drew level with the head of the line, he saw that what they were waiting for, was food and water.

He passed through the empty shopping precinct, where the shop windows had been tagged with white-wash. The words 'Ruptured stock' and 'Closing down for good sale' had been sloshed across laminated glass, with six-inch paint brushes.

Ahead, where several major roads met, there was a messy junction, a roundabout, flyover and subway. He crossed the four-lane thoroughfare by ducking into the stinking subway. There were A to E exits underground, ramps and stairs which made him lose his sense of direction and then brought him back up to the surface again. He trudged up the wheelchair ramp and found himself standing in front of bus-depot architecture: a red brick building, grey-mortared together to form the four floors of the administration complex.

Leonard entered by a revolving door and stood alone on polished granite. The double-height space had labelled corridors leading away from the reception area. He approached the pale figure who manned a marble-topped desk.

'Hello, I'm…'

The clerk held his hand up in order to silence Leonard. He then pointed to the corridor marked 'Interview Rooms' and said, 'Move your arse, sir. You're late.'

Leonard jogged along the corridor. He passed windows which looked back onto an unbroken stream of cars circling round the roundabout and passing over the flyover. His footfalls caused short, dry echoes. His long shadow was thrown forward and to the left, broken in two like a stick of firewood in the right angle made by the wall and the floor.

He found the door to the Interview Room. He knocked and took off his coat, gathering it into his chest with a rolling-folding action, which squeezed two wispy feathers into the air. Leonard watched as they floated slowly toward the ground, almost reaching the floor before they were whipped up again in the vacuum created by the opening door.

He was shown into a large, oak-panelled room, which had a tiered gallery of seats up at mezzanine level, full of people gazing down. Leonard crossed the room towards one of two empty chairs placed opposite each other. He thought it an overly theatrical set up and he felt utterly exposed before the general public. When he sat down, the people in the gallery began to whisper softly to each other. They cleared their throats and shifted in their seats.

There's always an audience, isn't there? Silver-haired and respectfully honed into men and women of reason. These people were no doubt the descendants of the drunkards and the toothless hags who hung around the guillotine basket. Leonard had read somewhere that those decapitated heads could remain conscious for several seconds after separation from the body. He wondered what such a head might have to say in those seconds, given that the Duke or Duchess had enough throat left to say anything at all? 'That fucking hurt!' probably.

Leonard sat and stared at the other empty chair. There was such a projection of personality sitting there opposite him that he decided to close his eyes and think positive thoughts. He was determined to do well, although the question he had for himself was difficult. It was, 'How do you do interviews?' Do you find out what they want to hear and regurgitate it? Or do you go in with your own entirely new way of looking at things? Leonard was not at all sure he knew. He felt like a remote controlled aeroplane which had flown out of range of its controlling mechanism. He was on his own now (when wasn't he?) and he would have to rise to the occasion and make his case.

Fluorescent green strip-lights buzzed high above his head and a pale, bluer light shone in through the windows. In one corner of the interview room, a fifty-year-old woman in a grey woollen suit sat behind a typewriter. She was on standby, the court recorder: ready to take down anything and everything Leonard might have to say.

Eventually the door opened and an old man entered, a tall, skinny old man with a candyfloss mane of white hair. He was wearing loose sportswear and he hobbled into the room with the aid of a walking stick and thick-heeled, jazzy trainers which took the spinal compression out of his steps. There had been a fair amount of cosmetic tinkering to his appearance, tints of bottled sun and whitened teeth. He sat down in the waiting chair and there was a short, silent pause during which time Leonard felt rifled through by the old man's eyes, optically frisked. Then quite suddenly the words started spilling from the old man's gob-hole.

'Right! I expect you know the form, Mr er...' (he referred to a list of names he was holding). 'Gopaul. I'll remind you that places on the survival programme are very limited. So, can you tell me why you are here? Be concise, state your case. Just explain why, of all the people on this God-forsaken planet, I should consider you eligible. Why you, over and above any-bloody-body else!'

That's all he said; he then settled back into his swivelling chair, jangled a loose-fitting gold wristwatch around his forearm and waited. Leonard looked around the room, brushed his hair off his forehead and tried, as honestly as he could, to imagine, why on earth.

'Well, now that you have asked me so directly, I find it difficult to explain. I don't feel particularly special or particularly worthy.'

There was a pause while Leonard adjusted his sitting position and thought about how to continue. The old man piped up.

'Have you not read any of the advisory material?'

'No. I didn't know there was any.'

Another awkward pause.

A cough was lobbed out of the gallery and the old man spoke again.

'You are, of course, free to leave without further explanation. It makes no difference to us at all.'

'No, no, I want to explain. I've come a long way.'

'Do go on, then. Time waits, as they say, for no man and we've a lot of people to get through this afternoon.'

Leonard leaned forward and rested his elbows on his knees.

'Well, to be honest, as a child I can remember that I was constantly moving, upturning every stick and stone and running on to the next. I explored every new object and sensation, I was like a kind of magnifying glass focused on the wonderful. But when I try to look closely at the world these days, my breath seems to condense on the glass and I am no longer able to see. And I used to be able to see so clearly; the green veins of a leaf revealed in the sunlight and after a rain shower, the smell of the dampened dust and the perfect limpid clarity of raindrops hanging from the lowest points of everything. I don't recall exactly when all of this stopped, but I have somehow left this facility behind me, locked into my childhood.

'I was not reckless as a young boy and I know that I did not misspend my youth, because when I arrived in my adulthood, I still had all the money that I should have squandered in my pocket. I have not really misbehaved as a grown man, either. But I do feel that I have somehow failed, somehow missed the point. At the very least, I have lost the plot. And here I am now, standing before you, thoroughly confused and, I suppose, what I am looking for, what I need, is the chance to put things straight, the chance to start over again.'

The old man rubbed his chin, nodded and pursed his lips.

'Is that it? I mean, is this supposed to be relevant?'

Leonard shrugged.

'Look, are you in the right room, Gopaul? Do you know what we are doing here?'

'Yes, of course, survival selection.'

'But what do you have to offer us? What services can you provide? What good are you to anyone?'

Leonard felt like he was right out on a limb, which was about to break.

'I... I don't know.'

'Good Lord, where do we get them!'

The old man stood, walked slowly and deliberately, like a wading bird picking its way through shallow water. He stopped beside his typist and checked the notes, then he wandered back and offered his hand for Leonard to shake.

'Thank you for coming to see us, Leonard. Now, please leave and stop wasting everybody's time.'

Leonard put his jacket on, smiled, glanced at the faces in the gallery and left the room.

He set off back down the polished corridors again, but before he could get clear of the building, just in front of the revolving glass doors, he was waved down by the clerk and ushered towards the reception desk.

'Perhaps you have not been told, but did you know that you are actually forbidden to leave the city until decisions have been made?'

'Yes, I know, but I didn't do too well back there.'

'I'm not interested in that, sir. You will be notified of the results, but you will have to leave your passport with us.'

'If you insist.'

Leonard took his passport out of his jacket pocket and handed it over.

'Thank you. And just a general warning, sir: do be careful out there. They are a nasty bunch, a desperate lot!'

'I'll bear that in mind.'

One laminated glass rotation put Leonard outside on the pavement. He sucked in some fresh air, eyed the sky for rain. He hoped the old man was in some way able to see what he'd been getting at. Who could say what sort of person they were looking for? Now he would have to take his chances and wait like everybody else, wait in a city full of hopefuls, each with that sharp-eyed sense of competition oozing from their skin. He was miles from home, in a city filled with strangers. He'd travelled a long way to get here, several hundred miles by train and bus, and what he had to do now was find his hotel.

This had not always been a city of strangers, but it had quickly become a kind of dormitory town, a place where four-storey houses had been cut to bits and boxed off with plasterboard to form tiny bed and breakfast rooms for the rising population.

He passed a newsagents' with a bold headline black-waxed onto a paper stand. It read: KILLER BLOND SEX MANIAC STILL AT LARGE!

The sub-headline read: OIL PRODUCTION GRINDS TO A HALT.

Both stories intrigued him so he took a copy and tucked it into his bag.

He had an address in his pocket, his only piece of inside information, hand-written on a folded scrap of paper, given to him by his friend Jerry, who had been to the city in the spring. He had Jerry's map too, unreadable in the worn out folds but with useful places ringed in red pen. Leonard followed the map toward a place which Jerry had circled more times than the rest and written 'pucker nosh' in the middle of the circle.

When the restaurant came into view, Leonard realised how hungry he was. There were a few tables set up outside but it was October now and the temperature had dropped sharply through the afternoon. Leonard stepped inside onto the polished boards, dropped his bag beside the bar and noted the gleaming white table-linen and church candles. He worried that it was way past lunch and too early for an evening meal, but it was busy enough, with a calming background noise of cutlery scraping china. He sat down facing the door and a waitress dropped an origami menu onto the table as she passed.

The thing was, even in that swift dropping gesture, there was some anomaly, her feminine swiftness was over-acted and he was sure that this waitress was, in fact, a waiter.

Leonard began to scan the menu.

'Excuse me, couldn't help noticing.'

Leonard lowered the menu.

'Couldn't help noticing?'

'The knot in your coat. It's one of mine!'

'What?'

'Do you mind if I pull up a chair?'

Leonard shook his head.

'No, I don't mind.'

He had black eyes, this man, and a bottomless gaze. His checked shirt was uniquely colourful; it looked as if he had drawn the pattern on himself with felt pens and steel rulers. This man leant forward over the candle and with squinted eyes drew on a cigarette until it was alight. He held out his hand for Leonard to shake.

'Ian.'

'Leonard.'

'Pleased to meet you.'

'And I you.'

Ian lifted a carafe of water and poured some into a glass, then fished a bottle of pills from his inside pocked and twisted off the top. He tapped a couple into his hand and swilled them down.

'So, how are we going to do this?'

'I don't follow.'

Ian pointed at the drawstring of Leonard's coat.

'Half-hitch, see. May I?'

Leonard shrugged.

Ian reached forward and examined the knot.

'Yes, it's like I thought.'

'What is?'

'Look at the way you've tied these cords.'

'What of it?'

'Well, the knot is one of mine!'

'What are you talking about, "yours"?'

'I own the copyright on every major knot in common use; the bends, the loops and slings, the twists and, of course, the hitches.'

'But I've been tying this stupid knot all my life, since I was a child.'

'Well, that's really very honest of you. I don't really back-date and the rate on that knot is reasonable. Just a small charge this time, then.'

'But I haven't got any foreign currency cashed in yet!'

Ian smiled.

'Oh dear, you are a freshman. There's no currency here, Leonard, no cash changes hands at all. The whole place operates on a system of barter and credit note, like I.O.U's. You'll learn soon enough, you juggle them, swap them, beg, borrow or steal them. Like for my knot here, you give me a credit note and I'll pay for my meal with it.'

'But where do I get a credit note?'

'Ah, well, see that's the same old same old, isn't it!'

'What?'

'Problem. That's the cash part of the sums, and as always there's two solutions. You've either got to earn it same as anywhere else. In which case, you'd better start offering your services. What can you do?'

Leonard hesitated.

'Or you borrow.'

'Borrow from who?'

'From you, from yourself, your future. It's a credit note, see! You write one out and that's it, you've paid. That is, you've promised a piece of your future to whoever calls in the note, see?'

'Ah, but…?'

'Never mind, you'll think of something.'

He sat back, Ian did, and puffed hard on his cigarette. The waitress passed again, then turned and confronted him.

'Oh no, there's no smoking in here.'

'No smoking? All right, darling, you're the boss.'

Ian pulled a light canvas sack out from beneath the table. He fished his hand into it and brought out a length of rope twisted into a knot. It was tagged with a string and card labelled, 'Half Hitch'. He took another look at the knot tied in the drawstring of Leonard's jacket.

'It's definitely one of mine, I'm afraid.'

He placed the sample knot in between Leonard's knife and fork.

'Bit hard to swallow, I know, but there it is all the same. Take a look, she's a beauty. I found out nobody owned the international copyrights a few years ago. So I bought the lot.'

Leonard picked up the knot.

Ian handed over his business card, which backed up what he'd been saying: 'Ian Marble, knots, shirts and fuel grade diesel oil'. Leonard examined the knot and label again, with its little 'c' inside a larger circle.

'Copyright! You can pay per tie or a one-off licence fee for a fixed tying period.'

Ian puffed at his cigarette; Leonard looked bewildered.

The waitress passed again.

'Look, I said no fucking smoking!'

'OK, OK, don't get your knickers in a twist. I'm going now, anyway.'

Ian raised his voice so it was loud enough for the whole restaurant to hear.

'Mind what you order, it's extremely expensive here. It's the bloody import-export gangsters trading black market because of the high border tariffs.'

'You know the waitress?'

'I don't, no.'

'She's a he, right?'

'I'm not blind, Leonard. Can I call you Leo?'

'If you like.'

'Good. Of course she's a he. It's a great thing in life, don't you think? To achieve what you set out to achieve, whatever it is? Can you imagine the busting great big thrill this chick-with-dick gets when he is mistaken for a woman?'

'Yes but…'

'So, where are you staying, Leo?'

'I don't know yet, maybe the Mirabelle.'

'Oh dear no, not exactly the best inn in town, that's for sure. I wish you good luck, although there is probably not enough luck in the whole world to protect you from the Mirabelle. Never mind, it's too late now!'

Ian stood. He handed Leonard a slip of paper stamped with red ink which read, 'Ian Marble Knots, Half-Hitch, unlimited tie certification.'

'There you go, I'm feeling generous this evening. See you around.'

Leonard watched Ian stroll out through the door, watched him lean on an aluminium beer barrel and finish his cigarette with one side of his face lit by the last of the day's sunlight. The exhaled smoke rose in a plume of gold above his head, he flicked the butt into the kerb and kicked off up the high street.

The waitress came marching back to Leonard's table.

'Ready to order?'

'Well, how much is the Bethany Omelette with Anatolian vegetables?'

'That works out at two hours, miscellaneous, manual labour.'

'What about the Stuffed Ichthys with Fayyum rice?'

'A night shift.'

'Zimrah compote?'

'Two van deliveries, multidrop!'

Leonard refolded the menu.

'I don't have a van. It's all pretty expensive.'

'What do you expect, we are practically living under martial law!'

'Well, I'm not that hungry.'

'Not yet, you're not.'

Leonard stood. The waitress raised an eyebrow and sprung her hip. Leonard left the restaurant.

He found himself in lively streets, unusually European streets, with lit shop windows and passers-by stopping and looking in at the goods on display. Maybe the Spanish came here in the past, blown off course into the North Sea and shipwrecked; maybe boatloads of stray refugees fleeing some inquisition, because the place felt influenced by Spain, there was something in the architecture, in the iron-work balconies. On these balconies were washing lines with dangling clothes and caged yellow birds hanging in domed metal frames. Guitar music was spilling out onto the streets. Heart-felt music it was, with strangled flugelhorn solos and a fretless bass playing underneath African drums. Leonard stopped to listen; he stood in the doorway of a tavern, ignoring the bar-top TV. A female shape pushed through the standing crowd wearing red, all red, low at the neck and long right down to her ankles, split so she could walk. Black hair with loose curls, the kind of curls which wrap around your finger tips, looping over and under the knuckles. Her hair framed her face, a face already smiling because she knew the God-given value of beauty, how at every new introduction she had this unearned upper hand.

She stopped just one step before physical contact with Leonard, she put her hands on her hips and looked straight in, right in until his stomach kind of lurched. That must be the famous butterflies, and it shocked him a bit, a childish phenomena happening right there in his own stomach.

'Hello, what's your name, then?'

'Leonard.'

'What can I get you then, Leonard?'

'A beer, please.'

She turned on her heel, lifted the flip-up lid of the bar top, stepped out of bounds and poured his beer.

'Can you tell me what this music is?'

She put his glass down on a small round tissue stamped with a logo.

'It's called elephant music, psychic elephant music. Like it?'

'I've never heard anything like it.'

'Here!'

She pushed the beer towards him.

'How do I pay? I mean, what do I owe?'

She raised a black eyebrow. Then he remembered, he pulled the knot certificate from his pocket and flattened it out on the bar. She took a look and smiled.

'Does that cover it?'

She shrugged and took it.

He picked up the glass with its tissue stuck to the underneath and drank it straight down, showing her his pale, swallowing neck.

He watched her duck out of the bar and move away back into the crowd which parted and closed again behind her. He followed, he could see the red flag of her flank bending as she whispered into a man's ear. It had to be a husband's ear, an older man, twenty years older. He laughed at what she said and glanced around the room in the same arc that you would use for an automatic weapon, then he turned back to his conversation.

Leonard moved in a bit further, excusing the bulk of his bag as it knocked against one or two people. One of the men in the crowd looked like the old man, the interviewer from the Administration Building. It was him, flanked by two assistants carrying files and unbound papers. Ian was standing there too, Ian Marble, smoking and drinking, wearing a doubtful face. Leonard felt like he'd got close enough, he was at that window-shopping distance, where you could still turn and go without obligation to buy. The old man had a beer in one hand and his walking stick in the other; he was leaning on his stick to stay upright but it also served to nail his assistants to the one place, the gum of grey rubber at its tip holding fast to the polished floor.

Leonard was hungry and he was tired. The journey down from East Anglia had been uncomfortable, he'd not been able to sleep because of the lack of leg-room. He fished the street map out of his bag and made his way back to the door. As he did, the girl in the red dress brought his exit to the attention of the crowd. The old man turned in a slow kind of three-point-turn, an about face just in time to see Leonard leave. The girl came back through the crowd and rammed the knot certificate down onto the bar-top spike which held a thick pile of credit notes.

It was blowing up outside, flat, sheet-rain blowing straight in the face. The map was soon turning into blue and red porridge in Leonard's hands. He just about found his way to the Mirabelle before the colours melted and the roads folded in on themselves.

The Mirabelle was a sort of four-storey seaside building, with round corners and a white-washed plaster finish; the large aluminium window frames were dappled with oxides. It was one of those buildings that didn't fit in the street, probably built on top of a bombsite where the existing building had been flattened in the war. It looked clean and ship-shape but up close there were thousands of surface cracks. There were a couple of handymen outside squatting on their haunches with wrenches and blowtorches, finishing up a day's work. They'd done a really neat job of fixing a double-sized central heating radiator to one of the outside walls of the building. Leonard thought about asking them what the hell they hoped to achieve by this, but instead he let it go because they looked professional, like they knew what they were doing.

Leonard walked into the reception area where the air was overheated, stuffy. He struck the bell on the counter top but nobody came. There was an office behind the desk. The door was gaping open so Leonard called out.

'Hello, anybody there?'

A man stepped out from behind the doorframe. He was naked to the waist and wearing three sets of body toner pads stuck all over his upper torso. Blue, saucer-shaped pads connected by criss-crossing wires taped to his back.

'Hello yes, Harry here. Can I be of any assistance?'

Leonard was not sure. The man walked towards the desk but as he reached the limit of his extension lead, he abruptly stopped and stood still with his stomach, chest and upper arm muscles flexing involuntarily.

'What are the ah…?' Leonard pointed.

'I'm working out!'

'But what?'

'Fitness regime. It's OK, I'm perfectly capable otherwise. Can I help you?'

'I booked a room.'

'OK, righto. Name?'

'Leonard Gopaul.'

Harry flicked through his reservations book.

'Yes, here you are. I'll show you upstairs.'

'It's very warm in here.'

'Yes, some of our guests like it hot.'

Harry disappeared into the office and reappeared carrying his own plug.

'So, when are you up?

'Up?'

'Have you had your interview yet?'

'Yeah, I went today.'

'How'd it go?'

'I couldn't tell.'

'Well, that's good.'

'It is?'

'Sure it is. I've seen thousands come and go, that's a good first reaction. And you're taking your room, fulfilling your obligation despite our reputation, I like that.'

'He said we might talk again.'

'There you go, see. Warden's a difficult nut to crack, don't loose heart.'

'Warden?'

'The old man.'

Harry left the stairwell at the third floor. Leonard followed.

'I've got two rooms free, shall I show you?'

Leonard nodded.

'Now, if you want my advice, forget luxury living and think practical. You'd better take one of these rooms because you won't find anything else, not this late in the day.'

'Right, OK!'

Harry turned left off the corridor. He opened room 45, walked in, switched the light on and plugged himself into the socket beside the vanity mirror. The muscle toning pads started to twitch, making Harry seem nervous and uptight when really he was just fine.

'What do you think? Need to see the other one?'

It was hard for Leonard to concentrate with Harry's tits flexing every few seconds. He didn't really look at the room because it didn't really matter. There was a bed in the background, nothing too offensive colour- or odour-wise.

'This'll do fine.'

'Good, bathroom's down the hall.'

Harry glanced at his watch.

'Curfew in twenty minutes.'

'Curfew?'

'Well, yeah. I wouldn't advise cutting it too fine if you're going out for something, the police are not very forgiving. See you around, then.'

Harry unplugged and left the room.

Leonard sat down on the bed, knackered and hungry. He unzipped his bag and reached into it, digging around in the rolled up socks for an airtight container. He peeled off the lid and inside were six snow-white duck eggs and a packet of bacon. The room, being just a bed, a chair, a table and one window, had no cooking facilities at all. But there was a kettle and an iron, so Leonard plugged them both in and took a look out of the window while they heated up.

It was a significant view, a square courtyard with light industrial workshops on two sides and a gate to the street. Down below in the lowering light, a bored, brown dog was circling around one of its own turds. Between the buildings, there was a viewpoint of the border post with guards checking the arriving and departing cars. The fences were high and barbed at the top; the striped barrier across the road lifted slowly when the counter-weight was leaned on.

The water was boiling so Leonard lowered an egg down into the kettle and let it settle against the heating element. Then he balanced the iron upside down and laid a rasher of bacon against the face. He gave the egg five minutes and turned the bacon twice, used the lid of his plastic container as a plate and rummaged in his bag for salt and pepper. He ate with a teaspoon, working the blunt steel through the meat and scooping out the thick, creamy yolk.

Leonard unpacked as best he could, then he left his room, walked along the corridor for a quick shower and turned in very early, sleeping without dreaming.

It was two in the morning when the noise of it woke him up; glass smashing in the street, followed by the brown dog barking in the yard outside. He rolled out of bed in unfamiliar darkness and couldn't find his way to the light switch. Instead he pulled the curtain aside and peered out through the window. He had a clear sightline along the street which lay back off the main approach to the border. There was a terrace of houses and a row of street lamps. One of the lamps was dark, and there was some movement at the base of it which was difficult to make out.

Leonard, his eyes now accustomed, walked across to his bag, opened it and pulled out a pair of army surplus 'night-vision' binoculars. He snapped them on and focused in on the figure of a woman in a black leotard standing at the base of the lamp, very close to the border fencing. She started to climb, moving easily hand over fist up the lamppost. At the top she took what looked like a length of carpet and threw it over the barbed wire. Leonard took the binoculars away and rubbed his eyes, then he re-focused on her. She was crossing from the top of the lamp onto the carpet when there was the sound of a gunshot. In response, she rolled back off the top and hooked her fingers into the fence lower down. She tried to control her fall but she landed heavily.

A patrolling police car turned into the street and switched its headlamps on to full beam. She jumped up quickly and ran, the car sped up and followed her as she sprinted away. She cut down a side alley and the police car tried to follow but it side-swiped a parked van. The doors flew open and four policemen got out and ran down the alley after her.

Leonard didn't think she would be able to get away. He pulled on some clothes and left his room. He ran along the hallway, to the far end where there was a fire escape. He opened the door and stepped outside onto some rusting, cast-iron stairs. He couldn't see the woman or the police anymore. He listened for a clue but there was nothing. He took the stairs to the yard and walked to the gate, his heart was beating in his throat and the hairs on the back of his neck felt electrified. There was a low growl behind him. He turned to see the brown dog looking much larger at street level and baring its yellow incisors, the muscles in its legs taut with wanting to lunge.

Leonard lifted the lock and opened the gate very slowly, eased himself outside and closed the gate behind him. As the locking bar 'clicked', he realised that he'd locked himself out. Now he was no bloody good to anyone, he was just a danger to himself. He crossed the street and looked around the corner; the woman, with her arms pumping, was sprinting towards him. Leonard waved, he gestured that she should follow him but she just screamed and waved a knife in his face. He stepped back and pressed himself out of sight into a darkened doorway. She ran past, breathing hard and looking over her shoulder, terrified. The policemen, all in a line according to fitness, came into sight, but they were not so much men as boys, the oldest no more than seventeen. They ran by, laughing and swearing as they went; the leader looked back and encouraged them with a wave of his arm.

'Come on, you bleeders, let's get her, then!'

Leonard looked for a way back into the Mirabelle. He rang the night bell but nothing happened, he couldn't be sure that it was working. He weighed up his options and decided he would try and find the tavern. It was the only place he'd seen people that he'd met before, and maybe they had a lock in and drank on after hours. A drink would be a very good idea.

He retraced his route and found himself quite easily remembering his way back to the Spanish quarter. The problem was that the bar was empty and pitch black, there was just one light coming from a first floor window and that looked like a bathroom because it had that frosted, crinkly glass. Through the window, Leonard could make out a peachy skin-tone with long dark hair; a woman moving to and fro underneath a silver highlight, which was most likely a chrome shower head.

He dragged a dustbin over to the building. When he stood on it, he could get a leg up onto a wall and from the wall he could reach the window with his outstretched arm. He tapped on the glass with his fingers and the shape inside jumped, disappeared for a moment and then returned, blue from the neck down. The window opened slowly. It was her; he'd hoped it would be her, ever since he had the stupid idea of coming here.

'What the hell are you doing here? Are you fucking crazy? My husband finds you here, he will kill you and I don't say that for drama, no. He actually will kill you.'

'Sorry, I am very… I don't know, sorry OK? I didn't know where to go because

I'm locked out of the Mirabelle and it's curfew and I thought you could tell me where I could find Ian.'

'You're staying at the Mirabelle?'

'Yeah, it's all I could get. I need your help. See, I wondered if you could tell me. I saw Ian Marble in the bar this evening, do you know where his house is?'

'Ian doesn't have a house, he's a visitor like you. He lives up on One Tree Hill, there's a row of old houses on the north side. His is number 4, flat B, I think.'

'How do I get there?'

She pointed south, to a piece of moonlit ground with swaying trees at the top.

'See the high ground? Well, that's it.'

'Thank you, thanks very much.'

Leonard turned to go but he was caught on her arm because she held his lapel.

'What's wrong?'

The streetlight lit up her face and her eyes glittered like crushed and flattened foil. She pulled him hard into the wall and stuck her tongue into his mouth. He could do nothing but let himself be kissed. He hadn't worked out if this was OK and he was so taken by surprise, he didn't think to kiss her back. Her skin was hot and perfumed, her lips and cheeks made of soft membrane. Cold drips of minted water fell from her wet hair, ran down her face and onto her collarbones. When she broke away, he had an overwhelming urge to close with her again. But she pushed him back and stood there, reading the aftershock in his facial muscles. She smiled, as if she had just added an important column of figures and got the sum she expected.

'There you go, swashbuckler, that should give you something to think about.'

She smiled again, longer this time, and then she closed the window. She knew the image she would leave him with, she wanted to burn it into his retina, she wanted it to go deep into his long-term memory, it was an image of her brightest, most beautiful youth. She needed this because sometimes she felt as if she was already old. She wanted to know that such beauty, her own fragile beauty, had heated another's blood and had not gone unnoticed.

Leonard watched her blurred outline move away into the bathroom and then the light switched off.

Leonard jumped down awkwardly, stinging the tendon beneath his left foot. He felt numb, heckled and somehow robbed of his own free will. He started off uphill without a backward glance. The walk was doing him good, moonlight was silvering the black roofs, and the look of it seemed to calm him down, seemed to help defuse the booby-trapped bomb ticking in his chest.

Ian's house was too close though, he was there too soon and his heart was still revving. The row of houses on the hill was well placed in amongst tall trees, there was no through traffic and the houses had that gloss of accommodating the people who were doing better than most. The buildings were elegant; long windows from floor to ceiling, with some carved stonework details on the façades.

The main door was painted a glossy red and it was unlocked, so Leonard stepped inside. Flat A was on the ground floor so he took the stairs up to B. He knocked and something seemed to fall over inside, then it sounded as if shoeboxes were being closed in a hurry. The door opened an inch until the security chain tightened. Ian's right eye appeared and did the investigating; the door closed, then opened and Ian stood there looking guilty, red in the face and wearing a paisley print dressing gown. In the pause before he spoke, Leonard studied the scar along Ian's breastbone, a thin line of pale skin with looping stitch marks.

Ian drew his dressing gown together, covering his bare chest.

'Ah, hello Leo, to what do I owe the pleasure?'

Leonard told him how he'd been locked out of the guest-house and had nowhere to sleep.

'Come in, then. How did you find me?'

Leonard sat down into a padded leather sofa.

'The girl at the tavern.'

'Adeline?'

'Is that her name?'

'That was stupid of her, you might be anyone.'

'I still might be.'

'No, I don't think so. I can see who you are, and I don't think you are very dangerous.'

'I don't know if that's good or bad.'

'How exactly did you get locked out?'

18

'I tried to help this girl. She climbed a lamp-post and tried to get over the border.'

'Ah yes, that happens every now and then. You must learn to keep yourself to yourself, Leonard. The woman is obviously not very clued up; residents have border passes and it's simple enough to beg, borrow or buy one on the black market.'

'But I thought people were trying to get into the city?'

'Yes, but there are the odd few who have this urge to go the other way.'

'And what happens if they're caught?'

'That depends. All strange behaviour is punishable by imprisonment. She'll be dumped into a cell, out of the running. Just like you if you get too interested in Adeline.'

'She likes me.'

'She's way too good to be true, Leo, you must have realised that. She's actually quite dangerous, likes to bring men in close enough to rile her husband. She likes to be fought over. Wants her old bastard of a husband to become so angry that he bludgeons her suitors to death. And the husband, Tony, there's an idiot for you. Likes the cuckold pain, I've seen him thrive on it. So Leo, do you want to be the next plaything, the next amusement?'

'Now that you mention it, not really. But then again she is as horny as hell.'

'Then maybe I should tell you something. People here like to kill each other; it passes the time and, as you might guess, it shortens the odds. Do you see what I mean?'

'Have you killed anyone?'

Ian's eyebrows hurdled.

'How dare you!'

But his tone was playful.

Ian filled his kettle and took some mugs out of a cupboard.

'Can you tell me something, Ian?'

'Fire away.'

'Why are the policemen here children?'

Ian shrugged his shoulders and held his open hands out, palms upwards.

'Well, I don't know, but they might as well be, mightn't they? None of the adults are to be trusted, are they?'

He spooned coffee granules into the mugs.

'You've got a lot to learn, Leonard. You'd better get up to speed or you'll be going back over the border, in need of remedial treatment.'

Leonard was hot under the collar. He got up and paced around the room. He noticed a pile of boxes stacked up behind the door, one had the cuff of a checked shirt poking out.

'What's in the boxes, Ian?'

'My shirts. I told you I made shirts, yes?

'No, I don't think so.'

Ian lifted one out of its box.

'Feel the quality. I sell them on the black market. Do you like them?'

'Yeah.'

Ian handed Leonard his coffee, then he showed him some work in progress; a white shirt was laid out on the ironing board with red stripes down one arm. Ian picked up a ruler and a felt pen, he drew a series of blue intersecting lines across the arm and on to the shoulder. Leonard didn't know what to make of all this; Ian's work was a pure madness and watching him work those indelible pens made Leonard wonder how long it would be before he too found his own particular form of underlying insanity.

'Would you like a shirt, then?'

'Yeah, OK.'

'Here.'

Ian pulled an intricate blue and black one from stock and passed it over.

'I'll take a blank docket, say half a day?'

'Ah, I don't understand.'

'The price, credit me half a day's labour and the shirt's yours.'

'But I thought…?'

Ian handed Leonard a pad and paper.

'Write this down. I promise to pay the bearer, half a day's labour. Then sign!'

Leonard wrote the credit note and handed it over.

'There, now you understand the economy. And you've got yourself a handmade bargain in the process.'

Ian handed Leonard an inflatable bed.

'If you blow this thing up, you can sleep here quite comfortably. I'm turning in now. Good night.'

'Can you tell me what to expect, Ian?'

'I told you she likes toys, life sized toys, action men with moving parts.'

'Not Adeline, I meant with the other thing, with the Warden?'

Ian stopped grinning.

'Why don't you start blowing that thing up?'

Ian left the room, so Leonard unrolled the mattress, squeezed the teat and blew into it. Ian came back a minute later with a bottle of whisky in his hand. He poured a measure into both their mugs.

'You know that I can't say much, see my hands are tied, but I've heard you did quite well in front of Warden. I am not supposed to tell you, but there you go, you asked.'

'Really? I thought I was useless.'

'You can feel reasonably pleased with yourself, he'll give you a recall I'm sure. There are all kinds of tests to follow you know, medical tests, cognitive tests.'

'But how do you know all this, and aren't you trying to be chosen too?'

'Yes, but it's been so long since I thought I might have a chance that I don't think I care anymore. See, my health sort of ruined it for me and now? Well, I just do some security work, I make ends meet, that's all.'

'What's wrong with your health?'

'I'm just not A1 that's all.'

'What do you know about Warden? I mean, who is he?'

'He's connected to the Americans. His funding comes from a Californian charity.'

'But what made him do this? What made him decide?'

'Well, he's a scientist.'

'Yeah, I heard that, but do you believe in him? Do you believe the survival project stands a chance?'

'I've seen the vessel!'

'I thought that was prohibited.'

'I've just told you that I've seen it.'

'Do you know how it will be done, then? How it will happen and when?'

'Of course not, no one knows. Anyway, I've had it for today. I'm tired and I'm going to bed. Goodnight.'

'Wait, can't you fill me in on a few details? What's the latest on the impact?'

'I can tell you right here and now, in short-hand - that the future is fucked.

But if you really want to bask in it. Here…'

Ian picked up the remote control and switched on the TV. He backed out of the door, mumbling something beneath his breath.

Leonard blew some more air into the mattress and focused on the screen. Computer generated images of what was going to happen played and replayed. A massive asteroid was bearing down on the earth from deep in space. Lines of trajectory marked the most probable point of impact. The screen cut to documentary shots of mass refugee movement and United Nations conferences. A graphic appeared on the screen which read 'TEN WEEKS TO IMPACT'

CHAPTER TWO

You feel like a stranger for less than a day here, because everybody's a stranger and nobody gives a shit whether you live or die; it's all the same. There's a mean population level, a kind of aggregate or net number that stays roughly the same, apart from some minor seasonal differences. There are exits and entrances, the people come and go, they're rejected or just disillusioned, then they head back to the midlands or down south to the capital. They are home before their 'had enough' postcards arrive, and they will not come again.

You are not welcomed and you are not told to go away either, the place reluctantly tolerates your passing through, that's all. What you face when you get here is that old favourite: indifference, professional indifference. That's what it is and the only way to get yourself a foothold is to do well in front of the Warden and become a 'contender', a 'maybe'. This is not so great either because being a maybe, being in the running, might just get you killed. The happiest medium you can hope for is to doubt if you've been successful, not have any hope and consequently not have any fear. If you have no hope, that is if you are just waiting for your notice of rejection, then you are in the position where you offend the others the least, and you can socialise, you can even relax a little. You don't matter any more, so you are acceptable and this is when you may go into the public gallery and watch the new arrivals present themselves.

Leonard shortened his steps on the approach to the Administration Building, timing his entry so he could walk through the revolving door without stopping. He followed the arrows to the left this time, up to a sweeping, panelled staircase which curved upward to the public gallery. The steps were awkward, though. The rise was set to a municipal distance; it's a shorter rise but a longer step than domestic treads. So Leonard watched his scuffed shoes as he climbed the red carpet, pock-marked by cigarette burns. Funny how all this wood gave the building a legitimacy, like it was a legally binding material, seasoned with age, absorbing the evidence.

Leonard was one of the first into the gallery. He took a front row seat, a well-padded seat with those awkward, shared armrests. The mezzanine was at the same level as the dust-coated lights which dangled above the chamber. The acoustic was good because a woman down on the ground floor was Sellotaping something together and Leonard could hear everything; the end-finding, the tearing, teeth ripping and sticking, all clearly defined. His seat was comfortable; there was plenty of legroom and a good raking angle to the seat backs. The capping rail, which ran along the top of the balcony, had been carved into, whittled out by knives, which must mean that the public had knives on them all the time.

People started to file in; ten, fifteen then twenty people took seats in the gallery on steeply banked seats that made you feel like you might fall forward.

The door into the chamber was knocked upon, knuckled three times, loud to quiet with decreasing confidence. There was no one to say 'come in', but after a pause the door opened and a woman appeared below. She looked ahead at the chairs and then straight up at the public gallery. She was dressed very badly; thinking about her clothes had obviously never been an issue, they were there to stop her being naked, that's all. She wore a green, ankle-length, pleated skirt and a black woolly jumper; it really didn't matter. Same with the hair: cut short because it was naturally curly and would not hold a stylist's instruction. You had the idea that with this woman, the charm must all be on the inside. Maybe she kept someone up nights saying how beauty was only skin-deep and in the eye of the beholder.

She was carrying a black, arrow-headed section of iron railing, which was about waist high and approximately two metres long. She moved forward a couple of paces then planted the railings upright and stood still. A man followed her in, a husband-type character, and as he walked in with her he ran a stick along the railings. When he reached the end, she lifted the metal and walked it forward so that he could move further into the room accompanied by the comforting rattle of wood against steel. Very odd, but that is how it was. There were murmurings coming from the seats behind, and one high-pressure guffaw leaked out of someone's mouth. All eyes were on the chamber though, as Mr and Mrs Burton moved in short stages to the seats and sat down. Mr Burton tucked his stick, drill-sergeant style, underneath his arm, crossed his legs and grabbed his kneecap. He sat there quite stony-faced and hook-nosed, turning slowly to listen to Mrs Burton's whispers.

The Warden entered, limped to the centre of the room and then he saw his problem: both seats were taken. Mrs Burton saw the problem, too, and stood, but Warden gestured that she should stay put.

'That's all right, we'll get another.'

Another chair was brought in and he sat down heavily into it.

'Now then, there are two of you. Why the hell's that?'

'We're together. One won't go without the other.'

The Warden left it at that; it didn't seem likely that logic would carry any weight here.

'And so what do you have to say then, the two of you, to back up your application?'

She looked across at Mr Burton; it was his cue to stand, so he stood. He tapped his nose with his stick and dragged it along the railings until he was as close as possible to the ear he wanted.

'We are good people, we mean well and want the best for all concerned.'

A silence then grew, with the Warden seeming quite comfortable to let the quiet become deafening. Mr Burton showed signs of doubting; he retreated back along the railing and sort of looked up at Mrs.

She stood up and took the floor.

'We do have a plan, based on experience gained working for the voluntary services overseas. We've worked on this plan, so that we will know how to go about the reinsertion of the population. We have drawn up proposals but the gist of it is that we have researched similar scenarios, made projections, looked into the why's and wherefores, the pros and cons, and we have the overview now. We know how to proceed and given the chance, we would, if we only could, we surely would!'

'That's it exactly, it's exactly as she says. Do you see?'

Leonard was thinking how it wasn't a bad end to a poor start.

The Warden wrote something down.

'Thank you for coming. Please see the receptionist on the way out.'

He stood and shook their hands then sat down as they left. He glanced up at in the gallery, expressionless. He had a mannequin face, a sunken, male model's bone structure but he was too old to model anymore. If he had an opinion of Mr and Mrs Burton, it would be easy enough to see it, but there was nothing, not a tick, not even the slightest twist of the lip.

'Leonard.'

She whispered close up to his ear.

'It's lunch time, do you want to get something to eat?'

It was Adeline, wearing black and in glorious close up, and unmoved by the coincidence of them both being there. She did not believe in synchronicity, she just wanted to know: did he want to go to lunch or not?

They bought sandwiches from a van and ate them sitting on an outside wall. Her bare knees bothered him, he kept seeing his own hands on them, saw her dress riding higher, her legs parting. He had to stop this, because with some women, it was already too late; as soon as you meet them it's too late, you know already that it will happen. Sooner or later it was bound to. It's a foregone conclusion, regardless of the hurdles they will have to jump over and drag themselves across. Two bodies with a kind of parallel static charge, opposite and equal, that can only be earthed through sexual contact. Some spark of nuclear energy is to blame, some fundamental wires that the almighty intends to cross, will be made to cross.

'How did you get on with Ian the other night?'

'OK, he was good enough to put me up for the night.'

Adeline smiled.

'Why?'

'You know that he's a secret policeman?'

'What? Why didn't you tell me?'

'Well, it's a secret.'

'So why tell me now?'

Adeline shrugged. She put down one half of her sandwich, wiped her hands on a paper towel and took an envelope out of her bag. She emptied a handful of black and white photographs onto the wall beside her.

'Take a look at these.'

Leonard picked them up and shuffled them in his hands. They were aerial photographs, rivers and roads like pencil marks, winding through valleys, around mountains. Each photograph in the sequence was at a higher magnification, and the last one showed a dark cluster of circles beside a group of rectangular buildings in the middle of a valley.

'What's that?'

'That's what all the bloody fuss is about. That's the vessel complex.'

Leonard studied the pictures close up, so close that focusing his eyes made the back of his head hurt.

'Really? It's the vessel? Are you sure?'

She didn't answer, she just gave him the lowest, gravest look.

'How'd you get these?'

'I paid a chain of liars. These are classified images, satellite photos.'

'So there is a vessel.'

'Did you ever doubt it?'

'I never really believe anyone or anything until I see some hard evidence and with my own eyes!'

'So why did you come here? What if the whole thing was just a rumour?'

'Well, I thought I might save my life. And I came to find out the truth. The pictures are a good start but I still need to see the thing for myself.'

'That's impossible.'

Adeline snatched the photographs and stuffed them back in her bag.

'I'm going back to the gallery.'

'Hang on, I want to ask you something. Why did you show me the photos anyway?'

'It seems you like to help ladies in distress. That's what you were doing the other night with the lamp climber, right? After curfew?'

'Yeah but...'

She turned away from Leonard and headed off back towards the admin building. Leonard followed and took her arm at the elbow, by that small bone there, that feels like a pistol grip.

'Are you in trouble, Adeline?'

'No more than anyone else!'

They entered and started to climb the stairs to the gallery two at a time. Her neckline was low and he gazed at her back. Her exposed skin was scattered with freckles, like the night sky in negative.

✦

There was a noise below, the light footsteps of the next applicant as he shuffled into the chamber.

He was a jowly man, a curly-haired, short man with square shoulders and short arms, arms thick in the uppers, tapering to thin wrists. He looked like a habitual grump in his tight yellow T-shirt with the maker's logo stitched over the left pectoral. He had over-long fingernails, which hooked over into curling claws. He placed a small wireless on the floor and switched it on. The voice of Frank Sinatra singing 'Fly Me To The Moon' filled the interview room.

He fished some strips of blue rubber out of his pockets, then with his sharp hands he inflated and tied the balloons into various animal shapes. He made small, blue balloon dogs: spaniels, setters and poodles with bob-tails. He popped a few with his fingernails but carried on undeterred, blowing up, stretching and twisting; plain balloons they were, nothing written on them.

By the time the Warden entered, the applicant had a hunting pack of a dozen or so obedient blue hounds at his feet. The Warden wasn't fazed, he took his seat and started with the routine.

'Mr Newman, is it?'

Newman switched the music off and nodded.

'Go ahead then, please. I take it you know what we are doing here and the question is the same as ever.'

'Yes, I know. I'm sorry about the…' he pointed at his blue dogs, 'only I'm an entertainer and I…'

'That's fine, Mr Newman, I like your act.'

'It's not an act, it's a way of life.'

Newman twisted a hind leg onto a body.

'Do carry on then, Mr Newman.'

'Well, I suppose I've come here because I think I'm the man for the job. I have certain qualities in that, I am sensitive, caring, relatively intelligent and genetically robust.'

An exploding balloon finished his sentence.

'Excuse me, Warden, but I gather from what I have read that you get to ask all the questions. But my very best quality is that I am curious. I want to know more about you and the project. I need to see some evidence. I suppose I need to know what I am getting myself into.'

The Warden's face registered some lack of patience.

'The facts are well publicised, Mr Newman. What we do here is selection. We give you a chance to be involved in this undertaking, your job is to rise to the occasion, not complain at the outset. I will add one word of, well, warning really. It's not your business or anybody else's to know the details. Don't try to get to the bottom of this; all that you will find down there will be your own, lifeless body.'

The Warden looked up, his eyes sweeping across the public gallery. He was speaking not only to Newman but to everyone in the room.

'When will you people learn? All I require is that you talk to me so that I can see who you are, then I can make my decision, file you under "maybe" or send you home. So, Mr Newman, please just talk to me, tell me about yourself.'

Newman picked up a handful of uninflated balloons and started to mumble...

'It just hasn't been the same, has it?'

'What?'

'Not since Frank Sinatra died.'

'Do go on, Mr Newman.'

'Well, it was good to know he was out there, wasn't it? Out there somewhere in the back of a limo, in a black Cadillac, going from conquest to conquest, laughing on the phone to some big-wig, sipping bourbon on the rocks, with his bow-tie undone and his hair slicked back. It was good all that, wasn't it?'

The Warden smiled.

'I would have to agree with you there, Mr Newman.'

'Soups, I like soups. Tins, I buy two tins, different flavours and I mix the two so I've got my own flavour. Sometimes it doesn't work and I have to throw it away; sometimes it's so good I think I must telephone the company to give them the idea.'

'Are you a tea or coffee drinker, Mr Newman?'

'Well, I like both, but they've got to be separate. They don't mix at all well, though I have tried. If I'm making refreshments for visitors and some want tea and some want coffee, I don't even stir with the same spoon, there's contamination.'

'But what have you been doing with yourself all these forty-three years? Tell me about your career path, your background?'

'Moving around, wandering, you know. I never like to stay in one place for too long. I'm no good at business, I don't think I'll ever have any money. I like new places, new vistas. I'm not a professional man, that is you couldn't really say "there goes Newman the plumber" or "Newman the dentist" because I'm not, I'm not any of those things. I'm… well, I'm just Newman, the man with his eyes and ears and heart open, and that's all.'

There was a pause. Leonard could tell that the Warden was listening carefully; he seemed to be hearing a kind of music to his ears.

The sound of Adeline's chair scraping as she stood, put a kind of full stop at the end of Newman's interview. She turned to leave and as she passed close to Leonard she dropped a blue envelope into his lap. Folded inside was an invitation to the tavern, to celebrate her husband's birthday: 'Tony's Fiftieth Birthday Bash! Fancy Dress Essential!' There were plenty of glittering stars, glued and sprinkled on the card, but the presentation had about it a kind of hand-made impatience. Leonard felt pretty awkward about how this was shaping up, he felt like he wanted to stop knowing Adeline and concentrate on why he was here. But it was too late for that. After all, she had shown him photographs of the vessel and he wasn't about to forget that she had already stuck her tongue way down his throat.

Leonard wanted to get back to the Mirabelle. His bag was there, his other shoes and washing kit, his bed and the familiar view.

He headed home but took a route that swung further south than usual, through a newer but more temporary district.

People walking through the streets here carried dark briefcases and leather handbags, not the customary plastic shopping bags. It was nicer here too: the streets were wider, there were fewer but nicer cars and on the horizon there was an arc of blue coastline. Prosperity, that's what it was: the polish of high tech industries. There were glowing computer screens visible through the office windows. Small businesses, lots of one-, two- and three-man 'Ltd' and 'Incorporated' companies housed in 'overnight success' buildings made from sheet steel bolted together. They had wooden window frames and quite small front gardens. Each building was freshly painted, white with red oxide roofs, sky blue or custard yellow front doors.

Sometimes a roofline swept up into a Balkan dome or a red minaret with flaring oriental shoulders. There was an atmosphere of arrival and departure here; company names, like 'Voyager Handling' or 'North Star Services' suggested long haul flights and sleeping carriages.

All the while, taxis and motorbike couriers arrived to deliver and pick up parcels. One rider in blackened leathers flipped open the luggage box, which was strapped to the rear of his seat. He lifted a metal flask out of the box, checked his clipboard and started looking for the address. He flipped his visor back and approached Leonard.

'All right? Don't know a company called "I Q Germ Cell", do you?'

'Sorry, no. What's in the flask?'

'Sperm, genius sperm.'

'What?'

'You asked.'

The rider caught sight of the company logo and stepped through the entrance door.

Leonard scratched his head and turned to the north. In twenty minutes or so, the city became more familiar again, and the Mirabelle came into view soon enough, with an ambulance parked outside, lights flashing.

Harry was leaning on the reception desk, looking very nonchalant. He was reading a newspaper and wearing a t-shirt this time, but he was still plugged in to a power source. His body, of course, jerking rhythmically underneath his shirt.

Standing in the double doorway which led up the stairs, was a policeman, police boy really, a child with his legs wide, stomach in, chest out, eyes staring straight ahead. Harry watched Leonard cross the reception area. He nodded, but gave no clue as to what to expect.

The police boy broke the silence.

'Good evening, sir.'

'Evening, officer.'

The boy took it as a compliment and the skin around his eyes creased as he grinned.

'Yes ah, there's been a death in the building. Forensic scientists are dusting for fingerprints all over the place. If I could just ask you not to wander into room twelve until they're finished?'

'That's not a problem. What happened?'

'We haven't got a monkey's, sir. Your guess is as good as ours, unless you did it, then your guess would be spot on. Did you do it, sir?'

'No, of course not.'

The boy stepped aside and Leonard climbed the stairs. It would be tricky all this. In a closed environment like the hotel, everyone was going to be a suspect.

He walked along the first floor landing to take a look at the crime scene. There were no guards outside the room, but inside, two men in blue boiler suits were down on their knees and dusting for fingerprints. The room was a mess, like there'd been a prolonged struggle, strangling and blows though, no blood bath, no evidence of knives or guns puncturing the flesh. The room was the same as Leonard's: same carpet, same bed, same window on the same wall. There were thirty or more wooden canes scattered all over the floor and leaning against the walls. And, in amongst the canes, were pieces of broken china, half smashed and completely smashed plates. The body was lying on its side, turned away from the room and kind of snuggled up against the skirting board.

Leonard moved closer and saw, for the first time since he'd arrived, the true nature of the city. It was ugly, the way the end would be. This was a foretaste of the way the whole world would look, the way people would behave when time suddenly ran out, all at once.

One of the boiler suits noticed Leonard.

'Oi, what you doing here?'

'Ah, just wanted to know what happened. I live upstairs.'

'Name?'

'Leonard, Leonard Gopaul.'

'Any papers?'

'They're with Admin.'

'I see. No big deal here, you should move along, Mr Gopaul. There's nothing for you to see here.'

Leonard pointed at the body.

'I beg to differ.'

'Ah, well yeah, the plate spinner. Imagine the scene if you can, she must have had thirty or so china white dishes spinning above her head. I know what that's like. She would have been completely absorbed by the rotations and the timings, she wouldn't have noticed the intruder, see. Nice girl by all accounts, caught short with her hands full, easy target.'

CHAPTER THREE

It came through the fog, this man-made noise, a regular tone splicing through the mind at rest. Tony listened, then remembered what it was. His ear ached from the tiny earpiece but it had done the job and woken him in the middle of the night. The audio lead ran from his ear to a small alarm clock, the face in lime green fluorescent saying 04.31. Tony turned and looked at the mound of duvet which masked the shape of Adeline. He raised himself up on one elbow and looked at her face. It was expressionless now, such a marked difference from her awake state. Normally her face was such an acute barometer of the way she felt about him. She was so terribly capable, so in control of her own destiny. Tony raised his hand and hit Adeline hard around the face, then dropped back onto his pillows and resumed a fast asleep position.

Adeline came to in confusion. She brought her fingers up to her numb face, which was tingling on one side.

Tony bit his lip; he loved this moment. He kept very still, kept his deep breathing slow and regular, even though he was completely awake. He could hear her brain, by a process of elimination, going through the possible causes.

This was beautiful, an outright score, a sharp blow and she could say nothing. It was a crushing victory, not one of those arguments he never felt he could win, where he could never make her shut up and concede. Her logic would not allow him any kind of upper hand, not because she was so smart, but because her arguments were always so biased in her own favour.

After a while she managed to over-ride the tingling nerves in her cheek and fall back to sleep. Tony also returned to his own deep and delicious, well-deserved slumber.

Tony had gone off early in the morning for the first treat of his birthday, a round of golf with his brothers. He played the kind of slugged-out golf weekenders play, hacking turf into the air, bending the high irons onto the wrong fairways, losing balls in long grass and water hazards and pulling his neck muscles. A great game, golf; a cold and wet preamble, all in aid of getting into the bar, tanking up and driving home knackered. The shoes were good, though, the metal spikes made a great sound over concrete and you got to wear a leather glove on your left hand.

Halfway through the round, Tony stood up on the ninth tee and addressed the ball. He waggled his club, waited for his blood to boil then took a murderous swing at it. It was a good contact and the ball sailed off up the fairway. Tony punched the air and shouted, 'Yes!' to egg himself on.

Tony's brothers kept on saying, 'Look! Look!' long after his ball had landed. When Tony turned he saw that what they were pointing at was a flaring, white projectile, which was burning a low arc in the eastern sky. They stood there in a tight group and just watched the event unfold. Eventually Tony had to ask.

'What the hell is that?'

There was an explosion of sorts as the object hit the earth a couple of miles away. A faint, but detectable tremor came up through Tony's toes and a ball of smoke lifted up out of the open farmland. Tony was the eldest; it was up to him to say.

'Come on, let's go and have a look.'

It took them ten minutes to get to the site, they were the first on the scene. The hole in the ground was about the size of a car. The earth smouldered; it smelt acrid. Tony's middle brother Danny spoke up.

'It's an impact crater, an early warning. It's a piece of the asteroid. They've been telling us that we should expect this kind of thing. I've been trying to kid myself that all this wasn't going to happen.'

Tony jumped down into the crater and fished out a piece of hot rock with his golf club.

Adeline had worked all day decorating the bar. She'd wired up the flashing lights, stirred up a swirling bowl of punch, hung balloons, organised food, music, taxis. She'd soaked herself in a bubble bath for an hour, then she'd pulled on her costume. By seven in the evening she was all through with the preparations.

She stood outside the tavern and waited to welcome the first guests. Tony, as far as she knew at this stage, was still frolicking in the clubhouse at the golf course.

It would be rude to refuse, right? That was the mantra Leonard had in mind as he stood and looked at his reflection. The surprising sight of a cavalry officer, in full parade regalia, looked back at him. A horse-guard in red jacket with silver buttons, dark trousers, riding boots, diagonal belt and ceremonial sabre. All of this topped off by a chrome helmet with a white plume. Stupid really, a tomato coloured, cocksure knob, is how he would have summed up anybody else dressed like this. But he'd left it late before going to the hire shop and it was either cavalry officer or the ape suit and well, the ape suit had seen too much action and it didn't have any pockets. He reckoned it would get hot and he would have to remove the head and carry it around all evening, and what's the point of that?

Leonard felt ridiculous as he walked up to the Spanish district. He was worried about moving closer to a wary husband because he had no excuse from this point forward; he was making the choices, his actions were self-propelled. He knew it, we all know it; past the first kiss, the gradient steepens and fucking, more often than not, will follow.

Adeline was standing on her own outside the bar, wearing a wide-brimmed hat and carrying a mask on a stick. She wore a puffed-up, pale-blue skirt with a blue and white bodice. Her face was powdered and her lips rouged, a prominent beauty spot high on her left cheek. A solitary seventeenth century figurine, standing on a twenty-first century street corner, and she didn't look at all out of place. How could anyone look out of place here? It wasn't possible, the usual rules did not apply.

Her face was not the way he remembered. With all the make-up, it was mask perfect, between oval and heart shaped. Her straight nose and buoyant cheeks were blessed by those green eyes, which were glowing with all the hyperactivity going on inside her head.

She smiled when she recognised Leonard. She curtseyed but her heart wasn't in it, she seemed concerned.

'Good evening and how are you, Mademoiselle?'

'Sober, and I'm waiting for the birthday boy who is sure to be hammered.'

'You look good enough to eat.'

'I know, and you look like an idiot!'

'Oh, I do love your honesty.'

She grabbed his arm, and led him in. The heads turned, the Romans, Egyptians, Aliens, Frankensteins, Draculas, Fairies, Nurses, Pilots, Werewolves, Zorros and Pirates. They all gave Leonard a glance, just to see who Tony would have it in for, later on.

Adeline ladled punch into a glass and Leonard started to knock it back. The music got louder and the first 'don't care if we look like fools' started dancing.

Adeline looked around at how things were going and weighed it all up very quickly. She placed her arms on her hips and tried to straighten her back.

'It's the corset; it's choking my insides. I'm going upstairs for a few minutes. Do you want to come?'

She walked along the hallway and Leonard followed. The hoops in her skirt were bending around people and furniture, then she seemed to be gliding like a small hovercraft up the stairs. Leonard followed on self-consciously behind. He knew that everyone in the room kept an eye on who climbed the stairs. He knew that more than one witness would be timing their disappearance, breaking the news of it in a whisper to Tony later on.

Leonard had a friend at junior school who lived above a pub, above The Bell in Markhouse Avenue, Peter something. He remembered how big the rooms were. These rooms above Tony's tavern were the same, huge and square with high ceilings and big windows. Deep pile carpets, extra fridges and chest freezers, oddly positioned in hallways and living rooms, to carry the overflow from the bar.

Adeline was sitting on the arm of a wingback sofa in front of a switched-off, wide-screen television. Leonard felt awkward, way too close to the heart of someone else's life, way too soon. Tony's things were all around: Sunday football trophies and framed photographs, books about commandoes and special service escapades, masculine ornaments, horse brasses and a rack of polished cedar-wood pipes. Leonard had been told about Adeline, he was forewarned and therefore forearmed, it should have put him off. But that never happens, does it?

She turned to Leonard and wrapped her arms around his waist. She started to undo his belt, her hands moving slowly but surely.

'Hang on, what about getting to know one another first?'

'Haven't you noticed that the world is about to end? There's no time and no point in building a lasting relationship.'

'But I…'

'Ssh, Leonard, that's coming along nicely. Shall we investigate?'

'I'd like that but…'

'But what? Let's get on with it!'

'To be quite honest, Adeline, no, I don't think so. I mean I don't think we should… It's quite lovely what you're doing, by the way.'

'You say no but your cock says yes. Look at it!'

'Yeah? But what does my cock know, eh? He has a simple soul.'

She redoubled her efforts.

'Well, it obviously knows better than you, Leonard!'

He stepped back and she let go. Leonard's pulse was making his extension twitch and she laughed at that. He regretted it when she stood up and made her way to the door.

'What are you afraid of, Leonard?'

'Same as always: getting caught in the act, caught with my trousers down, doing something I shouldn't be doing, a very long way from home. I'm here to save my skin and that's all.'

'You're an idiot, Leonard! Don't tell me you actually believe you stand a chance of being selected for survival? Selection is a farce. Warden is the biggest phoney of them all. He gambles, fucks around, hoovers up the class A drugs.'

'Well, then what's he doing in charge of the passenger list?'

'He's not in charge, he's just like some kind of middle-man. He's just admin', he doesn't decide anything.'

'Well, who does then?'

'The project has a whole committee of managers, there's always two or three of them in the public gallery, and even they have to report to a selection board.'

'Jesus, I was way off.'

'Looks that way.'

'But what about Tony? I've been told he's the murderous, jealous type.'

'Look, Leonard, who can afford to be jealous? We're living out the last few weeks of the history of the world.'

'Yes, but as you have noted, I am trying to play my cards right against lengthening odds. I'm trying not to die sooner or even later. I want to get onto the vessel and have a chance at survival.'

'Don't we all, but let's face it, the odds aren't good and the system is corrupt. There are ways, I'm sure, more circuitous routes, alternative passenger lists. There's bound to be plenty of bribery going on, but I don't imagine you have the goods necessary to negotiate that kind of a deal!'

Leonard felt he'd been exposed as a naïve fool, a greenhorn.

'I need a drink.'

Adeline turned and headed back towards the party. Leonard sat down on the sofa and switched on the television. He began to flick through the channels with the sound down. There were shots of mass refugee movements, unchecked rioting and clever men standing before computer generations of the solar system.

Leonard turned the sound up until he could hear the expert commentator say:

'It is not easy for any of us to forget that we are living in a state of international emergency. Of martial law. This spring an asteroid of huge density will collide with the earth. The disruption will be unprecedented and all-pervading. Anybody who cannot find effective shelter from shock waves, earthquakes and the subsequent after-effects will be wiped out in one fell swoop. There are several, state-organised survival projects: there are moon shots, underground chambers. But I think we all understand now that the world as we know it will come to an end.'

Yes, there were plenty of survival projects, some were moon shots, some were underground chambers, but the Warden's vessel project had been given the best chance of success, and it was in this vessel that Leonard hoped to avoid a premature death.

He held his thumb on the channel changer through the blank 70's, and on through 100, before the pictures came back again in the single figures. This is where the escapist channels were, back-to-back melodramatic movies from the world's heydays, romantic comedies from the 1960's, food fights in the labour-saving kitchens of affluent Americans.

Downstairs, the party was underway because Tony had at last arrived. He breezed in and made a point of not being in the least bit surprised by his own surprise party. He carried his golf clubs in one hand and the lump of asteroid in the other. He downed a glass of punch, listened carefully as an informer whispered in his ear and then headed for the stairs.

The door burst open and Leonard spun around. Tony waltzed in wearing cranky golf gear: a red jumper and tartan trousers.

Before Leonard had a chance to figure out what was going to happen, it happened. Tony hit him hard across the head with the rock. Leonard rolled onto the floor and lay there clutching his head in his hands.

'There you go, how's that for a taste of things to come?'

Tony hauled Leonard back up into the chair and Leonard sat there assessing the damage.

'I'm bleeding.'

'Yes, and it really suits you.'

'Have you lost your mind?'

'Of course I have, we all have. Now then, Mr Gopaul, I have a little business proposal to put to you.'

'Like what?'

'I believe that my lovely wife would quite like to go to bed with you.'

Leonard felt a sting in his chest and scanned the room for a weapon.

'Really? But I assure you I have not acted improperly, I…'

'Hang on, listen to my proposal. What I said was, my lovely wife Adeline came to me to broker a deal. She tells me that she would like to go to bed with you. Therefore I would like to offer you that opportunity. What do you say?'

'But why the hell would you do such a thing?'

'It's strictly business, of course.'

'What kind of business?'

'I would need you to pick up a certificate of debt someone has been threatening to call in.'

'What kind of debt?'

'It's an outstanding demand I have not been able to pay. What do you say?'

'What kind of a demand?'

'What I owe is, well, I have been asked to leave the city. So that's the deal. For spending the night with my wife, you will have to pick up my tab and leave the city!'

'Why are you doing this?'

'Adeline has not been feeling herself lately; well she hasn't felt well for quite some time. She's been down in the dumps.'

'How long has she been feeling like this?'

'Four years.'

'Four years? And when did you two meet?'

'Four years ago.'

Tony smiled.

'Well, she moved in with me and then of course we got married.'

'But what do you think is causing the problem?'

'Beats me, maybe its hormonal. Will you spend the night with her? It's what she wants and I only want what's best for her?'

Leonard was feeling slightly woozy from the weird logic, the unresolved sexual contact and the alcoholic punch.

'Look, I came here to get on the survival programme. I can't afford to mess this up, I need to stay in the city.'

'This survival rumour, it's way oversubscribed, success is highly unlikely. So, think about the offer, will you?'

'OK, OK, I'll think about it.'

'Good. Now if you'll excuse me I'd better go and enjoy my party. And you had better leave.'

Leonard woke in the middle of the night, hot and bothered, his throat bone dry, and sweating like a pig. His hair was matted to his face and in one movement he threw off the layers of bedding and stood swaying in the dark. He touched his forehead to check for fever, but it wasn't that. The room itself was overheating, the temperature was up way too high. He tried the windows but they would only open a crack. His nose was blocked and his eyes were stiff with dehydration. He emptied water from the kettle into a glass and drank it down; he gagged on chips of mineral scale and spat them out.

The radiators were boiling, scalding hot to the touch. They were those heavy, cast-iron ones they use in schools, covered in years of paintwork. The metal edges and the controlling valves were caked in coat after coat of yellowed emulsion. Leonard took a coin and scraped at what he thought might be the temperature control. As the flaking paint came away, a bright, brass-work tap was revealed. It wouldn't budge and it burnt the palm of his hand when he tried to twist it. He got down on his knees and followed the pipe along the top of the skirting board until it disappeared into the brickwork. He was only wearing pyjama bottoms, so he pulled on a t-shirt and stepped into his slippers.

Outside in the hall he followed the pipe for five metres before it disappeared through the floor. The pipe then snaked through the building with a kind of hydraulic logic, the route followed the path of least resistance ending up by disappearing into a locked boiler room in the sub-basement.

The basement was the arse and heart and brain of the building, all in one place: a junction of wiring, fuse boxes, soil pipes. It was a place that showed how closely the building mimicked human systems. It had a kind of biology, with pipes and ducts, waterways, electrical currents and gases, bringing in all that was needed, and evacuating the by-products.

It was even hotter down here. Leonard hoped that the thermostat control would be easily visible on the boiler itself. There was loud rhythmic noise coming from inside the boiler room, and every so often a whistle or a bird hoot. One of the door panels had been broken and patched with a plank of wood. Leonard pushed the plank to one side, reached in and unlocked the door. It was dimly lit inside but the boiler was easy enough to find, it was a scorched rectangular oven made of heavy, cast-steel. There were several controls down the right-hand side, all with ancient needle dials. Leonard reached up to turn a promising looking disc, and was hit hard across the knuckles with a stick. He screamed out, more in shock than pain, and spun round to see who the hell had hit him.

'Don't touch that!'

It was an old lady, a sixty-year-old lady, with a gnarled walking stick in her raised hand.

'What are you doing in here?'

She was quite a large lady, draped in blouse and skirt, a careful wave in her hair and big, square, horn-rimmed specs. She had a high colour and peachy cheeks, her nose small and rounded. Her eyes cut through, though; they were shallow, narrow eyes, with the shape echoed in surrounding wrinkles. There was no avoiding or mistaking that these were the piercing eyes of greater experience.

'I was just trying to turn the heat down! It's too hot!'

'Says who?'

'Says me. I've got a room up on the second floor and I'm roasting!'

'Don't touch anything in here, I've got low blood pressure, poor circulation and I need to keep the temperature turned up high, or my blood stops turning. My fingers and toes will freeze up.'

'But what about the rest of us?'

She'd gone, walked off into the room heading towards a piece of clattering machinery. She stood close by the machine, quite comfortable next to the spinning, tucking and rolling-moving parts. It was a printing press; Leonard had never seen one working. Most paperwork was spat out of an electronic machine these days. The old lady sat and watched the fresh sheets coming off the press. Then she took a deep breath and made a noise, it was that shrill hooting noise he'd heard from outside, birdlike and high pitched. She saw Leonard giving her the sideways glance.

'Don't look at me like that, Mr…?'

'Gopaul, Leonard Gopaul.'

'My name's Beryl. My hoot? Well, it's my locomotive whistle, and this?'

She pointed at the printing press.

'This is my little train of thought!'

'Yes, I see…'

'What happened to your head?'

Leonard touched the wound.

'I had a run-in with someone.'

Beryl peeled a sheet of paper off the inking plate.

'You ought to be more careful. Here, have a look at this.'

She handed him a single white foolscap sheet, with a fold in the middle. A tiny, black headline read: Mutating biotech virus may force Asian quarantine. And then in big, bold, red headlines: ROCK STAR AND FASHION MODEL TO MARRY!

'Rock star and Fashion Model. Is that news?'

'Don't fret, it's just a hook to grab the punters. A headline is like a good spread of jam all over the front page, it's what makes a newspaper sell like a hot cake.'

Leonard studied the paper.

'Not the anti-government propaganda I'd expect of a print shop hidden away in a basement.'

'It's business, that's all. I slip the odd fact in once in a while – but I don't want to run the risk of losing my readers. This is my livelihood we're talking about.'

'I take your point.'

'I'm always on the lookout for new material, Mr Gopaul. What's your story, have you been up before the Warden yet?'

'I have, yes.'

'And?'

'God knows, I've heard the whole project is a scam, anyway.'

'Well, of course it is.'

The press ran out of paper. It kept on running though, printing the page onto black, rubber rollers.

'Excuse me, but could you let yourself out? I've got to change the roll. Sorry about the radiators, I just can't help you there.'

CHAPTER FOUR

Leonard wanted to stay in bed really, it was safe and sound, warm and neutral beneath the covers. But some kind of night-time conclusion had dislodged itself from the back of his mind and was now rolling down the stairs and becoming conscious. It was the realisation that he'd always been one of life's assistants, looking over shoulders at what was going on and holding the other end of the piece of wood. But the thing was that from now on, he would have to be the active party, the innovator, now he would have to think like a virus to survive.

A lorry was beeping in the street as it reversed, a distant train rumbled by and a fading aircraft passed overhead. Leonard unbent his left arm so that some blood could flow back into his fingers; he had red marks on his chest where he'd been holding tight to his own body while he slept. He lifted himself up onto his elbows, then he laid his head back down and just listened for a while, building a mental picture from the sound clues. A car hacked through a gear change as it climbed the hill. A diesel engine stalled, started up again and idled unevenly.

He got up and got dressed. He swallowed two Aspirin, hiked his belt in an extra notch, did his bootlaces up tight and left the Mirabelle.

It was early Sunday morning, church bells in the distance, a thin layer of ice underfoot. He felt at ease on the street, even though he'd heard how dangerous the city was becoming.

They sold great big meringues in the baker's shop, sugar-white mountain tops. He munched one as he walked, licked his fingers and wiped the front of his coat. OK, so it was dangerous here; wherever you were in the city, all you needed to do was turn left and then left again and you were likely to get stabbed! He thought about testing the theory, then thought, 'What am I doing here? Why don't I just go home, all the way home, back to the Norfolk Broads and carry on like I did before, like nothing was going to happen?' If he could just accept the fact that one day soon, the world was going to come to a sticky end. Well, that wouldn't be so bad, would it? He could probably live quite well on what was left of the borrowed time.

Leonard could imagine himself taking it easy back home, driving carefully around the traffic islands, sucking on a jelly baby. The glucose syrup, the gelatine and acetic acid would be dissolving in his mouth, the artificial flavourings seeping into his thin blood and he'd feel fine. All he would have to do would be to brush up on that diversionary skill called 'kidding yourself', and then he could just sit tight, ignorant and blissful.

Leonard was embarrassed by who he had become; he was so petty-minded, so accommodating, so mild mannered. He was never embarrassed by the enormous amount of pleasure he felt when he was able to park outside his own home. Often, back home after work, after parking, he would draw the curtains and just sit there in the dark with his eyes open, and his bladder full. He would then see very clearly that he was not who he thought he was, not who he wanted to be, but what the hell? He tried; he sometimes left the house determined to commit an act of kindness, but he was rarely successful. He was not a good man, not an exceptional man. In fact, it sometimes dawned on him that he was the most ordinary man in the world. Even though his internal voices kept on insisting that he was somehow special, somehow different, he had to admit that just about everybody thinks they're different, and anybody who thinks they're different is likely to be more 'the same' as almost anybody else in the world.

Maybe coming here had been a bad idea, but he wouldn't leave the city, not yet. The only way forward was to find a heroic angle. He came here because he had vowed to amend his mediocre life with a last, up-tempo act of faith. He would find the vessel, he would secure his place and he would try to make himself useful by rebuilding the world.

He finished the meringue and picked up a newspaper. The headline read: FOOTBALLER CAUGHT IN THREE-IN-A-BED ORGY! The sub-headline, in smaller, black lettering: Rogue asteroid will rain down from the heavens in just eight weeks' time. Global violence spreading unchecked!

Up ahead, the business quarter loomed with its flat blue backdrop of coastline. The level of energy was markedly different here; it was vibrant and industrious. He studied the passing pedestrians, looked into their faces for clues as to how they were feeling, and they didn't look that concerned. No 'end of days' panic, despite the fact that pieces of ruptured asteroid were likely to rain down from the sky in something like eight weeks time.

The people here seemed preoccupied, they were busy ferrying supplies; couriers were arriving, delivering and picking up. There was a visible sense of security here. Square-shouldered men answered doors, took in parcels, they had radios tucked into their belts, they worked efficiently and silently.

Leonard carried on walking. He turned a corner and the road widened, and the tarmac receded to reveal cobblestones, green polished stones, which sloped away towards the docks. Walking down the slope, trying not to twist an ankle, he was flanked on both sides by industrial buildings, sheet steel warehouses with angular rooflines and rust bleeding from rivet holes. These buildings were fenced in by plastic-coated diamond wire. Above the rooftops red cranes marked out the docks, they turned, dipped and lifted bulging cargo nets, Heron-like.

Leonard had this reflex to turn and look behind, and when he did, he realised that he was being followed. He didn't look like a street criminal, though, this guy. He was in his mid-sixties, one of those invisible, 'I would never have thought it was him' men. Small, thin and pale faced, wearing retirement colours, he looked as if he'd been wearing beige all his life. That was the way, though, with surveillance operatives; they were the most ordinary men, they were the ones who got the cloak and dagger assignments, because they were forgettable people, who lacked distinguishing features. Leonard felt vulnerable with the man at his back, so he decided he would turn and head back towards him, meet him head-on.

The little man showed no surprise at Leonard's about-face, he just kept walking straight and tidy, all the way 'til just before he crossed Leonard. Then he sort of shrugged his canvas rucksack, and in order to avoid Leonard's eyes, he glanced through wire fencing at the arse-end of a factory. But as he passed, he said something, something like, 'Leonard Gopaul?'

Leonard stopped in his tracks and turned. The little man was young in the face but with greying eyebrows and a fixed but anxious grin.

'Are you Leonard Gopaul?'

'And who are you?'

'I'm a runner.'

'A runner?'

'Are you Leonard Gopaul?'

'You know I am. You must have been following me since I left the hotel. Why would you want to do that?'

'I'm a runner.'

'What does that mean?'

'Means I issue demands.'

The runner handed Leonard a slip of paper. Leonard recognised his own signature, it was the credit note he had given Ian two weeks ago in payment for one of his checked shirts.

'What's this got to do with you?'

'It's a cod!'

'What?'

'C.O.D. Certificate Of Debt. My client needs some work doing out at his place and I'm just delivering the notice, calling in the debt.'

'And what if I tell you to go stick it?'

He pulled out a two-way radio.

'Well, I get on this radio and call your reaction in to the police. At best you'll be deported. And remember, I say at best!'

Leonard looked at the certificate again. In small print on the reverse side, it had those familiar words, 'I promise to pay the bearer on demand all sums, deeds, goods, as indicated.'

'Look Mr Gopaul, I have the credit and the means of enforcing the credit and you have the shirt, right? So where is the ambiguity?'

Leonard shrugged.

It's horrible when a man with the upper hand introduces an element of humour and needle into a deal.

Leonard was two heads taller than the runner, but he sensed that the little man would not have a soft centre, not in this line of work. He remembered too that he had turned left and left again and he was, therefore, dreadfully exposed to the possibility of attack.

'So, do I call in your refusal?'

'What do I have to do?'

'Half a day's manual labour. You'll be given the details on the job.'

'When's this for?'

'No time like the present.'

'But?'

'Here, here's the address.'

The runner passed him a slip of paper with some printed information.

'Thank you for your cooperation and have a nice day, sir. Oh, and here's my card in case you have need of my services.'

A green hill, up above the bay, exposed to prevailing winds. There's wood-smoke on the breeze and soft mud on the drive. The city is visible across the water, on the opposite headland several miles away. This part of the country was still within the southern jurisdiction, still within the patrolled border and controlled by the city police.

Leonard approached a whitewashed farmhouse with a moss-green roof. He knocked on the door and a man with red cheeks answered.

'Yeah?'

'Hello, I'm Leonard Gopaul.'

'Yeah? And I'm Reggie, so what?'

'You hold a C.O.D. credit note against me, a cod.'

'Well now, you're keen. Normally have to squeeze it out of 'em. Come in then, I'll give you your chores.'

Low ceilings inside, smoke-aged plasterwork between wooden beams, an open fire ticking away in the corner of the room.

Leonard followed Reggie through the house. He was a heavy man, and the floorboards underfoot were shifting beneath his stomping gait.

He arrived in the kitchen and filled a kettle.

'Cup of tea before you start?'

'Yeah, OK.'

'Have a seat then.'

Leonard sat up close to a cast iron range and warmed his hands.

'Got any work clothes, you know, outdoor clothes?'

'No.'

'Oh dear.'

Reggie lifted the latch on the back door, covered his bald head with a hat and disappeared outside. A long steel bolt scraped a grey arc into red floor tiles as the door pulled shut.

When you first meet someone, who just as quickly leaves you alone, they leave a vivid afterimage, a clear and accurate likeness. The farmer's green cardigan had tilted buttons straining to do the job of covering up his rounded stomach. He'd knuckle-cracked his fingers and his hands were ready at his hips, like they were hovering above holsters. His eyes were watery blue, and seemed to follow on sharply behind his quick mind.

The kettle boiled; Leonard lifted it off the stove and made the tea, leaving out Reggie's unknown spoonfuls of sugar.

The latch lifted and the door swung in.

'Here you are, then. Put these on and we'll get to it!'

Whilst Leonard pulled on some blue overalls, the farmer stood over his mug of tea with the bag of sugar in his hand.

'Have you sugared?'

'No.'

'Three, see.'

He spooned in the three sugars and started sipping, blowing and sipping.

They walked across the yard and entered a brick barn. There was a stinging odour in the air, of fermenting straw, piss and shit. While Leonard's eyes took a moment to adjust to the dark interior, his ears were telling him that a large animal was breathing heavily and moving around inside. Light from a stable door half way along the barn spilled in and reflected off the animal's wet nose. It was a bull with wiry red hair, its ears were scanning forward as Reggie started to make some reassuring noises.

'Move over then, you. We're going to have a spring clean-up today, eh, boy?'

The bull breathed out through its nose, leaving a cloud of vapour. It moved away a few steps, moving slowly because the floor was slippery. The bull's legs were black with mud all the way up to his chest. He turned and looked back, happier at a distance, then yawned, showing Leonard his muscular, pale-pink tongue.

'Here you go, then.'

Reggie handed Leonard a shovel and cracked a smile.

'Know what this is?'

'Well, I...'

'It's bullshit, real, honest-to-God bullshit. Clear the stuff out the door, and then get it into the trailer. You can use the wheelbarrow if you want.'

Leonard stepped through the mud and grabbed the barrow. He checked the route he would have to take, out into the yard then along a plank of wood, which ran up into the trailer. He pushed the shovel under eight inches of soiled mud, lifted and felt the weight: it was heavy, he'd have to pace himself. As he snatched the shovel up to the lip of the barrow and twisted it, he could feel his hip joint opening up and the tendons in his back straining.

Reggie climbed up a ladder and started pulling compacted blocks of straw down from a raised platform.

'You live here on your own, Reggie?'

'Uhh?'

'Are you married?'

'Yeah, but, well she's gone back to her family in Australia.'

'How long for?'

'Oh, you know, she ain't coming back. She heard on the telly that there was more chance of survival in the southern hemisphere.'

'And what about you?'

'I'm staying here.'

Reggie dropped three more bales of straw to the ground.

'Aren't you interested in the survival programme? I mean aren't you going to try and get onto the vessel?'

'Yeah right, as if I stood a chance in hell, with all the back-handers going on.'

Leonard stopped scooping and leant on the shovel.

'What do you know about that, then?'

'Nothin', I don't know nothin', I don't want to get in any bloody bother, do I? Shovel's not an ornament, you know.'

Leonard lifted the blade and kicked it into more shit.

'Look, Reggie, I need to get some capital together. If I come back tomorrow and help you out, will you give me a credit note?'

'Well I don't know if…'

Leonard pointed across the yard at the beat up, canvas-topped vehicle parked in front of the farmhouse.

'Or maybe you could lend me your Land Rover for a couple of days?'

Reggie carved off a couple of thick slices of bread and buttered them up, then ladled out some soup, leek and potato soup. As he turned, there was a gyroscopic effect going on in the soup bowl: he was turning and the bowl was turning, but the soup stayed still. Reggie put Leonard's down on the table and sat in his armchair, balancing his own bowl on his lap. Leonard was kneeling down by the iron grate, he hadn't set an open fire burning for years and he was enjoying the process of getting it going. The newsprint blackened his hands as he screwed up the broadsheets. There was something so comforting about burning newspapers, he felt like the lord of hindsight sending all that non-libellous opinion up in smoke. All those carefully edited quotes crackling into life and all that arch phraseology crumpled to dust in his own bare hands.

Up close, the chimney acted like a great big ear, funnelling sounds in from the outside. Leonard could hear the wind noise and mixed in with it the sound of a cuckoo, far off, out in the fields somewhere.

'Soup, Leonard.'

Leonard turned and Reggie lifted his head in the direction of the soup, to show where it was.

He got up and sat at the table, scooped up a big spoonful and blew on it. He could taste something lovely, something from a long time ago: it was pearl barley.

'That's good stuff.'

Reggie nodded.

'Making my nose run.'

'Look then Leonard, if you come back here tomorrow and do the pigs, I reckon I can let you have the Land Rover for a couple of days, long as I ain't gonna need her. Alright?'

'Course it is, thanks a lot.'

'Alright, then.'

CHAPTER FIVE

It's all very sober, the way 'Warden' is stamped onto the door in gold leaf, a black border outlining the letters, giving them false perspective. Just below and between the 'r' and the 'd', is the tiny lens of a spy hole.

Raymond made his way along the corridor, with Jennifer following on behind. He turned and looked at her to see how the drugs were doing. She looked compliant, but she needed her smile back. Warden only wanted to see happy faces; he wanted girls whose only personality trait was that they smiled a lot. Raymond brushed Jennifer's hair back off her face, smiled at her, and right on cue she smiled back. He had loaded her up with stimulants, ready for the matinée performance. She'd been pumped full of dreamy drugs which would stop her from seeing too clearly. The Dextrone would distort disgust and the Phenulase would turn it into erotic desire.

Raymond lifted his thin fist and knocked on the door. Up close, he saw the narrow beam of light jetting through the spy-hole from the large window opposite, on the far wall of Warden's office. The view looked out over the church and the market square, but the glass was always clouded with condensation in the winter.

Warden heard the knock, but sat still in the armchair. He looked across his desk at the sparkling mineral water bottle. It had been squeezed in the middle when the screw top had been done up tight, so the plastic form had a tucked in waist, flared hips and shoulders - the hour-glass. He was a sick, obsessive old bastard but he was, however, quite chuffed at his own, enduring libido. It kept him looking on the bright side, even in the middle of all this shit. And there had been a ton of shit recently, with men of influence badgering him all hours of the day and night, asking big favours, promising good terms and then underlining them with threats.

Being Warden on the project gave him a position of power; he had influence. But to have power was no protection at all, everyone was subordinate to someone else and there was a brutal pecking order. He mustn't grumble, though; the job did come with the only wage worth doing anything for, a place on the vessel, a chance at survival. He kept thinking how his life, and for that matter how everybody's life was a kind of long, slow walk out of the corner of the ring, toward a far more experienced opponent. There were three ways of dealing with this: (A) on the way out of the red corner you picked up a very big stick and started swinging; (B) you took off your gloves and offered a hand to shake. In this case you were only going to get booed and pick up a broken nose, cauliflower ears and black eyes. The only sensible thing was (C) the famous ducking and diving we hear so much about, the bobbing and weaving and giving as good as you get kind of thing. This was all shit though because theories and philosophies were just pies in the sky. Opinion bored the living crap out of Warden; actions were the only things that counted, actions and events. The door knocked again.

Out in the hallway, Raymond noticed that the stream of light coming through the spy-hole had cut out. Obviously a beady eye had been levelled there on the other side of the door, it would be the Warden's eye, taking a gander. The door swung back but they were not exactly welcomed with open arms. Warden didn't say a word; he just backed away along the hall.

Jennifer reached for Raymond's hand, and holding her fingers, he felt that he should be on her side, he felt bad, felt like a pimping bastard, like he was fencing his own daughter.

He shook her fingers off and let her walk forward. Warden looked her up and down, drew a flat circle in the air with his finger and she spun around, twirling and giggling. She was looking to him for her instructions now. Warden looked past her at Raymond, he nodded.

'I'll be a while, Raymond, but you'd better wait here, we have something to talk about afterwards.'

He turned and led Jennifer into the sitting room, kicking the door shut with his heel.

Raymond's nerve endings were frayed. He tried to shrug off the feelings of guilt by walking over to the big window and taking in the view of the city. It was raining and the daylight was phasing out, dropping the streets into deep shadow. There was a muted yellow haze above the horizon, a dozen industrial buildings with grey smoke trailing from chimneys. The evening traffic was circulating down below, people walking underneath umbrellas, and city life carrying on, almost as usual.

It seemed, for some reason, that Jennifer wasn't able to feel that the Warden's hand had been squeezing and un-squeezing the soft skin between her legs. She was kneeling on the sofa, her back to him. She remained silent and distracted until he redoubled his efforts. Then she felt she had to say something.

'What are you doing down there?'

She giggled and wriggled. Warden's blood was pumping, he wanted a quick hit, so he could get back to business. He lifted her waist, reached around under her skirt and pulled her knickers down to her bent knees. He undid the knot in his training bottoms and fished around for the almighty rod. Not quite there though, was it? He'd had this half-baked trouble before, too much tension in his shoulder blades; he only ever had a short window of opportunity, a few split seconds of green light before he remembered that he was a farcical old fool.

Jennifer asked again, 'What are you doing now?'

Warden hated to hear them, he hated it when they said anything, so he lubricated himself with spittle and fed the flaccid thing in, but she buckled at the knees and fell forward leaving him way behind. Shit! That was all it took to turn the tide, it made the whole circus too real, seeing her so young and remembering that he was so bloody old. Warden knew that he wouldn't be able to manage it, not now the spell had been broken, not now that he was on the wrong side of desire. This was the downhill slope, and well, he couldn't pull it off any more, could he? He thought it better to change tack, so he yanked up his jogging bottoms and yelled out.

'Raymond! Get in here, will you!'

Raymond was examining the condensation patterns left by his lips on the windowpane; he was being intimate with himself, he was trying to absolve his own sins. His breath had left a fat 'X' shape with a thin lip line and a nose dot. He turned to the sitting room door, knocked and entered the room, still wearing his overcoat. He saw the girl rolling around on the sofa and watched as Warden tucked in his shirt and patted his wild hair flat.

'Ah yes, Raymond, I'm finding that she's not really my type. Would you step in, there's a good chap?'

'Step in?'

Raymond was afraid of this, it was not the first time and he knew he would have to do as asked; he was not at all happy. He thought quickly back to those soft porn epics, where the copulation is mimed, maybe he could get away with some sleight of hand and make believe. He took his trousers off and sat on the arm of the sofa. Warden lit a cigarette and sat into an easy chair.

Jennifer was wide eyed and completely stoned, she was groping around for a body part, and finding Raymond's leg, she began to kiss his skin. Raymond wanted in some way to save her, to reduce harm to her if he could. The problem was that now, she was completely out of her mind, she wanted a conclusion to what fear and drugs and sexual contact had started. Raymond saw, with some concern, that she had one single purpose in mind: she wanted to fuck, and anybody, even his body, would do. She kept hauling away at his limp genitals and he felt very uncomfortable, knowing that the old man was seeing all the nasty, uncouth angles of his bare arse from the chair beside the sofa. He turned Jennifer around so that her head was pointing towards Warden, then he got himself in between her legs and started to thrust at a pathetically unconvincing rate. Jennifer was pissed off, she turned to look back at Raymond and he watched as pure anger tightened the pale skin around her eyes. Raymond stopped and she whispered softly in his ear.

'What are you doing, you useless fuck?'

She hit him hard across the face and he rolled off her. At that point Warden yelped with laughter, he snorted and cackled, kind of jumped up and smacked his hands together like a golfer sinking a long, tournament-winning putt.

The only saving grace for Raymond was that he fell right next to his trousers, so he slid into them and belted up. Jennifer bundled up into a foetal position; she moved to the corner of the sofa and started to rock herself to sleep. Warden was tap-dancing across the room, grinning as he opened the bar.

'Bloody hell, that's a laugh eh, Raymond? Pathetic pair of old bastards, aren't we! Come on, let's have a drink!'

Raymond stood and joined Warden, watching passively as the malt whisky was poured out.

'Ice?'

'No, no thanks.'

Raymond buttoned up his shirt and sipped the whisky. He felt like a low-life.

'Why do you keep on with the girls, Warden?'

'One of the perks, isn't it?'

'But what if they don't like the way you carry on? What if they take away your place on the vessel?'

'I won't be taking my place.'

'What?'

'Look, forget I said that.'

'But I don't understand…'

'I'm ill, Raymond, not long to live sort of thing. My blood has become a brackish sludge, it runs around my body like ditch water. I'm sort of beyond help, but I don't want you telling anyone, you hear? You should also bear in mind that I have been thinking very carefully about who I'd be leaving my place to.'

Jennifer mumbled something; Raymond knelt down next to her and checked her pulse.

'OK then, "stunt-cock", on to further business. I need you to keep close tabs on a new arrival.'

Raymond stopped counting and nodded.

'I want you to find out about one Leonard Gopaul. I quite liked him at interview, but I don't think he's going to be a very good citizen. Something tells me that he's not here to play by the rules and I don't want to allow the boy too much freedom to do whatever he's planning to do.'

'I know who you mean, I made first contact a few days ago, I served him a certificate of debt.'

'So from now on, you follow him. Can you do that?'

'Of course I can.'

The telephone rang. Warden finished his glass and picked up the receiver.

'Hello? Yes hello, Max… I know but I'm a busy man.'

Warden waved his hand at the glasses and the whisky; Raymond got up to do the refilling.

Warden despised the voice on the other end of the line, it was whining, paused and mannered, a sort of newscaster-inflected plea. It was Max, a fifty-year-old 'fixer' who made his living by 'brokering' seats on the survival programme for high profile clients.

'OK Warden, but hey! These are top of the tree people, I'm just here to tell you that the offer still stands. You've had time to consider, so what do you think, do you accept the bid?'

Warden yawned.

'Money don't count anymore, Max, you know that. What can you offer instead?'

'Hey, this asteroid impact, it's not one hundred percent either. Money still matters, and when that thing sails by, all the poor bastards, buried in caves and under mountains, are gonna come flying to the surface and pick up where they left off!'

'I'm not a betting man, Max. I've watched all the documentaries about the asteroid, I've seen the trajectory forecasts and it doesn't look good.'

'Yeah, well Vicky and Eddie have asked me to tell you that they've got this art collection, and well, I told them you'd be considering the offer. I need to know what your thoughts are, I've got to get back to them today. So what can I tell them?'

'You tell them you can't help them. I don't need a pop singer and a bloody footballer. The people I'm taking on board have survival skills, they are reconstruction experts, engineers and all-round wise guys.'

'Bollocks they are! I know the way things work up there, they're all bloody crooks and back-stabbing politicians, so that's enough crap from you, Warden! I've listened to that kind of bull long enough! Now you can shut the fuck up and start saying yes to me. If you think you can cut me out, you've got another thing coming. I have contacts too, I can apply pressure if needs be. Think about what I'm saying here, you jumped up shit face!'

Warden laughed; it was refreshing to feel no fear. Ever since his terminal diagnosis, he'd felt this kind of aloofness: the future would be getting along without him. Anybody who threatened harm did not know that they had come up against a brick wall. They had no idea that they were trying to inflict the fear of death on someone who was dying anyway.

There was a knock at the door. Raymond set off to open it but Warden waved him back to the bar. Max was still shouting in Warden's ear, so he put the receiver gently back down, cutting the line. Warden left the room and walked along the hall, with Raymond trailing behind. He got his eye up to the spy hole and squinted - nothing? He raised himself up on his toes and looked again.

'It's my grand-daughter.'

Warden turned.

'Shit, Raymond, it really is my grand-daughter! Go back into the sitting room, tidy up the girl and get her dressed! If Lena spots her, say she's your wife or something!'

Raymond grimaced.

'Does it matter?'

'Of course it matters! I'm not keen on the idea of Lena finding out that I'm such a sordid old sod. Plus the fact that she tells her grandmother everything and I don't want to give that old bat anymore rope to hang me with!'

Raymond nodded and did as he was told.

Warden opened the door and there stood Lena, wearing blue jeans and a red turtleneck. She smiled and he smiled.

'Are you ready, granddad?'

'Ready?'

She understood that he had forgotten, but would that mean 'go home' or 'come in'?

'Bugger, lunch! Yes, I'm supposed to take you to the "Chrome Caravan", right?'

'But you're not!'

Her arms had been hanging at her sides but now she folded them. Her hair was longer than last time, straight and reddish-fair, her skin not good for the sun or for hiding her feelings either; she reddened.

Warden started to offer some excuse.

'Well, see, you know I'm...'

He stopped, reached for her hand and led her in. She was twelve, or was it thirteen, and she was becoming immune to tall stories.

'I simply forgot!'

After shaking off Warden's hand, Lena walked into the room and sat on the window-sill. She was a very pretty girl, but you could see how she would be plump and plain by the time she was eighteen, and not beautiful again until forty or so, when her cheekbones would return. She looked around the place, logging every detail, especially the whisky bottle standing on the hall table. Lena saw all, she noticed and she absorbed everything. The place was cluttered with paperwork, but it was also stuffed full of Warden's things like pieces of gnarled wood, pictures and furniture. Not like grandma's basement workshop, which was dominated by the boiler and the printing press.

Jennifer laughed loud enough to be heard through the wall.

Lena pointed toward the sitting room.

'Who's in there?'

'Well, that's why I forgot our lunch, Lena, I've got a business meeting and I...'

'You should have a secretary, someone who writes it all down.'

'Yes, I know but look, I've got to get back to it.'

Warden led her through to the kitchen.

'I'll finish up as soon as I can and then I'll see if we can get booked in at the restaurant, OK?'

'OK.'

Lena stood on her own in the kitchen, a bright and white fitted kitchen, with underused appliances. It didn't smell of cooking, of food; maybe the kettle and the microwave saw some action, but that was it.

Beryl had explained to her that if she was left alone, she must follow her instructions to 'go through any desk or cupboard, especially if it's locked or unusual-looking'.

If she was discovered prying, Lena was still young enough to use 'just looking' as an excuse; she was, however, old enough in her head to understand what she had to do. She knew what to look for, she would know it if she found it.

In between the sink and a tall freezer there was a door, a black door with a long aluminium handle. She went through and found herself in Warden's study. The room was arranged around the desk, the desk arranged to make the best use of daylight, which angled in through a skylight. There was a computer on the desk, so Lena sat in her grandfather's chair and moved the mouse. A blonde girl appeared on the screen, wearing a shiny, red bikini. She bit her bottom lip, and then stripped her clothes off. She did some stretchy floor exercises, then the screen flickered and she was dressed again. Lena watched the loop of video play one more time, but she didn't touch the keys, she had been told not to touch the computer.

She scanned the room by swinging herself round in the swivel chair; a ceramic fruit bowl, fired a deep, glossy red, was sitting on a side table, filled to the top with green apples. A CD cabinet stood beside a music centre, a black box sat on the floor. The alcoves each side of a small chimney-breast had shelves stacked with books. She pulled the sleeve of her sweater over her hand, so it covered her fingertips, and then she pulled open the right hand desk drawer. Floppy discs, sunglasses, the computer manual, brown envelopes, bank statements and a pipe. The left-hand drawer: insurance documents, two watches, some photographs, string, keys, paper clips and clothes tags.

Lena walked to the corner of the room and knelt down next to the black box. Its lock was undone so she flipped the lid back and found a tight stack of records inside; Barbara Streisand, West Side Story, Brahms, Chopin, Mozart and 'The War Of The Worlds'. He must play them a lot, but why didn't he use CDs?

She walked over to the music centre, it was stuck on the wall and had flat blue speakers attached to the same unit. She opened the CD cabinet, it was empty, just a flat, metal box with heavy hinges. She lifted the box out and flipped open the lid; there was a gun inside. It wasn't a metal revolver, it looked more like a pistol-grip for a garden hose, but this was it, the thing she'd been told to look out for.

She was exposed now; this was not something she'd be able to explain away. She ran to the side table and took an apple from the fruit bowl, held the gun up against it and fired. There was a snap of compressed air and the apple rolled out of her hand, intact. She gathered it up and inspected the puncture marks in the green skin. Lena felt sick in her stomach now because she had promised her grandmother that she would do as she was told. She pulled her top lip away from her teeth, held the pistol up against the wet and tender underside. Her heart was racing but she squeezed the trigger anyway. She felt like she'd been slapped in the face; a focused tingling spread up through her nose and made her eyes water. She held her hand to her lip as she put the gun back into its box and placed the box inside the CD cabinet. Then she stuffed the apple into her pocket, went through to the kitchen and sat down at the table.

Warden was trying to help Raymond lift Jennifer off the sofa; her limp body was a dead weight.

'Gonna break my bloody back, this is useless!'

Raymond lowered her back down.

'Why don't you just leave with Lena and I'll wait for Jennifer to get her breath back?'

'Don't say Jennifer, you know I don't want to know their names.'

Warden lifted the girl's legs back into a more natural position; her calf was warm and soft to his touch.

'My idea is that you could take Lena to lunch and leave me to take care of things here.'

Raymond didn't like the idea of leaving Jennifer alone with Warden.

'Look, Raymond, I love my grand-daughter, but she makes me think of my "x" wife!'

'And?'

'And well, alright, I'd like to take another crack at this Jennifer girl.'

Raymond picked his coat up off the floor and started to slip it on. He spoke up, it was time he spoke up.

'I'm taking her home.'

'Who?'

Raymond pointed at Jennifer.

'Why?'

'It's for the best. You'd better take your grand-daughter out or she'll never forgive you.'

Warden was staring into Raymond's face; it wasn't common for anyone to disagree with him. He felt confused, deflated.

'Get her out of my sight!'

'Who?'

'Jenni-bloody-fer!'

'Right you are, sir.'

'Give me something before you go.'

Raymond took a pillbox from his inside pocket and handed a couple over.

'Thank you, Raymond.'

Warden slammed the sitting room door shut behind him. He paused to grab his glass and swallow the pills then he headed towards the kitchen. When he stepped inside, he saw that Lena was standing on a stool and going through his cupboards.

'What are you doing?'

Lena turned; she looked scared but covered up with a quick smile.

'I'm hungry.'

'Is that so?'

Warden walked across to Lena, took hold of her waist and lowered her to the floor.

'Come on, let's go and eat.'

CHAPTER SIX

Adeline felt stupid standing in the kitchen and doing this stuff. It worked in Drohobycz, her mother insisted that it did, so maybe Slavic Sorcery would work here too. The first thing she had to do was to pour water from a jug into a bowl that she had to hold above her own head. It was not easy to do and it felt odd; as she listened to the water filling the bowl, she felt a pressure on her scalp.

She went back through the parcel her mother had sent. There were other props: a man's shoe, a glove, a bag of wheat. There were very clear instructions as to what to do with this stuff and although Adeline was a sceptic, she followed them to the letter. She took hold of the worn leather glove; it was soiled and smelled of sour sweat. She opened up the wrist and poured in the wheat seed, shaking and bending the fingers so the tips filled right up. She held the wrist shut with her left hand, and as she took hold of it with her own right hand she had the peculiar sensation that she was meeting someone.

Her mother's letter lay open on the kitchen table, a Carpathian postmark stamped onto the envelope. The instructions then asked that she put on the flat-soled shoe, just for one foot. She pushed her foot into the brown leather shoe and laced it up. On the other foot, she had to wear a high heel, a glossy, going-out shoe. Adeline flexed her toes and pushed her left foot into the blue stiletto, buckled the strap and stood up.

The door swung open and Tony walked in. He was carrying the lump of asteroid in one hand and an empty plate in the other; a ceramic plate with the glaze chipped and orange clay showing through. He looked at Adeline's feet then up to her face; he thought about saying something smart but he couldn't think of anything. He shuffled up to the bread-board, cut himself another slice of fruit-cake and crossed the kitchen, chewing on the first mouthful.

'You hit him with that?'

Tony allowed plenty of cake crumbs splutter out of his mouth as he spoke.

'Well, of course I did.'

'He didn't do anything, Tony.'

'He didn't?'

'Well, no. He's a sort of bloody gentleman type, if you can believe such a thing.'

'No, I don't believe it, and I don't like him.'

'Well, I do.'

Tony let go of his plate, which fell to the floor and smashed into hundreds of pieces. He said 'Ooops' and 'I am sorry' then he left the kitchen.

Adeline tried to walk in her odd shoes but it was very awkward, even with her right foot on tiptoe. Her mother had remarked that it would be easier once she was outside in the street. What she had to do was to stand in the kerb with the flat shoe on the pavement and the high heel on the road surface. This would level her up and enable her to walk the block, around the house. She would have to do this once a day now, until the man who would be the father of her child approached her and took her by the spellbound hand.

The one-way system was quiet because there were only ten minutes left before curfew. The only other car on the road was the police car, which had been following Leonard for the last few miles. They were obviously hoping that he would not make it home in time, then they'd be able to make an arrest. Leonard drove as fast as he could; he hoped he was below the speed limit, but he couldn't tell because the dashboard clocks were all out. He could see the police in the rear-view mirror, there were four silhouettes in the car; their heads were rocking back and forth like they were listening to music, and they were swapping their helmets, just for a giggle.

It was raining and the knackered windscreen-wipers just pushed dirt around the glass like a builder's trowel. One deep scratch right across his sight-line split the verticals, made lamp posts resemble x-rays of fractured tibias.

At the bottom of the hill he slowed, indicated and pulled in next to the Mirabelle. The police car slowed as it passed, they looked in then sped off, skidding round the first corner.

Leonard's plan was to leave by first light; he had the Land Rover for three days but he didn't know how far he'd be driving yet. He knew that he had to be cautious, what he was doing would certainly be classified as subversive behaviour. If he were caught he'd be deported, beaten up or worse.

He stepped down onto the pavement and started to climb the steps up to the Mirabelle. Someone was sitting outside, wearing a raincoat the colour of cardboard and slumped over, either dead or taking a nap. Leonard nudged the man, and as soon as his eyes lifted, Leonard could see that it was Ian.

'Ah, there you are, been waiting for you.'

'What d'you want?'

'Now, now, don't get all defensive. Can I come in?'

'Not now, Ian, I'm off to bed. Plus the fact I've heard a nasty rumour that you are some sort of secret policeman.'

'Tis so, tis so. But I'm a free agent, Leonard. I work for myself and have my own best interests at heart. Don't get me wrong, I'm for hire, but my loyalty is to a certain Ian Marble and nobody else.'

Ian climbed down the steps and crossed to the Land Rover, he kicked the tyres and looked the vehicle over.

'Where you off to, then?'

'Nowhere in particular.'

'Intriguing.'

Ian tugged at the lashings, which dangled from the bottom of the canvas roof. He studied the knots.

'Half-hitch! Nicely done, Leo. Just as a matter of interest, let's see your paperwork.'

'That's enough, Ian, I had to use the certificate.'

'I know you did. You're still tying the knot though, aren't you!'

Leonard hadn't tied the knots, they were Reggie's farmyard half-hitches, but there was no point landing Reggie in it.

'OK, what do you want?'

'You're going up-country, aren't you? I'd like to go along for the ride.'

'I'm sorry, Ian, but I can't do that.'

'Really?'

'No.'

'You could get into quite a lot of bother, you know, going all on your own. We'd make a good team.'

'The answer is still no.'

'Look, I can help you, Leonard. I know you want to see the vessel, and I know roughly where it is.'

'You do?'

'Yes, it's up in the north-east, but you won't find it without my help. You'll just get yourself arrested, that's all.'

'Look, Ian, the Land Rover is for getting to work, I'm not intending to go on some wild goose chase. So goodnight!'

'OK, have it your way, but don't come crying to me and don't say that I didn't warn you!'

The Mirabelle was hot and dry again, the lounge was empty and the screen of the fat, coin-op television set was a mute, khaki green. The tops of Harry's arms were visible behind the reception desk, his feet were crossed and resting on the blotting pad and the rest of his body was leaning back in the chair. As Leonard approached, Harry's head came into plain sight; he was wearing headphones and mouthing something silently. Leonard whacked the bell hard and it rang out shrill and lasting. Harry didn't budge until Leonard tapped on the soles of his feet.

'Evening, Leonard.'

'What are you listening to, Harry?'

'Oh, it's personal stuff, self-help.'

'Can I have a go?'

'Go on, then.'

Harry handed the headphones over; Leonard put them on and leant on the reception desk. It was chanting with bells, that's why Harry hadn't heard the reception bell. The voices were low and grave but solid and comforting.

'Om ah hum vajra guru padma siddhi hum, Om ah hum vajra guru padma siddhi hum, Om ah hum vajra guru padma siddhi hum.'

Leonard uncovered his ears.

'What's all this, then?'

'Put them back on.'

Leonard put the headphones back and listened carefully.

'When we meditate, we are trying to calm the confusions of a chaotic age. It is

therefore useful to compare the mind to a jar of muddy water; the more we leave the water without interference, without stirring it, the more the particles of dirt will sink to the bottom, letting the natural clarity of the water and the brightness of the mind shine through.' [1]

Leonard took the headphones off again and Harry asked, 'Do you think it'll help?'

Leonard shrugged.

'Maybe.'

'Good, good. And so, how are you doing these days then, having any luck with things? Heard any whispers through the sulphurous old grape vine?'

'There's plenty of whispering going on out there. Everybody's whispering something to someone. But I think you're better off listening to the self-help.'

'You might be right there.'

'Night.'

'Night, then.'

Leonard stripped off his clothes as he climbed the stairs, his coat and his sweater, even his T-shirt. It was stuffy and airless in his room; he opened the windows as much as he could and kicked off his shoes. He splashed some water over his face and lay down on the bed; his head was too full to sleep. He lay there trying to fend off the nagging doubts, trying to remember Harry's tape.

It took him a while to get comfortable. He yawned and his eyelids were heavy, but there was this persistent, metallic clanging. He realised that the noise was coming from the central heating pipe-work; it was Beryl tapping on the pipes, trying to get his attention, three floors below.

Leonard pulled his shoes and his T-shirt back on and went out into the hall.

By the time he got to the basement, the clanging had stopped. He stood by the door into the boiler room and listened. Nothing, not a whisper, so he knocked against the frame.

'Yes?'

'It's Leonard.'

'Come in, boy.'

1. Sogyal Rinpoche: 'Meditation'

It was dark inside and even warmer than upstairs. There was a lack of oxygen in the air, and a distant humming of contained flames. A faint ticking of thermostatic control told Leonard that somewhere inside the machinery, a fire was roaring. He moved through flickering shadows, past the bed of the printing press and on towards yellow light shining from two standard lamps.

'We're through here.'

He followed the voice until he could see a pair of hands, a young girl's hands frantically tying something up in her lap. Beryl looked up, then away again. She was doing the same thing, she was focused on her hands, nodding and raising her eyebrows as she tried to go faster.

'We're having a knitting race, bear with us a minute.'

Leonard leaned against the wall and watched the child: she was numb with concentration, all her energies were focused on her efforts, and she was going as fast as she could. But Beryl was working effortlessly, her hands moving with fluid, unfaltering speed.

The girl did not take her eyes off her needles, but Beryl was relaxed enough to look across at Leonard.

'Haven't got yourself beaten up or bumped off, then?'

'I'm doing my best, watching my back.'

'That's good. This is my grand-daughter, Lena. She's going to lose.'

Lena smiled but she was not happy; she didn't like to be chided and she was annoyed that her grandmother was able to talk and knit at the same time. She tried to break Beryl's concentration by asking a question.

'Do you think that ducks have heart attacks?'

Beryl swept the question aside.

'Probably, dear. Yes, I think that could be possible.'

Lena could see now that she couldn't win; Beryl was unrolling more blue yarn and going even faster.

'Oh, Nan!'

Lena stopped and stretched out her blue band of knitting. She ran over to Leonard and sized the wool up against his waist. Beryl stopped casting off.

'Ha, is that a surrender, dear?'

'Yes, alright, alright!'

Lena looked up at Leonard and asked, 'Turtle or crew?'

'What?'

'Neck, you fool! I'm going to knit you a sweater.'

'Don't be impolite, Lena.'

'Sit down in Lena's chair, Leonard, she's going to make us a nice cup of tea.'

Lena stuck both of her knitting needles back into her ball of wool with bullfighting force, then walked off further into the basement.

'She is a terrible loser.'

'Why don't you let her win?'

'What kind of a lesson is that?'

'Well, yeah I…'

'Somebody tells me you've got yourself some transport?'

'That's right.'

'What are your plans, then?'

'That'd be telling.'

'So tell me.'

'I'm leaving at first light. I'm going to look for the construction site. I want to see the vessel for myself!'

'You're a brave one. Do you know where it is, then?'

'I've got a rough idea.'

'That's no good, is it? Sounds a bit half-arsed, if you don't mind me saying so.'

'Well, a man I know said I should head up into the north-east. I'm going to get hold of some aerial photographs from a woman I know.'

'You're such a fool Leonard: "a man I know, a woman I know"!'

'Ian, Ian Marble!'

'Are you mad? Marble's a maniac!'

'I know that, I know what I'm doing!'

Beryl smiled.

'Be honest with me, you haven't got a bloody clue, have you?'

'Not really, no.'

'What do you know about Marble?'

'He's alright, he let me stay one night to avoid curfew.'

'Did you know, for example, that he has a pig's heart in his chest?'

'What?'

'He had a transplant about a year ago. He's got the heart of a pig.'

'You're joking.'

'You see, Leonard, you don't really know very much at all, do you? Haven't you worked out that you can't trust anyone here, including me? Nothing is done on trust and nothing should be taken at its face value. If you want to get anything done you've got to trade, make mutually beneficial deals, like the one I'm going to offer you.'

'I'm listening.'

'Before we move on, this "girl you know", her name's Adeline, isn't it?'

'Yeah. She's got these photographs, they could be useful.'

'She got any influence over you, Leonard? You lusting in her direction?'

'No.'

'Don't lie to me! You are pathetically transparent. Do you know what a hard cock is, Leonard?'

'Well, I...'

'I mean, what it really is?'

Leonard shrugged his shoulders; she was going to tell him what she thought it was anyway.

'It's a handle, a bloody saucepan handle and once the lady in question has a hold of you, she can put you wherever she wants! She can heat you up over the hot plate see, or empty you out into the bin! Do you see what I'm saying?'

Leonard saw himself being picked up and put down in his mind; funny but not at all that funny, really.

'I know what I'm doing, Beryl.'

'Why doesn't that reassure me?'

'Look, the most pressing and most urgent thing is, this bloody asteroid is going to hit us in something like eight weeks time. Right?'

'That's what they reckon, boy. No mistake this time, they've given the rock a name. They've started calling it the Ice Moon.'

'OK, what's the deal then? What were you about to offer me?'

Beryl stood up and rested her hands on her hips.

'Now, Leonard, I need you to trust me. No, in fact it's more than that: I need you to indulge me.'

'Right.'

'Stand up and don't think too much about what is going to happen next. I am not a lusty old cow with misplaced longings. I just know my horse-flesh.'

Leonard stood and Beryl approached him. She reached for his genitals and

Leonard flinched.

'That's alright, now just relax.'

'What the hell are you doing?'

'What do you think I'm doing? I'm weighing you up, Leonard. I'm trying to find out if you've got the bloody balls for this.'

'For what? Are you allowed to touch me like that?'

'Yes I am. These are unusual circumstances and this is absolutely necessary.'

Beryl looked onto Leonard's eyes, then she removed her hands and took a step backward.

'Are you quite satisfied?'

'You could do with a little more fire in your belly. But I suppose you'll have to do.'

'Thanks a lot.'

'I want you to look after Lena. I want you to get her onto the vessel. Now excuse me a minute, I am going to check on the tea.'

The room behind the laundry chute was used as a kitchen; there was a microwave, a leaking fridge and an electric frying pan. There was a sort of worktop propped up on bricks, it bowed in the middle but that didn't matter. The floor wasn't level either, patches of repaired cement overlapped, forming ridges which the blue rug couldn't really cover.

The kettle boiled but it didn't switch off, so the steam just rolled off the ceiling and back down around Lena. She had a big knife in her hand and she was cutting open the green apple she'd taken from Warden's office.

'Be careful with that, Lena.'

Lena sucked in a sharp breath. Beryl kissed the top of her head.

'Don't creep up on me, Nan! You make me jump!'

'Have you got it?'

'Yes, I've got it.'

Lena picked a metal tag out of the apple and wiped it with surgical spirit.

'You know how to do it?'

'Yes!'

'I'll take the tea, you bring the biscuits.'

'Yes alright, Nan, you go on back to him.'

Beryl knew how to handle a tray; it had been her life, this fetching and carrying. She set the tea down and poured, and Leonard helped himself to sugar.

'Are you still printing the newsletter?'

'Of course, not that it has much effect. It's gone too far for that now.'

'What has?'

'The scramble. The gloves are off, haven't you noticed? It's going to get nasty now.'

'What is?'

'Just staying alive.'

Lena entered with biscuits piled up on a metal plate.

'Would you like one?'

'Yes please, I'd love one.'

Lena was pleased; she crossed the floor to Leonard.

'Close your eyes and open your mouth.'

Leonard didn't really want to, he didn't want to start a long running weirdness with the girl, where Lena would think him willing to play the kid in her games. But then Beryl joined in.

'Oh go on, Leonard, be a sport.'

'OK, OK.'

Lena approached with the tray ahead of her. Leonard looked at the pink wafers and the jammy dodgers, then closed his eyes and opened his mouth. He felt something cold slip underneath and over the top of his lip, then a sudden, localised pain. He screamed out and opened his eyes; something like a bee sting had cut into his upper lip!

'Fuck!'

Lena was standing over him, her concentrated face up close to his. She was lifting something away from his mouth, something like a staple gun.

'What the fuck are you doing?'

Leonard jumped out of his chair. He couldn't hit out at her so he kicked the table over sending tea and biscuits flying everywhere. He took Lena by the shoulders.

'What are you doing?'

Leonard turned to Beryl.

'What the hell is she doing?'

'I'm sorry, Leonard, she's got this thing with the staple gun just lately. I know it's terrible behaviour but it's not her fault! She has… problems.'

'Problems?'

'Emotional problems. Come here and let me have a look at you.'

Beryl pulled him over to the light and brushed his hands away from his face. She lifted his top lip and rolled it over to look at where the blood was coming from.

'Is the girl mad?'

Lena was sitting in her chair knitting again.

'Keep still! She's not mad, no, and I can't see anything wrong with your lip; there's a little cut but that's all.'

'Yeah, but why in the hell would she do such a thing?'

'I'm sorry, Leonard, she is prone to bouts of instability. Her parents were killed rather violently and she sometimes just reacts like this. Please don't be angry with her, she doesn't know why. You're a stranger and she just needs to get used to you, that's all.'

'What do you mean, her parents were killed?'

'Car crash, good old granddad was driving, newted to the gills on cheap whisky, he drove straight into a wall. The car rolled over and the roof collapsed. He was the only one to get out alive.'

Beryl sat down again and picked up her knitting. Leonard rubbed his fingers across his lips and tried to salvage a cup of tea.

'Well then, now we know each other a little better, I'd like to talk to you about Lena. I'd like to get back to settling the terms of our agreement.'

'I'm listening.'

Leonard rinsed his mouth with tea; he swallowed, tasted blood.

'As I said, I find that the best policy these days is to trust no one, not a living soul. So in keeping, I am not going to trust you either. However, as I need your help, I am prepared to offer you a deal.'

Beryl's hands were looping around the needles, drawing up the blue yarn.

'This rather careless granddad I've just mentioned, is the Warden.'

'He's your husband?'

'"X" husband. The thing is, he used to talk in his sleep, he probably still does but I am not the one who lies awake next to him any more. He is a keen debaucher of young girls, so they are the ones listening now. I heard enough though, before I finally left him and the result is that I know more than most about the vessel project.'

'What do you want from me?'

'It's simple; I want you to check out the construction site. I'll keep Lena with me until I have a favourable report from you. Then I will ask you to make sure that she gets onto the vessel.'

'But why can't you use your influence with the Warden?'

Beryl laughed.

'Even if he wanted to, and he doesn't, he still couldn't help. He has to do what the selection board decide. So I need someone like you to make sure that Lena is safe.'

'What makes you think I'm the right man for the job?'

'Give me some credit. I may be a silly old cow, but I know a good man when I see one. Is it a deal?'

'I'll think about it.'

'Listen to me, Leonard: if you think you've got a chance of getting onto the site without help, forget it. And the possibility of being selected for the list? Forget that too, the thing was filled a long time ago. The places have been bought out by the rich, the powerful and the murderous. This selection process is just a scam.'

'Well, if that's the case, how could I promise to get Lena on board?'

Beryl lifted her glasses off her nose and looked at him squarely.

'It's a challenge, Leonard, something to rise to! And you should realise one more thing, at the outset.'

'What?'

'This is the greatest challenge in your life. You must not wait these last few weeks out running around in a tiz, in a flat spin. Now is the time to act, to make your presence felt. The great moments in the history of the world were not won by the innocent bystanders, no! The future has to be fought for and taken, the future has to be won with heroic deeds!'

She was being fierce, but not foolhardy. She meant what she said because there were tell-tale goose bumps on her arms and an emotional intelligence radiating from her face.

'That's it, then, that's what's on the table. I've already arranged the paperwork.

I've arranged a pass which will allow you to go back and forth across the border. I will also supply you with a document that will grant you access to the construction site. This is the only way you will get past security. I'll give you some goods to trade, some whisky and fags, and I'll draw you a map and explain how to get there. In exchange I will expect a full report on the vessel site. Well?'

'I'll think about it.'

Beryl smiled.

'You think you have a choice?'

'Alright, if Lena can promise to behave, then yes, we have a deal!'

Leonard looked across at Lena; she was singing softly. She smiled and waved a ball of wool in the air.

'Crew or turtle?'

Leonard thought about it for a moment and then said.

'Turtle.'

From now on, Leonard would have to be very careful. From here on in, he had stepped over the line to the other side, where official opinion would conclude that he'd earned the consequences, that 'he'd had it coming to him'.

He'd heard Warden's warning along with everyone else in the interview room. There was no mistake; he was now, officially, playing with fire.

It was just after first light when he stood beside the Land Rover and looked up. A pale blue break in the cloud to the east was the brightest point in the sky, there was a smell of rain in the air. A few windows in the Mirabelle were lit, insomniacs and early birds fixing breakfast. Leonard guessed that many of the guests just stayed in all the time, had food delivered and never ventured out. It was bad luck, but as he threw his bags onto the passenger seat, someone pulled their curtains aside and looked straight down on to Leonard's clandestine departure.

Leonard did not normally worry about bad luck omens, apart from not putting new shoes on the table, or when dressing, if you accidentally put something on inside out, you never took it off and put it back on the right way. In Leonard's family, this was, and always had been, a 'no no'.

No point now in doing the rolling start he'd planned. The Land Rover was a noisy vehicle and he'd wanted to start the engine downhill of the hotel. That was pointless now, now that he'd been seen from above. He could feel the unknown eyes burning into the roof and putting the two's and two's together as he pulled away from the kerb and headed off up hill.

The gearshift was awkward, the suspension rock hard, the steering was heavy and the tyre bolted onto the bonnet was distracting, but it climbed and accelerated. It was taking Leonard where he wanted to go!

They were Raymond's eyes, up on the fourth floor, looking down. He'd been chewing on a part-burnt piece of toast as he watched the Land Rover pull away from the Mirabelle and climb the hill back towards the centre of town. He was expecting as much, and he'd notified Warden the previous evening that he expected Leonard to take a trip up-country any day now. The view was good from the fourth floor, and with binoculars, Raymond was able to follow Leonard's progress until he looped a roundabout and disappeared.

He dialled Warden's number into his mobile and waited for the tone to be answered. He looked in the mirror at his bloodshot eyes and grey skin; you could say that he was fed up with being Raymond.

Leonard stopped short of Tony's bar, parked up, switched the engine off and watched the petrol gauge fall back slowly to zero; at least that worked. It was just before seven o'clock and the only place with any lights on was the baker's shop. When he opened the car door he could smell the new bread on the air. He walked to the window and looked inside. The glass was all steamed up but he could just make out a couple of figures working in the background, white hats and white overalls carrying silver trays to and fro.

Leonard carried on walking until he was standing outside the bar. He wasn't sure whether to knock, he didn't want to have to explain himself to Tony. But he wanted to talk to Adeline, he needed the photographs of the vessel. As he stood there thinking over what he should do, the top bolt slid back and the door handle turned. Leonard moved away and took cover in the baker's doorway. He heard the door slam and then he heard footsteps, odd, limping footsteps. It was Adeline. He saw the side of her face as she passed, she had her head tilted forward and she was looking down at the ground.

Leonard let her pass, then stepped out behind her and started to follow. He looked at her feet and wondered if she had lost her mind because she was wearing one flat shoe, one high heel; flat shoe on the kerb stone, high heel down in the gutter. She was walking steadily though, fairly fast, and behind her back she was carrying a leather glove, a fat-fingered glove like a scarecrow's hand. She walked to the corner and turned right, still straddling the gutter. It seemed as if she might be off to join the circus, this was her act and she would never look back. She stepped around a lamp-post and realised she was being followed. She spun on the ball of the flat soled shoe and grimaced at Leonard. She was embarrassed, like she'd been caught sleepwalking, or something similar.

'What do you want?'

Her voice was different, filled with anxiety, so Leonard shrugged his shoulders and kept quiet. Adeline walked towards him, looking tired and unhappy without her make-up, and wearing middle-aged colours. She looked the way younger wives do, when they ugly themselves up a bit so that the much older husband doesn't feel so bad. She looked threatening though, holding onto the big club hand; maybe it was one of Tony's hands, severed at the wrist.

'I've been expecting you, Leonard. I have something to ask you.'

That was ominous but Leonard reckoned that if she had prepared something to say to him, then he ought to let her say it, let it happen the way she'd rehearsed it in her head. If he let it go as planned, she would feel that she'd given a good account of herself, she'd feel that she'd been understood. Then the mood would at least be ordered and calm when he said, no, that he couldn't, that he didn't want to.

She held out the big hand, the idea seemed to be that he had to shake it. That seemed OK, so Leonard gripped tight, and shook. Adeline let go of the glove her end, and thousands of seeds came spilling out of the wrist, raining down onto the paving slabs, bouncing and rolling, making a showering monsoon sound. He watched this happen in a kind of slowed motion. She was watching, too, her face bright with glee, as if a prank had paid off.

God knows why, but it made Leonard smile, he was grinning shyly as Adeline skipped forward two steps and jumped into his arms. Leonard swung her round. It was the first time he had held her like this; he felt her weight, her mass, and had a better idea of what she consisted of, what she amounted to in the flesh and blood.

She kissed him lightly on his mouth with her dry lips.

'You know what this means, Leonard?'

This was not just a statement of fact; it was, Leonard figured, some kind of a forecast, panning out.

'What's going on?'

She stepped away from him.

'It means that sooner or later, no matter what, you will be the father of my child.'

'Ah, but what about Tony?'

'Tony can't, he can't have children. It's a medical problem and it's a shame.'

'Listen to me, Adeline, you may not even see this year out. The Ice Moon is going to hit the earth in less than two months.'

'Yes, I know all that but there's a lottery for the last places on the vessel, it's a state residents' lottery, and you can only enter if you are pregnant. I've never really thought of myself as a mother, but now, with all this space clutter shit, well, now it's different.'

Adeline was standing crookedly on the pavement, her whole body involved in making her case.

'Do you know about the deal Tony has offered? The price, if I sleep with you, is that I will have to leave the city. Don't get me wrong but I would be committing suicide if I took that kind of a deal.'

'Stop dreaming about rescue, Leonard, it's very unlikely you stand a chance of winning a place. You've not been recalled and it's been a while since your interview, right!'

'I know. Look, that's why I'm going out to the construction site. I want to see if there are any other ways to get on board, any back doors.'

'But you'll never find it.'

'I will, but I need the pictures, the ones you showed me, the satellite shots.'

'Yes, I've still got them. Come in for a minute, they're upstairs.'

Leonard followed her into the bar and sat down where the air was sour. Daylight is not flattering for a nightclub, all the scratches show, all the vague nocturnal references stand out in ugly fact: the scorched lampshades, the atlas of wine stains on the carpet, the edges of the velvet seating polished black with wear and tear. Without the cover of music, the fridges hum, and without cigarette smoke, the pine cleaning fluids sting the nose.

Adeline came down the stairs moving gracefully without the stupid shoes and passed him the envelope. No more was said; all the cards were on the table, the whoie pack. She stretched one corner of her mouth into a quick smile and showed him the door. She wasn't sad, no, she was quietly confident. She walked half way to the car with him and held her own elbows as Leonard slapped the gearshift into first and gunned the pedal, leaving her in a cloud of milky-blue diesel smoke.

CHAPTER SEVEN

The routine was that on the first of each month, a selection board inspector would call, always a different inspector, but with similar questions. He would want to take tapes of candidates away, and to discuss schedules. However, March was not a routine month, the inspector didn't turn up until the twelfth, he didn't want to see any videotape, he just wanted a strong, sweet cup of tea.

They were on the top floor of the Administration building, Warden was sitting opposite the inspector, who had views out over playing fields and into far-off countryside. They were seated in straight-backed, straight-talking chairs and Warden was trying to suss-out the inspector. This one was a reddish haired man in his early forties, with a high colour and thick, horizontal eyebrows. He had pale eyes and red marks round his nostrils, where he'd been fingering his nose.

'I don't need to know about any more priority cases. The book's just about closed and we have begun to sign off certain sections of the passenger lists.'

Warden nodded, listening only, letting him say what he'd come to say, letting him get it off his chest.

'They're not saying how the intake will be organised, there's not even a whisper about the procedure so I'm here to just suggest that you complete the induction within the next week to ten days and wrap it up, really. That's about it! After that, who knows? I'm in the dark, too. All we've been told is to go home and panic-buy, stockpile whatever supplies we can get hold of and just wait.'

The inspector's mobile phone rang. He held the receiver to his ear and stepped away toward the far corner of the room, into a personal space, a sumo circle of space where he kicked at the ground and had his whispered conversation.

Warden took the opportunity to make his own call. He dialled and the phone rang just once before it was snatched up and answered.

'Hello, sergeant Hayes?'

'That's correct, ID please.'

'East Anglia, ward thirty six.'

'Yes, sir, how can I help?'

'Has my man been on to you about our nosey parker, Leonard Gopaul?'

'Yes, sir, we have description of vehicle and probable route. We'll pick him up this evening, give him something to think about.'

'Good work. Let me know how it turns out.'

'Will do.'

Warden settled the receiver back but he felt uneasy, it was a dangerous time to fuck up. Martial law was not long in coming, and when his job was finished, he'd be very vulnerable. And these blokes like the sergeant were OK, until they changed their minds and decided that now was the time for you to be the enemy! You never knew who was whispering sweet nothings into their ears. You could never be sure about mercenaries; they had no loyalty, except to themselves. They were with you one day, against you the next, no arguments, no disagreements to tip you off, just the about-face of the gun barrel and good bye Vienna.

There were massive holes in the road filled with black water and there was a border of rubbish on each side of the street as Leonard drove through the outskirts of the city. Squashed traffic cones marked ditched and burnt out vehicles but the worst thing was that nobody stuck to their own lane anymore. It wasn't clear whether you were supposed to drive on the left or right, so Leonard straddled the centre line, kept his speed up and his headlamps on full beam. Cars weaved past each other on both sides of the road but Leonard held his line, and mostly the on-coming cars did all the evasive stuff. Maybe they thought he was driving a military vehicle and didn't want a burst of machine-gun fire hacking into their tyres. The duel carriageways and then the motorways were even worse, like great unmarked car parks with idiots going in all directions, swerving around broken-down vehicles and slow-coaches.

The Land Rover was noisy above about sixty, but the heater worked and he felt like he was getting somewhere at last. If he could just make it out to the construction site and see the thing, make sure it existed, then he would be able to imagine a strategy, devise a way on board. If the application procedure were bullshit, he would go round it and find another way!

Every single streetlight and road sign had been removed, there were no mileage markers or junction indicators; there was nothing to go on. Leonard figured he'd just have to keep going until he met one of the landmarks detailed in Beryl's directions. She'd started her map in the middle of an A4 sheet, which was a problem because a lot of detail had been squashed in to fit at the bottom of the page. The scale was all over the place and it would be difficult to work out exactly what she meant. Her writing was quite neat, though, a throw-back to severe 1950's schooling.

By dusk he saw the 'cement works' off to the right of the motorway, and knew that this was where he was supposed to exit. He took the slip road and spotted the 'wide brick bridges over the railway lines'. He drove alongside the tracks until he saw the older and narrower 'stone bridges over the river'. The river snaked its way downhill, twisting black and silver with the shadows of overhanging trees dappling the surface of the red, iron-rich water.

As daylight fell, the road climbed into higher ground, and each time the Land Rover climbed, the petrol gauge fell right back to zero, a warning that he'd have to find fuel soon.

He slowed and pulled off the road. He needed to stretch his legs and open up his flask of coffee. He sat up on the bonnet and looked out at a peaceful, undulating landscape of low green hills. As the sun set, he climbed a bank up to a pile of jagged green rocks and filled his lungs. The tops of the hills were dusted bright with snow, dark streams running out of the ice flowed down through rust coloured bracken and on towards a lake. The lake was gunmetal blue with faint, polished bird traces criss-crossing the surface. Leonard's stress level had dropped; the high altitude seemed to unravel idiotic fears, untie stupid knots in his stomach. He held Beryl's map up against the landscape, and figured that at this rate, he should reach the site in about an hour. He stepped back down the bank and opened the driver's door.

A flat, rhythmic battering of the air made him stop and look over his shoulder. A small, red helicopter came out of the sunset, and started to turn in toward Leonard's position. He jumped in and started up, crunched the gears and took off. He had his pass to get onto the vessel, but it was not fool-proof, he didn't know what he was getting himself into and his cover story was pretty shallow. He drove for a couple of miles with his lights off, until it became pretty impossible to see. Then he caught sight of a very welcome neon sign: it was the petrol station which had been detailed on Beryl's map. He slowed and turned onto the forecourt, pulled up close to the black diesel pump and the Land Rover shivered to a halt.

He unscrewed the cap and jammed the pump into the tank. He stood there with his hand on the roof, watching the fruit machine numbers tumble. He reached into the back of the cab to fish out a litre bottle of whisky, hoping that would cover the gas.

If you've ever had your arm pushed up your back, you will know that the pain is profound. You realise that you can't move, and must not move for fear of the last shove which will dislocate your shoulder. Leonard had been taken by surprise; he'd been thrown forward by two heavy figures that had approached silently except for a slight whisper of their nylon waterproofs. Both Leonard's fists had been hauled up into the middle of his back; his reflex was to lift his foot and kick back, hoping to drag it down the front of someone's shin. He was lucky to make contact, lucky and very stupid, because he was spun round and belly punched, the kind of deep punch that moved your internal organs around.

Now he could see who was doing this: there were two of them, big men in dark uniform, their faces covered with black balaclavas.

'That's enough of that, smart arse!'

Leonard noted the 'from nowhere' accent, the wide shoulders and the bull necks, their automatic rifles strapped diagonally across their chests. One of the soldiers checked his face against a photograph and turned to nod to his mate. Leonard was shit-scared, so scared that he wasn't thinking when he lifted his knee into the man's exposed crotch, and saw his shoulders lift up to his neck.

'There's some fight in the bastard, eh, Geri?'

Geri came over, took the diesel pump out of Leonard's tank and inserted it into Leonard's mouth. He had to force it in because Leonard was resisting, he could see where the idea was heading. Geri broke a piece of tooth away, held onto Leonard's nose and squeezed the trigger. Fluid was rushing down his throat. For a split second, it was just like the consistency of milk shake, but then some taste buds in the back of his throat caught on and he panicked. The diesel ran over his cheeks as he tried to wriggle free; his face was burning and he had to close his eyes, but worst of all, he couldn't help it, he had to swallow. Then everything went black; Leonard was unconscious.

The two soldiers picked him up, transferred him onto the back seat of their car and spun the wheels as they pulled off the forecourt.

Geri switched his head microphone on.

'Geri here, hello?'

A voice crackled through static.

'Use proper etiquette Geri, over!'

'Ah… this is three four south calling Horncastle, over?'

'Horncastle reading you, three four south. Sergeant Hayes speaking, over.'

Geri looked over his shoulder at the pathetic body on the back seat.

'Yeah, bringing in driver of Land Rover, fitting description of one Leonard Gopaul, repeat Leonard Gopaul. Be with you in thirty minutes, over.'

'Affirmative, three four. Horncastle out.'

Leonard was coming to; he was rolling and vomiting on the back seat, choking the poison out of his stomach. Geri looked round again.

'He's making a right fucking mess back there.'

'We'll hose him down when we get back to camp.'

The movement of the car threw Leonard's body around, but under the driver's seat was his first bit of luck, a box of matches. He reached out, opened the box and struck one. The regurgitated diesel started to burn, and he slipped his oil-soaked coat off, transferred his paperwork into his trousers and held the coat to the flames. The fire started instantly. Leonard got up from down behind the back seat and wrapped the melting, smoking nylon around the driver's eyes. Geri tried to unstrap his rifle but by the time he had taken aim, Leonard had leant on the door-handle and rolled out of the line of fire, onto the road. As he tumbled to a halt, he saw the car skid off the road; it hit a stone wall and burst into flames.

Leonard was still emptying himself out. He was on his knees and still gagging diesel, his throat burning and his head spinning.

He got to his feet and wandered off the road, knelt down and cupped his hands in shallow ditchwater beside the road. He sucked the water down, rinsed his mouth and spat it out; he washed his face, cleaned as much of the stuff off as he could. He was cold, shaking with fear but glad to be alive.

He knew that he should keep moving, so he picked himself up again and started to stumble along beside the road. His elbows were bleeding and his shoulders and hips were cut and grazed.

Staying close to the road, though, was not a great idea; he was visible and maybe the burning car would bring in more soldiers. Leonard just wanted to get away, get some distance between him and the car wreck. He cut back off the road and made his way uphill through long, wet grass and spongy soil. He climbed up over the first ridge in his sight line. Only a glimmer of daylight remained as the red sun was already way down below the horizon. He followed a narrow path across a long, steep slope, down into boggy ground. The path split in two, giving no clues as to which was the right way. A phrase which he'd never quite understood came to mind - 'died of exposure'. Now he could see how something like that could happen. He was cold without his coat and unsteady on his feet, the aftertaste of diesel made him wretch and spit.

A sweet, musky smell hit his nose; it had wafted in on the breeze blowing from Leonard's right. He turned off the path and headed upwind into the fragrance. It was a citrus smell, an unnatural and pretentious, Saturday night whiff. Leonard could see a man walking along a track fifty metres ahead, going left to right. He had a rucksack on and a coat with a hood. Not a soldier, he looked too small and he was wearing civilian clothes.

Leonard shouted out.

'Hello!'

The figure turned his head and stopped.

Leonard explained.

'I'm lost.'

He started to walk towards the man, but the figure turned away and carried on walking along his path, faster than before.

'I need help!'

The figure stopped and turned again but made no move towards Leonard. He took his hands out of his pockets and lifted some binoculars up to his eyes. Leonard was really feeling the cold now, his legs shaking with downhill fatigue. His head was splitting open, he had a searing pain behind his eyes which throbbed in time with his heartbeat. The figure called out.

'What d'you want?'

It was a young man's voice, quite a thin, passive voice.

Leonard approached.

'I had a car accident and I need to get myself seen to, that's all. Do you live round here?'

The figure lifted his wrist, pulled back the arm of his coat to look at his watch.

'I'm late for a split shift.'

Leonard stopped in front of the man, looking pretty fucked.

'You don't look too good.'

Leonard offered his hand.

'Leonard.'

The man's grip was reluctant.

'I'm Dave.'

'I know I look like shit. I'm lucky to be alive, though, and I need to clean up and get warm.'

Dave knocked his hood back off his head and rested his hands on his hips.

'You'd better come with me, I think we've got a first aid kit at the factory.'

'Thanks.'

Dave kept his head down and led the way; he never once looked over his shoulder to check if Leonard was following. And he didn't say a word apart from 'shit' or 'fuck' a couple of times when he stumbled on muddy ground.

The path eventually met a road and the road ended at a fenced off group of brick buildings with steep, slate rooflines.

Leonard followed Dave down alongside the first building, past empty wooden packing cases and sacks of polystyrene chips.

As they approached a double door, savage barking came from a security van parked beside the building. The black tip of a dog's nose pushed itself up against the glass and snorted the air coming in through a small gap. Leonard recognised the crinkly black skin around flaring nostrils, it was the nose of an Alsatian guard dog.

'Reception' consisted of one leatherette swivel chair and a low smoked glass table with copies of 'Forecast News' stacked in the centre. As Dave walked through, he nodded his head towards a mousy girl in a black trouser-suit, sitting behind a metal desk.

'Alright, Halima?'

Halima replied, 'Hello Dave' back at him and looked Leonard up and down.

He tried to look harmless and followed Dave through a door marked 'Factory Floor, no unauthorised personnel.'

Dave took his rucksack and coat off and sat down at his workbench. He rested his hands on his thighs and took a moment to himself before he started.

On the work surface in front of him were cutting tools and paint pots, fret saws and jigsaws, mitre blocks and G clamps. And then some examples of his labours: various weather forecasting symbols in different stages of completion. There were cut-outs of storm clouds, grey with lightning flashes, or a paler shade with pearly raindrops falling, white cumulous with peek-a-boo yellow suns trying to break through, snow flakes, Fahrenheit and Celsius temperature indicators, wind direction arrows and whole yellow discs of sunshine with jagged rays. Dave flicked a wall switch on and somewhere beneath the bench, a compressed air pump buzzed into life. He started heating glue, arranging paints, clipping clouds into stands, and positioning stencils.

Leonard tapped Dave on the shoulder as he pulled on his eye protection and tested his airbrush.

'Yes? Oh, sorry, I'm on price work so have to get stuck in from the off. First aid's in the green box over there on the wall, and make yourself a cup of tea if you want. You'd better not hang around too long, we've got security here and they swing round a couple of times each shift, they'll probably want to ask you some awkward questions.'

Leonard nodded and turned to the window. The bench beneath it was cluttered with rejected work; spare flood warnings, spiralling anti-depressions, tangled isobars and unlikely long-range weather fronts.

Leonard opened up the first aid kit, cleaned his wounds and rubbed antiseptic into his cuts. He swallowed Kaolin and morphine, bicarbonate of soda and three Aspirin, then he washed it all down with a gallon of tea. He ripped off the top of a Tupperware box and ate what was left of the chocolate roll inside. He looked into Dave's rucksack lying open on the floor: inside was a bottle of after-shave. Leonard dropped down to retie his laces and lifted the gold-topped bottle into his pocket as he stood up.

Dave was completely focused on his work, turning a rain cloud in his hands, checking for faults, so Leonard started to move off, back towards the reception.

'Leonard?'

'Yeah?'

Dave pointed to the other end of the factory floor.

'It's better if you go that way, the receptionist's a nosey cow.'

'Right, thanks.'

'Don't mention it!'

As Leonard walked the length of the factory floor, a couple of men looked up from their work, but most kept their heads down, their scalpels concentrated on a clean cut-line.

He pushed through the exit door into a white-washed hallway with faded red floor paint. Concrete steps led up some stairs to his left but he turned toward the emergency exit instead. A grey-green fungal bloom spread from the edge of the door; it was padlocked shut but the frame was wet, rotted through. Leonard gave the frame a kick, and flakes of soft timber dropped and wood lice ran out the bottom. He kicked again and this time, with a push as well, the door broke open.

Leonard made his way along the side of the building, crouching down low when he passed the windows. As he approached the security van, the dog kicked off again barking, howling and jamming its nose to the open section of the driver's side window. Leonard wanted to make sure the dog wouldn't be used to hunt him down. He took the bottle of aftershave out of his pocket and squeezed a good dose of it straight down into the dog's sniffing nostrils. The barking immediately changed pitch, became inquiring and almost musical, then there was silence followed by snorting and heavy sneezing.

Leonard ran uphill from the factory, his knees were still wet and he was feeling the cold again without a coat. He made for high ground in the hope of getting his bearings, in the hope of maybe seeing some lights that might lead him to the construction site. His map was useless, it only worked from one direction and he had no chance of matching up landmarks in the middle of a field at night. His right knee was throbbing as he got to the top of a ridge and he was starting to limp and favour one leg. In the darkness he could just see the shape of the landscape, dark hills overlapping and receding into deep shadow. The snow on higher ground bounced some hazy moonlight into the valleys, but he still had no idea which way to go. A hard wind was blowing over the ridge, Leonard was walking straight into it, and the cold was running round his jaw and setting off an old twinge in a badly crowned back tooth.

He took out a pocket torch and shined the thin beam over Adeline's aerial photographs. He wasn't sure but there was a rough match to the main features of the surrounding geography. He figured out the lie of the valleys, the way they ran away from the higher ground to the east, but it was confusing. Glacial features fanning out across the photographs were not easy to identify at ground level. He scanned the horizon, turning slowly until he noticed a haze of orange electrical light. Leonard smiled; it was maybe an hour's walk away but it was probably the most likely place for the construction site. He decided to stay high on the side of the valley and cut the distance with a long diagonal track, then get onto the road that ran along the valley floor.

He lost his bearings as he made his way down along the side of a hill, but when he climbed up again, the lights coming from the centre of the valley were stronger. A helicopter came over the brow of a hill and flew fast and low overhead. Leonard didn't have time to dive for cover. He took a bearing on the flashing tail-light and realised that he was on the right track.

An hour later the construction site was visible: five domed enclosures, huge curved spans clustered together. Leonard decided to pick his way down the slope and join the road.

His stomach rumbled with nerves and hunger, fear of further security patrols and worries over whether Beryl's paperwork would carry any weight.

The road, when he jumped down onto it, was wide and smooth and stained with oil. Large pieces of shredded tyre lay alongside the road, the cast rubber from heavy vehicles; those articulated trucks with doubled-up wheels. Under heavy loading, the tyres locked up and just peeled off.

He kept moving. He passed a line of floodlit helicopters parked in a landing field off to the left. After twenty minutes, wire fences sprouted up on each side, with security cameras mounted on top of ten-metre poles. He was in sight now; on a monitor somewhere, he was being pointed out, discussed, anticipated.

His shirt and the bottoms of his trousers were caked with mud, he knew that he must look a mess so he made an effort to brush his hair down with his fingers. There was noise on the road behind him, engine and tyre noise, then a row of headlights approached. He stepped aside to let the Chevrolet pass.

The driver stared at him so Leonard thought to wave; the man, a Chinese man, smiled and waved back.

There were signs wired to the fence, presenting information in an assortment of languages, the way it is on ingredients labels: Arabic, Hindu, German, French, Spanish and English.

The door of the guard hut ahead opened, two soldiers stepped out and walked towards Leonard. They were wearing black combat clothes, body armour and helmets with full-face protection.

'Halt! Stay where you are. Raise your hands above your head!'

The first soldier had his gun levelled at Leonard's chest. He covered the second soldier who switched a piece of hand-held equipment on, and approached Leonard.

'Are you tagged, sir?'

'What?'

'Do you not understand the question, sir?'

'No, I don't.'

As soon as he had given this wrong answer Leonard was pushed to the ground and told not to move. The first soldier screamed out.

'Scan him.'

The second soldier moved the scanner back and forth over Leonard's head and shoulders. It was some sort of detector, a bar of metal with ultra violet light shining from it, the fly killing colour. He took it away and read a number that came up on a screen.

'OK, he's numbered.'

The first soldier dropped the assault rifle and they both eased off.

Leonard offered his papers.

'Get up, you idiot. Why didn't you tell us you'd been tagged?'

'I don't know, I couldn't think straight.'

'Why didn't you just sit tight? You're not supposed to turn up like this, unannounced. We come and get you when the time is right. That's our job!'

'I'm sorry, I...'

'Alright, now just follow the road up to the intake hall. They'll check you in.'

The soldiers turned their backs and walked away, Leonard didn't think they were supposed to do that, not ever.

The building up ahead was a rectangular mass of concrete with a recessed entrance; it was lit up low and wide by large spotlights sunk into the ground. Leonard stood and waited as the door slid away to one side, then he entered, and his shivering stopped as heated air washed around his body.

The floor was covered in a thick layer of sponge rubber, the pimpled texture of a professional table tennis bat. There were illuminated clues beckoning him forward, a flashing orange rectangle was obviously the place to head for, so he walked forward into the large featureless space. Thankfully there was a human presence, albeit behind thick, green tinted glass. Another soldier stood off to the left, unarmed this time and with his face revealed. All he did was to wave Leonard towards a second flashing light above an arched structure in the centre of the room. It was another scanning unit, maybe a metal detector. Leonard passed through and out the other side. The soldier waved him on again and Leonard did as he was told.

The wide reception area narrowed to a point where Leonard had to step onto a moving walkway, a rolling conveyor which whisked him out of the first area. The artificial light cut out as the conveyor moved into a warm and moist enclosure, the air perfumed by natural smells; tropical, night-flowering plants. Leonard was moving through a glass-roofed structure, a greenhouse filled with foliage.

On the other side of the room, there was another door with light spilling in around the edges. The conveyor stopped, Leonard stepped off and walked through the door.

On the other side of the glasshouse, a woman received him, an attractive woman in her late twenties. She directed him towards a middle-aged man, who was sitting behind a computer at a wooden table. His face was broad and tanned; he was dressed in a short-sleeved, white shirt, a striped tie and black trousers. He stood to welcome Leonard.

'What happened to you?'

'It's a long story.'

'Aren't they all? But we can't have you wandering around like that, now can we? Get yourself a shower as soon as possible. But first of all, perhaps you'd like to take a seat.'

Leonard had to ask a question first, though; it was something that had been bugging him.

'They said that I'm tagged, the soldiers. What does that mean?'

'You don't know what that means? How odd, most people seem to remember that they've been shot in the mouth.'

Leonard felt like he'd just made it into a friendly embassy after crossing through the badlands.

His details began to scroll down the screen.

'Ah, there is a mistake here, but not a big one. We don't have your history on file but that's not a problem. I see you're North 4?'

He looked for Leonard's confirmation.

'Yeah, that's right. Do you need my paperwork?'

'No, I have what I need right here on the screen. How are things in the city?'

'Well, it's a pretty unpredictable place.'

'Yes, I'm sure. That's a southern accent you've got there, isn't it?'

'Yes, my mother was from the South.'

'I see. Well, go through and relax, you're in good hands now.'

He stood to shake Leonard's hand. It was the training course reflex, the mark of modern customer care.

Leonard was given his own room, a single room for a single man. A large and comfortable cube of living space with grass cord flooring and maple-wood furniture. After being shown in, he experienced that rare luxury of being left alone. Nothing surplus to requirements here, an en-suite bathroom, a television, a desk, a service intercom, but no need for a telephone or a window.

Leonard sat and soaked away the aches and pains in a hot and bubbly bath. He peeled the plasters off his elbows and rubbed small pieces of grit out of the grazes in his knees. He was in bits really, his back ached and he felt so exhausted that only a good night's rest would put him back together again. The buoyancy was comforting, but when he pulled the plug, his body weight returned and gravity took hold of him again. He got out and sat on the edge until a sensation of dizziness settled. He stood, stared into a mirror and managed to smile at himself. The vomiting diesel trick was a stroke of luck and the fact that he hadn't been arrested as soon as he presented himself at the gate was unbelievable.

He grabbed a thick towelling robe from its hook and wrapped it around his body, then he pulled on the shaving mirror which extended laterally on a length of chrome trellis. The bathroom cabinet contained a complete kit of toiletries, own label shampoos, tooth brushes, hair gels.

This was the sort of place where you needn't have a care in the world, there was a restaurant nearby or there was room service, a swimming pool, gym, piped-in music and not one mention of the bill, not a whisper of how much all of this was costing.

After his shave, Leonard rolled onto his bed. He ordered and ate a freshly cut sandwich and then he fell into a sound sleep.

CHAPTER EIGHT

Adeline had this way of looking at things that made you want to watch her looking at the thing, whatever it was, whatever was holding her attention. Tony watched, he liked to use her as an object of focus, a diversionary mind game that pushed the fate of the world into the background. She was moving around the bedroom, animating the place, picking up enough laundry to make a full machine-load. What made her so fascinating was her own focus on what she was doing: it was complete and utter. She sorted and shook out the whites only, held them bundled at her breast. The moment she walked out through the door, the stagnation returned and Tony remembered how he'd been becoming morbid, how he'd been thinking that everyday now had this sour aftertaste. Tony felt that because of these unforeseen solar circumstances, he could no longer catch up with the way his life should be going and he, along with everybody else, was moving into a penalty clause. Just lately, the consideration of death was at the front of his mind. He'd been trying to come to some understanding of this strange arrangement. He had been noticing how it was possible to learn about death in the nighttime, when all those scattered segments of the day were being jumbled up and tied together, mismatched into dreamed sequences.

The thing was that while he was sleeping, his investment in the dream was total and everything in it mattered, but the next thing he knew was how easy it was to let go of all those concerns in the moment of waking. What was troubling Tony was how easy it may be if at death we can look back at all our connections to life and untie them as easily as we can discard the fading importance of the dreamed world. What if it was like that? What if? Was that a comfort? Why wasn't that at all comforting?

'Are you going to lie there all day?'

Adeline was back again and doing the colours now.

'Sounds like a pretty good idea.'

The seam of her black skirt was split over her hip and the thin white band of her knickers showed through. She handed Tony a cup of tea and he reached up from his prone position but his coordination was off, he spilt the tea onto the quilt and couldn't hide it from her.

'You idiot!'

'Don't call me an idiot, shit head!'

'You jerk!'

'I said don't!'

'Prick!'

'Tart!'

There was a knock at the door so Adeline had a look out of the window.

'It's the postman.'

Tony rolled off the bed.

'I'll pay the bastard.'

'What with?'

'Booze, what else?'

Tony ran down the stairs, picked up a bottle from behind the bar and opened the door to the postman. He was a new man, a big guy with a helmet and visor.

'Letters from overseas.'

'Right, what do I owe you?'

'What you got?'

The whisky did the job, and Tony watched him go back to his van and pass the bottle through to his driver, then they both drove a short way up the road to make the next delivery.

Tony was disappointed; it was another letter from Adeline's mother. Always when the letters came, Adeline would take herself off for hours to study the thing and then there would be new spells, new trials and tests around the house. This time maybe, it would be better if he dealt with the correspondence, so he slipped his finger in and tore a ragged split in the seam. To start with, it smelt good, the envelope was full of lavender flowers and the writing was in English and legible too.

Daughter,
I hope this letter finds you well.

My spirits can't decide but how are yours, high or low? I've been trying to see all of life as glory and light but it doesn't seem to work anymore. I have been digging deep into my notebooks for some fundamentals and I have found something for you, something fitting this oddest of occasions. Please promise me you will make this spell, promise me so that I may sleep at night.

Tony was about to read on but he could hear the descending footsteps and felt spooked.

Adeline arrived at the bottom of the stairs and turned to pick up a dropped sock.

'Well?'

Tony stuffed the letter into his back pocket.

'Nothing, he asked me if I would take a parcel in for next door, but would I pay and sign receipt? No bloody way!'

Adeline had nothing to say. She walked past Tony and on through the doorway towards the whirling washing machine.

CHAPTER NINE

The morning was slow to start. Leonard lay in bed clueless, half expecting a knock on the door, but it never came. Eventually he got up, stood beside the closet and slid the door to one side. He flicked through the clothes: lots of grey marl sportswear, one size fits all stuff, several light coloured shirts, dark trousers, a navy blue, waterproof jacket. There were several pairs of shoes in the bottom of the closet: polished black dress shoes, blue Goretex trek boots and plump white trainers. He slid the door back the other way to reveal shelves and boxes containing folded sweaters, rolled socks and assorted underwear. All of these things were still packed in their cellophane wrappers. Leonard unwrapped a pair of blue jeans, T-shirt, sweatshirt, and the blue jacket; smart but casual, ready for anything.

The mirror was kinder today; his hair was conditioned and he had some colour in his cheeks, his gaze was steady and measured.

Out in the hall, sunlight washed in through a glass ceiling as he slung the blue jacket over his arm and headed in the direction of the restaurant. The corridors felt something like hospital walkways; they were a similar dimension and had the same plastic slap-shut double doors. The route to the restaurant led onto a mezzanine level, then down a fast escalator running past a wall of glass. The restaurant door opened automatically for Leonard and he crossed a highly polished wooden floor to an area that smelt of fresh coffee.

A few linen-covered tables were placed beside a row of rectangular windows. The tables were decorated with yellow, Ikebana flower arrangements in glass jugs, and filled with clean water.

Five or six solitary figures sat spooning jam onto toast or sipping orange juice. Leonard crossed to the self-service bar and took what he wanted. As he walked back and sat down, he took in the view out of the window and had a clear sight of the valley with the sun glancing into it. He could see the domed construction hangars with their chrome flue pipes carrying bright exhaust vapours into the still, cold air.

He didn't know how much longer he should keep himself to himself. He supposed that the best thing would be to play along like he understood the drill and gather any relevant information.

The man sitting closest to Leonard was sipping orange juice. Dark skinned and curly haired, he looked Greek and he had that air of a business magnate, an opinionated but off-duty bore. He was wearing a tan leather jacket and dark glasses, brilliant white shirt cuffs with gold links sticking way out of the armholes.

On the next table, a woman in her late thirties, tapping into a hand-held organiser, lifted her head and met Leonard's stare without a flicker. She looked as long as she wanted, and without expression, lowered her eyes back to the machine again.

The people at the other tables seemed to be more like staff than guests, they were short-sleeved men with slicked back hairstyles and thick glasses. They stared into their food and kept the fork moving. They were quiet and focussed, like they were taking a break from something far more hectic. They reminded Leonard of NASA personnel, grabbing a break from mission control.

Leonard peppered up his Kedgeree and ate it while it was still hot.

'Ah, there you are!'

Leonard swallowed and dabbed his lips with a serviette.

'Hello.'

'Yes, good day. Settling in OK?'

'Yes, I have everything I need.'

'Good. Now I had a look at your papers and it seems everything is in order. You have a tour pass, yes?'

'That's right.'

'Well, you must be guided around, and that will be my pleasure. My name is Patrick.'

Leonard shook Patrick's hand.

'Bear with me a moment while I deal with the formalities.'

Leonard looked the guy over: mid-sixties with a bald crown half-heartedly covered with a throw of hair. He had watery, jellied eyes, a brush stroke of red on his cheeks and a small, smiling mouth. He wore gentrified clothes, cords and brogues, cashmere woolly over the top of a pink, pinstriped shirt. His head hoola-hooped very gently clockwise, like a brushed cotton dog in the back window of a car; maybe this was the first sign of Parkinson's disease.

'First of all, let's be clear that nothing I tell you and nothing you observe, can be communicated to a third party, by any means whatsoever.'

'Yes, of course.'

'And so then, as matter of protocol, I must ask you to sign this legally binding document.'

'Of course!'

Leonard signed. Patrick grinned then stood up.

'Let's be having you, then! You're from North 4, aren't you, down around Boston? Is everything running smoothly there?'

'Yes, I think so.'

'You think so? Tut tut, you should yes or no, so.'

Leonard followed Patrick, and Patrick started to explain. He led the way out of the restaurant and down a flight of stairs.

'Of course, what you have to realise is, the first thing the designers were instructed to do, was to break down the stages of the event. They didn't have to worry about such things as selection, or indeed secure intake, that was and still is, a military matter. They had to think only of the safety of the passengers and cargo.'

Patrick pushed down on a steel door handle and they were outside standing in the short grass.

Leonard was looking and learning, trying not to be distracted by Patrick's running commentary.

'So then, let's not beat about the bush. The point is, the Ice Moon and how to survive it! It's really a question of the degree of impact and the consequent after-shocks. Now in the past, survival structures have been based solely upon the idea of a large protective enclosure, say like the hull of a battleship. This worked well enough in certain environments but with the problem we faced, this was no longer the case. A large and autonomous single structure is completely vulnerable if its outer shell, or hull, is damaged or holed. Indeed in such an instance, the integrity of the entire vessel is lost and the structure will cease to offer any protection.'

Patrick stopped outside one of the main domes, swiped an ID card through a reader and the door popped open.

'At all points, what we had to focus on improving was the probable survival rate.'

Leonard stepped into the dome and Patrick locked up the door behind them both. Inside the yard, the sound quality was different; there was a faster, shorter echo than outside in the valley. The various sounds of heavy construction were contained and multiplied by the curved roof. Hammer blows, steel falling onto concrete, arc welding flashes, shouts, crane engines, all of these sounds were doubled up and bounced off the sloping walls. There was no great steel ship, no immense curving hull dominating the space.

'The production line is divided into task specific zones, and if you look to your left, you can see what all the fuss is about.'

Teams of men in white overalls were gathered around rows of metallic spheres, each with a radius of approximately four metres.

'Contrary to popular belief, there is no "vessel", as such. What you see here, Leonard, are the survival pods, designed to keep a single human being alive for a period of no less than thirty days. The outer casing is Titanium steel, wrapped around a carbon fibre shell.'

Leonard followed Patrick over to the production line.

'But how will they work?'

'When the occupant finally closes the door mechanism, the pods are sealed with explosive bolts. The construction has been designed to resist violent shock, temperature change, submersion; they have an independent air, water, power and food supply, and they are fitted with distress beacons which will be satellite-tracked. The moulds are a standard size, they allow minimal movement, and can be self-adjusted. If you take a look inside, you will get a clearer impression.'

Leonard climbed a short, three-step ladder and looked in. The spheres were hinged vertically, in two halves. In section, the layers exposed were: thick steel and even thicker carbon fibre, then a honeycomb of aerated foam padding, with wiring and plastic tubes running to the air supply, water feeds and human waste unit. The padded restraining harness was gimballed like a ship's compass, so the occupant would be able to stay upright, even if the sphere wasn't. Leonard couldn't help but start to agree with the logic of it all; this was a hedged bet, a numbers game. There was no big ship.

Patrick piped up again.

'You see, if some of these units are lost, not all are lost; it's a damage limitation exercise. What we've got to make sure of, is that enough of the population survive, so that we have a chance to re-colonise what might be left of the planet, do you see?'

'Yes, I see what you're getting at.'

'As you probably know, there are projects designed to go out of earth orbit, but our American parent company has been reluctant to go that route. We concluded that we wanted to stay attached to the earth's landmass. We hope to hold our solar orbit, so we are at least in line for approximate survival temperatures and weather patterns.'

'How many are there?'

'We planned for three thousand, but we don't have much time before the Ice Moon hits. We think we'll manage to complete just over two thousand five hundred. And we expect to lose thirty percent.'

'The pods are not even joined together?'

'No but they are designed to move like a single fluid mass which can change its shape, and fit into any survival space which might present itself during the impact and through the subsequent aftershocks. Even if there is a huge upheaval of the earth's surface, we calculate that there will be some survivors. There are also specialised pods, medical units, food stores, seed banks, water purification units and habitat construction pods.'

'One more thing, Patrick.'

'Yes?'

'Who has been chosen? Who will be saved?'

Patrick rounded on Leonard, looking fazed.

'As one of the so called "chosen", that is a rather foolish question.'

'I mean, who else?'

'Ah yes, right I see. Well, why not come along to the clubhouse, socialise a bit and see for yourself.'

They stepped out of the construction dome and Patrick seemed thrown for a minute, unsure of the direction he should take.

'It's this way.'

He skirted the curve of the dome and pointed to a structure built into the side of the valley.

'That's where we're going, that's the clubhouse.'

Leonard followed Patrick, until they reached the foot of a flight of steps, brushed aluminium steps with wooden handrails. There was a gun-shot up above, and then what looked like pieces of a smashed-up dinner plate rained down onto the steps.

'Ah, they're shooting on the terrace, do you like shooting?'

'What d'you mean?'

'Clay pigeon, they fire the clays from the roof. That one was good and powdered. Do you shoot?'

Leonard didn't answer.

There were more gunshots as they climbed further up the steps. When they arrived at the decked landing, Leonard could hear some muffled music and chatting voices, then he turned and got his first sight of the clubhouse.

The building was a very contemporary steel and glass affair, arranged on four staggered levels. The structural supports were wired up like sail boat masts and the different floor levels were slung from horizontal braces.

More shooting came from a cantilevered platform up on the roof. He could see the spinning target clays, heading fast and low out over the valley before they exploded or sailed on untouched. Other projectiles came from the roof, small and white this time. They were golf balls slicing and hooking their way towards a patch of grass marked with a red flag pole.

Patrick waved him on and they stood outside the entrance. Through the windows on the ground floor Leonard could see the cocked, bare elbows of several women with drinks in their hands. It was eleven o'clock in the morning but they were wearing evening dress and moving along a buffet table.

'I'll leave you here, Leonard. Just make yourself at home, get acquainted. Any more doubts or concerns, just ask.'

'Thank you, Patrick.'

Leonard stepped onto a pressure-sensitive mat and the door slid open for him. Inside, all the way down the right hand side of the ground floor was a curved marble bar-top and behind that, a very exotically stocked bar. At the far end of the room, a huge video screen was lit up with images which promoted the effectiveness of the survival pods. These images were cut against computer-generated sequences of the asteroid impact.

Leonard took his hands out of his pockets and perched himself on a stool. The barman stopped twisting a white cloth into the neck of a glass and asked.

'Can I help you, sir?'

'I don't know.'

'Cocktail, sir?'

'Yes, OK.'

'Pina colada, sir?'

'Yeah, OK.'

He got to work and Leonard rotated his stool away from the crushed ice and chrome shaker. He faced the valley, took in the whole view of the construction site through the windows, then pulled focus and watched the passengers at the buffet table. They were laughing and chatting, but it was that stiff and formal, self-protective laughter. It seemed like they were relative strangers going through the process of re-introduction; they were exchanging pleasantries, trying not to be nasty. If they didn't have anything nice to say, they were not going to say anything at all.

The cocktail was perfect, pack shot condensation on the glass with a subtle umbrella, a taller finer one than the usual squat pink jobs.

Leonard, glass in hand, moved through the crowd and picked at the buffet. The problem was that you couldn't do that without people wanting to know who you were. They were clever because they explained who they were first; so then they had a kind of right to ask the probing questions. A lot of them seemed to be based in Switzerland, they were multi-lingual, multi-tasking folk, prettier and taller than the average, consensus slice of the population. Leonard kept his own details sketchy; it was easy enough to leave those gaps about personal wealth and position wide open because the 'folk' were eager enough to fill in what they thought anyway. He felt uncomfortable enough in their company to make a blatant exit. He headed for the stairs and made his way up to the first floor. Here he entered another open-plan space, a busy, light-filled restaurant, with champagne coolers standing beside the tables and animated diners gesturing with their hands and scanning the menus.

Leonard carried on around the landing and up onto the second floor. There was less glass here, more modern veneer, great panels of waxed walnut and doors with oversized hinges. Through the first of these doors was a lounging room, partitioned off with shining furniture, leather sofas and tilting, easy chairs. Leonard sat into an armchair close to the windows; he sipped his cocktail, rested his head back and closed his eyes. Then he started listening in to a nearby conversation. He'd seen the group when he entered, four middle-aged men and a couple in their mid- to late-twenties.

The girl was trying to make herself understood, there was a point she was trying to make.

'We need to create a much more humanitarian society. We have to put an end to the ego-centred way we've been carrying on.'

One of the middle-aged men interjected.

'We all know what you are trying to say but, well, it's the way you say it that's the problem. It's pretty half-witted. You really should not be trying to make sense of things you are clearly not qualified to analyse.'

The girl blushed, but didn't move a muscle.

The man then counted out the salient points he wanted to make, on the fingers of his right hand.

'Selfishness, greed, the desire to win, the desire to then rule and impose one's own favoured conditions. That, my girl, is what makes this goddamned world go round.'

'You think so?'

'Oh I know so. And after impact, we will in any case be making the best of the opportunity to reinstall the accepted norms.'

The girl stood up, her heart was obviously racing.

'This is not some unique opportunity to shape the future. We are facing a terrible global catastrophe! There's no point in speaking to any of you.'

Leonard couldn't resist taking a look, so he tipped forward and rotated the chair. He had turned into the group and quite suddenly included himself in their business.

'Excuse me, didn't mean to butt in.'

'Yes, yes, hello, and who are you?'

'My name's Leonard.'

'And what are you?'

The first, and Leonard thought the most relevant thing he could think of, was: 'I am a survival strategist.'

Silence, a total lack of interest from the girl until she asked, 'So what's your strategy?'

'Every man, every woman, for themselves.'

Some chortles and nods of agreement from the old guys, and a frown from the girl. The man who had been arguing his point spoke up.

'I'm Derek Dunbar. I'm an information architect.'

The others listened but the idea of introducing themselves did not move around the group. Leonard looked across at the girl and asked her, 'And you are?'

'I'm Vicky, I'm just somebody's daughter.'

Leonard finished his drink and thought about spinning his chair back out of trouble. But then she asked, 'Do you want to come up to the roof?'

Leonard stood, trying not to seem too keen. The old men seemed disappointed, they didn't like the girl, but she was something to look at, especially as her skirt had a habit of inching further and further up her thighs as she shifted in her seat.

'I won't be long, Eddie.'

'That's alright love. No problem, show Leonard around.'

She flattened the creases in her skirt, picked her jumper up off the arm of the sofa and wrapped it around her shoulders.

Leonard followed her up the last flight of stairs and out onto the roof. She seemed excited, at the very least she was relieved to be out in the daylight and away from the group. She made straight for the edge and looked over.

Leonard stood behind her, and when she turned, she was much happier than before, her eyes were wide and elegantly shaped; she looked familiar.

'I'm sure I've seen you somewhere before.'

'I'm a singer in a band, you've probably seen me on TV.'

'Are you OK?'

She seemed wrong-footed by the question.

'What's it to you?'

'I'm sorry, I…'

'I just needed to get some air, that's all.'

'Who were those people you were talking to?'

'Oh, they're so pompous. They want their women to be intellectually submissive and nymphomaniac!'

'But who are they?'

'Power brokers, very wealthy industrialists, European fat cats…'

'You mean like politicians, businessmen?'

'No, not really. These guys are a cut above all that. They invent scapegoats, they stand behind the fall guys. In a few months, after the impact that is, they will make up a good part of the emergency government.'

'Look!'

She pointed at the queue of golfers waiting to tee up and drive off into the sky; they wore caps and tartan trousers and were constantly practising their swings.

'What does your husband do?'

'He's a footballer. I suppose we're quite unusual here, nearly everyone else I've met is a king or a Duke of somewhere. I just got a good PR man on the case and we made it in!'

Leonard leant on the balcony rail.

'This passenger list, it's not exactly a democratic cross-section of society is it?'

'Don't tell me that surprises you at all? You made it in, didn't you?'

'Yes, but that just makes me uneasy, I'm not so sure I want to be a part of it. It takes all sorts to make a world, right? But I fail to see how the heads of corporations and the military capitalists are going to help. What we are going to need very soon are essential personnel. Doctors, engineers, men and women who can pull other men and women out of the rubble.'

'Are you essential personnel, Leonard?'

'Maybe, maybe not. I don't even know if I'm going to be a passenger.'

'Of course you are, you can't get security clearance if you're not chipped.'

'Chipped?'

'Micro-chipped!'

'What are you talking about?'

'The ID tag embedded in your lip.'

Leonard grabbed hold of his top lip and felt the skin between his fingers.

'Oh yeah, that. The first thing I knew about that was when I was stopped at the gate. I had no idea I had a tag, I was tricked into it by a couple of very clever ladies.'

'What?'

'Sorry, but I'm only just finding out how this whole thing has been put together.'

'God, you're a beginner. Wherever you are in the world, if you've been tagged, you'll be picked up. The microchips are linked to a Global Positioning System.'

'Yes, as of yesterday I know all that.'

'So you are saved. Why so glum?'

'Well, now I'm here I'm getting the feeling this place is overrun by mean bastards, Aryan scientists and career criminals. The meek aren't going to inherit the earth are they, it'll be this bloody lot!'

'It's only what you'd expect though, isn't it?'

'Well, yeah, but it's just about the worst thing that could happen.'

'So what are you going to do about it?'

'I don't know'

'They see the Ice Moon as a marvellous opportunity to clear out the old order and build a brave new world. They think it's a chance to cut out all the dead wood, restructure society!'

Vicky tilted her face up to Leonard's; her big eyes engaged his.

'Tell me, Leonard, how do you feel about being a part of this? Why is all this happening?'

Leonard's eyes flinched as a shotgun blast rang out somewhere over his shoulder.

'I can't say. It's like all those times when you say to yourself - surely this can't be happening to me, but of course time and time again, it is happening to you, it just is.'

It was late March and the sun was warm on his face. He didn't know what he could do about the bastards who would survive. The fact was, if the predictions were correct, eighty percent of the world's population would be wiped out by the impact of the Ice Moon. Particles of the earth's mantle would be kicked up into the atmosphere and would block out the sun for several years to come. It worried him, the whole thing worried him, and what he was supposed to do about it, for the moment, eluded him.

Vicky moved away and turned her attention towards the group shooting clays. They had the west facing roof space screened off with Plexiglas panelling. The clay trap was basically a big green catapult, worked manually by a keen young man. After each firing, he cocked the throwing arm and reset the next clay disc. Then he waited for his queue to 'pull', which he did, sending the projectile screaming out over the valley. The people waiting their turn to shoot stood in a semi-circle behind the firing line watching the action, offering jeers and snide remarks. Every so often the man on the trap changed the flight of the clay and this time the disc was raked back, firing high into the sky before dipping down again. The man shooting had his back to the Plexiglas, he was wearing ear protectors and a fawn coloured, tweed jacket. He followed the arc of the clay as it rose into the sky, fired one barrel as the target reached the top of its curve, and missed. As the disc started to fall back, he followed the descent, waiting so long that by the time he was ready to fire the next cartridge, the barrel had levelled out. The gun went off and the buckshot struck a body; a man spun around, lurched backwards and dropped to the floor.

'Shit!'

Leonard looked to Vicky but she said nothing. The golfers stopped playing for a few seconds but then went back to their own business.

The dead man was rolled off the edge of the roof and the shooting resumed.

CHAPTER TEN

The bar-top TV flickered into life. It had been switched off earlier, after the hardcore drinkers had turned up, but now it was way past midnight and the last few old soaks who had braved curfew were sobering up with self-inflicted slaps and black coffee.

Ian stretched up and adjusted the volume control; he twiddled the aerial and tried to tune in the set. These days it seemed like every channel was a news channel, more than ever before, twenty-four hour news. It was great television though, the production costs are kept low because they are met accidentally by the whole world and the script just seems to go on and on, episode after episode, producing hour after hour of unequivocal truth. There's so much of this truth being produced these days that the underlying lies have been lost in all the noise.

Ian sat back down, lit up another cigarette and tuned his ear into the political commentary. The TV screen showed a good moving picture of the prime minister, talking down to the audience once again. His body was arranged behind a polished desk, he wore a dark suit and a touch of mortuary style make-up for the benefit of the cameras. He looked a little bit over-rouged though, and punchy, like he'd been in a play fight and escaped a head-lock. He had that face on, the face they all wear, the one that registered the discomfort of having an unseen hand way up the arse. A hand which worked the eyes, the ears, the mouth, but circumvented the heart, a good heart really, one that started out with all the best intentions. He'd had a good career, this one; he'd been earnest and brave, saying all the right things, rallying, giving hope and strength. But today he was hedging; he was saying all he could, except what everybody suspected. He wouldn't say what he should say, he wouldn't admit that he knew, that we knew, that it really was time now for him to go through the garage and dig out 'the end is nigh' sandwich-board from his student days.

To wind up, he at last delivered the line everyone had tuned in to hear: 'the heavenly body will impact with the earth in seven weeks time'.

Tony had noticed Ian messing with the TV. He hated it when a punter worked the controls, switched things off and on; it was his job to set the levels, his job to tinker with the atmosphere!

Tony just didn't like Ian; he didn't like his pink and puffy skin, his clammy handshake or even the smell of him. He hoped it didn't show, but he didn't like the overall look of the man, he found him long headed and flat in the jaw line, like he was already wearing dentures. And whenever they had a conversation, Ian was only ever half listening, daydreaming. Tony suspected that the dream Ian was mostly dreaming was of how to fuck you over. You just couldn't trust a man like Ian. He rubbed Tony up the wrong way because Tony was the kind of man who, when he found a stray piece of something which had fallen off something else, he picked it up and asked himself, 'where's that come from?' And then he would get some tools and set about fixing it. Ian though wouldn't bother, and weeks later when something critical rattled and then fell off, he would just wonder why.

Ian sipped his coffee; it was smooth and smoked and had no beery bitterness to it. He emptied out his pill bottle onto the table and felt a tightening in his gut when the last two oval capsules bounced out. He popped them into his gob and washed them down with the dregs. He could see Tony out of the corner of his eye, shuffling around in the background, stacking chairs up on the far tables. He knew how to handle a chair, did Tony. It was not too big a step to imagine him in the circus ring with a family acrobatic act. All he needed were a few gymnastic relatives in leotards, that would suit Tony. Ian could see it all, it made him smile to think of the way they would say 'hup' with each leap. Hup, and then someone else would be somersaulted up into the chair that Tony would be balancing on his head. But none of this was possible for Tony; he had the necessary brothers, but not the one very beautiful, very heavily made-up sister.

Tony was a roughly hewn man, the eyes of his hangdog face slid away over the top of his cheeks and his ears looked plasticined onto his neck. He was a broad-shouldered man carrying a bit of extra weight, a bit of a light heavyweight, around the midriff.

Tony stacked the chairs until only Ian's table was left, then he ducked behind the bar and came back with his own mug of coffee. He sat down with Ian and turned his head towards the television.

'How's the other half then, Tony?'

'She's fine, thanks.'

'One thing I've never understood, is just what in the hell you were doing with a woman like that? Alright, she's very attractive and all but she must be a right bloody handful.'

Tony grinned as he replied, to blur his anger.

'Are you pissed, Ian?'

He shook his head and raised his coffee.

'Not today, no.'

Tony tried to let it go but couldn't, it soaked in, the question did, it made him uncomfortable because, well, what was he doing with Adeline?

'What's it got to do with you, anyway? I didn't ask for your opinion on my private life.'

'Just being sociable, Tony, making chit-chat, that's all.'

'You don't think we're suited?'

'I didn't say that. She's just… well, she likes to play the field, wouldn't you say so?'

'What do you mean by that? I wish I knew what you were getting at.'

'I'm not getting at anything in particular. I'm just mouthing off, poking fun.'

'Look Ian, it's shutting up and chucking out time. So if you'd like to kindly piss off, that would suit me just fine.'

'Yes, yes, yes. Listen, it's just that I'm a confirmed bachelor right, I don't understand relationships. I was wondering if you could shed any light, that's all.'

'God, do we really have to have this conversation?'

'Why not? Why not indulge me a little?'

Tony felt stuck with having to elaborate.

'I don't know! We met, we found that we liked the same things. We concluded that we were very similar people, so we got married.'

'And then what happened?'

'Well, pretty soon after that, we discovered that we were just not happy in one another's company. We tried a few things but…'

'Oh yeah, like what?'

'We thought that maybe we were too similar, so we tried to change; we tried to make ourselves opposites so we might attract? But that was just confusing, it just didn't work out.'

'But there's something else, isn't there? I mean, that's not the heart of it, is it?'

'What are you getting at?'

'Oh come on, you know what I'm talking about, you know that she's a witch.'

'You are pissed!'

'A white witch.'

'Don't be ridiculous, you can't know who's a witch.'

'She must have told you, Tony?'

'Look, if a witch ever says "I am a witch" then all her spells come undone.'

'Well, that's confirmed it for me. Seems you know about this stuff too, so maybe you're in on it. Maybe you can tell me: can men be witches too or do they have to be wizards? That sort of thing can lead to a lynch mob, very nasty...'

'There's the door Ian. Go through it would you.'

Ian skidded his chair back and stood up. He had an urge to throw Tony the chair and step back for some applause, but he didn't, he only waved and walked, light headed to the door.

Tony locked the door behind Ian and lifted his own chair up onto the table. That Ian knew something about Adeline was a problem; he would use it against the both of them if he could. It was true that Adeline's mother was known as a 'guesser', which is a kind of watered down way of saying witch, but that was in another part of the world. Tony had intercepted some of her letters and he'd seen stuff lying around the house before now, like candle wax and bowls of water, photographs of the Milky Way and the polar stars ringed in red. If they went for a walk in the woods, she would ask him to urinate in the open air, as a mark of respect for the forest and sometimes, in the summertime, she bathed in ice-water.

It was none of Ian's business but he was right, there was far more to Adeline than meets the eye. Sometimes he felt that she didn't mean anything she said, that she didn't mean it even when she smiled; when she looked, she wasn't really looking, and maybe it wasn't even black for her when she closed her eyes.

She'd gone up to bed hours ago and when Tony finally hauled himself upstairs after tidying up the bar, he trod gently, made every effort not to wake her. He looked down at the white skin of her trailing arm; it was locked out against the elbow joint, in a ballet dancer's gesture. He had the idea of sitting on this outstretched hand, which would quite easily break her arm. But instead he kissed the exposed blue arteries of her forearm and then her right cheek; she stirred, lifted her head and turned onto her right-hand side. Her breathing was slow, she was taking long, deep breaths, her face registered nothing; she was switched off.

Tony dropped his clothes in a pile, T-shirt inside shirt, inside sweater, then he lifted the covers and slid in. Her body lifted as he set himself down, but she was fast asleep. He switched off his bedside lamp, waited as long as he could (maybe ten minutes) then slapped Adeline hard on the side of her face.

She woke slowly, in a daze, and rubbed her cheek. The room was dark and still; she waited, then settled her head back again into the depression in her pillow. Though her blood was boiling over, she managed to give a perfectly understated performance of bewilderment and Tony was quite happy to fall into a reassured sleep. But Adeline had heard his every move, the way he'd crept into the room, the sound of fabrics sparking off each other as they were whisked over his head. She felt the lifting and tipping as Tony performed his stealthy hippo crawl into the bed, and of course the weight of his hand as it stung her face.

CHAPTER ELEVEN

The following morning, Leonard stood in front of his wardrobe for fifteen minutes, not really looking at the clothes and not realising that he was in a kind of delayed shock. The point was that, well in simple terms, he had achieved what he'd set out to achieve. He was now relatively safe, he'd gained a place on the vessel, and he had his own survival pod earmarked. All he had to do now was sit tight for the next fifty days and take his chances with the others at impact.

But it wasn't that simple was it, not now that he had to consider Beryl and Lena. The survival pods were being systematically hi-jacked by the rich and powerful, an elite ruling class of casual murderers; did he really belong?

The entire course of human evolution was about to dogleg God knows where and Leonard was wondering whether or not a simple end to the human race might not be just as well. The hominid eye had been opened for a few hundred thousand years, now it would be closed again and why not? That seemed to be the shape of all other manifest life anyway. It starts and then it finishes, that's it, trying to last it out forever was a terrible pressure, and it was bringing out the worst in all of us. Even if he did survive impact, how safe would he or anyone else be in an environment where the law would be enforced by mercenaries, acting as henchmen for a bunch of extremist leaders? What pissed Leonard off most of all was this great big, highly publicised lie, which had people flooding to the city in the hope of being judged on their merits and included in the survival programme. There were fifty days until the impact, at least that was a known and fixed parameter. If he was going to do anything at all to influence the programme, that was the amount of time he had left.

The thing was, the coming events were lined up and on their way, and Leonard had a very particular and privileged position within them. If you looked at it like that, what he had to do was simple. He would have to upset the way things were developing, upset the apple cart and do what he could to make a difference.

Leonard stayed away from the breakfast bar, he called room service instead and ordered coffee and sandwiches, scotch eggs and chocolate. He packed the food into a sports bag, then dressed for the great outdoors in plenty of layers, with the waterproof jacket over the top. He sat on the floor and pulled his boots on. He checked the room before leaving, but he had no personal effects.

He made his way through a series of bright, top-lit corridors, looking for an exit. He wanted to get outside into the cool air so he could think things over and get his head on straight again. He turned away from the directions offered by the sign-posts and found that he was making his way downstairs. The ground floor of the accommodation block didn't seem off limits and Leonard moved quickly through a less spacious layout, multiple corridors flanked by unmarked offices. The windows ran out, but the interior of the building was still brightly lit with overhead bulbs. The wooden floors ended and spotless, white Linoleum took over. The only sound was the faint squeaking of his rubberised soles as he turned the sharp, right-angled corners. Eventually he reached a dead end corridor with 'Alarmed' and 'Emergency Exit' pasted onto the door. He walked back a few paces and tried one of the office doors. It opened into a quiet laboratory space. There was a metallic smell in the air which was strong enough to have a taste and it was cold, too, colder than just no heating, it was probably refrigerated.

Leonard entered and stepped in between two long benches which had steel racks sitting on top, starting at waist level and finishing above his head. Labelled metal tubes were contained within the steel framework, each tube a few centimetres long and held into the frame with safety-wired locking screws.

'Yes, hello?'

An old man in a lab coat had entered the room carrying a smoking box of the same metal tubes. Leonard moved away from the frame and smiled.

'Hello.'

He stood in the doorway with his head, hands and feet covered in elasticated cloth bags. He was looking over his glasses at Leonard, wondering how to proceed. It upset him because this was not the usual sequence of events. He worked alone and nobody else came here. Usually he entered the lab, loaded the tubes into the frame and went straight back, uninterrupted, to get some more.

He asked the obvious question.

'Who are you?'

'Well, it's ah… Patrick sent me on ahead to have a look around. I'm not disturbing you, am I?'

'Isn't it obvious that you are? I have had to stop what I was doing and I am now having to listen to you and respond to what you say.'

'Please just carry on, act like I'm not here.'

He did; without further reference to Leonard's existence, he carried on walking into the room, sat the rack of steaming tubes onto the bench and began to load the frame.

'What are those, then?'

'Seeds.'

'And what are you doing with them?'

'Loading them into this frame.'

Leonard realised he'd better try and work it out for himself; this old man didn't want anything to do with him. He was obviously a kind of lab assistant and he wanted to be left alone so that he could be of assistance to the lab, that was all. He lifted the metal tubes very gently from the rack and slid them into place.

'But what are they exactly?'

The lab assistant's shoulders were hoiked up around his neck; he really was very uncomfortable with Leonard just hovering there beside him. He finished placing the tubes.

'If you really must know.'

He bent close to the labels and wiped condensation from the stamped letters.

'These are Avena Fatua.'

He giggled.

'Is that funny?'

'Yes yes, very funny. Avena Fatua, the common name is the wild oat.'

'And what about those?'

'Moringa Oleifera, horse radish tree.'

'How many seeds are you going to preserve?'

'The project has 24,000 plant species, that's only about ten percent of all the seed-bearing flora. We're trying to protect as many species as possible. We need to hang on to some biodiversity.'

'It's for after the impact?'

'Well, of course.'

'So how will you grow seed in a densely polluted atmosphere?'

'They'll be transferred into the artificial light propagators as soon as the immediate after-effects of impact have passed.'

Leonard walked along the frame reading the species names.

'Well, I've got to go and prepare more samples.'

The lab assistant didn't want to leave Leonard in the room, he was standing in the doorway with his right arm held out, showing that he wanted to sweep Leonard into the hall.

'Where's my nearest exit?'

The old man pointed.

'Go that way 'til you meet a corridor on your right, follow it and you'll find your way out.'

Outside, the air was cold and sweet and thickened by a pale mist which was lying in the bottom of the valley. Leonard walked towards the construction domes, across stems of emerald green grass, caked in ice like frozen green-beans.

The chrome chimneys venting the buildings were pumping out clouds of smoke, vertical plumes which rose straight up into the still air until they evaporated in the sun's rays.

A black and white football rolled out from between the construction domes, leaving a dark trail in the frosted grass. Then a man skidded after it, turned tight and flicked it back the way he came. It was Eddie digging up the turf, and all the time he was talking to himself like he was a radio commentator looking on, describing the action. Leonard turned the corner to see Eddie curl a long cross in toward Vicky. She caught the ball at head height and threw it back out, over-arm. She waved to Leonard and Eddie trapped the ball, then looked over his shoulder to see who she was waving at. He smiled and laid the ball off towards Leonard; it rolled downhill fast and stopped when it hit his feet.

When he looked up from the ball, he could see that Eddie was bothering Vicky in the goal mouth, dodging around her, crowding her out, looking towards Leonard and pointing at his head. Leonard put down his bag and tapped the ball forward a bit. He tried to figure out whether he should strike it on the inside or the outside of the foot to give it lift. He knew he only had a few good kicks in him before his knee would start playing up, so he skipped three short steps and punted his toe into the leather. It was good, had good flight and reasonable direction. Eddie fixed the thing in the air and started to run on to it; as it hit the top of his head, he lifted and twisted underneath to touch the ball on, deflecting it in the direction of the goal. It flew past Vicky and bounced off the curved wall of the dome. She started to clap, while Eddie punched the sky and started to sing a song with the same tune as a Christmas hymn called 'Noel Noel', but with the words changed to: 'Twelve nil, twelve nil, twelve nil, twelve nil, la la la la la la la la la la.'

Eddie jogged over to Leonard and slapped him on the back.

'Nice one, here you go.'

Eddie handed over a stick of chewing gum and Leonard stripped it with his cold fingers and bent it into his mouth.

Eddie had mud-splashed shorts on over his track-suit, football boots and thick gloves. His skin was glowing hot and his eyes were keen and squinting as he focused in on Leonard's face.

'That was a toe punt, wasn't it?'

'Yeah, well.'

'Nearly took my head off.'

The ball bounced by, then Vicky arrived in her red tracksuit with its thick plastic zip which she kept running up and down to make a whizzing sound.

'Hello, Leonard, are you leaving us?'

'Maybe, have you got a car here?'

Vicky answered.

'Yeah, we came in the Merc'. It's in the garage, isn't it, Ed?'

'Yeah.'

'Can I borrow it?'

'Course you can, we're not going anywhere.'

'Are you sure? See I might not be able to bring it back?'

'Look, at the end of the day, we've got to help each other out, right? Vicky thinks you're an all right bloke and I trust her opinion so, OK!'

'Thanks. Can you show me the car?'

'Course, but I don't understand why you don't stay put. It's safe here, and well, it's gonna get a bit dodgy out there, isn't it!'

'I'm going back to the city. I'm going to see what I can do to level the playing field.'

'What do you mean?'

'I've had it with being polite and inoffensive.'

'You've what?'

'I've always been passive, I've lurked in the background, I've let others lead. I've been a kind of neutral observer and that makes me feel guilty.'

'Guilty for what?'

'For not doing anything.'

'At the end of the day, I mean, with that kind of game plan, well that's fair enough. Come on, then. I'll show you the car.'

Vicky kissed Leonard and jogged off towards the goal. Leonard followed Eddie back towards the garage. He stopped at the rolling metal door and bent down to the handle.

'Do you want to know what I think, Leonard?'

'Yes, I do yeah.'

'I think the world's on its last legs, it's gone to pot.'

'You mean fucked.'

'Yeah, alright, it's fucked and you know what else!'

'No, what?'

'I just don't believe all this asteroid crap, not a hundred percent anyway. I've heard rumours in the clubhouse; some people think it's all in our heads. It's like a mass hallucination, or a conspiracy, do you know what I mean? It's like some long shadow of all that can go wrong and will go wrong. It's mass hysteria, really, I'm sure that's what it is.'

'You're saying there's no Asteroid?'

'That's right, it's a scam! It's like a symbol that's all, of the future coming early and all at once.'

'I just wish you were right, Eddie.'

Eddie blocked the garage door up with a piece of wood so it wouldn't unravel. The Mercedes, with its piece of occult jewellery stuck on the bonnet was waiting quietly inside. Eddie opened the driver's door and Leonard climbed in.

'It's a three litre, fuel injected engine. It goes like shit off a shovel, so watch yourself. You're going to need petrol pretty soon, it's a gas guzzler.'

'Thanks, Eddie.'

'See you, Leonard. Good luck.'

Eddie turned and walked away. He cart-wheeled his arms and broke into a run, heading back to Vicky.

There was no trouble on the way out of the site, Leonard just raised his hand to the gate security guards and they lifted the barrier for him. He drove out of the valley, picking up speed as he got used to the way the car handled. He was speeding through a moody landscape, towards a stormy weather front. He felt like he was in a car commercial, like he was being filmed from high above and in extreme close up. All the oblique angles were being covered, the airflow whipping up and over the bonnet, washing chrome raindrops from the galvanised body work. He felt like one of those drivers they employed too, 'x' rally drivers; you never saw their faces because they were always kept in anonymous silhouette, hidden behind flaring reflections on the windscreen. Every time he kicked the accelerator down, the engine responded and the car lurched forward. He was having to concentrate on the narrow lanes which were cut into the sides of the valleys. The bends were tight and blind, sometimes he'd round a bend and two or three sheep would clamber up a slope, moving as little as possible to get out of harm's way.

He tried the radio, turning up the volume and dialling through the presets, but there was nothing but white noise.

Leonard hit the brakes hard, stamping on the pedal with the ball of his foot to avoid smashing into someone walking across the road. It didn't quite work and the figure avoided impact by jumping up onto the bonnet and rolling off the passenger side.

Leonard got out and ran round the front of the car. The man sat up. He had a long green coat on with a snorkel hood zipped up right to the end. When the head turned and pointed at Leonard, the face was hardly visible behind the fur, it was way back there like the last pickled onion in the jar.

As Leonard got closer, the man unzipped and folded the hood back off his face. It looked like Dave, the same straggly hair and the eager face of a foot soldier.

'Dave?'

'Leonard.'

'What are you doing out here?'

'Walking home, I did a night shift.'

'Are you alright? I could have killed you!'

Leonard grabbed Dave's hand and hauled him to his feet.

'That might have been the best thing that could happen to me. I'm fed up with my useless life; I'm such a drain on limited resources.'

'What's wrong?'

'They've stopped paying us, I just go in for something to do. Seems like all anyone's got to do now is wait, and go fucking crazy waiting.'

'Get in the car, Dave, it's bloody cold out here. I'll give you a lift home.'

Dave didn't move. He seemed a bit slow on the uptake, like he was thinking with a blunt instrument. Dave, for some reason, thought that now was the time for a handshake. His hand was crushing, too bold because he'd been thinking about it too much. He went to the passenger door and climbed in. Leonard flipped the sun visor down and looked into the mirror mounted on the underside. You get a crisp image from these small mirrors; Leonard had some pinkness around his eyes, some anxiety in his fixed expression.

He started up and pulled away, they were soon up to eighty.

Dave undid his coat and settled in his seat.

'You've got to turn right at the next junction.'

'OK.'

Cars are not only built for getting you from A to B, they are for conversation too. Speaking your mind comes easily with the landscape flowing by.

'Bit hot in here, isn't it?'

Leonard adjusted the heater.

'Strange days.'

'Huh?'

'I said strange days; we're living in strange days.'

'You could say that, Dave.'

'Food for the soul though, isn't it? When you think about it, you've got to confront your mortality with the end on its way, hey? It's taken the pressure off though, hasn't it? I mean my natural endowment is minimal; to be honest, I am a flawed and incapable individual, quite worthless in fact. But I don't worry about the future anymore. I don't expect to win, I don't expect to lose, I just live day to day, hand to mouth. And of course, this must be the fated path of my eternal soul so, what can you do? Go over the bridge and follow the road, I'll tell you where to turn off.'

Leonard followed Dave's directions and listened in on his curious mumblings, a mixture of daytime TV slogans, agony aunt phrases and random truisms. The last time they met Dave hardly spoke, he was timid and introverted. Maybe he meant well, but Leonard wished he would shut up. Things like the soul were being mentioned far too often, and with far too much conviction.

Dave may not be an educated man, but he's not stupid either. He's rank and file, keen but in need of leadership.

'What will you do, now the job's finished?'

'Not much. Hey, it's getting cold in here, isn't it?'

Leonard turned the heater back up.

'Do you want me to take you back with me, into the city?'

'No, I don't think so.'

'Well, think about it, weigh it up in your own mind'.

'I'd rather not, I'm not so hot at making my own plans. Can't you tell me what to do?'

'Well no, you've got to decide.'

'I've got a bit of a stomach ache.'

'Do you want me to stop the car?'

'No, 'course not. Look, where the road turns left, you take the track up hill on the right.'

Leonard turned in and dropped the auto shift into drive one. The track was steep and muddy; he would have to use his momentum to get up to the drier ground ahead.

'That's it, just park in front of the window there.'

The house was built of solid stone, tightly puzzled grey-green stone with pale reddish veins. It had a long, low angled roof, a ridge of black slate, splattered with yellow-green lichen.

Dave tipped himself out of the car and walked to the door. He didn't knock or look for his key, he just pushed heavily and it opened. Leonard followed him in and closed the door. It moved stiffly under the weight of a piece of machinery attached to the door. Leonard stepped through an ankle-deep carpet of shredded paper, he looked around and saw that the hall table, the stairs and banisters, the top of the picture frames, they were all coated in a layer of shredded paper and cardboard fibres.

'It was my parents' house. It used to be a farm.'

'But what's with all this paper and shit everywhere?'

'Ah, that's, well that's just the way it is here, it's the way it's always been.'

'What?'

'Look, Leonard, just wait for me will you? I'm going to pack a bag and come with you into town, OK?'

'Good, good decision. Pack some working clothes.'

Leonard turned left into a small sitting-room which had an open fireplace with a plastic flower arrangement stuffed into the grate and a bay window seat. He sat in the bay and watched the postman arrive; he parked his van at the bottom of the lane and started to struggle up the path with a handful of letters.

As Leonard stood and walked into the hall, he could hear the postman step up to the door. A crack of light shone in through the letterbox as it was pushed open and three brown envelopes were posted through. They dropped into a wide basket positioned directly beneath the letter box. A loud electrical revving started up from the machinery attached to the door, followed by a short sequence of violent 'zings' as each of the envelopes were shredded to bits and sprayed into the air.

Dave came down the stairs, threw his bag for Leonard to catch and Leonard caught it cleanly. People love to throw things and then have you catch them; it feels like something has been communicated without the aid of language.

Dave locked the house up and tucked the keys under the coconut mat.

'There's a garage a few miles east of here, do you know it?'

'Ah, yeah, I think so.'

'We need to get over there and pick up a Land Rover that I left there.'

'OK.'

When they got to the garage, the Land Rover was sitting on the lot with a 'For Sale' sign stuck to the windscreen. As Leonard peeled off the letters, a mechanic strolled out of the shop.

'You interested in the vehicle, Sir?'

Leonard handed him the rolled up words.

'It's my vehicle, I left it here a few days ago.'

The mechanic smirked then dropped his gaze to the floor.

'It was abandoned, sir.'

'I'm taking the Land Rover away with me.'

'Look, don't you get it?'

'What?'

'Finders keepers.'

The mechanic took a pistol out of his dungaree pocket, shook his head and made a lip sucking sound. Leonard wasn't thinking straight, he was too fuming mad to think; if he had taken the time, it might have killed him. Before the mechanic could raise the weapon and take aim, Leonard had punched him squarely on the nose, as hard as he could. The mechanic toppled backward and dropped to the ground and as he cupped his hands around his nose, blood came dribbling through his fingers.

There was no comment from the mechanic when Leonard went into the kiosk and came back with the keys. Dave brought the petrol pump over and waited for instructions.

'Fill her up please, Dave.'

When both cars had been filled he settled Dave into the Land Rover. He looked keen but not that capable and Leonard worried that he might well crash into the back of the Mercedes. That was always more likely to happen when someone was trying to follow and not lose you.

So Leonard drove slowly because the Land Rover had a top speed of about sixty-five, seventy. Dave stayed a fixed distance off the tail gate, gripping the wheel tight, and his face in the rear-view mirror showed his eyes bulging in concentration. Leonard smiled at that, like Batman proud of Robin.

When they reached the motorway it was clear of traffic. They drove south and at the top of a long climb, they reached a point where they could see clear across country to the suburbs. In the far distance, the city tower blocks were surrounded by a low, grey fog. It was like looking in on an art class, a perspective drawing, with closer buildings in sharper focus, some foreground detail and just the one fixed light source rolling away to the west.

Before they made it into the suburbs, Leonard turned off the motorway, switched off the engine, and had a chat with Dave, a pep talk. He had a go at building Dave's morale and then explained how he'd had the Land Rover for much longer than he said he would and that maybe Dave could offer his services out on the farm to make up for it. Dave seemed keen on the idea of making himself useful. Leonard gave him the border pass but hung on to his travel permit; that would get them both through the checkpoints. He gave clear instructions on how to get to Reggie's farm and sent Dave on his way.

CHAPTER TWELVE

The Mirabelle stood out in silhouette against the setting sun, a few pale electric bulbs lit up the windows. It was a dull light though, rated in single figure candle power.

Each time Leonard had returned to the hotel, he'd had the feeling that this was a seafront building, and each time he'd been disappointed by the fact that it was not. The area was just a straggling, indecisive, commercial, retail, wholesale mix up.

On the pavement outside the hotel was a neat and tidy pile of soil. Up close it looked like an artist's colour, a burnt umber pigment. It was a small pile, like a molehill or the diggings from a vole hole. Three steps up to the entry door, there was another pile of the earth and then inside, in reception, a pair of tiny earth mounds standing a stride apart.

There was no-one in reception, Harry's office was empty and there seemed nothing more to do than go to bed. But as Leonard passed the reception desk to take the stairs, he noticed an envelope in his pigeonhole. He reached over and pulled it out. It was from Administration, a notification signed by the Warden: Mr. Leonard Gopaul had been granted a stage two interview. Leonard expected something like this; it was a simple tactic, a means by which he would save them the trouble of bringing him in. He'd simply present himself for arrest.

He climbed up to his room and lay flat out on the bed. He was tired and bored, an antagonistic mix that could mostly be fixed by masturbation. Tonight, though, was not the night for those dull fireworks. For the first time in a fair while, he felt like company, random human company, 'warts and all' people, not the polished, perfect citizens of the construction site. He would have a shower and venture out into the curfew, find something to eat and quite a lot to drink.

It was just an idea, but no match for Leonard's fatigue. He rolled onto his side, pulled the duvet up over himself and fell asleep.

On Monday nights the bar closed early, there was no lock-in after curfew, so Adeline and Tony had the whole evening to kill. Tony had put the chairs up on the tables by seven o'clock and stomped off to watch sport on TV. This was Tony's treat, Tony's down time, and he ordered himself take-away Chinese. Adeline hated the stuff so she cooked for herself in the kitchen downstairs.

Tony was beginning to relax, everything was going fine, he'd settled into his chair. The carefully placed beer- and sports- related advertising was cutting back and forth and the picture was crisp. He could hear Adeline downstairs rattling pans, he liked to hear her down there, and be entertained up here.

But suddenly the screen faded to black and white, and words appeared saying that due to unforeseen etcetera, the third round replay had been cancelled.

'Bollocks de bloody bollocks!'

They kept doing this lately, and didn't bother to explain why anymore. He had Chinese on the way, for Christ's sake!

He flicked around the channels a bit but he couldn't find any emerald green, no natural or Astro-turf, no sign of the lovely colour, marked with white lines, or bunkers or flags or stumps; it was useless.

The only thing for it was to go down and watch Adeline. He quite liked to watch her when she was kicking around the kitchen. He preferred her morning fixture though, that was his favourite; she was at her best just after she'd woken up. She'd arrive slowly in the kitchen ready to be insulted and attacked by all the inanimate things. Every morning, the world conspired to work against her: the coffee would be too strong, she would burn her finger on the toaster, there would be a funny smell in the air, she wouldn't be able to find her slippers and there wouldn't be any post. Adeline would be angry but it would be a level anger, one which would not rise to a fever pitch. She would discuss all these annoyances with herself, in between taking tentative looks in the mirror. She would be saying shit and shit! But after her first cigarette and the second coffee, she would manage to turn things around, she would try out a few dance steps, with her arms bent and head bowed, her face hidden by her tumbling hair.

Adeline sat down again at the kitchen table and ate her pasta with olive oil, parmesan cheese and pine nuts. It was one of Tony's dishes, one his mother had shown him when he was a boy. She ate the food and drank a glass of not very good red wine. These days wine, beer and spirits were being supplied very erratically by the black market, their stock was low because the monthly delivery was three weeks late. She flicked through some out-of-date lifestyle magazines. She liked to flick through and study the perfect faces, all blasted with ecstasy. She liked to let the advertising draw her in, and believe it all again, even if it was just for a little while longer.

When she'd finished eating, she walked to the window and had a look-see at how the seeds she had gathered from the spilled glove were doing. They were germinating, the first leaves showing. She picked one, bit into it and tasted an acidic sap.

Tony crept down the stairs until he was standing at the open kitchen door. Adeline had her back to him; at first he thought she was smoking with a cigarette holder but it wasn't that. She had a thermometer in her mouth.

'There's no bloody football. No TV at all, in fact.'

Adeline took the thermometer out of her moth and read it.

'What's the matter, are you poorly?'

'No, I'm ovulating.'

'Oh, congratulations, I'm very happy for you.'

Adeline turned to fill her glass. Tony took careful aim and lobbed his screwed up take-away menu at the back of her head. He liked the look she gave him as she glanced back over her shoulder. She swallowed some of her wine and hurled the glass at Tony's head. It hit the wall level with his eye-line and shattered, making a loose artistic statement and a perfect sound effect.

This was good sport for Tony, his short attacking move had been countered with flourish and vigour. The exchange had sent his pulse racing up nicely. He laughed and put his best foot forward, his left foot, as he climbed back up the stairs.

Adeline switched the kitchen lights out then went to the fridge. She liked the way the box of light lit the room, it made the place stagey and theatrical, it made her want to act out her fantasies, made her want to perform miracles. She reached into the door for a carton of milk, took a few sips and then went upstairs.

The bedroom lights were out so she climbed in beside Tony and listened to his breathing for several minutes. It was steady and even, so she rolled over. She wanted it to look like an innocent, sleeper's gesture, part of that endless search for a more and more comfortable position. As she rolled, she aimed her tensed arm and hammered her snouty elbow into the bridge of Tony's nose.

She waited, but there wasn't much of a reaction, he murmured and sighed but that was it. She looked and there was some blood running from his nostrils onto his top lip. He was still breathing, though, and his heart was still pumping. She figured that it must be possible then, to knock someone out while they were sleeping.

She brought her lips up close to his ear and said.

'Sleep well, my love.'

Raymond had spent all day trawling the streets; it wasn't that easy for a man like him to proposition beautiful young women. They didn't want to stop and talk sex to a pensioner, that was just too weird, that was asking for trouble. Truth is, Raymond was having difficulty hiding his contempt for the job. He couldn't help himself, but he was kind of seeing the world differently. He was slowly becoming a man who not only disliked Warden but, to a greater extent, didn't actually like men at all. The maleness of men was sickening, so out in front and expecting to be deferred to. They were always so self-aggrandising, and always lying to themselves about what they wanted. They thought that all they had to do was to rustle up some show of character by rushing in, taking charge and fucking things up.

He spent some time in a couple of coffee shops where he'd found girls before, but his heart really wasn't in it. By the time the street lamps were lighting up outside, he was enjoying a feeling of benevolence that was washing over him, as he watched the girls come and go in all innocence.

Warden wouldn't ring to see how he'd gotten on, he hated Raymond knowing that he was horny. He always treated his sexual arrangements like take it or leave it amusements, like he wasn't fussed either way. Raymond had decided to keep on the right side of the old man, though. Warden had alluded, 'tongue in cheek' to a place on the vessel for Raymond.

The streets were clearing ahead of curfew and he decided to head back to the hotel on foot. It was a cold night so he flipped his collar up and tucked his scarf in around his neck. The walking generated some body heat, enough so that he could loosen his scarf by the time he got there.

The lights in the reception area of the Mirabelle were dimmed and in the half-light the place was almost welcoming. Raymond looked in at the reception desk and noticed the envelope that he'd left there for Leonard was gone. That was good, he'd head off now he had something to tell Warden. It would dilute the fact that he'd had no luck finding him a new girl.

Morning sunlight was shining through a lime yellow curtain. Leonard was sitting on the bed, pointing the nozzle of a hairdrier into a sock. He had discovered this method for drying wet socks as a student. It worked brilliantly and the sensation of slipping a scorching hot pair of woolly socks onto cold feet was not to be taken lightly. He slipped his outdoor boots on over his warmed feet and stepped out into the hall. He took the stairs automatically whilst he was doing up his watch. The boards creaked as he turned left at the bottom of the stairs and entered the lounge. The room was brighter than normal because three sets of French windows at the far end had been opened onto the garden.

Leonard recognised the two people who were sat chatting at one of the tables placed in direct sunlight, but how did Dave know Ian? As Leonard approached, Ian looked up.

'Ah, there you are then. We found out that we were both waiting for the same man, young Dave and I.'

Dave stood and smiled, and offered his hand so Leonard shook it. Ian piped up.

'Let's get some breakfast, shall we? It's on me.'

Ian turned to the waitress and tried to get her attention. She was standing in the corner of the room, drying cutlery. Each time she dropped a knife or fork into the tray, it made a kind of cymbal crash, like a terrible drummer struggling to keep time, very slow and improvised, jazz time. She didn't notice Ian, so he got up and went over to order the food.

Leonard leant in to Dave.

'What have you told him, Dave?'

'Ah, oh, just that we met up north and I'd decided that I'd rather die in company than up on the hills.'

'Did he ask about the vessel?'

'Yeah, now that you mention it, he did mention it, yeah. What's the vessel?'

'Never mind, don't give him any more information, OK? And don't tell him where you are staying.'

'Well, shit he knows that, first thing he asked.'

'All right, just be civil and boring, maybe he'll leave. What are you doing here anyway?'

'Well, Reg sent me out on a fuel run. It's hard to find diesel, and I'm using up the last quarter of a tank looking for more, it's ridiculous.'

Leonard leaned back in his chair as Ian returned.

'It's on it's way, tea all round and a full English brekky, the lot.'

Ian sat down, took his sunglasses out of his top pocket and settled them over his brown, poker-playing eyes. His shirt was loose at the neck and rolled to the elbow; he tipped his chair back so his face was in the sun.

Leonard closed his eyes and let the sunlight heat his face. For a moment they looked like old friends taking their ease outside a clubhouse somewhere.

Thin lace curtains hanging in the French windows swayed gently in the breeze, the air did not carry the seasonal wind chill.

'It's warm, isn't it?'

The waitress brought the tea and settled the cups.

Dave didn't take sugar so he was sipping first; he swallowed, and then spoke.

'Yeah, it's one of the side effects of the Moon.'

Ian dipped his sunglasses and stirred sugar into his tea. He took the hot spoon and placed it on the back of Dave's hand.

'Ouch!'

'What about the moon?'

'The weather's all wrong: winter and summer, back to back. Look down the path there, the two trees on the corner, cherry trees they are, well they're in blossom!'

'But it's way too early…'

'Yeah, well, that's what we've been saying at forecast, it's going to be a forced spring, a very short and early spring then straight on to the hottest summer we've ever known. Except most of us will never see the summer, of course. It's the side effect of the mass of the Ice Moon. It's kind of realigning the earth's angle of rotation, the gravitational field has shifted, the year is being brought forward.'

Ian leaned in closer to Dave.

'How fascinating! It's really quite clever of you to know all this stuff, David.'

'Well, you just pick things up at the centre, it's coffee break chit-chat.'

The breakfast arrived and Leonard sauced his eggs and bacon, peppered his grilled tomatoes and mushrooms, and hogged it down, keen as a hungry dog. He couldn't be that sure yet but it seemed as if Ian was trying it on, trying to seduce Dave, and Dave was happy enough, or naive enough, or both, to let Ian pay him fool compliments.

Leonard ate gratefully though; it had been a long time since he'd eaten so well.

'So, Ian, what do you want?'

Ian took a long time chewing on his mouthful, then said, 'What do you think I want? I want you to tell me how you got on up north.'

'It was interesting, it was educational.'

'Care to elaborate?'

'No.'

Ian stirred three sugars into his tea and then placed the back of the hot spoon against Leonard's forearm.

'Ouch! What are you doing, you idiot?'

'What I can't understand, Leonard, is why you weren't killed snooping around up there in the hills.'

'It was a waste of time, a wild goose chase. I never found the vessel, I just got kicked around by security patrols.'

'That means you must have been close.'

'I don't think so. I sort of don't care anymore. If these are the last few weeks of our lives, I don't want to spend them chasing around the country for nothing.'

'I don't believe you, Leonard. I'm a good judge of character and you are just too ambitious to give up this easily.'

Leonard stood and tucked his chair under the table.

'Thanks for breakfast.'

Ian rose too.

'Do you mind if I have a word with you outside, Leonard?'

'All right.'

Ian offered his hand for Dave to shake.

'Do excuse us won't you, David, and do come and see me. I'm sure that I can arrange some diesel for you.'

'Thanks, Ian. Yeah thanks, that's great!'

Leonard stepped out into the garden and walked onto a lawn that needed mowing.

Ian followed with his hands on his hips; he looked out of breath.

'Now then, Leonard, all joking aside, tell me what you found out!'

'I have told you, wild goose chase.'

Ian moved closer to Leonard, far too close for comfort. Leonard raised his arms, it was a reflex action but Ian didn't like it. He took hold of Leonard's shoulders, and turning away he rolled him over his hip and onto the ground. Leonard was now looking up at the sky; he was winded and felt his breakfast in his throat. Ian pressed his knee into Leonard's chest, reached into his pockets and searched through his wallet.

'What are you looking for?'

'Shut up! I'm serving a curfew violation on you.'

'But you're not a policeman.'

'Oh, aren't I?'

Ian dropped the wallet like he'd remembered something more important. He was flushed in the face; he placed a hand against his chest and started breathing heavily.

'You alright?'

Ian couldn't say anything for a minute, it was as if he was having to shut up while he swallowed something that was really difficult to swallow. He walked to the garden wall and steadied himself.

'You alright, Ian?'

'No, I'm not. It's my fucking useless heart, it's had enough of me.'

'What should I do?'

'You've got a car outside, haven't you?'

'You know I have, Ian.'

'Get it started, you're taking me to Hospital.'

Ian didn't speak in the car, he just sat in the back crumpled up and breathing heavily. It wasn't far to the Hospital, just down into the business district but by the time the building came into view, Ian looked pretty rough. Leonard drove in and tried to figure out the colour-coded departmental blocks; there were big signposts everywhere to explain what red, blue, green, orange and pink were. He parked up and waved some people over from accident and emergency. They ran across the forecourt in their green jumpsuits, uncurled Ian and laid him out on a stretcher.

'What's wrong with him?'

'I don't know, he had some sort of attack.'

Ian was trying to raise his hand; he managed a finger, to signal that he could shed some light. The nurse leaned down and Ian whispered something like: 'It's my heart you arseholes, it's my pig's heart! I ran out of immuno-suppressants, get me into intensive care!'

The nurses wheeled him off, mechanics of the human body getting on with another routine pit-stop.

It was true, then: Ian had this animal centre, his blood <u>was</u> pumped around his body by a bag of pork gristle. It was no wonder that he didn't look that good. No wonder that he lacked some of the most essential human characteristics.

CHAPTER THIRTEEN

The good thing about Adeline's mother's letter was that it was very specific, very clear. Thank God the old girl wrote in English or the whole thing would be impossible. Tony left the bar early, with the excuse that he was off to play a round of golf, so of course Adeline thought nothing of it. He did go to the golf course anyway, it was the nearest woodland and early on a Wednesday morning, apart from the odd junior champion, it would be deserted.

The first instruction, when he got to the edge of the trees, was to urinate, which was fair enough as he needed to anyway. He moved through the deep woodland to the right of the fourteenth fairway. The air was sweet and moist, purple flowers sprouted from the rich, red soil. The letter said to find a substantial tree, an Ash tree, with a regular spread of branches and a full crown. He would have to match the drawing and leaf diagram up to the real thing, because he had no idea what an Ash looked like. Why an Ash tree anyway? These were all oaks. He found two lost balls and put them in his pocket; a Dunlop 65 and Slazenger with a smile sliced into it.

Where the golf course boundary met some private houses, Tony found his Ash, or as the letter specified, Fraxinus; It is written that the human race will be protected and restored by a man and a woman who find shelter in the branches of the Ash. A man and a woman who have eaten the honey-dew secreted from its flesh. Adeline's mother talked the most bollocks he had ever heard in his life, but to be honest that didn't matter anymore, he had decided to do this. He followed her instructions, picked up the measuring tape and started to mark out a circle.

Leonard had a couple of days before he had to turn up at the Administration interview. If they left him alone for those days, maybe he could set a few things up, get a few things in place.

First of all he had to go and see Beryl, tell her about the vessel and ask her why she hadn't told him everything she knew before he left.

He took the stairs down to the basement and knocked on the boiler-room door. There was nothing, not a sound and the room was locked shut. He couldn't do anything until he'd spoken to Beryl and asked about the stapler and the microchips, he couldn't make any plans until he understood what was going on. He couldn't bear to sit waiting in his room either, so he went out into the street, determined to enjoy the good weather and the forced spring. And it did feel good; he squinted at the sun, absorbed its warmth and walked west this time. There was nothing else to do but kill some time, time that was running out anyway.

High grey clouds seemed to be floating down from the north and below these, creamy cumuli were caught in a southerly breeze. As Leonard watched and walked beside the open green of a public park, the criss-crossing clouds seemed like a silent screen pie-fight going on above his head.

He stepped in through one of the park gates, a place he usually loathed, because it was the place the urban planners wanted you to go to unwind, and the idea that an urban planner could second-guess how you wanted to unwind, really pissed him off. Flower beds laid in grids, Bristol fashion, made him feel physically sick. No matter what the old folk said, they were not, 'Oh, look at that, that's lovely isn't it, Leonard!' No, they weren't, they were an insult, a ground zero of hope, a reminder of how governed and how empty an average life could be.

Up ahead, a man in a dark jacket stood in front of a wooden bench. He looked eccentric, a bit 'navvy' in the lived-in blazer, glossy chip-fat hair, string belt and heavy shoes. Leonard watched him; he was just standing there, minding his own business. That was another thing about parks. It was not a place where you could mind your own business because all the other poor bastards in the neighbourhood gathered there to mind theirs too. And then there was that fairly accurate rumour, that people who hung out in parks were most often, well, almost certainly certifiable and at the very least, up to no good. Mostly though, they were just cases of almost catatonic boredom who'd just popped over the park to get out of the house for a while.

But there he was, this man. His hands were in his pockets so his jacket was flaring out over his hands, and the vent in the back of the jacket, open wide. He shifted his weight from time to time, one foot to the other, and beside his feet, there was earth rolling out from his trouser legs and collecting in piles.

He stamped his feet a couple of times, then looked up at a copy of the 1957 bylaws stuck to a metal pole, and like he'd decided not to wait any longer, he walked off. He didn't walk far because he stopped to put bicycle clips around his ankles, then he picked up a ladder and threaded his arm through the middle rung so that it balanced. He settled his arse onto a hard old leather saddle and peddled off amazingly slowly, so that the piece of window cleaner's scrim tied to the back of the ladder hardly flapped at all in the wind.

Leonard walked across to the bench and picked up a handful of soil from the pile. He rubbed it through his fingers and smelt it, it was the same stuff he'd found in the Mirabelle. What was this bloke doing, trailing soil from his trousers? He must have drawstrings in his pockets that worked the open ends of long, thin bags strapped to his legs. Leonard had seen this sort of thing before, he'd seen the movies about the prisoners of war, hiding tunnel dust from prison guards, scattering it in the camp grounds.

Raymond was standing about a hundred yards away, looking through his binoculars, sweeping Leonard's position and following as the man in the dark suit walked away. It looked like a classic 'drop'. The dark suit had left something and Leonard was now picking it up. It had all been very out in the open, though, and not the sort of technique he would ever recommend. Raymond was nicely hidden by the thick trunk of a Plane tree; parks were usually very good places to work because the perimeter trees gave excellent cover and good visibility over an open central area. It was good to be on Leonard's trail again. Although he'd evaded capture and gone on a jaunt in the prohibited area, he was back now and Raymond was on his tail, taking notes and filing reports. It was only a matter of time before Warden asked Raymond to kill Mr Gopaul, he was a security risk now, and although things that used to matter were being increasingly overlooked, people like Gopaul were not.

The target was on the move again, walking faster (as you would expect after a pick up) heading for the nearest exit.

Birdsong has a 'hurry up' quality to it because they streak across the sky with no time to spare. It makes you think that you should be doing the same. Thing is, they were probably right; even with their walnut-sized brains, they knew better than Leonard. And Leonard now had to think about his route back up to the Spanish district because he was disorientated by the detour through the park. This tends to happen, because the alternative exits throw you out into new and unknown neighbourhoods which are actually just the same old neighbourhoods seen from a new angle.

He was standing in a side-street he hadn't seen before, a street of very old fashioned houses, square and flat roofed, made of blackened bricks, with white plasterwork borders around the windows. There were a couple of throttled, rusting cars dumped in the street and lots of taxis, like it was somewhere they used to repair taxis.

Each house in the row had a metal rubbish bin and eight polished steps up to panelled doors with sombre, lion-headed knockers. Short runs of arrow topped railings neatened off and squared up the front gardens. Through the front windows, Leonard could make out a grand piano and rows of photo frames placed onto a polished table-top. Each frame had a thin, beige rudder of cardboard at the back, to hold the loved ones upright.

Leonard made his way along the street, which led into a crescent and once out of the crescent, the familiar landmarks started to re-present themselves.

Raymond followed, making sure that he was just rounding the street corners as Gopaul left his sight-line. You could lose someone like this, but they were certainly not going to realise they were being followed, and this was the most important thing. Gopaul was cutting back towards the centre of town, and Raymond settled into the best part of his job. He liked surveillance because when he was following people, he pretty much vanished, he forgot who he was and blended in with the surroundings. The city lost its hard edges and became an architect's plan and he was just an incidental figure, a line drawing walking beside the buildings or between the alleys of sketched trees. A man who entered at the entrances and waited at the pedestrian crossings.

Gopaul was an interesting subject; he hesitated here and there and seemed unsure of himself, and when he reached the Spanish district, he hung around the baker's shop. He bought a meringue and ate half of it out on the street, then licked his lips, brushed his hair back and went into a bar.

Tony was serving, and he looked tired but it was more than that, he had black eyes, those prize-fighting eyes, both ringed with blue-green bruises. He looked a bit sheepish, sorry for himself, so he stayed focused on what his hands were doing. He pulled at the lager pump, picked up glasses, lemon slices and ice cubes. Leonard couldn't help but ask the obvious question, it would have been rude not to.

'What happened?'

Tony finished topping up the pint glass he was filling and set it down on the bar top, then he lifted his battered face.

'Allergy.'

'To what?'

'To stupid questions. Do you want a drink?'

'Ah, no thanks, I don't have any credit.'

'Who the hell does these days? The system's breaking down, the brewery keeps delivering the beer so we're just writing up slates for any poor bastard that comes in. Can't last for long though, can it?'

Tony moved along the bar wiping beer spill as he went. He got to the tape deck, ejected the thing and turned it over.

'I wondered if I could see Adeline?'

'She's upstairs.'

A deliberately minimal reply, a statement that was also a dare; she's up there, but from here on it's up to you, on your head be it!

'I'll just go and say hello, then.'

Leonard felt a bit of a jerk heading for the stairs, but once he'd turned the corner out of sight and climbed up above ground level, the hard bit was done. When he reached the landing he could see clear through to the living room, he could see Adeline balancing on top of a stepladder in her work clothes. She was holding equilibrium over the centre of gravity but she didn't look at all stable. She was reaching up for boxes on top of a wardrobe, trying to see what was inside. Leonard walked through, but way before he got to her, she turned.

'Leonard!'

She looked younger with her hair tied back off her face, wearing a paint splashed sweatshirt and ten-year-old jeans.

'You're back and still in one piece. How did it go?'

The ladder wobbled and creaked as she turned and started to climb back down.

'You could say that I found out what I needed to know.'

'Really?'

'Yeah.'

'Well, yeah what?'

'There is a survival project and a vessel of sorts. But it's a dangerous place, ruthless and corrupt. It's a bloody free-for-all up there.'

'Are you surprised?'

'Not anymore I'm not, no.'

'Not a nice spectacle, is it, the human race clambering over one another for advantage.'

'I'm not like them.'

'Yes you are, Leonard. Don't kid yourself about that.'

Adeline was leaning on the ladder, wiping her hands on her jeans. She lifted the bottom of her sweatshirt and wiped her face with it. Leonard looked at her exposed stomach, her soft, pale skin with one mole above and one below her navel.

'How have you been, Adeline? You look shattered.'

'I've been scared. I'm always scared, like everybody else. I just don't know anymore. I try to control myself; I don't want to lose control. I make my hands into fists before I leave the house. Tony and I are just trying to hang on to our routine. We carry on like we always have. The bar fills up, so we keep on opening. Nobody really talks about what's going to happen anymore.'

Adeline stepped away and Leonard followed, noticing her height, how the top of her head was level with his jaw-line.

'I wanted to see you. I can't say for sure, but if you want, maybe I can help you get a place on the vessel.'

Adeline turned.

'You can?'

'Maybe.'

'Really?'

'I've got to do some running around first, but I think I can get my hands on what I need.'

'You know something, Leonard?'

'What?'

'You look a bit knackered yourself!'

'I know.'

'Your eyes are troubled, you need a shave and your hair's a greasy mop.'

Leonard smiled and dropped his head.

'Why don't you have a shower, and get out of those mail order clothes?'

'OK.'

Leonard took his shower. He soaped up and washed down, then he just stood there with the running water splitting over the top of his head. He felt like he didn't matter much, like he was just another hungry, panicked soul spread way too thin. If only he had the resolve of his own heart, the way it continued to beat, whatever was going on in the outside world.

He tilted his head back, let the water flood into his mouth and overflow. Six weeks now, that was all the time he had left. He could leave the city, go at any time he liked and sit it out at the construction site with a very probable chance of survival. But that wasn't good enough. He hated the idea that the arseholes were going to win, that they were going to be in charge. If he made an effort now, he had a slim chance of doing something about all the bullshit.

He reached out for the dangling light switch, a length of string, grubby near the bottom but clean above Tony and Adeline's reach. He cut the bright yellow light that was flooding the bathroom, in favour of semi-darkness. He couldn't see very clearly but the very last of the daylight coming in through the window was easier on the eye than electricity. Through the half-opened window, he caught sight of the sky; it was a gentle, minimal palette of silver blue, with tall trees on the hill, half-orange in the lowering light.

The door opened and closed, he turned and looked at Adeline. Hers was a frank face, a kind of Canadian face, with long flattened eyebrows and a straight nose, a shallow vertical scoop between her nose and her upper lip.

She locked the door and started to remove her clothes. Leonard watched her, letting the fact of it play out as she dragged her shirt off, not bothering with the buttons. This was no striptease; it was a practical act like before a dive into a swimming pool. She was ready now, she just stood still opposite Leonard, and he looked at her through a thickening fog of arousal.

He kissed her dry lips, which tightened into a smile and then softened as she became serious again. He dropped to kiss her shoulders and down along her arms, across her stomach. He noticed temperature differences as he brushed his lips over her body. As he kissed her, he imagined a thermal image of her body, the skin a cool blue over her hips and along her shinbones, orange around her neck and between her breasts, fierce red when she opened her mouth.

She was whispering, trying to say something, undefined, involuntary. There were long pauses and he hadn't noticed before, but maybe you had to be this close; with her mouth at his ear, her voice had a sudden beauty to it. She spoke in half tone, barely pronouncing the explosive consonants, softening them. When she said 'stop', 'back' or 'not' the P, K and the T were muted, elongated like a softly hit drum. Leonard held her close, feeling a kind of perfect calm in her arms, a rare calm that she was loaning him; he knew this would pass quickly, like the eye of the storm.

Adeline took hold of his hand, opened the bathroom door and stepped out into the hall. The bar noise from downstairs was a loud and familiar sound effect. Adeline crossed to the opposite side of the hall, opened the bedroom door and moved into the darkness. Leonard followed, moved around the door and closed it behind him. Low lamp-light from the bedside blinked on, lighting her left side; her outline looked retouched, especially at her waist, a long and gradual curve which flared around her hips. Her breasts were small, the nipples pale, and the red whip marks of her clothes had not yet faded.

Leonard hesitated but too many switches had been thrown now, the analytical faculties of the brain were choked off and he let go, gave over control to unknown forces. Leonard did as he was told, did what he wanted. Adeline touched herself, stroked her own shining skin; she used her pale fingers, opening a kind of ring-pull opening.

The fluid in Leonard's inner ear slopped around the spirals as he fell forward onto the bed. He had stopped processing any more information; what they were doing now was locked off, stolen from misery. They were catalysing enzymes now, and the sounds came from the gut and off the top of the head. Leonard felt like he was running very fast up to the edge of death and then he discovered something more hopeful than he had ever expected.

He felt a subliminal reduction of the constant need, a loss of atmospheric fear. As Adeline pulled him close and held his head in her hands, there was a temporary cessation of a life's pitiful objectivity.

When Leonard woke, the room was black and quiet, and he didn't want to move, he wanted to leave it alone, to leave it for now, as it was. A sweet breath of cool, fresh air made the curtain billow and sway. They had been sleeping back to back with the soles of their feet touching. Adeline moved. She put her arms around him and squeezed, Leonard could hear her teeth grinding as their heads touched. Her fingers absentmindedly pressed into his back, tapping out stanzas against his spine!

He was very hungry; he fancied fried chicken with pickles and potato salad and corn on the cob. Adeline lifted her head off the pillow and propped herself on her elbow.

'Do you want something to eat?'

'Yeah, I'm starved.'

'I'll have a look downstairs.'

'What about Tony?'

'He's gone out.'

She leant across Leonard, smiled and whispered in his ear.

'I'm exhausted.'

She sat on the edge of the bed, then stood and walked to the door, went through silently except for the cracking of her ankle bones.

Leonard rolled across the bed into the space she had left; he stretched out his arms and legs and felt relatively calm. There was a nagging doubt, though, sparked off by the fact that he was alone in the other man's room. He felt a chill and wondered what this would cost? These were weird times and Tony was an unreadable man.

Adeline called up the stairs but what she was saying was muffled and mopped up by the carpets and paintwork. Leonard opened the door and her voice was clearer.

'What about a bacon sandwich and a glass of Sambuca?'

Leonard made his way down the stairs before he answered, he didn't want to shout through Tony's house.

Adeline was still naked, she was sitting on a barstool sipping from a shot glass, and her right leg was crossed over the left, twitching very slightly in time with her pulse.

'I love being up when it's dark, see I never want to go to bed when it's night time.'

'I know what you mean.'

'Bacon sandwich and a glass of Sambuca?'

'Yeah, go on then.'

CHAPTER FOURTEEN

Daylight entered from above, shining down through glass cubes which had been cemented into the pavement up at street level. The light brightened one wall of the boiler room, the far wall behind the printing press. In one of the alcoves behind the press and beneath the glass cubes, Lena had placed her bed. Lying flat out, it was possible to look up at the glass and watch the footsteps of pedestrians as they walked across the skylight. It was quite noisy during the morning and evening rush, but it was always interesting to watch the way the people moved. Lena could get an idea of who they were from below, because after all, everything we do is intricately linked to who we are, even a snap-shot of three footsteps can reveal something.

'Don't you want me to help you, grandma? Isn't that what grand-daughters do?'

'Don't say grandma, I know you're saying it because you know I hate it.'

'I feel lazy watching you work.'

'I want to do this myself, work at my own pace. I haven't got time to answer lots of questions from a silly young girl.'

'But aren't you supposed to be passing on the benefit of your experience, handing down your wisdom?'

'You're doing fine, believe me.'

'But I'm wasting my time.'

'That's not true, and you should know because I have told you often enough, that a full and indifferent immobility is one of the secret weapons.'

'What?'

'Don't be afraid to waste your time, Lena. Use it up doing nothing sometimes, that way you'll notice it passing, you'll know its value. That's better than rushing around and scoffing it up like a greedy pig.'

Beryl was inking up a new plate, you couldn't read it back to front, you had to wait until it was reversed. She finished wiping off and clamped down the drum, then had to load another roll of paper.

Someone had stopped above Lena's head, which was a bonus. He'd planted his big feet slightly apart and Lena watched, grinning, as a shadow grew and became a bag placed on the ground next to him. Sometimes the strangers stood there for ages hardly moving, then the orange butt of a cigarette would land nearby, still alight, and then the feet would move off.

'Nan?'

'Yes, dear.'

'This might be a stupid question, but do you believe that the choices we make, I mean what we actually do in our lives, has anything at all to do with what actually happens to us in our lives?'

Beryl was struggling to lift the roll of paper onto its locating bar. She managed to get the end on and it slid down gently.

'Yes and no.'

Someone knocked on the boiler room door.

'I'll get it.'

Lena rolled off her bed and ran to the door. She checked who it was through the broken glass, then opened it.

'Hello, Leonard! Come in. Leonard?'

'Yes?'

'When you were young, what did you think you would be doing when you got old?'

'I'm not old.'

'You know what I mean.'

'I don't know, I think I wanted to be an expert in something, something not too hectic, maybe a violin teacher. I wanted an ordered, genteel life, with a bust of Beethoven on the mantel, and climbing plants flowering on the outside of the house, and students jogging past in pairs from the nearby university.'

'So it didn't work out then?'

'No, not really.'

Lena walked through the boiler room and Leonard followed. She ran over to her bed and came back with a blue bundle.

'Here.'

Leonard shook out the material and held it up in front of him.

'It's your jumper!'

'Looks great.'

He pulled it over his head and stuck his arms through the sleeves.

'Feels good.'

'Looks very, very good.'

Beryl was bending over the printing machinery watching some test sheets roll off.

'How's our hero, then?'

'A bit pissed off, really.'

'Do you really like it?'

Leonard rolled the roll neck over and turned back the sleeves.

'Yes, it's great. Thank you, Lena.'

Beryl came towards Leonard waving an empty sheet of newsprint.

'Come on then, give me a full report. If I get going, I can run a last minute newsflash in this edition! You can be my roving reporter, my man on the ground. It's quite a scoop to have inside information on the survival project. Well, what's it like up there?'

Leonard looked at her; he smiled at her energy and her intention. Political activism had never been his thing.

'In a nut-shell, it's kind of disturbing.'

Beryl took off her glasses and rubbed her eyes; she looked him over.

'Been in the wars, have you?'

'Got chased around a bit, yeah. The place is full of dog-eat-dog characters, God knows how they'll run things if they do survive the Ice Moon.'

'Same as before, I should think. Don't forget, Leonard, you are just one man and one man can only do so much.'

Leonard hadn't thought of that. The history of the world was pretty sordid and the rise and fall of empires would probably continue. But it still pissed him off.

'I'm a fool for coming to the city in the first place.'

'Oh, I don't agree, lad. It was either that or wait for doomsday at home with your feet up.'

'I'm a bloody coward, Beryl. I've always been a terrible coward.'

'Oh, I don't think so, not from what I've seen you're not. At worst you're a bit of an introvert, but that's no bad thing. I think you're about ready to show your true colours.'

'I'm not sure I've got what it takes to be a bloody hero.'

Beryl held her hand up to stop him speaking.

'Something's burning.'

'What?'

Leonard followed her through to the kitchen where she adjusted the dials on the cooker, fine-tuned them as if she were cracking a safe.

'Where were we?'

'I haven't got what it takes.'

'You'll be marvellous, I know you will. Now what about a catchy headline for the paper? What about something like: Gangsters buy out survival project!'

Beryl grabbed Leonard's hand and walked him back to the printing press.

'Between you and me, Leonard, this was never going to be a fair fight, was it?'

'Why the hell didn't you tell me about the tag in my bloody lip?'

'Hah! Bet you were glad of it when they scanned you though, eh? Did you know that anyone who turns up uninvited at the construction site and without a tag, is disposed of!'

'What?'

Lena stepped up and peeled back her top lip.

'Look, I've got one too.'

Beryl shushed Lena away.

'They take themselves very seriously up there, Leonard. They're far too paranoid about security to let anyone who isn't tagged live after seeing the site. You found it though, so now you should believe me, and you should thank us, Lena and I, we've given you your ticket to the future. Sit down, Leonard. If you don't mind me being direct, you look shagged out.'

He slumped down at the table and rubbed his face in his hands.

'Why didn't you tell me about the stapler gun business?'

'Well, it was a bit of a test, really. If you did come back after finding out, you really didn't have to, well then you were the right person to take care of Lena.'

'Why didn't you ask me to take her along, we could have gone up and just stayed there 'til impact.'

'First of all I wanted to be sure that the site was operational. Second, it's too soon, there's likely to be all sorts of monkey business going on over the next few weeks. I want to keep my eye on Lena for as long as I can.'

'I can make sure Lena gets to the site.'

'We'll see, but you'll have to watch your back you silly sod, I don't want you being arrested now, do I!'

'I'll do my best.'

'Do you want to eat with us?'

'OK.'

'Lena, set the table.'

Beryl waited for Lena to disappear, then she turned on Leonard.

'If I'm not very much mistaken, you've been a busy boy, haven't you?'

'What do you mean?'

'You know full-well what I mean. I told you to watch yourself. Didn't I say it was a bad idea to get involved with Adeline?'

'Look, it's my bloody business!'

'What's left of it is important to me too! I wonder what it's going to cost you, this bit of adult recreation? What's the C.O.D.?'

'Tony's credit note says that I have to leave the city. But I don't know for sure. If I get picked up now, I'll probably just be thrown in jail.'

'Brilliant! Well that's no good to me is it, not now your job is to look after Lena!'

'I had no choice, I'm sorry, I...'

Leonard's face coloured up.

'I understand, Leonard, you couldn't think straight and you made a mistake. Do you have any feelings for the girl?'

Leonard shrugged.

You wouldn't have imagined it but Beryl was a convenience cook, a woman formed by her time, stuck in the era of prawn cocktails for starters, where you make the sauce with half salad cream, half ketchup. Then Coq au Vin and a jacket potato for main course, and you finish up with syrup pudding and custard, whipped cream and ice cream, all the stuff that'll kill you.

Beryl had been quiet at the table, she'd let Lena go on about this and that. When Leonard had finished stuffing himself, he looked across at her and she seemed anxious. She was clearing up and she was worried because she couldn't find the top of the mustard. She backed her chair away from the table and excused herself. She found the lid in the kitchen, then washed up and wouldn't let Leonard help.

Lena stopped talking and watched him for a few minutes. They were still sat at the table, but with everything except the tablecloth cleared away. Leonard was studying the white weave up close because it wasn't just white, there was a foliage pattern hidden inside the white.

'You're a silly sod aren't you, Leonard?'

He looked up at Lena, with her elbows on the table and her head in her hands.

'Oh, and how did you reach that conclusion?'

'Nan says so, but you're quite nice, and the main thing is you're capable; Nan says that that's really the main thing.

'Lena?'

'Yes?'

'I've got a plan, but I need the tagging gun.'

'A plan?'

Leonard stood up and started to fold the tablecloth.

'Can you get me the tagging gun?'

'It's a pistol.'

'Where is it kept?'

'Warden keeps it in his apartment.'

'OK, I've got my interview tomorrow so Warden'll be busy and his apartment will be empty. So what do you think, can you get it?'

'But you said there was a plan, what's the overall plan?'

'I want to start an alternative passenger list, Lena. I'd like to add a rebellious element and tag some outsiders.'

The pudding was lying heavy in his gut but it was warming too, all that sugar and suet, high-energy food. So he was slow up the stairs to the lounge. He probably needed to sleep but the idea of lying flat out with his eyes closed was not good. He felt vulnerable now, it seemed like every avenue might lead to a sticky end.

Harry was slapping the top of the reception desk with his hands, in a rhythm known only to himself because he was wearing headphones. As soon as he saw Leonard, he stopped slapping and switched off.

'Leonard.'

'Harry.'

'Ah, there seems to be some bad news in your pigeon-hole.'

'Do you read my mail, Harry?'

'Of course I read your mail, how am I supposed to provide a first class service if I don't know what's going on?'

Harry passed the envelope over and Leonard opened it.

'What's it say?'

'You know what it says.'

'Well, yeah but…'

'It's the C.O.D. for last night, says I've got twenty-four hours to leave the city. When did this arrive, Harry?'

'I didn't see, but some time this morning I suppose. You'd better tread carefully.'

'Has anyone been in looking for me?'

'Well yeah, people have been in looking for you, all right. That one in particular has been keeping a lookout, on and off for days.'

Leonard turned and recognised Raymond sitting in one of the dusty, raspberry-coloured armchairs, with his head in a newspaper.

'Look, don't worry about it, Leonard. One day we'll all be sitting on a beach somewhere and we'll laugh about all of this.'

Leonard folded the envelope and tucked it into his back pocket.

'No, Harry, no, we won't.'

Raymond waited in the lounge while Leonard went up to his room. He lowered the newspaper and stuck a finger in between his shirt collar and his neck. It was warm and his throat was dry so he wandered over to the bar and asked for a glass of water. He just had time to knock it back before Leonard came through the lounge with a rucksack and a shoulder bag.

Raymond followed him out and watched him pile into a white Mercedes.

Raymond jogged across the street to where he'd parked his car. He loved his car, a blue Austin Morris 1300 with balding tyres. Not the standard model but the Vanden Plas, which meant chrome bumpers, tan leather seats and a curved, walnut dash.

Leonard had started the Mercedes and was pulling away from the kerb. Raymond twisted the key in the door lock and the thing that looks like a golf tee, popped up. He jumped in, started the engine and pulled away. He had to hold the choke out for a couple of streets but then it was OK, he stayed with the Mercedes, no problem. He rolled his window down and rested his arm on the mossy rubber sill and grabbed the roof trim. This was his favourite driving position, with his forearm braced in the window.

The Mercedes pulled into a petrol station. Raymond overshot and parked up. He watched Leonard fill the car, then pay the bill with three bottles of whisky. He'd been bloody lucky to stumble on a station that actually still had some gas. The car then rejoined the road and headed south out of town, picking up speed on the longer stretches of straight road. Raymond kept pace, but on the uphill slopes he was starting to fall behind, he was pushing the engine, over-revving really but he didn't want to lose Leonard.

When the Merc turned off onto a lane and stopped at a farmhouse, Raymond kept his distance and pulled onto a muddy track in between two brick barns.

Leonard felt quite a lot like a returning parent because Reggie had flour on his shoes and there was a smell of burning oil as soon as he opened the door.

'What's going on?'

Reggie had a tea-towel in his hand, and replied as he was walking back into the kitchen.

'Come in, we're making pancakes.'

It was true, they were. The boys had it all kind of loosely organised. There were eggshells and used bowls, packs of flour and a good few spoons and forks lying around on the work tops, with pancake mix dripping off them. Dave was standing by the stove, he had a hot iron skillet oiled up and Reggie's job was to scoop up a big spoonful of mix from the bowl on the table and pour it in. Dave then rolled the pan, so the mix spread out evenly.

'Hi, Dave.'

'You've got to try one of these, Leonard. Sit down and we'll do one for you.'

Reggie was on his way with the spoon. It was the unskilled part of the job, but he wanted to get it right. He scooped up and moved carefully past the TV that was on but with the sound down. He shuffled across the kitchen to the stove and tipped the pancake mix out into the pan.

'The pan's too hot.'

'It's got to be hot, you've got to cook them quickly.'

'I don't like 'em burned.'

'Just watch, I know how to do this, Reg.'

'Fair enough, but don't say I didn't warn…'

Dave held his finger up and Reggie didn't finish, the often-used phrase must have become a sore point. Dave turned to Leonard.

'He cooks everything in the microwave.'

'Yeah, and he puts bloody cumin and coriander in his baked beans.'

'Yeah, and you like them, Reggie.'

'Not that much.'

Leonard sat down and Reggie brought him a plate with a wedge of lemon and the sugar.

'Mind, plate's hot.'

Leonard tested the plate by tapping the edge with the palm of his hand; it was scalding hot. He pointed at the television.

'Are you watching that, then?'

Reggie turned and looked at the screen.

'We like the TV on in the background, but it's better with the sound turned off.'

The TV was tuned to a public information broadcast showing how to survive the asteroid impact by hiding under the stairs.

'You ready, Leonard?'

'Yeah.'

'How many do you think you can eat?'

'Let's see how we go.'

Dave turned and flopped the pancake onto the plate, and Leonard leaned in to smell it. Up close, it was like looking at a still photograph of the blistering sun, with dark spots and spiralling, solar flares. It gave off heat too, like on a summer's day, and Leonard had to douse it in lemon juice and fold it into quarters to get rid of the idea of the scorched star.

'Good?'

'Yeah, very good.'

Reg tipped another scoop onto the smoking pan.

'You two seem to be getting on famously then?

Reggie bent down to Leonard's ear and answered.

'Well, we've had a few poachers about, what with food being scarce, so Dave's been keeping an eye on the livestock. He's been pulling his weight, he helps out with milking and well, it's just good to have another pair of hands around the place. He loves to use the axe; he loves splitting the wood right down the middle. He brings the freshly cut logs down to show me. I think it's because I told him this old wives tale which says: when you split the log, you can see God.'

Raymond stood beside the barn, watching the house. He looked like a bit-part actor, a red herring in a detective series. He looked up at the sky and figured that it would be dark soon, so he'd probably be sleeping in the car. There was a sleeping bag in the boot but the seats weren't recliners, it was likely to be a very uncomfortable night. He had a thermos of sweet tea and a packet of Jaffa cakes in the glove box. These days, though, Raymond was not such a keen action man; he liked to crawl into a bed at night, preferably his own bed.

Nothing from the house, a puff of smoke from the chimney, that was all. He turned, walked along the side of the barn and stopped when he came to the edge of open fields. It was a banal landscape, laid out like an extended golf course with rolling hills, water hazards and screens of poplar trees. It was a man-made landscape, not good hiking country. If you walked through this, you'd feel no benefit, you'd just be bored to death. He stuffed his hands deep into his pockets and tried to imagine how he could make himself comfortable in the car. Thing was, before he could turn, he was grabbed from behind, his arms were trapped at his sides and a heavy hand covered his mouth and closed off his airways. He couldn't see who was doing all this. He tried to turn, but whoever it was, stayed behind. His vision was fogging up because he couldn't catch a breath, his legs buckled and he fell to the ground.

The action hadn't moved on much when Raymond regained consciousness, it was still the same episode with Raymond lying flat out on the floor and the yob standing over him. The yob wasn't a big fella but he was youngish and threatening. Raymond recognised the man, the froggy face was familiar and he'd seen him around, sucking up to the Warden.

'Who are you, you bastard?'

Raymond didn't say a word; he was trying to gain an advantage, pretending to be hurt more than he was. This brought the yob's face closer.

'I said, who the fuck are you?'

The yob's face was close enough for Raymond to push both his thumbs into his mouth and pull apart as hard as he could. The yob screamed, his top lip unzipped and blood started running into his distorted mouth. He backed off and Raymond got to his feet, but then the yob pulled a gun.

'Who are you? You cunt!'

'I'm sorry, I am unable to answer that question.'

The yob grabbed Raymond by the throat and backed him into the barn, kicked into the backs of his knees and Raymond was forced to the ground again. He was pushed face down and a rope was wound around his left wrist, it ran across his throat and down to the other wrist. Same with his feet, then a last bight of rope was looped around his neck again and back to his feet. There was tension on his throat, the rope tightened when he moved and wouldn't slacken off.

While he'd been working, the yob had been swearing and licking his own blood off his lips. He was an angry fucker now and his anger had been transmitted to the tightness of the bindings. He gave each knot an extra, fucked-off tug.

'Now then, smart arse, you're not going anywhere until you tell me who you are and what you are doing here?'

'I'm sorry, I am unable to answer that question.'

The yob did something behind Raymond's back; he was sliding a slipknot, increasing the choke.

'Stop it! I can't breathe!'

There was a pause then the tension eased as the knot was slackened off. Raymond tried to move his arms.

'Don't move, you idiot, that's a constrictor knot I've tied behind your back. The more you move the tighter it gets.'

'What do you want?'

'Why don't you just tell me everything you know, eh? It's that simple.'

'I'm a runner, an administration runner. I followed my target to this house.'

'What do administration want with Leonard?'

'He's breached security.'

'Do elaborate.'

Raymond stayed quiet until a foot pressed his shoulder and tightened the loop at his throat.

'He's seen the survival project, the construction site. He's got to be detained before he can jeopardise the programme.'

'And just where is this site, exactly?'

'I'm sorry, I am unable to answer that question.'

'How could he jeopardise the programme?'

Another pause.

'Come on now, you can tell me, nobody will know; nobody really cares who did it, in whodunnits.'

'I'm sorry, I am unable to answer that question.'

'Look, Leonard had to have been tagged. He could never have made it onto the site otherwise. So how did that happen, did Warden tag him? How did Leonard get access to the pistol?'

'I don't know. I can't tell you anything else. I don't know anything else.'

That was enough for Ian, his patience had run out and he knew what to do now anyway. He would have to confront Leonard and get his answers there. But he couldn't in all innocence do that now, he didn't think it was a great idea to knock on the farmhouse door and say he was just in the neighbourhood. Not looking the way he did with the blood still spilling from his opened lip.

He put his foot into the middle of Raymond's back and pulled on the tensioning rope, like he was loading a crossbow. The rope choked on tight and the body rolled away, looking like a very elaborate but primitive harp, a single-stringed instrument of suffocation and slow death.

Warden was sitting on his own, drumming his fingers on the desk; when he closed his eyes, he could imagine it was horses galloping. He could shift the sound by drumming in the middle of the desk or close to the edge. When he did this carefully, he could produce a doppler sound effect like the horses were approaching, passing close by and galloping off into the distance.

There was still a full day ahead and he wasn't feeling his best. He sat and looked into the computer screen with a file open for no real reason. He let his eyes lose focus and his head drop; the painkillers were doing a fine job, he felt nothing at all, not the slightest twinge. He knew that down in the bottom left hand drawer, were several tools of self-destruction. That reassured him, all he had to do was slide the drawer open a fraction and the edge of a pistol, pill bottles, fuses and high explosives would be visible to his naked eye.

His job was not a demanding one; it was like any other office of power, as long as you landed the position in the first place, you could then relax. Everything around you then made it seem as if you were the man for it: the office, the schedule, the helpers, the telephone calls, the respect accorded. But Warden didn't have to be the man they thought he was. Inside, he was his own man with his own ideas, and mostly he was able to forget what he was supposed to be doing entirely. The job was a kind of lie anyway, a public service bluff. The truth was that it was very hard, this close to a devastating, international incident, to care about who was doing what. If he weren't such a sick old man, maybe he would make more of an effort. But he was, so the idea of the Ice Moon hurtling toward the earth was oddly comforting. So comforting that it was this he focused his mind on at night, to help him get to sleep. The impending arrival of the thing, the idea of a great cleansing fire coming soon to a cinema very near you. The idea of it coming to crush his own sickness into dust, to clear it all away, was comforting. It was time for an end, and this would be quite a fitting end.

Adeline stepped out into the storm to close the boot of the car. Tony was loading up and he'd left it open. As she crossed the pavement towards the kerb, hail pelted down. It was a weird sensation because she felt dry for a while, until her body heat melted the ice. When Tony came out through the door again he was carrying a sack, a big billowing sack that appeared to weigh next to nothing.

'What you got there?'

'Rubbish.'

'What kind of rubbish?'

'Stuff we don't need anymore.'

'Like what?'

'What do you care, Adeline?'

Tony turned, dumped the sack onto the back seat, opened the driver's door and turned to her. The way he built the drama before delivering his lines was beautifully paced. He dipped his head and looked to the side before he said, 'I'm still in love with you, Adeline.'

Adeline's eyes looked for a safe focus.

Tony was actually shocked to see how far this had fallen short. How too little, too late was just embarrassing for both of them. He felt like shit, like a wanting, needful fool.

'I tried, Tony. I tried my best.'

He hit her sharply across the cheek with the flat of his hand. This time the blow was way out in the open, in plain daylight. Then he turned and climbed into the car, that was all. Adeline watched him drive off, watched his tyres clear black tracks on the whitened road surface.

Waves of wintry showers blew across the road so Leonard flicked the headlights on and tested his brakes. Up ahead, a man walked with his arm outstretched and his thumb up, a lost and indecisive Caesar, looking for a decision to make. Leonard slowed down, the guy wasn't wearing enough to conceal a weapon so he stopped and threw open the passenger door.

The head came in, surprised and flushed.

'Town?'

'Yeah, get in.'

The man hesitated.

'You're not mad or nothing?'

'No, are you?'

He got in.

'Ok then, thanks.'

Leonard had the feeling that the guy was trying to think up a conversation but never quite made it. So they were silent all the way in, until, all of a sudden he said, 'Here'll do. Yeah right here, this is fine.'

He leant on the roof, wrote Leonard out a C.O.D. and handed it over. When he'd closed the door Leonard took a close look at the spiky handwriting, it said: I.O.U one journey.

The Administration Building was just across the street and Leonard was standing beneath a telegraph pole with the cables fanning out above his head. The wires ran to the corners of shops and houses, looped around a black gadget and then disappeared through drill holes in window frames.

He'd parked the Mercedes several blocks back, door open, keys and Reggie's spare shotgun tucked under the seat. If he had to make a run for it, at least he'd be able to speed off sharpish, and at least he'd be armed. There was no point in avoiding the interview, they'd pull him in eventually and it also gave Lena an opportunity to get into Warden's apartment and take the pistol.

The big building was imposing; it had the psychological upper hand. Those inside were invested with a degree of power they wouldn't ordinarily have out on their own at street level. The building had a commanding position, overlooking a tangle of major roads. It was always intended to be an ugly building, a building that was purely functional. It was, though, unnecessarily ugly and the ugliness set the tone for the whole area. At the design stage, the architect had said that the building was supposed to be ugly because ugly was far more powerful than beautiful. Ugly will not give way on a point of order. Whereas, what does beauty say? It says - relax, come on in and be well treated, let us talk as equals, we all want an equitable outcome, we want to please, to contribute, we'll be accommodating. So the planners understood, and ugly it was and now nobody argues about the featureless brickwork and the smoked glass windows; the kind that never open and are cleaned from the outside by men in a cradle, on a year round rota.

Even though he knew all this, as soon as Leonard stepped inside the place, he felt picked on, he felt oppressed.

Warden's office was at the rear of the building, up on the top floor.

You reached it by taking, or in Leonard's case being escorted through, the ground floor to a private lift. He was left on his own to ascend and when the doors opened on the fourth floor, he was welcomed by a plush red carpet neatly vacuumed into cricket pitch stripes.

He hung around in the lobby for a while and looked at some of the beautifully framed pictures, all perfectly levelled, hung at head height and individually lit by halogen spots. Various subjects - an original crayon drawing of a woman's face by Matisse dated June 1945, a small, smudgy cityscape and a group photograph of a management celebration, the Administration's Christmas do. Leonard recognised a very young Warden sitting off to the side, in the background of the picture. The image had an unsettling quality to it because it reminded him of those second world-war photographs of Nazi socialising, where ten or twenty dapper faces in dinner dress looked off into the mid distance, half crazed with just being there. These were the only photographs Leonard had ever seen where it was possible to know exactly what the guests had been thinking, and what they'd been thinking was, 'I wonder how much longer all this is going to last? I wonder when all this will finally catch up with us, and kill us the way we've been killing all the others?'

Warden's office door opened and his secretary came out.

'Gopaul?'

'That's right.'

'We're waiting for you.'

Leonard walked into the outer office and turned to watch as the secretary used his big fingers on the intercom phone. The man looked as hard as nails, like he'd been hit around the head with a piece of wood on and off for several years. There was a whole history of scars on his face.

He finished with the phone and approached Leonard until he stood right up close. He put his hands on Leonard's shoulders and started to search his clothing for weapons. He dragged his hands down his chest and arms, over his back, abdomen, down each leg. Then he pulled back just far enough to smack Leonard one, around the chops. It wasn't a punch; just a token humiliation to say that there was plenty more where that came from, if he didn't behave.

'That's for nothing, now in you go and be polite.'

Leonard didn't say a word; he just turned to the door, knocked and waited. He heard, 'Ahh, hah', so he went in.

Warden was standing in the doorway of a washroom, brushing away at his teeth. He turned and yawned, which was not pretty with all the paste foaming up his gob. He gestured for Leonard to sit down and he rinsed his mouth out.

'Now then, Leonard, you have been giving us the run around, haven't you?'

Leonard stayed silent.

'What got into you? I thought you were a perfectly nice chap. You came across very well at interview. Well?'

Warden was still holding a hand-towel, dabbing his lips from time to time.

Leonard wanted to tell him to throw it in, to give it all up.

'I simply wanted to know what I was getting myself into.'

'I should have thought that was pretty obvious. I thought you wanted to get onto the bloody lifeboat, just like everybody else.'

'But that's just bollocks, isn't it? Not a single person you have interviewed will be given access to the survival programme.'

'And what makes you such an expert?'

'I've seen the construction site!'

'Now that is a pity. I might have tried to work with you on this, but well, that is a pity. Can't really give you any leeway at all now, can I?'

Warden pressed the buzzer on the intercom.

'What about your grand-daughter?'

'What about her?'

'I'm trying to keep her safe, make sure she'll survive.'

'Yes, well, she doesn't like me very much, she seems to have got the idea into her head that I killed her parents.'

There was a knock at the door and Warden's secretary looked in.

'That's alright, we're not quite through yet.'

The door closed again and Leonard had to ask.

'Did you kill her parents?'

Warden sat on the edge of his desk. His face was patchy, like he'd applied some cosmetic powders. Leonard noticed that his baggy tracksuit was not that clean and that it was draped over an increasingly skeletal frame. His mood had darkened.

'The world has grown foul Leonard, surely you would agree with that? What's right and what is wrong has become less significant, we have entered an era of blatancy, of kill or be killed. I can sympathise with you, I can see it is awkward for a man like you, you have a conscience, you think you have understood what is right and what is wrong. Well, I have to remind you that there is not a place for you here, you will be faced with impossible decisions where doing the right thing, doing the human thing, will get you killed. Now that's OK for martyrs but somehow I just don't see you as a martyr. I think you are smart enough to realise that there is no lasting value, no real longevity, in posthumous awards.'

'I'm not a hero, I'm Joe average, but I just can't stand it when the bastards get their way. I can't leave it at that.'

'Admirable sentiment, really quite admirable. And one more thing: if you must know about Lena's parents, I'll tell you. I was driving and there was an accident, that's all. My wife never forgave me, the mad old bat insists on blaming me and trying to do me harm!'

Leonard was fazed; the old bastard was far from being a fool.

'The "world", Leonard, will go its own very particular way, with or without you. You must find the humility to step aside and let those who are up to it, survive.'

Warden rocked himself forward and limped around the desk. He picked up his walking stick and braced it against his hip. Leonard saw that there wasn't really that much left of the man, he was shaky on his pins and down to featherweight. Then Leonard realised something.

'You're dying, aren't you? That's why none of this really matters, isn't it?'

'Well done, very astute. But listen, I asked you here to strike a deal. I want you to tell me how you were tagged and if I am satisfied with your answer, well, then I am prepared to let you keep your place.'

Before Leonard could think of an answer, Warden started to slide down his own stick, which didn't last long because he was the one holding the stick. He hit the floor. Warden's expression was not of pain, it was more that he was pissed off, like he'd taken a roller coaster that hadn't been thrilling and there he was on the floor, afterwards, dissatisfied.

He pointed to his desk, the left hand drawer. Leonard reached over and pulled on the handle. Warden managed a couple of words.

'Morphine, fucking morphine.'

Leonard picked up a handful of pre-loaded syringes and brought them over. Warden snatched one up, whacked it into the top of his leg and pressed on the plunger. The morphine went straight through the jogging bottoms, no time for a wipe with a piece of sterile cotton wool.

Leonard was hoping Warden's secretary would not appear at the door, there was a very good chance he would misread the scene. He returned to his seat and kept his eyes fixed on the old man.

Lena nearly always did what the adults asked her to do, and if she was going to get in trouble for doing what Leonard had asked, well she wasn't really to blame. She was a kid and if she were found out, well, that would be her excuse.

It would be easy enough because she knew that security would let her in, they would tell her that Warden was out but she would say that she was going to wait.

When Lena turned up at the reception desk of Warden's apartment building, the security guards were extremely accommodating. They gave her a key and let her make her own way up to the apartment. She opened the door, ran through to the sitting room, then straight through the musty smelling kitchen and into the study.

She crossed to the CD cabinet and flipped the lid open; the pistol was there in its place, so she lifted it out. She put everything else back as it was and left the apartment.

Warden stretched out his arms and legs like a newborn animal. He lifted his head and rested his weight on his elbows; he bent his legs and made it to his knees. He picked himself up off the floor, dusted himself down and smoothed his hair off his face. He didn't bother to turn and look at Leonard but walked the other way instead, into the washroom. He closed the door, braced himself over the sink and looked up at his own face in the mirror. Yes, it was him, but only just. He shook his head and rubbed his eyes, then practised the expression he often lived behind, the one where he looked like he was fed up with listening to limericks.

He heard the intercom buzzer go off out in the office, so he kicked the door open a crack to hear.

'Ah, Warden? It's three o'clock.'

He splashed his face and took a few deep breaths; he'd managed to pull himself back together.

Warden dabbed his brow with a towel and came back out into the office. He picked up his walking stick and made it to the door.

'Do excuse me, Leonard, but I've got interviews.'

'Can I come with you?'

'If you want.'

Leonard followed Warden out of his office. His secretary looked up at them as they passed; he rubbed his chin and watched Leonard help Warden shuffle along the corridor towards the lift.

The old man hit the call button over and over until it lit up.

'Leonard, I would prefer you to leave very quietly after the interviews. I haven't decided what should happen to you yet, but I would like you to, at the very least, get out of my sight. You should make yourself scarce, you have made some enemies as you well know.'

'OK, I understand.'

The doors opened and Warden moved off with a bit more spring in his step. It seemed like the distraction of the interviews was the thing that kept him going.

Leonard took the long staircase up to the mezzanine and went in through the door. The gallery was packed with strangers who were hogging the front seats. Leonard sat in the third row and looked down into the chamber.

Warden was settling himself in his chair; he had a whispering chat with the stenographer and took a quick look at some paperwork she'd shoved under his nose.

Then, without fuss, the door opened and an old woman walked across the floor and sat in the seat opposite Warden.

Leonard picked up the pair of binoculars chained to the back of the seat in front and aimed them at the old lady. She was frail but beautiful; she'd added some blue-green to her eyelids and a very subdued red to her lips. There was a small brown stain on her forehead, but no added colour to her cheeks, she had too much class for that. The shape of her face told you how beautiful she had been, how beautiful she still was.

Warden shifted in his chair, he had eye contact with the old girl now.

'So then, Magda, I don't know if you've realised but you are quite an old candidate, aren't you?'

'Oh, yes, very.'

'Is this not a moment for youth to come to the fore? After all, the next few months are going to be very hard physically?'

Magda was sharp, her head was still, and she waited for the right place to speak and then spoke clearly and concisely.

'I imagine they will be, yes. But I am tougher than I look.'

'If you can, and in your own time, please explain why you would be a valuable addition to the survival programme?'

Magda straightened out her dress.

'I've had a good innings already but I am concerned and well, I just wanted to keep my eye out. It's all very well having the fitness and energy of youth but dealing with so many unknown quantities requires another kind of strength.'

'Go on, Magda, we are all listening, even if you are talking bollocks.'

The use of 'bollocks' didn't seem to faze her; she had obviously talked publicly before, because she turned her chair and spoke, not only to Warden, but to the whole gallery as well.

'Well, what I could bring to the pot is the benefit of a lifetime's experience. I know that doesn't sound like much and I am not claiming higher knowledge. It's just that I've been around, I've watched the sun come up and the days roll by, I've kept my eyes open and I've remembered. The hardest thing is that you really can't understand until you've lived as long as I have. You can't get things into perspective until you have a way to measure, until you realise what's involved.'

She stood up, crossed her arms then dropped them by her sides.

'If I can be straight with you, the point is this; it isn't bollocks. I mean, what life teaches you over the years! Maybe I should remind you all, for example, that life is just a bit of leasehold, some rented time and space, that's all.'

Warden had been holding his bottom jaw for a while, scratching his chin by flexing his forefinger over and over.

'OK, Magda, OK. I'll warn you that we've had a lot of advice from candidates in the past. A good few have proposed guides to new ways of living. What's your pocket formula?'

She turned to Warden and gave him a look that would have killed him if he had not been looking up at the ceiling. She carried on though.

'I think several things are essential. I think we should set out goals and strive to achieve those goals.'

She could see that he was ill. Warden smiled, he knew she knew. It was not difficult for the old ones to tell, to see through the false front. He liked the old bird though and honestly, if he had his way, he might well include her in any surviving society.

A chair scraped and the court recorder stood. She walked to Warden and whispered in his ear. He then turned to Magda.

'Ah, much as I'd like to extend, we have to leave it there. I have a pressing matter to attend to.'

The court recorder held out a book for Warden to sign. He signed but the recorder didn't look happy. She flicked back through previous entries, looking at Warden's signature at the bottom of each page; it was the same name scrawled there but there was a problem.

'Is that your signature, Warden?'

He took the book in his hand.

'Yes, I know, it's a problem I've been having lately. Signature comes out different every time, I can't help it.'

He waved the recorder close again, he wanted her to repeat what she'd said, just to be sure he'd heard right. She handed him a fax and added, 'I'm sorry, Warden, but we've just received information that Raymond has been killed.'

Warden looked across at Magda.

'We've got to leave it there, Magda, thank you. A pressing matter... a dear friend of mine, you see... I am required somewhere else.'

Leonard got to his feet and made for the exit; this was going to be a useful diversion. If there were any plans to arrest him, it looked like they might be on hold. Something more pressing had just come up, but even so, Leonard would not leave the Administration building by the main exit. He didn't take the stairs back to the ground floor either; instead he climbed up one more flight and stopped beside a window on the landing. He reached up, snapped the security locks off the double glazed unit and opened the window. Then he stepped out onto a flat area and ran along the cracked roofing felt. He jumped to a lower level; the wind was freshening and flooding into his lungs. The sky off to the east was dark and streaked with rain spilling from thick grey cloud. He grabbed the top rung of a fire escape, jumped down onto the ladder and descended as quickly as he could.

He ran back past the front of the Administration building and up hill towards where he'd parked the car. He got to the corner of the street and stopped; up ahead he could see that the white Mercedes was crawling with cops. The kid cops, sitting inside and waving Reggie's shotgun around. The electric aerial was extending and retracting, going up and down in time to outbursts of music.

He turned and ran back the other way until he could take another route. He settled into a good jogging pace and tried to breathe evenly. He'd have to make it back to the Mirabelle on foot and it was raining hard, coming in at an angle over his shoulder and down his neck.

It was raining heavily. The driver held a big black umbrella above Warden's head and walked him across the car park, opening the door and helping him into the limousine. As the door closed and Warden reached for his seatbelt, the driver finished flapping the umbrella and jumped in. Warden asked him, very softly, 'What happened to Raymond?'

The driver looked over his shoulder.

'Sketchy details as yet, sir. Raymond's body was found lying in a field out near a dairy farm. Cause of death, strangulation.'

'Oh, God. Get going, would you please.'

The car taxied across the car park and stopped at the exit. When it paused before moving off, a figure appeared, opened up the back door and jumped in beside the Warden. The driver turned and screamed out.

'Oi, what's your game?'

Ian smiled and said, 'This is not an exercise. Everybody stay calm.'

Warden found enough energy to offer a measured response.

'I'm busy, Ian, I can't see you now, whatever it is.'

Ian hadn't stopped smiling. He proceeded to pull a pistol from his coat pocket and aim it at the driver's head.

'Now, tell your driver to do as he is told. We are going back to your place and you are going to tag me.'

'You are being very melodramatic, Ian.'

'Drive on, you shit!'

Warden nodded at the driver and the limousine pulled onto the wet ring road.

CHAPTER FIFTEEN

Leonard edged his way down the access stairs and into the boiler-room. He could see Lena asleep on her bed, with the covers wrapped around her legs and pulled up to her neck. He was soaked through; he shook himself off and moved out of shadow. The last of the daylight was shining in from above and bouncing off the back wall behind Lena's bed. Bounced light is soft light, it caresses skin and cotton, so much so that Lena looked like an artist's impression of who she was, lovingly painted into the corner of the room by an unknown apprentice of the Dutch school.

He had to wake her, though. He rocked her shoulder gently.

She woke with a sudden twist of her body.

'What?'

'It's alright. Lena, listen, did you get the pistol?'

She lifted the edge of the mattress to show Leonard that she had.

'Well done! Where's Beryl?'

'She's off with her friends, they're delivering the newsletter.'

Lena looked up at the pattern of raindrops settling on the skylight and smiled.

'Are we going to get in trouble, Leonard?'

'Yes, sooner or later I think we are bound to.'

Lena jumped up off her bed and started to pull her coat on.

'Wait, you've got to stay here.'

She carried on zipping up her coat, then pulled on her hood and sat there ready.

'I'd like you to wait for Beryl and I'll come by later to see if you're both OK.'

Leonard picked up the pistol and put it in his jacket pocket.

'But what if you get arrested?'

Leonard pressed the pop-studs on her collar shut, closing the neck of her coat.

'Look, I promise, I'll see you later.'

He kissed Lena and left the boiler room.

It was quiet on the streets, just a couple of cars passing with their brake lights colouring up the wet roads. Leonard had what he needed in his pocket, all he had to do now was to stay at large, avoid capture.

As he crossed a major intersection, he was aware of a uniform pattern to the litter on the pavement, the scrap paper was all the same. The same size and colour, the same news sheet with the same headlines reading: 'Survival Programme Exposed - The Corruption of Hope: Gangsters, Bribery and the Warden's Lies!' It was the latest edition of Beryl's newspaper, hundreds of copies strewn across the street, hundreds of cats let out of the bag all at once, all of them damning the Warden.

Warden had been called upon to tag a client three or four times. It was an official duty whereby the selection board would send him out to a corporate headquarters or to a private address. He'd have a four-man team escorting him through the tagging process. Ian's armed assault was more like a bloody hijacking; he'd been taken against his will, out of his 'high-security' work-place. It was a bloody kidnapping, really. He had no desire to be difficult, all he wanted was a quick turnaround - get Ian tagged, and get back to his own life again.

The car screeched to a halt. Ian waved his firearm at the driver and locked him into the boot. He then manhandled Warden into the lobby of the apartment building. They stood close and quiet while the lift ascended.

As soon as he'd unlocked the door, Warden limped along the hallway and headed for the bar.

'Would you like a drink, Ian?'

'Get me a stiff one, a bourbon.'

Warden gulped down his own glass and closed his eyes. A warm shiver, the most pleasant sensation of the day by far, crept around his back and up over his shoulders. When he opened his eyes, Ian was leaning against the wall with his hands stuffed into his jacket.

'OK, Ian, let's get this over with. Follow me.'

They made their way through to the study and Warden pointed out where

Ian should sit down. Ian perched himself on the edge of the chair and started wringing his hands.

'How does this work then?'

'Don't tell me you're having second thoughts.'

'Don't get smart, just answer the question.'

'It's a simple procedure and it won't hurt. The upshot of it being, that you are numbered for survival.'

'Get on with it.'

Warden bent over and felt the tendons in the back of his thighs tighten up and begin to shake. He felt as if he was on his last legs and when he opened up the CD cabinet and looked for a second time into the strongbox, he felt quite ready to die. After absorbing the fact that it was empty, he felt a numb tingling spread across his body. He laughed as he said, 'Oh dear, this is interesting. I'm afraid I won't be able to do much for you today.'

Ian watched and waited for the truth of the matter leak out of the atmosphere.

There was no point at all in bullshitting, so Warden carried the strongbox to his desk and sat the thing down with the lid open, showing just how empty it really was.

'The piece of equipment I need to tag you has been removed from this box. I don't know how, or by whom. I cannot guarantee your inclusion on the survival programme without it.'

Ian sat back in his seat.

'So what happens now?'

'I don't know.'

Ian's disappointment was like a third year drama student doing disappointment.

When he lifted his head he was having a go at outrage and anger.

'I will have to kill you, you see that, don't you?'

Warden could see that.

'Give me a few days and I will correct what has gone wrong!'

'Don't fuck me around, Warden.'

'I'm not, Ian. To be quite honest, I'd like to, but I'm not.'

'So what happens now?'

'I don't know. You got any ideas?'

'Yes, take a pull on your drink.'

'I can do that.'

Warden gulped some down. Ian bent forward, pointed the gun barrel at the toe of Warden's training shoe and pulled the trigger twice.

The temperature had dropped sharply after sunset, then the rain had tightened into a hard, dry hail. As Leonard looked along the lamplit street, he could see how it was falling in vertical sheets, pimpling up off the road surface, rolling along the black camber.

On a whim really, he ran through the middle of it. It cheered him up and put some oxygen back into his blood.

He was thinking, 'So now what?' He had the instrument in his hot little hand but he felt that his luck might be running out. He was sticking to the back alleys, slowly zig-zagging his way back across the city. A patrol car slowed and turned in, Leonard looked for an escape route. Further along the alley, halfway up the next turning, he could make out a strip of red fluorescent tubing which had been artfully twisted into the shape of a pint glass. It was a beer ad, up above a yellow door. As he approached he could hear music; he knew the tune, it was Frank Sinatra singing, 'Fly me to the Moon'. Leonard poked his nose in and listened to the peeling laughter and ripples of applause welling up from the basement.

He climbed down and found himself an empty table by the side of the floorshow. He picked up the shaker from the table, poured out some sugar onto his hand and licked the stuff off.

The guy under the spotlight was familiar; he was short and square-shouldered with curly hair. The radio was at his feet, with the music blasting from it. He had ridiculously long fingernails and he was inexplicably blowing up balloons. The audience were very amused and Leonard remembered he'd seen the man's interview with Warden. It was Newman, how could anyone ever forget a man like Newman? He inflated a long, skinny balloon with a single breath, then tied it off and twisted it, to form a dog's back legs. He'd already twisted together five or six, they were placed around the stage and Leonard could see that he'd been working on his act. He'd improved it by getting hold of different coloured balloons for the different breeds. All white for the Poodles, black and white spots for the Dalmatians and black and tan for the Doberman Pincers.

'Newman!'

Leonard climbed a couple of steps and squeezed round the back of the stage platform. He called out again and this time Newman turned. As he turned, he got a surprise and the air he was forcing into the next balloon blew back down his own throat.

Leonard placed the barrel end of the compressed air pistol against Newman's upper lip and squeezed the trigger. The pistol went off with a sound like a truck slamming on the air brakes. Newman reeled away, tripping on his own feet and falling onto his own dogs. There was some panic in the crowd, people stood and knocked over glasses, most everyone backed up to the walls and let Leonard scamper away back up the stairs.

As Leonard ran back through the alley and up onto the main road, the hailstones stopped falling. It had settled, though, so that all the parked cars looked like they'd been salted from above. He stopped and had a look at the pistol. He was worried because there wasn't a numbered readout, no way of knowing how full or empty the pistol was. It was a completely sealed unit, factory moulded.

But letting off that first shot felt good, he had struck a blow, a countermeasure that no one would be able to reverse.

He was grinning but his head was aching; the rain, the running and just the constant stress of knowing what he had to do, was wearing him down. He hadn't eaten much lately and he wouldn't be able to get back out to the farm without the Merc, he'd have to find somewhere new, somewhere safe to spend the night.

The sky was a damped down orange-grey, grilled from underneath by the radiating city lights. He doubled back onto familiar streets and tried to stay alert. He hugged in close to the doorways for cover.

In all honesty, he had become a sort of outlaw now, a fugitive, wet through to the bone and desperate to carry out some kind of half-cocked vengeance. Adeline, though? When he thought of her, he softened and when he rolled up outside the bar, he tried to tidy himself up for her sake. When you don't have a mirror though, all you can do is imagine how bad you look. You run your hands through your hair and straighten your clothes. You can only hope that will do.

As soon as Tony saw Leonard in the bar, his body stiffened and his jaw dropped. He stopped the downward pressure on the pump handle and rocked back to the cutting board, upsetting the cherries and the cocktail sticks.

'What the bloody hell d'you think you're doing here?'

Then Tony stepped into the wings and picked up the telephone.

Leonard moved through the crowd and took the stairs. When he got to the landing, he shouted out.

'Adeline?'

He jogged along the hall and as the noise from the bar faded, Leonard recognised the humming tones of a television set gabbing off in the living room. He pushed open the door and walked in; the lights were switched off and only the big TV tube brightened the darkness. It was throwing pale blue out into the room because the picture was of an Olympic-sized swimming pool. A tracking camera poolside followed the leaders and cut to the underwater angle for the racing turns.

Adeline was asleep on the sofa, curled up with her head on a cushion. A half-eaten sandwich lay on a plate on the floor and a full cup of cold tea beside it.

'What the fuck's going on!'

The room lights came on and Tony stood there with a nine-iron raised up above his head. Leonard pulled the tagging pistol and levelled it at Tony's head.

'Stay where you are, Tony.'

Adeline lifted her head and followed Leonard's aim to where Tony stood.

'Wait! Leonard, stop it!'

Tony stepped forward. He was holding up the certificate of debt with all the scribbled details, and pointing at Leonard with the golf club.

'You've got to pick up the tab, Leonard, honour our agreement! That was the deal, don't you remember? The police are on their way, and they'll enforce the terms! If I were you, I'd just turn around and piss off out of here!'

'Don't shoot him, Leonard.'

'I'm not going to shoot him, I'm here to help! I think I can get both of you onto the survival project!'

Loud pumping music arrived in the street outside and a car screeched to a halt. The passenger doors opened, the heavy muffled bass of the stereo grew louder, then cut to silence when the ignition was switched off. Leonard moved to the window and looked down.

'It's a police car.'

Adeline got to her feet.

Leonard ran to the bathroom and locked the door, then opened the window and clambered out. He had to lower himself, full stretch, onto the brick wall below, but from there he was able to jump down onto the pavement.

Tony broke the bathroom door down and ran to the window, Adeline following right behind him.

'You idiot, Tony, he came here to help us.'

'Well I didn't know, did I? It's not my bloody fault!'

Leonard cut across traffic and had a look back from the other side of the street. There were a couple of little heads at the bathroom window, looking up and down, but nobody seemed geed up enough to give chase.

Three military vehicles arrived at the scene, pulling up without fuss, without a skid, and a dozen big men were quickly deployed. A mix of men, some in khaki uniform, some suited up with flak-jackets over the top. Leonard recognised Warden's secretary among them. He was holding a mobile phone to his head, standing in the middle of the road to talk.

Leonard had seen enough; this was a lynch mob so he didn't wait around, he eased away along a wall, staying low and using the shadows for cover.

As he ran, he felt his guts heaving up and down with each stride. His lungs ached and the back of his throat hurt. He had to keep spitting stringy, thickened saliva. At least, though, he was running downhill and he did still have the tagging pistol.

He had to stop sometimes, wait for cars to pass; he couldn't just carry on across the main roads, the traffic was heavy and it was raining again. He was two blocks from the Mirabelle and getting nervous. What if they'd already raided the hotel?

You don't realise, you just think maybe they are standing or walking a little too close. You don't figure out until it's too late, that you are the target, that it's you they're after.

Two men had dropped a sack over Leonard's head, his legs came off the ground and he seemed to be rolling forward, attached to some kind of wheeled trolley. The only good thing about this kind of capture was not being able to see. You had to realise early on, that without your vision, you just had to let whatever was happening, happen. You couldn't make a run for it or fight back; you'd only hurt yourself. The people stealing your body, whoever they were, they had the eyes and it was up to them to look out for you, to duck your head into cars, steer you away from danger, or guide you off the edge of a cliff.

The trolley stopped and he was pushed forward from behind, his head making contact with a sheet of plywood at something like table-height, but he was outside in the street. How could a table be out in the street? They pushed him along the hard surface and then there was a banging, a rattling and a metallic clatter behind. He was lying awkwardly and dust from the sack was tickling his throat. He wasn't tied up but he preferred to just lie there and wait to be given permission to move. The floor rolled first one way, then the other, then there was a clattering, closing door sound.

As soon as the engine fired into life, Leonard figured out that he was in the back of a lorry. As it took a left-hand turn, his blood shifted, his head ached and the lorry bounced, probably the back wheel clipping the kerb.

'I hope that's you, Leonard?'

Leonard knew the voice.

'Beryl?'

'Help him out of that, will you, dear?'

Lena took hold of the corners of the sack and started to pull it off.

The lorry picked up speed as the driver gunned the accelerator and crunched up through the gears. Leonard held his breath as the sack was rolled up over his shoulders and off his head. Lena stood over him with her legs planted to keep her balance, grinning because this wasn't too bad a game at all. Beryl was a few feet away, sitting on a cushion with her back against a net made of seatbelt strapping. Leonard could feel his hair weaving about above his head, matted and electrified by the removal of the sack. He felt like a fool, but somehow he knew this reassured Beryl, it was what she expected of him. It even redoubled her trust in him.

She bounced more than he did because she was sitting over one of the back wheels. When the lorry slowed down to a stop, she stood up cautiously and looped her hand through a piece of the webbing.

'It's been a funny old day, hasn't it, Leonard?'

Leonard rested on his knees.

'It's had its moments, yeah.'

'I must say, I'm very angry with you, Leonard, because I found out what you asked Lena to do. You've put her in a great deal of danger!'

'I had to get the pistol.'

'That is debatable. Now, don't get me wrong, lad. I understand what you're trying to do but now Lena is in a lot of trouble. It's not safe for her to stay in the city.'

'I'm sorry, really I am. But I'll take care of her.'

'Bloody right you will! That's why you're here. The lorry will take you across the border and on to a safe house. You'll wait it out there until it's time to get to the project site.'

The lorry was climbing now and Beryl shifted her feet and took a better grip of the strap. She pointed at the cab end of the lorry.

'I've asked Pete and Danny to drive you.'

'Thank you.'

'You'll be staying with a good friend of mine in the south-east. You'll be alright there for a couple of weeks.'

'Why don't you come with us?'

'I don't have the heart for all that gallivanting. I'm staying here, where I can make a nuisance of myself. Lena?'

'Yes, Nan?'

'Get the driver's attention, will you?'

Lena moved along the floor on all fours trying to avoid getting splinters in her fingers. She giggled because the road was bumpy and when the lorry dipped and bounced, she experienced split seconds of weightlessness. She banged on the cab wall and the truck pulled up hard.

Beryl smiled.

'Pete and Danny are keen lads, sharp as tacks and eager to please. I trust them.'

Beryl let go of her hand strap and adjusted her glasses. Lena ran down and stood by her. Lena was serious now, not so confident that the adults knew what they were getting her into. Beryl tried to lift the tailgate, but it was too heavy.

'Give me a hand here will you, Leonard?'

Leonard took hold of the rolling metal shutter and lifted it. He jumped down onto the road and held a hand out for Beryl, who stepped down and looked back up at Lena.

'I'll see you safe and sound in a couple of weeks, and I want to hear good things about your conduct from Leonard.'

'Yes, Nan.'

'Take care of her, Leonard.'

'I promise you that I will.'

Leonard slipped the tagging pistol from his jacket. He took hold of Beryl's ample shoulders and in the confusion managed to snap a tag into her lip. She shouted out in pain and moved away from the back of the lorry as the flashing orange hazards and the brake lights lit her face. She looked accusingly at him.

'You silly sod!'

Leonard jumped back up into the lorry. Beryl looked embarrassed, self-conscious, she was not used to being included. She was flattered but unsure how all this would end. She said nothing more, but waved and licked her lip as Leonard pulled down on the metal roller.

He walked the six or so steps to the cab end and banged on the aluminium partition. He felt the handbrake coming off and the lorry pulled away. Lena was standing in the middle of the empty space, trying not to lose her balance. For a moment she felt like she was wearing waterwings, but this was the pressure of Leonard's fingers around her upper arms, keeping her upright as the lorry rocked away from the kerb.

'Will Nan be alright on her own?'

'She knows what she's doing.'

They flattened themselves against the side of the lorry, and hung on to the horizontal tie-bars. A dim strip-light screwed to the ceiling barely lit the floor space. Leonard looked around at the simple tools of the removals trade: bits of worn nylon rope, grey cord, sacks, blankets, bubble wrap and an 'L' shaped trolley on rubber wheels.

Lena had dropped to the floor and was trying to get comfortable by sitting on a folded blanket. Leonard went to look for more bedding, moving forward until he reached the cab. To the left-hand side, there was a ladder that led up to a door cut into a rectangular cupboard. He waited for the lorry to steady out on a straight stretch of road and climbed up. He pulled the door open and looked in: it was dark but carpeted, an empty coke bottle rolled into view. Leonard eased himself through the door onto a sleeping platform which ran horizontally across the width of the lorry.

Lena thought she could hear her name. She looked up and saw Leonard's head sticking out of the door above the cab. It made her laugh. What was he doing messing around, climbing up there? She stood and walked forward on her hands and knees, then climbed up the stepladder into the tiny nook.

She thought it was fantastic because they were right above the drivers, in the forehead of the lorry, speeding forward at double-decker height. Leonard tucked her into the bunk; she closed her eyes, grinning, loving the way the lorry rocked her body back and forth.

When she laid her head down, she could hear the men's voices coming up through the floor. Mostly one man's voice: one talking, one listening. She began to fall asleep, into an excited, contented sleep.

There were windows each side of the bunk and the glass gave some forward, but mostly sideways visibility. Leonard opened the short, pleated curtains and took a look outside.

They were still in the suburbs. It was probably too dangerous to cross the border in the city so they were driving east to cross at a quieter point. He lay down beside the viewing window, and the height of the ride meant that he could look straight out at the passing houses, straight into the first-floor bedrooms and dingy bedsits. The rooms flashed by and Leonard began to edit together the brief glimpses of the way people lived. He saw the televisions and the cups of tea, half-eaten dinners and booze bottles standing upright. Almost subliminal flashes of people in standing, seated or reclining positions. As the lorry picked up speed the rooms blurred together, like a strip of movie film. Scattered lives, all different but basically all the same, they would cut together nicely, into a hard-hitting documentary on the world's last days.

CHAPTER SIXTEEN

He'd enjoyed being an out-patient, it had given his life structure; but it didn't matter any more, and to be blunt about it, nothing much ever had. So what now, then?

The hospital could no longer provide the drugs Ian needed to keep his body from rejecting his own heart. The immuno-suppressants came from America and could no longer be sourced. They had told him (two of them, half-smirking) that, though they were sorry, there was really nothing more they could do for him.

Ian was very pissed off by their attitude and gave the only honest reaction he could think of: he inflicted heavy, blood-letting blows, one for each consultant, splitting their academic eyes and noses quite nice and sweetly. He felt a bit better to see them with their own, much more immediate health problems. He had taken a kind of on-the-spot revenge and equality had been restored. Vengeance is mine, that was the thing, nothing else was quite as sweet and that's why the Lord had tried to keep it all for himself. But Ian being a robust basket-case, didn't believe in all that.

On the way out of the hospital, he climbed into an empty ambulance and drove it off the emergency stand. He stamped heavily onto the accelerator and tipped the thing into the roundabouts at sixty miles an hour. He looked happy enough behind the wheel, capable, professional. A loose gas bottle was bouncing around in the back and when it rolled close enough, Ian grabbed it. He held the mask up over his face and drank down some deep gulps of pure oxygen. Light-headed and red-faced, Ian sang out loud into the windscreen.

'Hey ho, hey ho, it's off to work we go!'

He laughed and sucked down some more oxygen, then for a moment his face lost all its animation. A thought had occurred to him and the idea was, just how much he wanted to go to sleep and wake up as someone else.

In the woods, Tony picked his way along the overgrown paths. Hawthorn bushes scratched at his coat as he walked and he lost his footing in the soft ground. As he moved deeper into the gloom, the road noise dropped to a faint, intermittent hum. The acoustic buffer of foliage thickened until he felt quite alone and hidden enough to start acting like a madman. He ducked under a wet branch; he liked being here. There was the sweet scent of musk in the air and a humble colour scheme. In amongst the bare trees were evergreens and when he kicked at the ground, the composted leaves from the previous autumn showed a rich, reddish brown top-soil. He had that feeling too, as he walked over the humped ground, that there were hollows below, rabbit warrens or badger sets.

Tony could see the tree and when it came into view, he was impressed with his own handiwork. Adeline's mother would be very proud, the tree was exactly as she had specified. It had four well-spaced branches which arched upward at a similar angle and each branch with the circumference, roughly, of a man's thigh. Over the past days, he had completed a frame of vertical hazel sticks criss-crossed between the branches. And onto the hazel stick frame he had started to weave willow branches. He'd plaited each length into place, working in circles from the base upward. He'd already finished the floor and now he was up to knee height with the walls of the shelter. He'd cut plenty of willow and he was keeping it stored vertically so that it wouldn't rot.

He found the stepladder where he'd hidden it, picked it out of the bushes and clambered up into the tree. The structure was like a great big bowl now, a well-woven basket about the size you need for a hot-air balloon. Tony picked up a small, sharp axe and cut through a length of willow, then bent down and began to work in earnest. It was a good feeling, to be up off the forest floor, and when the wind blew, the tree swayed gently, its full crown caught in the south-easterly. Tony imagined how odd his behaviour might seem to the average ploughman or mill owner, how they might drum up a mob to punish him for taking part in such an occult ceremony. It troubled him that only a few weeks ago, he might well have been part of such a crowd, cursing and calling for a lynching, too. He picked up another stick of willow; it was green and supple and bent easily around and in front of the hazel frame. He began to work methodically, bringing the spiral weave up to waist height. Of course this was a very particular kind of behaviour and in these matters there was no justice. If he were to be discovered, there would be no live and let live. Those who revelled in rooting out all evil were convincing leaders and they were never very far away.

CHAPTER SEVENTEEN

Ian liked to think that he was a good judge of character, that he could read the average punter like that 'open book'. But these days one thing was certain, what he could not do was have any idea at all of himself. A numbing rage had blossomed inside his head, blurring his faculties of self-reflection. In any case, he had never been a benign soul, he desired conflict in even the simplest social situation and now there were these added difficulties. Now his bullish sub-characteristics were taking over and the dominant urge was to give in to it, let himself go more completely than ever before. It was way too late in the day now, to do anything else.

So, by Ian's reckoning, bad habits were good for you; they were a harmless and pleasurable indulgence, an important part of pain management. And wasn't it true that he had been warming to this idea of murder? It was his latest craze, it was the only thing which could take the sting out of his own impending demise.

Kernmantel climbing rope has a braided sheath and a plaited core of parallel fibres, it was Ian's most favourite tying rope, an exhibition rope really. The outer sheath was designed to resist abrasion, whereas the core material was chosen for strength and elasticity. For complex tying, Ian liked to use two different coloured ropes, because then it was a lot easier to follow what each cord was actually doing within the knot. He had a two-metre length of blood-red and the other was emerald green.

Ian had spent most of his afternoon practising the Zeppelin bend, a dependable, symmetrical knot that the US Navy at one time employed to tether their 'lighter than air'-ships. It was a simple concept; basically two interlocking overhand knots were blocked against each other. It was a beautiful thing to see lying there in his lap and when he was sure that he'd tied one or two absolutely perfectly, he turned to other business.

His apartment was a mess. Scattered clothes had been kicked into the corners, his cast-off slippers were lying alone in the middle of the room. A trail of biscuit wrappers and coffee cups had to be collected and a deep and whitening layer of dust which had built up on all of the horizontal surfaces, had to be cleaned off.

By six o'clock he'd hoovered, polished, showered himself and aired the flat; he'd yanked up two good fistfuls of daffodils from the communal gardens and stuck them into a cut-glass jug. It took a while to find the right place for them, but eventually he decided on the folding leaf table, in front of the lounge window. The curtains blew in and stirred around the flowers, which lent a kind of localised drama to that end of the room.

That was about it. He stood quietly, looking round the place like a foreman in the loading bay. He felt some dampness under his rings where there was some soap left; he twisted the gold bands forward, towards the knuckles and dried the few pale millimetres of exposed skin with his shirt sleeve.

He took a couple of chipped, ceramic bowls from the cupboard and filled them with almonds, olives and slices of dry-cured sausage.

He tried to imagine Dave coming into the room, and he placed the bowls within reach of his likely sitting positions. The last thing was a bottle; he wanted the bottle to stand on the silver tray, with the cork removed and two short, gleaming glasses standing by.

Ian had just one precious bottle left of a thick black liqueur made from walnuts. His uncle made the stuff, a hundred bottles each year. It was sweet and warming, contained a lavish complexity of flavours, which stirred even the most dormant taste buds into life.

The brakes on the Land Rover squealed dryly, eventually the thing stopped. Dave had to park on a steep hill, so he yanked the handbrake on, turned the wheels to full lock and left it in reverse gear. He had a look at his face in the rear view mirror; his eyes were evasive, not the evasiveness of the actor but the real discomfort that comes when some part of the self has been able to reckon the situation more clearly than the whole man.

Reggie had sent him off to do the delivery run; he had milk, cheese and eggs in the back and his last stop of the day was Ian Marble. Marble ran a food-for-oil scam, and reserves of diesel for the Land Rover and Reggie's tractor were running low.

Dave brushed his hair and squirted himself with aftershave. He slammed the door shut, grabbed a milk churn and a case of eggs, then turned and climbed the hill. The air was warm, warm enough for Dave to have to take his jacket off and sling it over his shoulder. He walked beside a row of brick houses, tall, elegant buildings with glossy, panelled front doors. He got to number four and entered, climbed the stairs and knocked.

The door opened swiftly and crunched against the security chain, then it closed a bit, the chain slackened off and the door opened completely.

Ian stood in the opening, one hand on the door, the other on the frame. He was dressed in flamboyant stripes, a blue cotton shirt with wide brown bands and thin, electric-blue piping.

'Well, well done for finding me. Come in and I'll get you a drink.'

'Thanks! Where do you want the produce?'

'Leave the perishables just inside the door, will you? I'll get you your diesel when you leave.'

Dave left the milk and eggs then followed Ian through the flat.

'Nice place.'

'Yeah, I suppose it is. The whole house used to belong to some kind of head doctor.'

Ian picked up the bottle and started to pour the liqueur.

'Nice flowers.'

'Aren't they just.'

He turned and handed Dave a brimful glass, then raised his own and sipped. Dave coughed as the alcohol slid down his throat.

'Bloody hell, that's good stuff.'

'Only the best for you, dear boy. Sit down and make yourself at home. How're things at the farm?'

Dave helped himself to an olive and drank some more liqueur. He was looking for clues in Ian's face.

'We had a problem with the police.'

'What happened?'

'They found some guy lying dead in a field out near the farm. He'd been strangled so they questioned me and Reggie. It was awkward, we didn't know what to say. They wanted to know if we'd seen Leonard. Do you know where he is, Ian?'

'No, of course I bloody don't, I was hoping that you'd be able to shed some light on that one for me!'

'Why are you so interested in Leonard?'

Ian poured himself another glass of liqueur and tipped it back.

'Leonard is a clever one, seems to me he's a born survivor. Do you get me? It's the Ice Moon, Dave, I'm sure he's found out how to stay alive through the impact. I've got to find him, get the truth out of him, before it's too bloody late. Do you get me?'

'I get you, but I don't know where he is. He came by the farm a couple of days ago, but there's been no word since. Nobody's seen him.'

'Fuck it!'

Dave stood and walked to the window; he looked at the daffodils in the glass jug. Lying on the table behind the flowers were two lengths of rope tangled together in an elaborate knot.

'Bloke they found near the farm, he'd been tied up, very fancy job they said. Skilful they said.'

'Really?'

'Look, seems to me I can't help you much. I've had a bit of a wasted journey and I don't know where Leonard's got to! I'd better go, I'll miss curfew if I don't set off now.'

'Nonsense, we've got this bottle to finish. You'll stay here tonight and keep me company.'

Ian wasn't a big man, he wasn't physically dominant, but when he said something, it sounded conclusive, like it was legally binding. And Dave had the idea that if things didn't go as he wanted, there would be a reaction, maybe even an over-reaction.

'Anyway you've already missed curfew and I've got a very comfy blow-up mattress you can use, OK?'

'Ah alright, no problem.'

Ian got up and sat down in another chair for no reason, just swapped seats for the hell of it and sat down again after topping up the glasses.

'You know something, Dave?'

'What?'

Dave shrugged and shook his head.

'Don't get me wrong, but there's something playing on my mind. It's quite difficult for me, but I've been meaning to tell you that… Well, you are a lovely looking young man, as angelic as a soap opera priest.'

Dave laughed and he blushed.

'A priest, eh? I'm not what you'd call a religious man, Ian.'

'No, nor am I. I suppose my only interest in the subject is fetishist.'

'What's that?'

'I'm interested in temptation.'

'What about salvation?'

'Oh, bugger that, no such thing.'

Ian drained his glass.

'I'll tell you what, Dave, I've been trying to forget how close we all are to extinction, but I'm crap at that. I'm a bit drained, bit exhausted by the whole thing.'

'Nothing we can do about it.'

'There's always something you can do, even if it's just to distract yourself.'

Ian got up, crossed to the radio and switched it on. He spent a moment wrestling with interference, before he settled on a signal.

The liqueur was heating Dave's head, his cheeks were flushed and his hands were hot.

'I'll tell you what I've noticed lately, as the Ice Moon becomes more and more inevitable.'

'What's that?'

'Well, haven't you noticed the amount of emergency sex going on?'

'Not so much, but I am living out on a farm.'

'Well, it's obvious, isn't it? They don't tell you because they don't want you to know, but it seems to me that the general public are beginning to realise that one of the greatest aphrodisiacs of all is impending disaster. It sets some sort of racial alarm off, a survival response is triggered. Do you see what I mean?'

Dave wasn't that comfortable with the theory. He was feeling light-headed, drowsy. The room was not as still as it should be; it was becoming fluid and weightless. The daffodils were scrolling to the left, moving behind Ian and Ian's head had vanished; it had dropped inside his collar as he struggled to pull his shirt off. Dave tried to get up, he wanted to get up and maybe get some air, but his legs wouldn't take his weight. He fell painlessly to the floor and looked up at the naked man. Ian lowered himself, knelt across Dave, pinning his arms down with his shins. He grabbed him by the ears, lifted him closer and kissed his mouth. He was mumbling in between kisses, and the words rattled around inside Dave's skull. 'You're a pretend person, Dave, you're not being honest with yourself.'

CHAPTER EIGHTEEN

The ceiling came into view, a flat sheet of metal riveted along a central seam. Leonard couldn't remember the last time he'd been able to sleep as soundly as this. His eyes had opened of their own accord. No screeching alarm clock, buzzing telephone, or heavy handed bedfellow rising.

The lorry was still roaring along, bouncing gently over patched repairs in the crumbling tarmac roads. He pulled the short curtains to one side and peered out. Trees and a flat horizon, that was all; the close things whipping past, the distant farmhouses hardly moving.

Leonard opened the hatch and climbed down into the empty haulage area behind the cab. His stomach was gurgling with hunger and he felt weak at the knees as he tried to stand still on the plywood. He placed his legs wide apart for balance and looked around in the dim light. The overhead tube had been switched off but rays of silver daylight were shining in through holes in the side panels. Leonard took a closer look at the holes; he pushed his finger through and realised they were bullet holes. On the other side of the lorry there were several closely grouped blast patterns from a shotgun. This allowed sunlight to scatter through onto the floor.

Behind the ladder that led up to the bunk, there was an access door to the cab. Leonard grabbed the handle, twisted and pulled on it. He found himself standing behind the seats with Lena sitting in between the drivers, looking out through the big windscreen. She turned and smiled, the drivers looked back and nodded. Lena made the introductions.

'This is Paul and this is Danny.'

'Alright lads, how's it going?'

Paul answered.

'We're getting there.'

'Where?'

'Where we're going.'

'How long's it going to take?'

'Don't know for sure yet, depends which roads are still open.'

Leonard rested his arms on the seatbacks and watched the road.

'We're going to have to go straight through the town up ahead because the ring road's blocked. It's getting a bit wild-west down through the high street, so we'll see how we go, eh?'

Danny took a shotgun from beneath the dashboard and stood the butt on the seat so it was visible from the roadside.

'We don't like slowing down too much here, they're a dodgy crowd.'

Leonard looked left and right. The landscape was kind of semi-rural, semi-detached, a few shops every now and then, a garage, a pub, net-less goalposts and fallow fields. There was a mid-morning mist hanging in the air, a thickening of the atmosphere like the day after bonfire night.

As the lorry climbed over the brow of a hill, the town came into view.

'Here we go, then!'

They were approaching a sort of market town that looked as if it had slipped back several centuries into the darker ages.

Danny piped up.

'Better pull over. Paul and I'll open up the back of the lorry!'

'Yeah, right.'

Leonard studied the lads: medium build, medium height, mousy-haired men in their mid-thirties. They wore scuffed white trainers, blue jeans and their removals company sweatshirts, with BARRY'S REMOVALS written in bold, three-D lettering.

'Why are we stopping?'

'We've got to open up the back to show them the lorry's empty.'

'Don't worry about all this, Leonard. The people here are just as uptight as you are, that's all. There's not much food around, not much petrol either.'

Danny jumped down, ran round and opened the back up. He was quickly back into the cab again and the lorry pulled away and picked up speed.

'Here you go, put one of these on.'

Danny handed Leonard a sweatshirt. As his head popped up through the neck, Leonard felt a rising nausea. Danny shook his head.

'Looks a lot worse than the last time we came through. Panic's really starting to take a hold.'

'Yeah, you can't really blame them, though, can you? Time's running out on all of us.'

Paul laughed pointlessly, his shoulders tightening as he gripped the steering wheel.

'Nobody really knows what to do with themselves. This used to be a nice quiet little town; look at it now! Look at that!'

Off to the left of the road as they drove down the hill, a vertical mast of wood had been driven into the ground. At the top was what looked like a wagon wheel. Lashed to the wheel was the body of a young man.

Leonard shouted.

'Shit!'

Lena looked up, then turned away.

Hundreds of people were milling about, cars competed with horses for road space and smoke rose from fires behind the high street. A gang of men wearing mix-and-match military uniform stood beside an oil-drum roadblock. Paul stopped and waved.

'OK, lads, how's things?'

'Fucking great, thanks! Got the toll?'

'Course we have.'

Danny opened his door and lifted a box out from beneath his seat. He handed it over and one of them cut the wrapping open to check the contents. He looked up and grinned; it was a case of good scotch.

Two of the gang members checked the lorry. They climbed in and kicked around in the back, then jumped off. They pulled the oil drums to one side and waved the lorry through.

Danny's ribs rose and fell as he breathed deeply again.

'It's going be a tight squeeze down through the high street.'

He turned to Leonard.

'Ignore them if they shout out, if they jump up, waggle this at them.'

He passed Leonard a second shotgun.

'It's loaded, but don't shoot anyone unless you really have to. It'll only slow us down!'

They slowed to walking pace and entered a one-way system. It was a chaotic scene, a mid-day chaos that had probably been building all morning. It looked as if they'd been laying out the tables and setting up the stalls for a Breugel painting.

Leonard turned as two kids were lifted onto the back of the lorry by adults. He raised the shotgun.

'We've nothing. See, we're empty!'

The kids ignored Leonard; they just searched the place with their eyes. They looked dishevelled, and their trademark tracksuits needed a wash. They couldn't see anything worth having so they started to lower themselves back onto the road.

'Cock-sucker! Yeah, cock-sucker!'

They jumped off and ran back into the market, watching each other's backs.

People were banging on the side of the lorry and a few stones came pelting through the rear door and rattled around in the back. In front, in the middle of the road, there was a burning car.

'Shit! That's torn it, the road's blocked.'

Paul pointed across the street at a café.

'See that café over there, Leonard? They're alright in there. Take Lena over and stay put until we get this sodding car moved, alright?'

'OK. How long will you be?'

'Don't know, it's a bloody red-hot piece of metal so we'll have to get some ropes on it or something. As long as we get out of here before nightfall, we'll be OK. After dark the bloody militia fuck off and people start shooting each other.'

Lena grabbed her bag, climbed over the seat and stood next to Leonard.

'Come on then, Lena, let's go.'

Out on the street, groups of people were crowding around the stallholders, like the four deep circles that grow up around fistfights. They were selling stuff off the backs of beaten-up transit vans, dealing food, drugs and guns. They had minders who stood a few metres away and aimed rifles into the crowd. The buyers and sellers weighed up the relative value of this and that. They argued, and then the swap price was bullied to a conclusion.

The crowd were subdued, they were swaddled into a kind of civilian uniform, layers and layers of dulled-down camouflage. They went about their business, but they weren't shopping in the usual family groups. Everyone seemed to be going their own way, looking out for themselves.

There was a constant sensation of angst in the air, of rush hour, and Leonard felt sick in his stomach. They passed two emptied out and beaten up chocolate machines, Lena looked inside anyway.

As they turned and walked towards the café, Leonard looked down at his feet. A water main must have burst because the pavement was flooded and the slabs were lifting, almost floating away.

'Don't bite your lip, Lena, it makes you look vulnerable.'

Leonard grabbed her hand, pulled her through the crowd and into the café. The place was decorated inside and out with white tiles and green grout, it was like graph paper, like sitting inside an exercise book. There were some arches against the walls, though, and inside the arches, naïve murals of the sacking of Rome. The tables and chairs were that bright yellow kind of pine, and the floor was a dark, stain-resistant plastic. Lena sat in the window and Leonard went to the counter. There was no one around, so he called out.

'Hello?'

'Oi oi, keep the noise down!'

It was a customer, an old guy sat at a corner table, huddled around his mug.

'There's nobody here, you idiot, and all they've got is soup, so help yourself to soup.'

'Is that what you've got?'

'Don't you worry about what I've got, you just get some soup down you and be thankful for the bloody small mercy of it.'

Leonard looked at the empty crisp boxes and up at the fluorescent lists of mixed-grill breakfasts. His stomach groaned. He took a couple of upside-down mugs off the counter and filled them from a hot chrome barrel. He carried them over to Lena. It was really just heated water, it was so diluted that only a faint trace of salted stock registered. Lena looked up at Leonard and made a sort of 'drink it anyway' face.

Leonard rubbed a patch of condensation off the window and looked out. The lorry was easy enough to pick out, with its sweatshirt logo painted huge along the side. They were OK those two, Paul and Danny boy; semi-skilled, salt of the earth, fly-by-nights. They were common-sense blokes; they reminded Leonard of dependable infantrymen, those lower ranks who were often a lot more capable than their commanding officers. They were throwing ropes across the smoking wreck of the car and tying them onto the crash bars at the front of the lorry.

'Leonard?'

He looked around at Lena. She'd really not said much all day, but he knew she'd been watching and listening, sifting through all the new information.

'What happens if everybody dies?'

Leonard shrugged his shoulders.

'What do you mean?'

'If everybody dies! You know.'

'Well, then the whole bloody world will have been one great big waste of time. Look, don't lose heart, we'll make it up to the survival pods, we've got a bloody good chance of getting through all this.'

He realised he was a long way from convincing her.

Lena smiled.

'Can we go for a walk?'

He looked through the window at the lads; they were still trying to drag the wreck off the road with the ropes, but they kept on slipping and snapping.

'Yeah OK, let's get some air. Paul and Danny'll be a while yet.'

They stepped out of the cafe and took a back alley away from the market. They climbed up past a Norman church, through some budding oak trees, up to a flat plateau above the town. The landscape sloped away to the west. The road Paul and Danny wanted to take zigzagged toward a flat horizon. Each side of the road there were fires, campfires, tents and makeshift shelters, stretching away into the distance. It was like a view of a medieval siege plain, a grey sky with black smoke from fires trailing off at forty-five degrees.

Lena had moved off downhill. When Leonard caught up with her, she was standing at the edge of a shallow film of water, which was rising out of the ground, then flooding down-slope from a burst pipe.

A man stood in the middle of the road, holding a baby in his arms. He was just standing there with the water rushing over his shoes.

They stepped around the flood and turned back towards the market. They passed mounds of black rubbish bags that were overfilled and spilling across the streets. A few cars cruised by slowly, with spare petrol cans lashed to their boot lids.

'Leonard!'

Lena's voice was fearful. A group of kids had ringed her, a dozen or so young kids, all under twelve. The colour had been washed out of their clothes and their cheeks were grey and blood drained. Their heads were tilted down because they wanted to hide their smiles. One kid lifted his head and the others listened, his voice was menacing.

'In your lorry. Where you going that's better than here?'

Leonard let Lena answer because if he spoke for her, that would be the first trigger.

'I said, where you going?'

'Don't know. Don't matter any more, does it?'

Leonard looked into their eyes as one by one the heads lifted. They had that compressed life experience of refugees. It was clear that they didn't give a fuck for what they did now, not after all they'd witnessed, not after all they'd learned from the adults. They moved closer to Lena and one of the girls got hold of her hair.

'I smell a virgin, Jinksy, we can get a rush for that!'

'Fuckin' yeah, trade her in no prob'. She's got to be worth something to someone, eh?'

'Wait a minute.'

'What?'

One of the kids took hold of Lena's ear. He ran his hand over her top lip.

'Fucking hell, Jinks, I reckon we've hit the jackpot here. She's chin-tagged!'

Jinksy looked across at Leonard because he had taken a step in their direction.

'She's ours now, wanker.'

The air exploded above their heads. Leonard looked up to see Paul waving and running towards them, aiming the shotgun before firing again. They let go of Lena and scattered back into the side streets. Paul was red-faced and breathing heavily, his hands were black with grease and his eyes were narrowed, searching for stragglers.

'For Christ's sake, come on, we've cleared the road! You shouldn't have left the bloody café! Let's get back to the truck!'

He turned and started running. Leonard grabbed Lena's hand and they ran after him.

Danny was driving and Paul was asleep in the overhead bunk. Leonard and Lena were sitting in the double bench seats, staring at the road ahead. It was engaging cinema and there was only the one simple storyline; they were the good guys and they were headed somewhere safe, for now that was all. The bends swept by and the landscape started to flatten out, the cloud cover was breaking up and the sky was brightening. Lena was squinting in the sunlight; she was too low in the seat to get any benefit from the green-tinted shading at the top of the windscreen. When she looked up at Danny and Leonard, though, their eyes were shaded and their skin coloured the same filtered green. Nobody had said anything for a while, so she did.

'Where are we, Danny?'

'We're running parallel to the coastline which is a few miles to the east. It's not far now.'

Lena was excited; she rubbed her eyes and squinted harder. She felt good in the middle, sitting in between them, she felt buffered and she didn't mind if they never got where they were going.

She turned and asked Danny a question.

'Do you think we'll all be killed, I mean by the Ice Moon?'

Danny's foot came off the accelerator a bit while he thought about that one.

'Buggered if I know, it's all down to luck now, isn't it? God knows what's gonna kick off when that big bastard comes flying out of the sky. They think it's going to pulverise China now, don't they? The facts are nasty, think about it - the asteroid will hit us at something like twenty thousand miles an hour! It's a flying mountain. I'm not trying to alarm you, Lena, but we are facing a mass extinction event!'

Leonard wound down the window and warm, fresh air blew into the cab. He looked over the top of Lena's head and said, 'Not trying to alarm you?'

Danny shrugged an apology.

'I'm sorry, but I mean that's what I've heard.'

Leonard drank from a bottle of water and offered it to Lena.

'Listen, Lena, look at it this way. The asteroid is just an unfortunate acceleration.'

'What?'

'Of what was going to happen anyway.'

'He means pollution and wars and stuff?'

'I suppose I mean the general, all-round, blind stupidity the human race specialises in. We were always heading for a fall.'

She looked like an adult when she nodded that she understood.

'Can we stop? I need the toilet.'

'I'll pull off the road a minute, if you like.'

The lorry stopped and Leonard stepped down into a different landscape. These were flatlands and the water table felt close, it was just below and sometimes broke the surface. Tall reed-beds stretched out on each side of the road, pale near the ground and deep green at the tip, swaying in the wind, in unison.

Danny lifted his arms above his head and stretched out his spine. He took a couple of steps, kicked a stone off the tarmac and pointed.

'Coastline's about ten miles that way. It's reeds, grasses and sedge from here on in. Nice, though, isn't it?'

'Yeah. I'm going to take a leak too, Danny.'

'Don't go far and mind your step, it's waterlogged.'

Leonard and Lena stepped off the road and walked into the reeds, she scurried off to the left and he went in a few metres further. He could hear hammering in the distance, a club hammer with a steady rhythm. As he listened, he started to anticipate the next blows and it was comforting for a while to be in synch, until the blows stopped.

When Leonard zipped up and stood still for a few minutes, the swaying reeds were taller than he was. He closed his eyes and let the sun warm his face. He'd been feeling nauseous for the past fifty miles; too much motion, and towards what? His stomach ached; it was restless and filled with excess digestive acids. He was probably just scared now. Like everybody else, the reality was beginning to bite, the weeks were counting down. Leonard was not sure that he had the time or the courage to do what he had planned. Maybe he was just kidding himself, following an unconscious urge, a fairytale myth of being the hero who saved the day.

Lena came back out of the reeds with wet shoes. She looked across at the truck and saw that scruffy-haired Paul and yawning Danny were speaking to two other men who were carrying guns. A black dog at their feet started to bark in her direction and she didn't know what to do.

Danny piped up.

'It's alright, come on over.'

Leonard waved at Lena and she ran across to him before they left the reeds and walked to the lorry.

The dog barked until it was told to shut up. It was a black, barrel-chested Labrador.

Paul was trying hard to lick-spittle his hair down, he introduced Ben and Trevor.

'This is Ben and this is Trevor, they're patrolling the area.'

They said the hellos and Leonard felt reassured, it was a brief and amicable exchange. Trevor was a big and heavy man, cheerful with it. Ben didn't say much, but he looked shrewd enough. They nodded a lot and wanted to know the story, then they headed off pretty happily into the reeds with their shotguns broken over their shoulders and the dog following.

Paul drove the last few miles, he pointed out their destination as he turned off the road onto a gravel drive. He kept the engine in first gear for the steep climb up to a group of mock-Tudor barns scattered around a big old house.

'It's not exactly a mountain, I know, but here we are something like a hundred metres above sea level, it's the highest ground for miles around. The original house was built on an outcrop of purplish granite, it was originally the site of a Danish fort.'

'Vikings!'

'Yeah, they put their settlement right here, funny how the same logic holds as true for us today as it did a thousand years ago. They built in wood, though obviously that didn't last. The archaeology lot from the university had the place dug up a few years back, they found all sorts of stuff.'

The outbuildings, like the main house, were wood framed. The blackened timbers showed through the rendered exterior of the walls. The plasterwork in between the timbers was tea brown, weathered and faded, with small, leaded windows and a steep roof. It was like arriving in a medieval hamlet, with the buildings wrapped around a straggling courtyard.

There were some modernisations though, some additions to the main house: a red brick extension, with a larger entrance door, Roman pillars each side and grimacing lion statues guarding the last few steps up to the house.

Leonard looked off to his left, he could see through to the ground behind the house, to a row of prefab' houses and a tennis court. Next to the tennis court were something like thirty or more brightly coloured luxury cars, a collection of all the cars that used to be sought after. Daimlers and Range Rovers, BMWs, Volvos, Audis; they were all shunt-parked into a rough circle. They were ditched really into a General Custer's last stand, left to rot where they'd ran out of petrol. The men and women who'd arrived in those cars appeared as soon as Paul hit the horn and switched the engine off.

Lena felt a bit nervous as she stepped down from the lorry, she didn't like to be the centre of attention. And some of the people looked a bit weird, there were lots of beards. They were nearly all long haired, even the men who were bald on top let their hair at the back and sides straggle down to lion-heart length. Leonard felt like they'd arrived on some radical university campus. When they started saying hello though, they were warm and smiling people, men with square shoulders and quick eyes. The women made a fuss too, they gave Lena and Leonard perfectly weighted kisses.

They must have had other things to do because after ten minutes or so they wandered off in different directions and eventually only Paul was left to show them into the house.

The hallway was dark and quiet, their footsteps fell onto thick carpet. There were portrait paintings hanging each side, dark backgrounds and pink faces, oil paintings, old ones.

They could hear music coming from a room further into the house. Paul led them through connecting rooms which were filled with antique furniture, Louis fourteen, fifteen, sixteen; not laid out for living but more for storage, all jumbled together in job lots.

The music was coming from the other side of the door just ahead, Paul turned to Leonard and shook his hand.

'I'll leave you to make your own introductions.'

He rubbed the top of Lena's head and headed off into another part of the house.

Leonard knocked but there was no answer.

'Whoever's in there won't be able to hear you knocking, the music's too loud.'

'I know that, Lena.'

Leonard twisted the handle and gave the door a shove. It swung open and across the room a big, bald man was standing in front of a loud speaker. He was standing very close to a big, rosewood Goodman, his lips were up against the pattern of concave, soot black hollows. It was like he was whispering in there or waiting for a kiss. He'd removed the mesh frame that is usually stretched over the front and he had his fingers resting inside, against the base and treble cones. He was moving his head in time to the music, flugelhorn music.

Leonard bent down and spoke into Lena's ear.

'I know this, it's that elephant music, psychic elephant music.'

The man started to dance. To begin with, it was mostly with his head, but then with his neck and shoulders. When the music reached a series of rising crescendos, his whole body started to spin dervish-like around the room. He was going too fast for his eyes to register that he had company. His arms lifted like a centrifuge and he spun, filling his fingers with blood, spilling his drink, dropping his glass. It was a laughable spectacle, but joyful, enviable even. He looked like a fool. A glad and quite glorious fool at the peak of his foolishness.

The track finished and the man steadied himself on the back of an armchair. He waited for his world to stop spinning, for the inertia to trail off so that he could walk across the room. He knew Lena and Leonard were there because he lifted his hand and said breathlessly, 'Sorry you had to see that. Be right with you, just one minute.'

So he crossed to them and they met on the sky-blue rug in the middle of the music room. This was Barry, and Barry had a bald, tanned head with six, deep and dry creases in his forehead. He wore a white shirt and dark tie, the whiter shape of a 't' shirt showing beneath. He looked like some sort of union boss, all beer-bellied up and ready to take the rule book in his right hand. A kind face though, well meaning and well rounded.

'So I bet you two could use a drink then, eh?'

Leonard shook Barry's hand and presented Lena.

'What'll you have then, ladies first.'

'Beer please.'

'Right you are, good choice.'

Leonard thought about making a fuss, but he suspected that sometimes you had to let the lesson be learned. Barry came back with a bottle and gave it to her.

'And you, Leonard?'

'I'll have whatever you're having.'

'OK but I should warn you, I always have plenty of nutmeg in my toddies.'

'I'll try.'

'I got the idea from reading about Nostradamus, he used to take a lot of the stuff because it's supposed to aid second sight!'

'Ah, well I'm not so sure I want to see anymore than I've seen just lately. I think I'd rather not know what the future holds.'

'Oh, come on now Leonard, ignorance is not at all bliss.'

'Isn't it?'

'Definitely not no, forewarned is forearmed.'

Barry dusted the whisky with nutmeg and handed it to Leonard. He raised his own glass and offered a toast.

'Welcome, and well done for making it out of that God-awful city alive.'

CHAPTER NINETEEN

It rained all the time now. There was probably some ominous reason for the phenomenon but Warden was, as in most other areas of his life, way past caring. At night, he liked to be driven around the glistening streets with the good old music playing, the big band stuff like Buddy Rich or Duke Ellington. He had big, fat cushions in the back and he slept now and then, waking in fits and starts to check that his driver was still at the wheel. He popped pills when he had to and they dragged him through indifferent black and white dreams of the celluloid heydays.

He was mostly only half conscious and he liked it that way, the pain threshold was higher and it helped him to be graceful and forgiving, helped him to be glad about giving up and giving in. Sometimes though, his brain was sharp enough to think things through, to forward a motion - and he would remember then, how he could no longer sleep in his own bed, it just wasn't safe anymore. He had picked up too many enemies and the few people he kept on his staff were paid very dearly for an uncertain amount of loyalty. The light though, at the end of the tunnel, was the Ice Moon. He spent all his spare time wishing on this star. It would come, all his hopes were pinned on it. He even prayed some nights that he might be killed outright by the impact, somewhere very near ground zero. This idea was keeping him alive, turning up the corners of his rippled mouth.

'Stop the car!'

The driver turned to check he'd heard right, then he indicated and pulled over, braking smoothly. They were in a wide, dark street with a tall building just to the right and behind. Warden kicked on the door but it wouldn't budge, so the driver stepped out and opened up. He reached in, slid Warden's body along the leather and helped him onto his feet. He snatched his cane and took a few steps across the pavement, then he stopped and swayed. The rain hitting the top of his head helped his eyes find focus. He spotted the sheet of paper but he couldn't bend down to it, not right down to the page. What was so weird was that it was his own, much younger, grinning gob staring back at him, a wet likeness flattened against the paving slabs. It made him chuckle this did, that someone somewhere had called out, 'Hold the front page!' and they had held it, until his portrait was typeset. So there he was, with his very own cover shot and the following headlines: 'The Man Who Sold The World'! 'Survival programme exposed!' 'The corruption of hope!' 'Gangsters, bribery and the Warden's lies!'

He looked good though, a lot better than he did these days and also somewhat immune to the present circumstances, in just two dimensions. More newspaper seemed to be falling from above, along with the rain, more and more mirror images ganging up as they settled. He craned his neck and looked up. Even with his underwater eyes, he could see that it was Beryl up there on the roof of the Mirabelle, tipping out the usual mix of anti-authoritarian propaganda.

Warden climbed the steps up to the entrance door. He hoped the lift was working because his legs were shaking and he had it in mind to get to the top of the building.

CHAPTER TWENTY

He woke early, stretched his spine, rolled over and pushed his feet into the tight, cool corners of the bed-sheets. He could hear someone moving around downstairs, rattling a cup, dropping a spoon, kicking a table leg. He heard the back door being opened and then closed heavily, which sent a minor tremor up through the floor and into the bed springs. Leonard turned the clock to face him, it was six thirty am. He sat up, put a finger in his ear and wiggled it, then he yawned and got out of bed. It was a bit of a shock to go from horizontal to vertical, and Leonard felt light-headed as he walked to the bedroom window. He pulled the drawstring on the roller-blind and peered out into the pre-dawn colours. Sea birds were crossing the sky and swirling clouds were evaporating. In the distance, the marshes were a shadowy mass, with the reed beds billowing this way and that, as the breeze stirred.

Barry was standing out on the lawn down below the window, drinking a mug of tea and sniffing out the weather. He wore khaki shorts and a sweatshirt, he had chunky calves and white trainers. He took a couple of swallows from the mug and shook out the final drop. He turned to face the reddening sky, held his arms out in front of his body with his palms turned upwards, and he started to say something. Leonard opened the window. Barry's voice was formal, well articulated.

'Salutations to the East.'

He cleared his throat.

'Thy dawning is beautiful in the horizon of heaven,
O living Aten, beginning of life!
When thou risest in the eastern horizon of heaven,
Thou fillest every land with thy beauty;
For thou art beautiful, great, glittering high over the earth;
Thy rays, they encompass the lands, even all thou hast made.
Thou art Ra, and thou hast carried them all away captive;

Thou bindest them by thy love.
Though thou art afar, thy rays are upon the earth;
Though thou art on high, thy footprints are the day.' [2]

When he'd finished, he lifted his arms up above his head then lowered them to the previous position but this time with his palms turned over, so they faced the ground. He repeated the movement twice more, then he started some stretching exercises.

Leonard pulled on a pair of trousers and a T-shirt, it was warm enough these days to wear shoes without socks. He splashed some water in his face and wandered along the hallway. He poked his head into Lena's room but she wasn't there. He went down to the kitchen to fill the kettle, then he opened the back door so he could see the pond. Just as he'd thought, there was Lena, crouched down beside the water, throwing stale bread for the ducks.

A diesel generator coughed into life. Leonard stepped out and walked along the side of the house until he could see what was going on. He joined two men who were shovelling sand and cement into a rotating mixer.

'Need any help?'

'Yeah OK, we've got to pour a lot of concrete over the next few days. Get yourself some breakfast first, check the chickens.'

It was true that they had a lot to do; they had to pour concrete into a flat cage, criss-crossed with reinforcing bars which lay below ground level. These were the last stages of a D.I.Y shelter project which had taken Barry and his crew the best part of a year to cobble together. They'd built an underground bunker big enough to house twenty to thirty people and hopefully keep them alive through the initial and the secondary stages of impact with the Ice Moon. This was the last stage of construction, the roof of the shelter. They'd welded a steel cage over the top of the structure which would add a final layer of blast protection. It was as heavy and as strong as they could make it, with the materials they could find. The clever thing was, although the whole site was built on solid granite, they'd found a fissure of softer limestone. This had been relatively easy to dig out, so the shelter was positioned in between two great outcrops of the purple-flecked granite.

They'd fill the reinforcing bars with a concrete lid, then cover it all over

2 Akhneten's Hymn to the Aten.

with earth in a few days time. Barry was outwardly confident, he reckoned the structure could offer them the protection they needed, but Leonard was not so sure.

He walked away from the shelter and swung around the back of the house past the neglected tennis court. It didn't look like it had ever been used. It had a loose, low-slung net and grass grew up through cracks in the tarmac.

The hen-house was behind the tennis court, where the ground started to slope away down to the level of the road and the reed beds. As he approached a couple of the chickens started to cluck, they all had something to say when he opened the door. He lifted half a dozen warm, tanned eggs from beneath the hens.

The black Labrador followed Barry all around the house, it stayed close on his heel and hurried through the opened and closed doors so that it wouldn't be left behind. That used to happen a lot, and the dog would find himself locked into a cold wing of the house, without food and missing a car journey. Barry opened the kitchen door and the Labrador shot through; the dog was excited because Barry was carrying one of the its favourite things - a wooden duck. It was a naïve bird shape, a decoy duck used by hunters.

As Barry and the black dog entered, Leonard and Lena looked up from their breakfast plates.

'Morning. How're you both feeling then?'

'Fine. And you?'

'So-so.'

'I saw you earlier, Barry, heard you chanting outside my window. What was that all about?'

The dog had been waiting patiently, long enough in fact, so he started to bark at Barry.

'Ah yes, it's a prayer, an old habit of mine. Its purpose is simple enough, it's a salutation to the dawn.'

He turned and gave the dog the wooden duck.

'He loves to chew on its head, see. It's the only one he's allowed to play with, the rest are on display in the music room. You must have a look at them, they're beautifully crafted objects, very collectable. They're antiques and yet they were just tools of a trade at one time, wildfowl decoys for the hunters who worked the droves.

'So, Leonard, what do you make of our last stand?'

'Your project seems well organised. And there is a good atmosphere here, a sense of community.'

Leonard finished his cup of tea and took the breakfast plates to the sink.

'If you don't mind, Barry, I'm going to give some of the lads a hand with the roof of the shelter.'

'That's good of you, it'll be a great help because we've fallen behind schedule. I'll show Lena the rest of the farm.'

Barry led the way out onto the ground behind the main house. As he walked, he pointed out how water was pumped around the property.

The circuit started at the pond, water flowed out through a buried pipe, uphill alongside the house and to the rear where the supply entered a walled garden. In the centre of the garden there was a stone statue, a naked woman called 'Siren'. She was supposed to spit water six feet into the air, but she really only dribbled like an imbecile because the water pump wasn't powerful enough and kept on clogging up with silt. Everyone called the statue the 'dribbler'. 'How are you settling in then, Lena?'

'Alright. I thought you were all kind of weird to begin with.'

'Why's that?'

'You just look weird.'

'Don't be fooled by appearances, these are very clever, very capable people. Independent, free thinkers and practical with it. These are my kind of people, Lena, men and women with bright ideas!'

'I see.'

'We are most of all a group of outsiders and I've always had a soft spot for an outsider, for an underdog.'

Barry pointed towards a small barn.

'We're going in there.'

They walked towards the building and Barry had to fiddle with a rusted padlock before he could slide the door open. As he rattled the steel, there was a single dry screech from inside, followed by a series of screeches, all at exactly the same volume and pitch, one after the other. The noise was not a complaint, it was more like a statement of fact, a cry to convey relevant information: I'm in here and I'm a fickle creature, remember? Barry lifted the padlock off and opened the door. Light flooded in, it excited the creature inside. Barry walked through the skewed triangle of light stretched across the concrete floor and into the shadowy interior.

'Come on in, Lena.'

Lena stepped in and strained her eyes, it took a while before she could see the interior. The space was quite empty, with spots of light coming in from the outside. One wall clad with vertical timbers let strips of light squeeze in through the joints. Barry was standing next to an upright wooden post with a crossbar, and he was whispering to a bird perched on top. He put something on the bird's head and then he pulled a long leather glove onto his right hand. The bird screeched four times, stepped onto his forearm and then stayed silent.

Barry turned and started to walk back towards Lena, some light bells hanging from his glove jangled like a pocketful of change. He had the bird standing on his hand and he spoke very softly.

'Lena, this is Maurice and Maurice, as you can see, is a very beautiful Peregrine falcon.'

Maurice had a leather hood over his head, it was polished red leather with toggles and a blue feather plume on top. He had lovely breast feathers, white and grey-blue, and his feet were butter yellow with spiked talons which dug into the leather glove.

'Come on then, let's take him out for a spin, get him up into his natural element.'

Barry walked away downhill with Lena and the dog following. The falcon half opened its wings every now and then to keep balance. Carrying him was like carrying a technically perfect machine, the latest version of something, an example of rare bio-engineering. Inside his hood, Maurice was calm, the leather blocked out the world completely and the dark acted as a kind of off switch. An antidote to the Peregrine's killing need. He was dead without his eyes, locked into a kind of buffering coma.

Barry stood on a slightly raised area with a clear view of the reed beds and scattered birch trees. The horizon was perfectly flat and the cloud cover was fast-moving.

'Stand here, Lena, I'm going to take his hood off now, so you can see how beautiful he is.'

Barry lifted off the hood and the bird appeared, as brilliant as an unsheathed knife. It didn't shake its head with over-excitement, it just blinked calmly and panned smoothly, left then right. It looked forward at Lena and she saw that his eyes were like shining glass beads, oil black and brilliantly reflective. He had yellow eye rings, the same colour as his feet, his head was grey-blue and his cheeks were a darker slate. The beak looked fish-hook sharp, scythe shaped for tearing flesh.

Without the hood, the space-age lenses recorded the surrounding visual information, he latched on to his immediate environment and felt the breeze ruffle his tail feathers. Barry took the tethers off his hand and held his arm still. There was a slight downward pressure on Barry's hand as Maurice kicked off, his wings whipped through the air and carried him low to the ground at first, before he tipped a wing and started to climb.

There was no confusion in Maurice's life, not a moment's doubt or indecision, flight was automatic and the reason for flight was to hunt and to kill his prey.

'Isn't he beautiful?'

'Yes, he is.'

Lena watched the Labrador set off into the reeds. Barry moved forward too, onto sodden ground, keeping his eyes on the sky as the Peregrine began to circle high above.

'You should stand over there, Lena, where it's dry.'

She saw what he meant, the ground was wet except for where reed stems from previous years had been cut back and laid flat, compacted down into a thick layer.

'Watch how the falcon and the dog work together, they're looking for waterfowl, or a shorebird. He's a duck hawk really, that's what he likes the best.'

Lena strained her eyes to follow Maurice. He worked hard, sometimes flapping furiously to gain height and then he slid, glided, or wheeled over in a gust. Head-on, his silhouette was like a flattened 'W', but sometimes hard light broke through the cloud and hit the underside of his wings. Then he glittered silver for a few seconds, his outline became chrome bright, like a speed-shape from the bonnet of a Polish limousine.

Out in the reeds, the Labrador advanced, he was soaking wet. He'd tracked a wide circle through the marshy ground, jumping across canals where he could, but swimming if he couldn't. Where the reeds thinned out, they gave way to larger areas of shallow water. Close to the sedge grasses, the water was still, but out in the channels, the wind whipped at the surface. The dog jumped into the water and three ducks started flapping and sprinting across the surface in a blind panic. Their wings lifted them and they scattered away in different directions.

Barry had just enough time to lift Lena into the air before Maurice went into a dive. He folded up like he'd been shot and he literally dropped out of the sky. Lena saw the falcon tear into the duck, very fast and hard with feathers flying where they'd crashed together.

'There you go, that's dinner I reckon, you're very lucky to see that first time out! Very lucky, two hundred mile an hour dive, that was!'

The falcon opened his wings fully, breaking his speed and flaring out into a stall as he approached Barry. Just for a moment, when he was air-breaking, he looked like a red Indian head dress. He set his feet very neatly onto Barry's forearm.

One thing Lena couldn't understand was why the bird came back after he'd been set free.

'Well it's all he knows, it's what he understands. Ever since he was a yearling, it's been me standing here with my glove on. That makes perfect sense to him.'

The Labrador came out of the reeds with the downed mallard dangling from his mouth. The duck's shimmering two-tone neck was broken because the head flopped around, the colour flashed peacock green, then deep purple. Lena wanted to pat the dog but his nature had changed. She didn't think it was the right time to grab his hot ears and scratch his head, not until he'd dropped the bird down beside Barry and become a domestic animal again.

CHAPTER TWENTY-ONE

The cement mixer rocked on three, uneven footings, it was tumbling a gritty mix of 3:1, with a flinty aggregate. Ben cut open a fresh bag with the blade of his shovel and threw four scoops into the mixer. Gary, a big dark-haired man with pale skin and flecks of grey-green cement stuck to his hair, stood over the barrel looking in.

'That looks more like it.'

Gary stood back and thought for a minute. He held his own nose between his thumb and forefinger, then he decided it was ready. Leonard and Ben got the nod and stood by with their shovels. Gary tipped the mixer forward and the cement poured out. Ben started to drag the stuff across the reinforcing rods, Leonard spread it out and knocked it down into place.

'How long will concrete this thick take to dry out?'

Ben plunged his hands into a bucket of clean water and rubbed the stuff off.

'It'll set overnight, take a good week to really harden up, though. We've got time.'

Gary took his turn at the bucket.

'Let's get some lunch.'

'Yeah OK, I'll catch you up.'

He washed his own hands and watched the two guys head off towards the house, shaking their arms to help dry their fingers.

The sun was high overhead, he could see the air flow moving across the wetlands in waves, swaying the reeds, fanning out as it arrived. It was an onshore breeze with a saline tang to it. There was something else, though, in the air, like a smouldering vegetation or a sweet, composting plant. Then he recognised the smell, it was Cannabis, someone nearby was smoking grass. There was no-one in sight but when Leonard started to sniff the trail, he saw a possible source. There were two venting pipes in the roof of the shelter and when he bent over the first, the fragrance became even stronger. He stepped down into a sort of trench, a gap between a granite slab and the main door into the shelter. The door itself was made of concrete, cast into a steel frame with three iron hinges. These hinges were really just welded loops, and the door had been lowered onto one long hinge made from a scaffolding pole. Leonard pulled on the door, it swung smoothly and he stepped into the dark. The air was damp and cooler than outside and the sound of his own feet seemed to be magnified. He couldn't find a light switch so he edged forward with his hand running along the wall ahead of him. He eventually found the corner of another door. This one had a long handle so he pulled on it and as he did, bright, fluorescent light came through the gap. Leonard was surprised by the size of the room. A polished red floor with racks of steel shelving along each wall, stacked high with numbered boxes.

'Who's there?'

'Leonard.'

He watched a woman with iron-red hair step out from between two aisles of racking. He'd seen her before, around the house.

'What d'you want?'

'I'm just having a look around I suppose, what's your name?'

'Gaynor.'

Instead of approaching him, Gaynor puffed on her joint, turned and climbed a steel ladder which was bolted to the side of a huge plastic storage tank. Leonard moved around to the foot of the ladder.

'What's that?'

She turned to answer.

'It's a ten thousand gallon water tank, there's another one further into the shelter. I'm running through the routine checklist.'

She held a wet tag of litmus paper up to the light and compared it to a colour chart. Then she popped some tablets from a foil sheet and dropped them into the tank via the access hatch.

'These will keep the drinking water stable.'

'What else is in here?'

Gaynor climbed back down the ladder.

'The essentials, food and water, medical supplies, the back-up generator and the communications equipment.'

She crossed the room and tapped her knuckles against a steel drum.

'And this is the air filtering system. It should keep our air clean even if we have to seal up the shelter and re-breathe for a while.'

'Re-breathe?'

'We circulate, re-use the same air. The drum is an air scrubber, it'll remove 99% of airborne particles down to as small as 0.3 microns, and the activated carbon trap absorbs the carbon dioxide.'

'How long can you live, sealed up like that?'

'We don't really know.'

She wrote something into her notebook, then walked away into the far corner of the room. She shouted back at him.

'I'm going to do a generator test, don't worry about the noise.'

'Right.'

There was a faint whirring, then a deeper thudding as the starter motor sparked up the diesel engine. It revved, turned at a constant pitch for a moment, then cut out.

She walked back to where Leonard was standing, looked up at him, half smiled, then offered him the joint. Leonard declined. She asked him, 'What do you think of our Barry then?'

'I like him, he's a good man and he's got a plan hasn't he, he's rallying people.'

'He's doing his best and he stays informed, he knows all about the Ice Moon, well, as much as there is to know. He studies all the reports, reads all the scientific papers. He thinks it'll help, knowing all the latest facts and figures.'

Leonard nodded.

'But he doesn't approve of cannabis. Says we need all our faculties, that we need to stay sharp. He says drugs are ultimately suicidal, but sometimes I just need to dull down, take the edge off, you know.'

'Yeah, I know.'

The idea of viewing a spectacular sunset filled Leonard with dread, he couldn't bear all the communal ooing and ahhing that goes on and how you had to agree that it was beautiful. It seemed to him that the only way to appreciate the phenomenon was by chance, in a rippled reflection, or against the side of someone's daydreaming face.

In the evenings though, after eating, Barry often wandered up through the courtyard with ten or fifteen of the others to watch the sunset. They watched the last few degrees of the solar arc, until a thin red stripe lay along the western horizon. Then the end of the day was declared, ticked off with a pen stroke through the calendar.

This evening, as the light faded and the shadows deepened, he felt glad of the ritual. They stood there for a while all looking the same way. Nobody said very much and as soon as the last patches of colour had faded, they turned back. A few children, still up after bedtime, asked to be carried.

Barry lit up a cigar and the ash-end glimmered in the half-light. Danny, Paul, Ben and Gaynor stayed where they'd been standing for the sunset. Their heads were raked back to spot the first starry pin-pricks that mapped out the night-sky.

Gaynor had brought her glass of wine up from the house. It was empty now but she still held the rim up to her lips, she bounced it there and looked off into the mid-distance. Her shoulders were bare and the wind chilled her. She snapped out of it and looked at Leonard. She raised her left eyebrow and let her mouth slide into a brave smile.

They'd started to walk back toward the house, when a flash of white shone through the reeds a few hundred yards back along the main approach road. Danny and Ben started to run and Barry shouted out some instructions. Leonard grabbed Lena's hand and jogged her off toward the house. He made sure she was OK, then he went back outside. Car headlamps flashed across the road. Leonard caught up with Barry down on the driveway.

A beaten up Saab had stopped in the middle of the road and turned onto the driveway. Ben walked forward ahead of the others, he bent down to the driver's window and rested his hand on the roof.

Leonard asked Barry what was going on.

'We're being cautious, Leonard, they could be dangerous.'

Ben looked over his shoulder and shouted out.

'They say they're lost?'

When his back was turned, all the passenger doors opened up at the same time. An internal map-light flickered on and Leonard could see that there were four men in the car, they were all armed and beginning to aim their weapons.

Ben threw himself to the ground and short bursts of automatic gunfire came out of the reeds along the roadside. Leonard could hear the bullets cutting through the sedge grasses and marsh peas before they slammed into the car.

Barry looked up from the ground, he had small pieces of gravel stamped into the heel of his hand and pressed into his cheek where he'd dived for cover. He looked up at Leonard.

'Raiding party, happens every now and then. Good job the boys on watch had their wits about them.'

The incident left the house haunted with what might have happened had the car not been intercepted. News of Barry's shelter had leaked out into the surrounding villages. More patrols were posted through the night but getting to sleep was not at all easy.

When Barry woke Leonard at something like four in the morning, he sat bolt upright in a panic. Barry pacified him, he apologised for shaking him up.

'Sorry Leonard, but you should come downstairs, there's something I want you to see.'

'Now?'

'Yes, now! Come on.'

Leonard got up and pulled on a pair of trousers, he followed Barry along the hallway and downstairs into the music room.

The television was tuned to a news channel, and the reader was looking flustered.

'Sit down and have a look at this report, it's coming in live.'

Leonard did sit, he rubbed his eyes and squinted at the screen.

'Do you want a cup of tea?'

'Yeah, sounds good.'

Barry poured the tea and dealt out the biscuits.

The newsreader was confused by last minute information which was being fed into his ear-piece. He sat up straight and said.

'Yes, OK we can now go live to that report.'

The picture cut away from the man behind the desk and switched to a fuzzy, sea-level camera angle with some foreground military hardware. The low grade video was obviously filmed from the deck of something like an aircraft carrier. The seas were heavy because the deck was lifting and falling. The camera lost focus, cut to black then went to tele-photo, it lifted away from the horizon and followed a smoking trail which scorched across the sky.

The commentary explained that the 1000-ton object was a fragment of the Ice Moon. The video followed the burning fragment across the sky and down into the sea, where it crashed then skipped off the surface; it literally bounced up off the Pacific ocean and climbed back out, fast and low-angled again, piercing up and through the cloud.

'Bloody hell, what's that all about?'

Barry piped up.

'A fragment of the asteroid, Leonard.'

The television image cut out of the video and into a computer simulation which showed the trajectory of the fragment. The commentary explained.

'As the fragment came through the earth's atmosphere this morning, the angle of flight combined with the glancing contact with the water's surface caused a most unusual continuation of the fragment back out of the earth's atmosphere and on into space.'

Barry laughed.

'Bloody hell, fantastic, eh!'

'Are there any more pieces?'

'Not that they are telling us about, have a look at this.'

Barry crossed the room and booted up a computer monitor.

'I'm afraid I've become a bit of an expert on the asteroid. It's become my specialist subject. I've got all these trajectory forecasts and plenty of these computer simulations and survival scenarios. Have a look at this, it's a live feed from the near earth asteroid tracking centre.'

Barry tapped into the computer and the screen shifted to blue, the main page clicked on and the first image appeared. In the corner of the screen a countdown clock reported that there were just eighteen days to impact.

'I'll run this and you'll see.'

The screen cleared to show a view of the earth from space.

'The last estimated position of the impact was grid referenced to 26°52'North 118°34'East. That's eastern China, a place called Fukien province. Did you know that some people are actually going there, they want to be right underneath the thing when it hits, silly sods.'

'I can sympathise with the logic.'

'Thing is, there's some doubt as to the exact position of impact. It could be anywhere in Russia or even through into eastern Europe. Look, I've got these sky surveys of the northern hemisphere.'

The screen scrolled down until Barry said, 'Ah there it is, look. I watched the radio telescope images first, before we got these visuals. Not that impressive is it, fizzing away like a cheap firework?'

Leonard put his finger on the screen.

'Is that it?'

'Yeah, looks harmless enough on this scale, problem is it's eighteen miles across. The energy released on impact has been calculated and it runs into hundreds of gigatons. It'll be travelling at something like twenty kilometres a second when it hits. And that's right off the Torino scale.'

'What?'

'It's like the Richter scale, only it measures the destructive potential of asteroid impact.'

'And it's off the scale.'

'Yeah, 'fraid so, right off.'

'So what does that mean? What'll it be like when it hits?'

'Catastrophic, it'll fuck us right up!'

Barry switched off the computer.

'Are you ready for another smashing piece of news Leonard?'

'Like what?'

Barry unfolded a piece of paper and read the short message out loud.

'This is a transcript of a radio message that came in this afternoon. It's from Beryl, it's short and sweet and it reads - Dear *Leonard, how is Lena? You must return soon... Adeline pregnant.'*

Leonard wanted to see the piece of paper himself.

'Does this complicate things for you at all?'

'I could use a drink, Barry.'

'Never a truer word.'

Leonard sat heavily into an armchair.

'Don't move a muscle, I've got just the thing.'

Leonard watched Barry go to his drinks cabinet and open the doors. A pale, yellow bulb flickered on and a row of bottles appeared. He took down a bottle and two glasses.

'This is a bloody good French brandy, it should do the trick.'

He handed a glass to Leonard.

Leonard swirled and took a sip. Barry stood by his collection of decoy ducks and did the same.

'I've got to get back. This business with Adeline, I don't know where I am with that.'

'Of course, I'll get you set up for the trip. Leave it to me.'

Barry slapped Leonard on the shoulder and topped up his glass.

'Now, now Leonard, keep it in perspective, lad. Don't lose your focus, deal with the problem and move on.'

'How do you deal with the stress of all this?'

'I have my feet on the ground, I have my philosophy.'

'Are you a religious man?'

'Heaven forbid.'

Barry smiled then crossed the room to his bookcase, where he placed his finger against the spine of a paperback. He tipped it off the shelf, then returned and looked for his page. He cleared his throat.

'I'll give you the reference because of course I don't wish to claim this pearl of wisdom as my own. It's a note from a chapter headed: "The Structure and Dynamics of the Psyche" by C.G.Jung. Page one hundred and thirty. He's talking about belief, life after death and all that gumbo. Here it is, he says:

'"At this point, just when it might be expected, I do not want suddenly to pull a belief out of my pocket and invite my reader to do what nobody can do-that is, believe something. I must confess that I myself could never do it either."* [3]

The only car still running was the one they'd shot to bits on the road the other night. It was a solid old Saab with a whistling turbo. Although it had been through the final scene in 'Bonny and Clyde' and was bullet-riddled, it had half a tank of fuel left and was still running well enough.

3 C G Jung: 'The Structure and Dynamics of the Psyche'

There wasn't much to load up, just some food and water for the journey. Leonard took some directions from Paul, and Danny handed him a shotgun and a box of cartridges. His advice was sombre enough, 'Shoot first, ask the questions later.' Paul pared that down even further to, 'Just shoot, don't bother about any bloody questions. And try not to get lost, just follow those routes and avoid the towns on the way. Keep your speed up and don't deviate from your sole purpose. What I mean is don't get sentimental about hitch-hikers or nothing.'

Leonard had a good look over the car; he'd popped the bonnet and crawled underneath. The oil and coolant levels were low but it would probably make the journey.

Barry rolled up with a more detailed map of the area and handed it over.

'Tell me, Leonard, and do be honest. Why won't you take your chances here and stay with us?'

'That's very kind of you, Barry, but…'

'Cut the crap now, and tell me.'

'It's nothing to do with you.'

'You don't think the shelter is going to work, do you?'

Leonard stored the map in the glove compartment.

'The shelter might, but also might not hold up to impact stress. Who knows how the shock waves will travel? There are a lot of unknown factors.'

Barry faced Leonard, he wasn't afraid of eye contact.

'Fifty-fifty?'

'You mustn't say anything to the others, Leonard.'

'Of course not, but look, you do have a very good chance here, that's better than most people.'

'Well, what's the alternative? If we didn't have the shelter, what then? We'd be at our wits-end wouldn't we, resigned to wandering the country like everybody else, on a hiding to nowhere, searching out some elephant's graveyard to curl up and die!'

'I've got a stomach ache!'

Leonard looked into the back seat and Lena was folded up into a ball.

'Don't worry, Lena, it'll ease off when we get moving.'

She sat up and rested her arms on the front seats, her head lolling through the middle.

Barry kissed her on the forehead and turned to have a last, quiet word with Leonard.

'It'll be chaos out there with the impact so close. Please be careful.'

Leonard nodded and shook Barry's hand. He started the car and waved to the small crowd gathered on the drive.

'Why don't we stay with them?'

'We've got to get back.'

'It's all your fault.'

Leonard looked at her in the rear view mirror.

'What do you mean?'

'Adeline is going to have a baby, isn't she?'

'That's enough chit-chat for now, get some rest.'

CHAPTER TWENTY-TWO

It was the first Friday night in five years that the place had been empty. Tony and Adeline sat at the bar, contemplating three newly invented cocktails. Tony went from glass to glass sampling each, trying to decide which one would be the 'Ice Moon'. Tony clapped his hands together.

'Tell me what you think, then.'

'I told you. The first is too sharp, you've got gin, bitters and lime juice. It made the glands under my ears hurt. The second one, Bourbon, apricot juice, tonic water and Vodka, well it's just nondescript. I like number three, it's the right colour, has the right amount of alcohol and the right punch.'

'Alright then, number three it is.'

Tony licked the end of a piece of chalk and scribbled the winner up on the bar slate:

'Ice Moon Cocktail': Take a tall, half-pint flute, add a double measure of white rum, a tablespoon of pomegranate nectar, one teaspoon of maple syrup: top-up with equal parts papaya juice and single cream and then shake. Decorate with one, just toasted, marshmallow.

There was a knock at the door so Adeline jumped down from her stool. She hesitated before opening and shouted out.

'Who is it?'

'Postman, I need a signature.'

She unlocked and opened but it wasn't post, it was Ian Marble and he didn't quite look himself.

'What do you want?'

'What you got?'

'It's a bar remember, what d'you think we've got?'

'Beer and a chat then?'

He pushed her out of the way and staggered across the room. He knocked a couple of chairs over and propped himself up against the bar.

'Service!'

'We are closed, Ian. Now sod off!'

'And it's so very nice to see you too, Tony.'

Ian banged his fists on the bar and hollered.

'Service!'

Tony ducked round the back of the bar.

'What'll it be, then?'

'The usual.'

Tony pulled Ian a pint.

'Have one yourself.'

'No, thank you.'

Ian raised his voice all the way up to a scream.

'Have a sodding drink!'

'I said no, thank you.'

'Sod you then!'

Ian made a great show of slapping a piece of paper down onto the counter.

'There, what do you think of that, then?'

Adeline picked it up and started to read. It was a C.O.D for a dance; she was in debt and Ian was collecting. It was her signature and she remembered that a few months back she'd given these out all over town to pay for this and that.

'Where'd you get that?'

'I've had it for weeks, been saving it up for a rainy day just like today.'

Ian reached up to the radio and switched on. The music was that smooching, slow stuff which allowed close contact. Ian clapped his hands together and shuffled across the bar. He grabbed her waist and slapped her flank like he was testing horseflesh.

'Let's dance, then!'

Tony came out from behind the bar but Ian had thought of that.

'Stay where you are, Tony, there'll be murders here if you don't!'

He got hold of her so that her cheek met his. He was clammy and cold, and he was clowning it up, acting the hip-thrusting jerk. He dragged her through the bar knocking back chairs and tables with his flailing legs. He had no idea what kind of dance to do, he just grabbed her neck and kept turning and turning. Adeline felt ill, sick in her stomach. He kept on spinning her around and she caught glimpses of her face in the mirrors behind the bar. It was a face that showed what all women think of men like this. It was a sort of infinitely patient disgust.

He looked terrible up this close; his skin was grey and swollen, broken open at the corners of his mouth. He was sweating and shivering at the same time.

'Let go of me, Ian, you smell terrible.'

'Of course I do, I've been sleeping in the cowshed. I'm obliged to do the milking these days, what with Reggie throwing in the towel.'

'What?'

Tony had made his way across the bar in Ian's blind spot. He was carrying a fire extinguisher up above his head, but just as he made to bring it down on the back of Ian's neck, Ian turned and threw a huge punch into Tony's face. Adeline screamed as Tony fell, the extinguisher bounced on its nose and began to spit a narrow jet of foam.

Ian grabbed Adeline again and resumed the twirling.

She thought she might at least try to roll him down onto the ground and run for the door. He looked weak enough but he was also as mad as hell and madmen always held something in reserve.

CHAPTER TWENTY-THREE

They'd driven all day and it was hot, too hot to keep the windows up so they were rolled right down, letting the wind blow through.

They were driving fast, heading north-east, but they were both uncomfortable. They'd used up their water supply and they were hot and bothered, dehydrated.

Half recognising the landmarks as they drove towards the city made them both nervous. Lena managed to find a radio station still transmitting, but it was a low-grade signal that faded in and out of the long wave. Leonard suffered the hissing noise for half an hour before he switched the thing off.

They were back on better roads with hardly any traffic; straight, tree-lined roads with badges of reflective red glass and warning stripes painted around the bark. Leonard was getting tired; the sun flickering through the trees was hard on the eyes. He tried to stay sharp, hitting a tree at speed would be like hitting a brick wall.

They drove into a small village and slowed to take a roundabout. Lena pointed.

'Look!'

Leonard went round again and took the exit, which opened out into a pedestrian square with tables and chairs laid out in the centre.

The main road passed down one side of the square and then onto a cobbled, central area. A good border of broad-leafed trees lined the streets and shaded the café tables. There was a circular fountain with tumbling water in the centre, which moistened and cooled the air. Leonard parked the car and they walked across the square and sat down at one of the tables. It looked like the kind of café where nineteenth century artists were supposed to have wasted time. Viennoise and café crème were on the menu along with fine, almond-filled pastries. Now things were different, the decadence was morbid and there was a heightened sense of mass anticipation in the air.

They expected a waiter to dawdle over to them, but nothing happened. They waited fifteen minutes before Leonard ran out of patience and went to get some service. Inside, five or six people sat at one long table, smoking, playing cards and not saying much. There was music playing, choral stuff, a requiem mass or something from Gounod. Leonard realised that these were the waiters. One was sobbing, lying on his folded arms, with one of the others giving him support. Leonard found himself thinking, 'Who waits on the waiters? Who brings them what they want?'

He backed out of the café, waved across to Lena and pulled an empty bottle out of a stacked-up beer crate. They wandered over to the fountain and filled it. Leonard splashed his face and the back of his neck. Lena did the same.

At night the motorway was treacherous, Leonard had to use his headlights to see where he was going, but that meant that the car was visible from a long way off. See, or be seen, which was the safest?

Lena was lying fast asleep, across the back seat, wrapped up in a sleeping bag.

Every so often they passed a harmless, abandoned car, but up ahead there was something more difficult to negotiate: a checkpoint. Leonard switched the headlights off, slowed and pulled in behind a burned-out camper van. He knew that if anyone had been watching, they would be able to figure out what he'd done, but what else could he do?

There was a rustle of nylon as Lena sat up, then the loud unzipping of the sleeping bag.

'What's going on?'

'I'm just being cautious. Looks like some sort of checkpoint up ahead.'

'Where are we?'

'About fifteen miles from the border, I think.'

'Should we turn back?'

'I don't know, I don't think so.'

Leonard stepped out of the car and looked into the darkness each side of the motorway. Not a clue, no lights, no slip-lane leading to a B-road. That's the trouble with motorways, once you're committed, you're a sitting duck.

'What's that?'

'What?'

'It's coming from over there.'

Leonard looked up at where she was pointing. The sky was black but there was something. An engine was disturbing the air, the vibration producing the tell-tale drone of an approaching helicopter.

'Come on, Lena, we've got to move away from the car.'

Leonard picked up the shotgun and led the way down the banked side of the motorway. He climbed over a low fence and lifted the wires so Lena could pass underneath, then they started to run across early crops, the thin blades of maize plants.

The sound was closer, it tickled Lena's eardrums but it scared her too. She couldn't really keep up with Leonard and a gap was opening between them. She could just make out his light trousers, bending and twisting forward as he ran.

The sound of the rotor blades was getting louder. Leonard could almost count the revolutions, and above that sound was the high-pitched whistle of the engine. Small orange lights blinking underneath the aircraft showed that it was crabbing sideways in the crosswind. They couldn't out-run a helicopter; their only hope was to find somewhere to hide.

'Lena?'

She wasn't with him anymore, it was too dark and then a downdraft whipped around his body. A blinding white light hit the crown of his head and threw a short shadow. He stopped running and watched the thing land. It was an old, coastguard sea-king. A pug-nosed machine painted high-visibility yellow and stuck all over with identifying labels.

Leonard dropped the shotgun because he realised that he was standing in the centre of a square with an armed soldier at each corner. They pointed assault rifles at his body, so he lifted his hands up above his head.

The soldiers came in from the corners and one of them held up a piece of equipment Leonard had seen before. It was the scanner which he'd heard them call the 'Murcator'. The soldier carried out the same procedure he'd seen at the vessel site. He waved the 'Murcator' over Leonard's jaw until it picked up the microchip.

'OK, he's tagged.'

The squad relaxed and led him back towards the helicopter. One of the aircrew gave him a lift up through a loading door. There was too much noise to ask what was going on or where was Lena. But to his great relief, as soon as he climbed in, there she was, quite happily strapped into her seat with a criss-cross harness. Leonard sat beside her.

The winch-man exchanged hand signals with the soldiers, it looked like they were going to stay on the ground and sweep the area.

Then the winch-man turned to Leonard and gave him an OK signal.

Leonard wouldn't confirm that he was OK. He shook his head and shouted out.

'I can't go yet. I've got to get back to the city. I've got unfinished business!'

The rotor noise picked up and Leonard's stomach lurched as the helicopter lifted off the ground and tipped forward. It picked up speed and stayed low, but it didn't take a straight line either; instead they weaved through the air, to the left and right of their heading.

The winch-man handed Leonard a headset and as soon as he was connected, he started to explain.

'Good evening, sir. As regards your unfinished business, that's a negative. There's no more "business" to attend to, sir; everything has been cancelled. My job's to deliver you come-what-may. Dead or alive, as it were.'

Leonard gave him a reluctant nod and the winch-man went on with his brief.

'So, welcome aboard. We are going to transport you to the survival site, for familiarisation with escape pod procedures. We've been ordered to pick up tagged individuals from all over because it's getting pretty cut-throat down there. We're having to stay low because the bastards on the ground are letting off surface-to-air missiles. God knows how they got hold of them but they are disrupting our routes. Just sit back and take it easy, stay strapped in at all times. The flight takes about an hour and a half, OK!'

Leonard nodded soberly.

'OK, I understand.'

'If we have to take evasive action, just sit tight and listen for instructions.'

Leonard gave him a 'thumbs-up' and the winch-man turned and sat with his legs hanging out into the night.

Lena looked concerned; she was quiet and withdrawn in her corner. Every so often she put her hands over her ears to cut the noise.

Leonard bent down to her and shouted.

'Are you OK?'

She shrugged her shoulders; she knew the problem and she shouted back.

'How are we going to get back into the city?'

Leonard couldn't say; he leaned forward in his harness and looked out of the open cargo door. A black night, a few stars were visible and about half a moon. Without warning the helicopter lurched violently to the left. Leonard's harness bit into his neck and a brilliant white flash tore down the right-hand side of the aircraft. They levelled out and the winch-man's voice came through loud and clear.

'Alright then, as you can see we have a problem. Sit tight, I am waiting to be advised.'

The helicopter came out of its forward lean and tipped back, the rotor noise dropping to a lower note as they lost speed.

Leonard unlocked his harness so he could see out. The winch-man turned and waved at him to sit back down.

'Stay where you are, we're close to some electricity pylons. We can't go higher, the surface-to-air radar will pick us up again.'

The winch-man went forward through a door that led to the cockpit.

Leonard looked out into the night; he turned to Lena and shouted in her ear.

'Look, Lena, you've got to help me. I have to get down to the ground. You'll have to stay here but you'll be OK, these people will take care of you, believe me.'

Lena looked doubly scared now, her mouth tightened and she was ready to cry.

Leonard pointed at the winch.

'See this machine?'

Lena nodded.

'It's the winch.'

Leonard stepped over to the unit, leaned out of the open door and tried to get his bearings. The moonlight picked out the web of electricity cables and pylons ahead. He waved at Lena to come over, then detached a steel rod from the rack beside him. He closed the door that separated the loading bay from the cockpit, then rammed the rod down into the cockpit handle, which jammed it shut.

Lena was crying but not sobbing, her tears ran freely. She put her hands around Leonard's waist and hung on. Leonard clipped himself to the winch cable, then hooked Lena's harness to a safety line.

'Please, Lena, I've got to get down and use the pistol. We'll meet up again at the vessel!'

'But wait, Leonard, I should go with you.'

'No, now listen to me. When you get to the site, look for a woman called Vicky, tell her who you are and she'll look after you.'

There was no reply from Lena but he knew that she'd taken it all in.

Leonard watched the steel rod bend as the winch-man tried to bash the door open. He grabbed the winch control that was on a long, curly lead like a telephone cable. He switched on and ran some cable out. A set of illuminated figures started to give a reading.

'Look, Lena, this is the cable payout indicator. We're going slow now so I'll be alright. You've got to lower me down, stop it when I get to the ground, then you have to remember to wind the cable up by pressing this button.'

Leonard took hold of her shoulders and kissed her cheeks.

'Don't fret, Lena, well see each other again soon.'

He stepped out of the helicopter and dangled in mid-air, then he started to spin slowly, anti-clockwise.

He smiled at her and she hit the button. It was OK to begin with, he was dropping slowly without too much movement, but as the cable lengthened, the pendulum effect kicked in and the swing became disorientating.

Lena looked down as he descended; he was twisting and bicycling in the air, trying to keep himself facing forward so he could see what was coming. The countryside was open enough for a stunt like this but the electricity pylons were getting closer. The winch-man was hitting the door hard now and the frame edge was opening up. The cable indicator was saying twenty-five metres but it suddenly went dead.

The pilot had cut the power to the winch and the winch-man was shouting at Lena through the gap in the door.

'Open the fucking door! Now! If you don't, we'll drop your mate onto the wires and fry him to a crisp!'

She didn't know what to do. The helicopter kept moving forward, heading straight for the pylons.

Leonard was spinning like a top, he felt sick but what was worrying him the most, was that every time he faced forward, the power lines were closer. They were going to try his nerve, that was clear. They wouldn't set the aircraft down on the ground because then he would be able to make a run for it. They were obviously very pissed off and now he was in a very difficult situation.

The gap in the door had opened up enough for the barrel of a gun to be poked through and pointed at Lena. This was an empty enough threat though, because she'd already reckoned that the winch-man didn't have it in him. And all she had to do was move to the left or right and he lost his aim anyway. He'd tried being angry with her, now he was reasoning.

'Look, love, what's all this about? We're taking you to the survival induction, we're saving your lives. For God's sake, what's going on? Come on, open the door and we'll sort it all out!'

The pilot was obviously a bit more of a bastard because the helicopter slowed as they reached the power lines. It climbed slightly and hovered so that Leonard was left dangling above a cats-cradle of high-tension cables, with 200,000 volts flowing through the national grid.

Leonard had to admit that up would be preferable to down. He hoped that Lena would weigh this all up and press the right button; he'd be no good to anyone if he was killed.

The winch-man had given up on the gun, he'd bent the metal back enough to get his hand through and he was reaching out for the obstruction. In the few seconds before he knocked the steel rod aside, Lena figured it out. She looked out at the black landscape, and down at Leonard hanging above the power cables. Then she looked back at the winch arm; there was a red box with 'Warning' stamped on it. She pulled a pin out so she could open the cover and underneath there was a yellow handle. The winch-man pushed the door open as she pulled on the handle labelled 'cable release'.

Leonard dropped and hit the cables, his body braced across three lines, but there was no spark, no flashing white extermination. Only his own weight ripping at his shoulders, pulling them out of their sockets as he tried to hang on. He swung his legs up and locked his ankles together above the cable. Then he passed the electrical wire hand over hand until he reached the nearest pylon. The released winch cable was wrapped up in the power lines, looped around them like a piece of spaghetti. There wasn't any power, of course there wasn't power, there hadn't been for days - clever, clever Lena.

He shinned his way along the power line until he reached the nearest pylon, picked his way between closely meshed steel, glass discs and ceramic buffers, then he clambered onto a metal platform and stood upright.

The helicopter had flown on and only a faint and vanishing drone remained.

CHAPTER TWENTY-FOUR

Leonard bent down to a man's body. It was just anybody, lying up against a low wall, trapped underneath a heavy motorbike. Another violent death, the face fixed into an expression of ironic surprise and inevitability. The biggest shock of all, though, was the mutilation of the man's face. The top lip was missing, leaving bared teeth and bloodied gums. Obviously it had been brutally cut away by an assailant who knew exactly what to look for.

The motorbike was a low-slung American make with tasselled, leather bags fitted all over it. Leonard needed some transport, so he hauled it up and straddled it. He checked for damage then he kicked it into life. He revved the engine, then dropped it into first and opened the throttle. He'd forgotten to lift the foot-stand so it scraped along the tarmac, sparking like the last match in the box.

He drove with the lights out, in case he was shot at.

He drove into the west of the city. This was familiar ground but things had changed, it was like a war zone. All the streetlights had been exploded and there were just a few candle flames, in one or two windows. Leonard's stomach churned as sirens came and went.

A few people staggered around the streets, carrying guns or swinging knives. Leonard kept to the back-routes so he could avoid human contact. He moved quickly in fits and starts, accelerating from corner to corner.

He made his way to the Spanish district, where he parked up and watched Tony's Bar for any signs of trouble. He waited twenty minutes before crossing the street. When he reached the window he lifted himself up on tiptoe. His calves shook with cramp but he managed to see in. Tony was sitting at one of the tables; he seemed to be in a solitary reverie. He was bent over a cocktail glass, smoking a cigarette. He was studying his own hands, as if he were checking for surface cracks, signs of deterioration.

Leonard pushed on the door gently and stepped inside. He stopped and waited, not wanting to take another step, not until the shotgun had been lowered.

Tony's voice came after a wheezing cough. It was a lower and thinner version of his old voice, minus the usual undertones of anger and malice. 'Leonard?'

Leonard noted Tony's busted nose, the broken glass and the ankle deep foam that had obviously bled out of the fire extinguisher that was lying on the floor.

Tony lowered the shotgun, settled both his elbows back on the table and rested his jaw against his hands.

'What happened, Tony?'

'We had a visit from Ian Marble. The man has lost his mind.'

'What?'

Tony's eyebrows lifted and he exhaled through his nose. He twisted a finger into his ear and scratched his nose.

'Gone to the dogs, haven't we! There's no hope left. The whole city has gone crazy, place is full of drunks, spun out soldiers and mercenaries. Know the first thing they did?'

'No?'

'They shot the police, all of them. So now they drive around in the old patrol cars. Gangs of bloody SS marines, shooting the place up! Have you got a weapon?'

'No.'

'Well I can't give you the shotgun, I need it, but you'd better get hold of a firearm as soon as possible! I just hope everything's gonna be alright.'

Leonard sat down, not at Tony's table but the next one.

'Forget about hope, Tony, hope doesn't have any effect on what happens!'

'Well why not? Mostly I only really hope for what's best! So why the fuck not!'

Tony finished his cocktail.

'D'you want one of these?'

'What is it?'

'It's new, I've dubbed it the "Ice Moon".'

'Go on, then.'

Tony crossed the room slowly, shakily. He had to think about his balance, but he made it to the bar and got some support there. He looked up at Leonard and spoke in a quiet and measured voice.

'Well, it seems congratulations are in order, aren't they, dad!'

'What?'

'Adeline's pregnant!'

'Yes, I know.'

Tony turned back to the bar and picked up a carton of cream.

'Where is she, Tony?'

'She's sort of unavailable at the moment.'

'Is she upstairs?'

Tony sniggered.

'Oh, if only, eh? No, you see Leonard, she's been taken hostage!'

He held out the filled glass and Leonard took it.

'What do you mean?'

'Well Ian's got her, hasn't he? He's a clinically insane, fucking head-case. And that's why it's good to see you!'

'Why's that?'

'You're the ransom, see? He knows you'll come looking for him. He knows you're in love with Adeline!'

'I'm not in love with Adeline.'

'Save it, Leonard, I'm not a complete idiot.'

'And I'm not an absolute bastard, either. Come here, Tony.'

Leonard took the tagging pistol out of his pocket. He pushed Tony up against the wall and made an attempt at tagging his lip. Tony ducked out under Leonard's arm.

'What are you doing, Tony? In case you didn't know it, I was about to tag you for inclusion on the survival programme. You'll be safe, you'll survive.'

'I don't want your bloody charity. I've got my own plans.'

'What do you mean? You'll die in the first hours of the impact like eighty five percent of the world's population. Let me do this for you.'

'Fuck off. Is that clear enough for you?'

'Alright, I hear you.'

Leonard sucked up the last of the foaming cocktail and stood the glass on the bar.

'So where is she, Tony?'

'Don't know. You find Ian, you'll find Adeline!'

Leonard didn't hang around; he went to the back door. He pressed down on the exit release bar and stood outside in the alley. He had to cover his nose with his sleeve because the place was stacked high with rotting, uncollected rubbish.

Leonard couldn't get used to the way the bike handled. Fine rain had wet the streets down so the brakes took a while to check his speed. The cornering was sluggish too and maybe the tyre pressures were low because the ride was spongy.

He drove up to One Tree Hill and propped the bike on its stand. Ian's apartment was in darkness but then again so was the whole row of houses. The street door was open, though, so Leonard went on through. He flicked on a torch and found his way up the stairs. He stood in front of the door for ages, listening and trying to figure out what to do. Ian always used a security chain, so kicking the thing off its hinges would not be easy. He raised his fist and banged on the glossy paintwork. He waited, and nothing happened. He knocked again with the soft part of his fist and he realised that the door wasn't locked.

Leonard moved slowly up the hall and searched through the whole flat until he was sure that it was empty. As soon as his adrenalin level had dropped, he felt exhausted and starving hungry. He hadn't eaten properly for days and his stomach was churning.

He shone the torchlight into Ian's kitchen cupboards, but he only found things to eat out of or with, until he checked the back of a waist-high unit. He grinned and pulled out a tin of peeled, plum tomatoes. There was another welcome sight when he pulled open the cutlery drawer and found the can opener lying there, just where it should be.

He spooned the tomatoes from the can; they tasted sweet and sharp, but were finished too soon. The only other food was a jar of dried spaghetti, the twist shapes. There was no way of cooking them but he tipped the jar into his pocket anyway, he could probably crunch or suck on them, one at a time, maybe the starch would keep him going.

He went and had a piss in the bathroom, rested the torch on top of the cistern and in its light, he caught several sights of himself in the mirrored walls. That was too much 'Leonard' by far, looking pretty shagged out too, dirty and drawn and most of all, desperate.

He twisted the shower tap and it worked. Tepid water and not much pressure but Leonard stripped off and stood under it. He managed to scrape some dried soap out of a dish attached to the wall, and he scrubbed himself down, head to toe. He found a couple of neatly folded towels in a bathroom cabinet and he rubbed himself down. His skin tingled, he felt a little newer.

He wandered back into the lounge and panned the torch beam around the room. On the table next to the window, a vase of dead flowers and lying on the floor, a blow-up mattress. Maybe Ian's house was not the obvious choice for a safe house, but Leonard had to sleep. It didn't look as if anyone had lived in the place for a couple of weeks and he just needed to put his head down.

He woke very early because he was so bloody uncomfortable, his face and all down his left side was stiff and numb. He went into the bedroom and opened a wardrobe, found some trousers and unpacked one of Ian's stock of striped shirts. He dressed and had a final look around.

On the way out, he caught sight of a milk churn standing in the hallway behind the door. He lifted the lid and choked on the smell.

He locked the place and went down to the motorbike; the weather was good and he was clean and less hungry than he had been. His new clothes lifted his spirits. He kick-started the bike and stuffed a couple of the pasta twists into his mouth, then lifted the stand and pulled away downhill.

The plan was to get to the Mirabelle and see if anybody knew anything. The old route was sprinkled with wrecked cars and the only people he saw were a couple of young children running in and out of the empty shops, back and forth through broken, plate-glass windows.

Leonard got to a T-junction and turned left. As he did, though, he saw a police car with its doors open and two soldiers hacking away at a boarded-up doorway. They turned and watched him pass, but then they went back to smashing the door in.

All along the approach road to the Mirabelle, people were sat out on pavements, with bits and pieces scattered across old blankets in front of them. They were trying to sell the last of their worldly goods, and if no one was buying, they would offer themselves. They would sell anything they could, in exchange for an object of immediate value, for food or a car ride, for drugs or just one night's protection.

Leonard tried to look as fucked as everyone else, but he felt a bit self-conscious arriving on the bike with a clean face and a new shirt. He jumped up the steps and walked into the reception of the hotel. Not much had changed, except that a few of the chairs were upside down and had been left that way. Harry was manning his post at the reception desk and he was looking straight at Leonard.

'Bloody hell, Leonard, I was pretty sure I'd never see you again.'

'Yeah, well, here I am.'

'Well, come on in, get yourself over here and tell me what's been going on!'

Leonard smiled.

'Maybe I could cut a long story and say that I've been on the run.'

'Well, I'll tell you what, you should have just kept on running! You're a marked man, I'm always being lifted up by the scruff of the neck and asked about you.'

'What's happened to your dancing tits, Harry, and your headphones?'

Harry looked pissed off.

'That's all over, no power. Like most things now, cancelled 'til further notice! I don't get post anymore, not even a bloody take-away menu comes through the letterbox!'

Leonard stood on the other side of the bar and rested his elbows. Harry was a nice guy, he hadn't lost his head or got it shot off, and he was still here minding his own and everybody else's business.

'I'm going downstairs, Harry, I've got to see Beryl, OK?'

'Well, ah I wouldn't if I were you, Leonard, see there's…'

'I'll see you in a minute, Harry.'

He went through and down the stairs. The door into the boiler room was closed but the glass was still broken so he reached through and turned the handle. It was dead quiet inside and smelled stale. Leonard took a few steps and walked round the printing press.

'Stop right there, shit-face.'

Leonard stopped. He looked across at the bed and came face to face with the Warden.

'What are you doing here, Gopaul?'

'Oh no, you first.'

Warden had never looked good, but he'd never looked this bad. His skin was grey, his bleached hair matted to his skull and the skull itself was visible through his colourless skin. Leonard took another couple of steps towards the bed.

'That's it, that's far enough. I have a gun, you see!'

Something underneath the bed-sheet was being raised up to a sharp point; it looked exactly like a gun. But then again, it also looked exactly the way a skinny, pointed finger does, when it's jabbed up through cotton.

Leonard was fed up with this kind of complication. He jumped forward and whipped the sheet off. But there was a gun, and it was aimed at Leonard's groin. Warden was fighting with the thing, but he couldn't quite muscle up the required trigger pressure, not even with two of his skinny digits looped through the guard.

'You bastard, Gopaul, I know you killed my friend!'

'What?'

'You killed Raymond!'

'I've killed no one! I had an accident with a South African soldier in the north a few weeks back. But who's Raymond?'

'He was one of my runners. I had him follow you for a couple of weeks.'

'Yeah, I remember, but I didn't kill him.'

'You didn't?'

'No.'

Warden gave up on the gun. He reached out for a bottle of water and took a sip.

'I need to find Beryl.'

'Well, that's interesting because they took her off in a bloody helicopter a couple of days ago. Dragged her kicking and screaming out of here. She was taking pretty good care of me up until then, nursed me on chicken soup. Now Harry has to sort me out.'

'She was air lifted!'

'Well, she's all right now, isn't she? Taxi to the construction site, red-carpet treatment. That your work, was it? The tagging?'

'Yeah.'

'Who did it then?'

'I don't follow.'

'Who killed Raymond?'

'I can't say for sure but at a guess I'd say it was someone we both know. I'd say it was Ian Marble!'

'What, namby pamby Ian?'

Leonard nodded. Warden got himself up on his elbows, his sunken eyes wandered around the room. He was still only half conscious and his lips were trembling.

'Our fucking viral nature, at last exposed, eh?'

'Our what?'

'Have you seen the way bacilli spread across a petri dish?'

'I don't understand?'

'Have you?'

'Well no, not lately.'

'...how it eats itself into a corner, eats itself right out of existence. Well that's our good selves, isn't it? Scavenging bastards all of us, not a noble deed left in any one of us, eh?'

Warden dropped back, as weightless as a charcoal drawing. He was losing his mind, rambling on, under the morphine jabs.

'Listen boy, way I see it, whole thing, and everything, history and all. Well...'

'Well what?'

'We... It's just one sodding step forward, two sodding steps back, that's the way of the world - self destruct, wholesale violence, that's the currency.'

He laughed and looked away. Leonard pulled out the tagging pistol.

'Listen, Warden, look at me!'

Leonard took hold of the Warden's jaw and turned his face back so he could make eye contact.

'How many rounds left in this thing?'

'Bloody cheek, you're the shit who stole it, now you want the manual! Bollocks to you!'

'Just tell me, how many shots are left?'

'Do the sums yourself. There were rumoured to be ten thousand escape pods, a thousand allocated to each area. We had ten pistols, one hundred silicon tags in each. All very decimal, eh?'

'OK, but how many left in this one?'

'Fuck knows. Your guess is as good as mine. Who gives a shit?'

Leonard turned and started to walk away.

'Oi, Gopaul, manners maketh the man, bid me farewell!'

Leonard waved at Warden but without looking back.

'Wait, listen you can do something for me, you can make sure that Ian Marble doesn't get anywhere near the survival programme!'

Leonard walked back to Warden and stood at his bedside.

'I think I might be able to arrange that.'

'Good lad.'

Leonard turned and walked out of the boiler room. Warden called out after him.

'Anybody that doesn't want to see the score, turn away now!'

Leonard made it back up to reception. He jumped over the desk, his trousers skidding easily across the polished counter. Harry had his nose in a book and he was drinking black tea. He looked surprised to see Leonard in the office, it was staff only this side of the desk. Leonard shot him in the mouth and Harry shouted, well, yelped.

'Fuck! Is that what I think it is?'

Leonard nodded and backed out of the office.

The streets were brightly lit, shadows deeply cast, the city set on high contrast. There was a yellow glow in the sky and although it was seven o'clock in the evening and the sun was low, it was shining harshly. The eastern sky was dark and against this backdrop, the high rise buildings stood out in stark relief. Rain began to pour from a ridge of cumulus clouds; it fell onto the rooftops and worked its way down to the streets. Leonard felt the first drops hit his face. He was driving along the kerb but his heart wasn't really in it, he was tired and hungry and unsure of his next move.

The shower stopped after wetting down the streets. As he drove down Mundania Street, he passed into shadow. The shop windows, if they weren't kicked in, showed his own reflection, his flopping head and hell's angel posture.

The road was shining oil-black and the sun was dawdling in the bright kerbside puddles, picking out the yellow kerb markings. He had that eye corner feeling, that cash machine sensation of heightened visual awareness. He'd seen a white van turn onto the street and he was pretty sure that he'd seen rifles sticking out the windows and they were being waved indiscriminately. He didn't think about trying to outrun the van, he just dropped the bike and stepped through one of the smashed up shop windows and found cover. He jumped down onto a flight of stairs and took the steps three at a time. He lost his footing and tumbled through a thin, make-shift door into a dark basement. Someone grabbed hold of him by the neck and squeezed.

'No noise!'

Leonard tried to speak.

'Shut up!'

Leonard stayed where he was, sitting down on the ground, a few moments of even pressure on his neck passed, then the tension eased off.

'Who the fuck are you, man? This is our dive!'

'My name's Leonard.'

Leonard looked around the candle lit room and picked out five or six figures bent close around a table. It was a crack-house, with fluids bubbling in spoons and hypodermics circulating. A couple of thin, black dogs sniffed and licked at Leonard's pockets. One bare female arm was being tattooed very badly with a compass needle and biro ink.

'Hey, I know you, you picked me up when I was hitching a ride one time. He's OK, Ned man, he did me a favour one time, let him be.'

Leonard couldn't remember.

'Like I said, I owe you, I even gave you a credit note for one free trip.'

Leonard saw that the syringe was loaded and circulating, but it didn't go past him like he expected because this guy that owed him a favour had jabbed the needle hard and he was emptying it into Leonard's thigh.

'This'll open up your heart, man.'

Bad to worse, this whole thing now, it was going from bad to even worse.

Gradually at first it came, and then for a while he had this weird point of view, like he was hovering out in space, still and silent with an even drape of stars all around. He felt good though, really good, like he could hang there forever not knowing anything at all and just smiling freely. But then there was this tipping forward feeling and a sensation of gathering speed, tremendous speed, until one star centred and became the target. He closed on the planet at what he knew to be the speed of light, until it grew larger and larger. The ocean blue and the cyclonic white of an atmosphere spread out beneath his free fall, the land masses expanded and he just kept on accelerating.

Beneath him now, though, were millions of tiny maggot-like worms which, as he got closer, grew into huge snakelike dragons with wide open mouths. One mouth so large it swallowed him whole and put an end to his descent.

In the back of the snake was an escalator which rolled him out onto a dead planet. A half submerged landscape under a black sky. Flooded mud-flats and a still, quiet, undulating plain, dotted with fire. He felt a light wind in his back; it blew across the road that led up and over a hill. He fell into a march and started to climb. When he made it to the top, he left the barren lands behind him. Instead, the sky lifted and he was walking a bright corniche bordered with pine trees. He cut through an olive grove and stumbled across the fertile soil; he was walking in between the mountains and the sea, and up ahead he knew there would be a house with fruit trees in the garden. And there would be a welcome from a woman and child he had learned to love.

There were 'pinking' sounds in his head, fluid underwater 'chinks' like glass beakers being tapped with a hammer.

They'd moved the body from the scene, his body, probably dumped him down here unceremoniously because his lip was cut and his tooth was loose. He was lying out in the open, on the pavement. He looked dead enough and that was some kind of camouflage. He picked himself up and tried to remember where he'd left the bike.

He had this idea that he should head out to the farm and see how Reggie and Dave were doing. He didn't want to spend another night in town and he needed to get off the street and find shelter.

Ian, though, where was the bastard? Leonard would have to track him down pretty soon, within the next few days in fact, because that's all there were, just a few more days. Leonard remembered the milk-churn he'd seen back in Ian's apartment, the connection between Marble and the farm set an alarm bell off in the back of his head.

On the way back to the bike he passed more bodies lying in the street with their mouths lacerated, more signs that tagging was now common knowledge. Leonard wiggled his loose tooth with his tongue and decided that he'd better get the hell out of town.

He drove out along the main route to the north, he felt so exposed astride the roaring engine, it drew attention to his whereabouts. He had to use his headlamp in the failing light and another thing was that he still didn't have a firearm.

He picked up speed through the suburbs and started to climb around the coast road. He felt better with the city laid out behind, and pushed his speed up along the long, clear stretches. He hogged the middle of the road because there were woods either side and it would be easy enough for someone to jump out and knock him off. He remembered how motorbikes were usually brought down by trip wires, which were set low for the bike, or high for the riders head. The idea of taking a wire across the throat made him bend forward and lie across the petrol tank.

A long, left-handed bend opened out and Leonard wound the throttle all the way open. The engine responded, and as the revs increased, he accelerated up the incline. The road sort of brimmed out ahead and as he went over the crest, the wheels left the ground and for a moment he was flying forward at about eighty miles an hour.

He came off the accelerator and let the speed die right back as the track leading to the farm was coming up on the right. He could make out the position of the farmhouse because he could see the roofline of the barn, and the pale yellow light coming through the trees was probably the kitchen window.

There was something else, though; a dark shadow moving through the field to his right, maybe a horse or something, he couldn't tell from this side of the trees. The woods thinned out and the creature tried to keep pace with the motorbike. Leonard realised it was Reggie's bull running and shaking its head. He had the ridiculous urge to call out and tell the thing it was running at exactly twenty seven miles an hour.

The bull had to pull up and stop at the edge of the field and that made him steaming mad. Mad enough to do a fair impersonation of some kind of fiery dragon with a flailing head and a rasping, pink tongue.

Leonard turned off the track which led up to the farmhouse. If Ian was inside and if he had lost his mind, he'd better be cautious. He had to wrestle with the handlebars because the ground was soft mud, with water lying in tractor tracks. He pulled the bike onto its main stand and the sharp points of steel sunk into the soil. Leonard made his way around the back of the house and stayed low. He approached the kitchen door along a line of bushes and then he watched and waited. The chimney was smoking and there was a light on in the kitchen. The place looked peaceful enough so he crept forward to get a look in through the window.

He had a cold pain in his back and his immediate reflex was to put his hand there. He found himself gripping a shotgun barrel, and turned to see Ian's big mouth grinning wide; he was so happy to see Leonard.

'So very good to see you, Leonard, your appearance is the stuff dreams are made of. And that, if I may say so, is a very nice shirt.'

He waved Leonard forward, all the while aiming the barrels of the shotgun into his guts. Leonard was for the moment at a loss for words.

'I know what a busy man you are so it's really very considerate of you to work us into your schedule.'

'Where's Adeline?'

'I'll be doing the questions, Leonard.'

He pushed the shotgun into Leonard's guts.

'You're looking somewhat the worse for wear, dear boy.'

Leonard stayed silent.

'Cat got it, eh? Your tongue?'

He still didn't reply. He studied Ian; he looked gouty and fanatical, his eyes were both zealous and fearful. Leonard felt very uncomfortable. Even in the soft, flattering light, Ian's face was all wrong.

The two zeros of the shotgun aimed into his guts were making him sick to the stomach. He imagined the damage and his skin actually tingled with anticipation. Ian grinned.

'Don't you want to know the state of play? Where all the pieces are? Don't you want to come up with a fiendish escape plan?'

Ian laughed but Leonard stayed silent, he didn't want to give him anything to go on, no clues to how he was feeling. The voice gives it away, lets the opponent know your strength, your reserves, your resolve.

Ian was losing patience; he made the childish gesture of breathing on his nails and polishing his fingers on his chest. This was supposed to be a self-contented gesture, but it was pathetic in these circumstances and Ian saw that Leonard was making him look a bit ridiculous.

'All fucking right then, boy scout! What happens now is, I take you on a little tour and then you do exactly as I ask.'

Ian jabbed him with the shotgun and pushed him forward.

'Off we go then, nice and easy, toward the barn.'

They trudged across the wet ground and stopped outside the barn door.

'Kneel down, Leo.'

Again, Leonard did as he was told; he kneeled and put his hands behind his head. He couldn't see what Ian was up to, but he worked out that he was moving around behind his back and off to the right. There was a tinkering mechanical noise, metal or hard plastic hitting something hollow. Then a generator started, it revved then idled. Leonard inhaled the petrol fumes and a strip of light switched on and seeped out from beneath the door.

'Get up.'

Ian pushed Leonard through the door, allowing the full glory of the interior to unfold. For a few moments, Leonard was numbed by the spectacle in front of him. The scale of it forced him to reassess the man behind his back! Just who the hell was Ian Marble?

You just can't tell from appearances, because it's what people do that defines who they are. It's difficult to know who you are dealing with, until they show you what they are capable of. And what Ian had prepared for Leonard was a thorough exercise in revealing the true workings of the inner man.

Leonard moved forward a couple of steps, into the floodlight. There was a straight-backed chair on the left with Reggie sitting in it and one off to the right for Dave. Both were tied up with their heads facing forward, towards the centre-piece. At the far end of the barn, Adeline was strung up above the ground, spread-eagled in the middle of a manmade web of rope. Leonard moved towards her and as he passed the first chair, he put a reassuring hand onto Reggie's shoulders. He felt solid but there was something wrong, he didn't move, and when Leonard searched his face, he saw that Reggie was dead, his head was pitched forward and there was no life left in him at all. He spun around to where Dave was sitting and his heart sank there, too.

Ian was getting fed up; he wanted some sounds now, some noises to show an appreciation of his handiwork. He felt like shit too, his balance was fucked and the earth kept tipping up at the edges. Whenever he moved, he felt like he was walking through the duty free on a rough ferry crossing. He'd been falling over a lot, falling to the ground just like that. He ripped the plastic off a pre-packed syringe and he jabbed some adrenaline into his blood, to keep his eyes bright. It probably wouldn't help much, he was becoming immune to the stuff. He stomped over to Reggie's chair and mumbled a few words of condolence.

'Poor old Reggie, eh? Didn't see it coming, did he? Too rural hearted to work it all out, see! And Davey boy, another of life's dawdlers, I'm afraid. I gave them both something to think about, they haven't answered me yet, in fact they've both been very quiet.'

Leonard looked towards Adeline and went deaf to Ian's taunts. The thing was that Ian did not realise what he had started. Yes, the spectacle was a shock to Leonard's system, but it was also blood-boiling. As he walked toward Adeline, Leonard had that feeling of arriving before the altar. She was supported by ropes running from her arms up onto the overhead timbers. Her legs were pointed down into the bottom corners of the barn. She was wrapped in rope coils and tied back against a spiral rigging that looped through the supports, all the way out to the edge of the barn.

Adeline was beautiful, even gagged and bound; her long, horizontal eyebrows gave her a level headedness. Her face, without make-up, looked even more vulnerable and the dark circles under her eyes made her even more fragile. It was embarrassing for her, the nudity, hanging in the position, her limbs parcelled so tight that her skin bulged in between the cord.

'Rare specimen, isn't she? Nice bit of rope-work, eh? That knot there is called a Zeppelin bend. The Americans developed it in the second world war, to tie down their airships.'

Leonard turned and took a few steps back down the barn. Ian looked pretty pleased with himself.

'Is enough, enough then? What do you think?'

Ian raised the shotgun up to Leonard's chest.

'OK, so now you've seen the floorshow, you can probably guess the rest. You know what I'm after, so shall we get on with it?'

'The tagging pistol is outside.'

'Where outside?'

'On the bike, in the saddlebag.'

Ian stepped away from the door.

'Go on then, you lead the way.'

It was difficult for Leonard to leave her like that, now that he was linked to her flesh and blood. She was not separate from him anymore; the child hooked into her placenta joined him to her and when he moved away, the distance seemed to double.

As Leonard moved back into the dark, he figured that Ian's eyes would be adjusting to the low light with each step. Leonard decided he had to take his chance; he dropped to the ground and rolled away to the right. The shotgun went off twice and missed, so now Ian would have to reload. Leonard stood and ran for cover, jumped a fence and sprinted into the dark. He ran carefully, though, he didn't want to break a leg over a rusted axle or a piece of abandoned machinery. He made it to the far side of the field and looked for a way over a high stone wall. He ran along beside it, going uphill, but it was all the same height and he couldn't find a way over.

'That'll do! Stop where you are right now! Not one fucking foot further!'

Leonard stopped in his tracks and turned. He was out of breath, his chest rising and falling. Ian approached, raised the shotgun and hit Leonard hard across the side of his face.

'There now, how does that feel? Not something it was designed for, I know, but it clobbers pretty well, all the same! Now, is it so hard for you to just do as you're told? Give me the pistol.'

Leonard was down on one knee and up close to the wall, holding his hand over the cut along his jaw. Ian was standing a few metres away with the gun raised again.

'Why so sad, Leonard?'

'You know why!'

'Just do as you are told, I know you have the pistol.'

'I told you it's back at the bike.'

'I don't believe you. You have it on you.'

Leonard was not doing well, his options were running out.

'Why are you doing this, Ian? You've become a cold-blooded man, a murderer!'

'What do you mean, I've become? These are difficult times and besides, you don't know me, you don't know my history. I've always been a murderous kind of maniac! As a kid I was fantastically nasty, and the interesting thing for me was that I was always forgiven. Every single time I created havoc, I was eventually forgiven and forgiven so warm and lovingly that I carried on being the bastard. It's the way I grew up see, I love the whole vicious circle of compulsive behaviour. It's so infectious, so enjoyable, it takes all the decision-making out of one's life. As for now, of course I want a ticket for the survival programme and then there's this medical problem of mine which needs expert attention.'

Leonard laughed. He was trying to stifle it but it was welling up from deep in the gut.

'I've never heard anything so pathetic, so weakly reasoned in all my life!'

Ian moved forward and hit Leonard again, in the same place as before but this time with greater force.

'There now, no more stalling.'

Leonard was laid out on his back, a numbing throb had started up, a stabbing pain in time with his pulse.

He ripped the Velcro tag and took the pistol out of his trouser pocket. Ian settled his own knees into the mud, held the shotgun against Leonard's chest and presented his face to be tagged.

Leonard resisted placing the pistol in position.

'Look at me, Leonard. They say you must confront your killer. You must look into his or her eyes. That way you have a value, you become someone and you are more likely to hang on to your life. If you avoid my eyes, you are nobody and it will be easy for me to shoot you.'

Ian hit Leonard with the gun barrel, then took the pistol, placed it against his own top lip and snapped a tag into his flesh. He groaned and clenched his fists, then looked down as Leonard looked up. He then managed a glorious, winning smile. Leonard rolled over in disgust and found himself lying face down, at Ian's feet. He reached forward and took Ian's shoe laces in his hands.

He untied the neat bows and knotted them together with a half-hitch. He felt sure this was too cheap a trick to work but that's all he could do with his nose down in the dirt.

Ian grabbed a fistful of Leonard's hair and yanked his head round to face him. Leonard rolled away, breaking Ian's grip. He got to his feet and started to run across the field. Ian laughed and took one step forward to aim the shotgun. That was all it took. Leonard watched Ian's face as he tumbled forward and he was sure that Ian had the time to register the half-hitch, the cheapest knot in the catalogue. The butt end of the shotgun seated itself into the mud and the barrel exploded into Ian's face. He slumped to the ground and lay there, an immobile, dead weight.

Leonard crawled back to Ian. He rolled the body over and saw that his face had taken the full force of the blast. His mouth and jaw had disintegrated and so had the tag.

The knife sliced through the ropes and Adeline dropped into Leonard's arms. She was exhausted and found it difficult to wrap her stiff arms around his neck. He carried her to the farmhouse and lowered her into an armchair. It was warm, but she was shivering with exhaustion. She held on to her own legs, tucked them under her body. Leonard took the throw from the sofa and wrapped it around her. She hid her face in her hands and sat there for a while rocking gently without saying a word.

He went through to the kitchen and opened up the fridge. He leant on the door frame and studied the shelves. There was nothing much, apart from a jug of milk. He poured out a glass and went back to Adeline, touched her head lightly because she was half asleep. She looked up at Leonard and took the glass.

'I'm so hungry.'

'OK, I'll see what we've got.'

'I'll eat anything.'

He'd started to walk away then remembered. He tipped his pockets inside out; there were pieces of crumbled meringue and although they were smashed to bits Adeline smiled. He handed the pieces to her, picking out fluff and pasta twists, and she crunched them greedily. She licked the last of the sugar from her fingers and swallowed down the milk in short sips. Leonard sat down opposite her, and as she lifted her glass to drink, a bright hoop of reflected light spilled off the rim, a kind of halo which shone across the floor and lifted up around the room, like a lasso.

'I never meant to actually feel anything for you, Leonard. But my plan, well I didn't have a plan anymore, I wasn't prepared.'

She smiled and stood up.

'Where are you going, Adeline?'

'There must be a bedroom here somewhere.'

'Yes, of course, but…'

Leonard got to his feet. He tried to hold on to her but she didn't want to be touched. She held up her arms, opened her fists and twisted away. She went out through the door and started to climb the stairs. He called after her, too late and with an inappropriate sentiment.

'You mustn't let life break your heart, Adeline, no matter what!'

He was exhausted, too tired to think straight anymore, but too fired up to actually sleep. He walked through into the room Reggie kept for his radio. Reggie had been one of those 'hams', he had a boosted receiver which could pick up even the faintest signals. Leonard wound the dial all the way to the left and then started to peel slowly back to the right. He settled into the tilting, easy chair and dialled through the news squawk. He stopped on a foreign broadcast where they were counting down in Italian, one hundred and something hours. The voice was female, a woman in her sixties maybe, he wondered when she would stop for refreshments and who would take over when she did?

Her face wore that extra year or so of morning, she was puffy around the eyes and red cheeked. She rolled off the bed and tried to find the bathroom. Her movements were slow and unsure, like she was taking cues from back-stage. She stopped at the sink and lifted her eyes to the mirror. Wouldn't it be better to live without mirrors? Her lips were dry and her heart? She wondered about her heart and her own motivation. She suspected that behind all her longings she was a simple creature. She moved from seduction to seduction, looking for anyone or anything which might make her heart beat faster.

Leonard pushed his hand through the waistband and placed his flat palm against the small of her back. Adeline's heart accelerated from a standing start to a full sprint. She turned and he looked like a thief caught without his stocking, he'd stolen up on her. She'd been thrown off-balance and she was breathing heavily, trying hard to catch up with how much she needed him. Leonard planted kisses far and wide but without that dull ring of text-book technique.

He carried her back into the bedroom. She closed her eyes, she didn't need to be a spectator in this, she just wanted to feel what was happening through her skin. Maybe it was the constant melancholy in the background that made him so tender, made the shortening future fade.

A block of sunlight the shape of the window frame fell onto the rose patterned bedclothes. She loved this rose pattern and the smell of lavender which came from the chest of drawers next to the bed. Leonard had been rummaging through because the big bottom drawer was hanging open. He'd found something. He turned to her, looking very pleased with himself, holding a pipe out in front of his chest and stuffing tobacco down its neck. He lit the thing and puffed some smoke, spat some loose leaves and settled the pipe into the corner of his mouth. The bowl burned red when he sucked, it was hot in his mouth and made him feel light-headed.

Adeline watched Leonard pace the room; he looked like some badly dressed Sherlock. Simply watching him made her happy, she thought about the way the best of life happens like this, despite and even against the rotation of the world.

Leonard removed his pipe, like he'd suddenly solved it! He bent down and kissed her below the navel.

'Adeline?'

'Yes?'

'This might sound ridiculous but I am very happy about the baby.'

Adeline felt there should be an audience for this. He had offered her such an uncommon show of support, that a kind of surprise reason for being, suddenly dawned on her. She didn't want to dwell on it, though; she didn't want to water down this moment.

'I got this concession for being pregnant. I had to present myself at an office downtown but...'

'But what?'

'There was nobody there, just an empty shop-front with a pile of letters scattered across the coconut mat.'

She stopped the story there, just shut up about it, just like that. Leonard liked that, he liked that she knew when to leave a conversation, where and why and how to back out gracefully.

She sat up and crossed her arms over her breasts.

'What happened to Ian?'

'He had quite a serious accident.'

'He'd been ranting on for days about some sort of pistol. He said you had this tagging pistol.'

'Yes, I do have it. It will provide the ID tag you need to get onto the survival programme.'

At the same time as he'd explained all this he'd walked over to his coat and taken out the pistol.

'Now, just tilt your head back and open your mouth.'

'Is this going to hurt?'

'Yes.'

Leonard adjusted the firing position then pulled on the trigger. Nothing happened.

'Is that it?'

'No, that's not it. There's something wrong.'

He checked the pistol, lined it up again and fired a second time.

'Shit!'

'What is it?'

'It's empty!'

They hadn't spoken since they'd left the farm. That was an hour ago and they'd travelled exactly sixty miles in that time. All Leonard could think about was the elementary maths of it, the certainty of their speed, their sixty miles an hour.

His eyes were fixed on the road ahead. He knew, and he knew that Adeline knew, that they had to get some driving over and done with before they could bear to talk about what had gone wrong.

The road narrowed and became high-walled. They took a sharp bend and forded a stream, then climbed and reached a fork in the road. Leonard stopped the car and Adeline looked across at him.

'So, Leonard, just what in the hell are we going to do?'

'I don't know.'

They got out and paced around on the clean tarmac. Leonard put his hand on Adeline's shoulder and made a mess of trying to massage her back.

'It'll be OK.'

Leonard's promise had that ring of emptiness about it.

'Do we have any options? What are our options?'

'Well, listen. We either head up to the survival project, take our chances there and I try to smuggle you in.'

'Or?'

'There is an alternative. I met this character, he's built a shelter in the south and it's a pretty good idea. It's a DIY project, though. I mean, they didn't have a structural engineer on board or an architect or even a qualified construction team. There'd be no guarantee we'd get through the impact. But we could take our chances there.'

'You're saying it's dangerous?'

'No, it's just that I'm not sure I know how well the shelter will stand up to what's going to happen.'

'So really there are no options?'

'Listen to me. Alright, the chances of staying alive are higher in the escape pods but they are ruthless people and it's an unstable place. I have my reservations about how they plan to carry on. They are clinical survivors and they have some dangerous ideas about the future.'

'You've got to get me to the project site, Leonard. I've got to take my chances there.'

'OK, but Adeline, just so's you know: it's not going to be easy to get in. In fact it's going to be nearly impossible. And they don't mess around up there, they shoot on sight if they suspect anything's wrong.'

They got back in, Leonard dropped the handbrake and they pulled away.

CHAPTER TWENTY-FIVE

The impact coordinates of the Ice Moon had been revised, and as the primary shockwave would be travelling from the east, the positioning of the survival pods had also been revised. The pods had been rolled out of the hangars and transported by truck to a valley a few miles from the construction site. The new site was a deep valley which ran north-south; the pods would be positioned on the valley floor and therefore in the lee of the prevailing blast forces.

The whole area looked like some kind of Formula One race day. Men in fire retardant suits dragged leads across to the pods – they hooked up water, oxygen supply and battery charging cables.

The spheres were in different states of readiness, some were open and empty, while others were already sealed and stood ominously quiet.

Lena was sitting on the bus, leaning up against Beryl's shoulder, trying to work out what all this meant. She stood up every now and then and walked up and down the aisle just to see if she could recognise anyone. It would be difficult, though, with everyone wearing overalls and their heads covered with close fitting hoods. The bus was parked on a flat piece of road halfway up the side of the valley, so she had a good view of the whole area. It was like being on the deck of an aircraft carrier, with swinging gantries lifting and lowering the last of the pods into place.

She stood blocking the aisle, one elbow resting on the left hand head-rest, the other on the right.

'There's no sign of him, Nan.'

Beryl looked up at her.

'He's here somewhere, mark my words.'

Beryl was uncomfortable in her suit; it was very close-fitting, like a one-piece leotard, but made of brilliant white spandex. In short, it was not a flattering get-up. Lena liked hers, it was laced with thermostatic wiring. It fitted her perfectly and made her feel like she was part of a science fiction epic and about to travel into deep space.

There was a sound of compressed air escaping and the door at the front of the bus swung open. The man who'd stepped on took a microphone from the driver.

'OK everybody?'

There were some mumbled replies.

'Now then, first thing to say is that we are in a secured area but there are some military police on hand should there be any last minute problems. So I'll introduce myself: I'm Patrick and I am the overall coordinator of this stage of the survival programme. I don't have any last minute technical information. That will be given to you when you are placed into the survival pods. I am merely touring the buses to wish you all well and to say good luck. We've thought long and hard about how best to make it through this emergency, so trust me, you are in good hands. I hope to see you all as soon as possible after impact. Then we will regroup and go on to the next stage of the programme, in which I hope you will all be very willing participants. We will shortly be proceeding to a secured area where each of you will be placed into the survival pods. Thank you, and goodbye for now.'

There was a ripple of applause from the back of the bus. It is funny how the gut reaction always comes from the back of the bus.

CHAPTER TWENTY-SIX

A full day's driving was finally rewarded with an encouraging sign: a helicopter. It passed to the left of the road, flying fast and low, with its flashing, red tail-light blinking evenly. Leonard wound down his window to change the air in the cab. He heard some shouts and then a rifle shot rang out followed by a slow echo winding itself around the night sky. Leonard switched off the headlights.

'What are you doing?'

'We can't keep driving with our lights on with shots being fired, we're too easy to spot.'

A red flare ripped a straight line up into the sky; it burst and started to burn brightly as it fell back to earth.

Leonard stamped on the brakes; three soldiers were standing in the middle of the road in front of them. They raised their rifles and fired warning shots into the air. Leonard slammed the Land Rover into reverse and started to go back the way they'd come. The windscreen shattered as shots peppered the bodywork. Adeline screamed. She had a lapful of safety glass.

'Shit!'

'Leonard?'

He took her in his arms and locked his hands behind her back. She looked close to collapse and Leonard didn't feel good either; he felt suddenly drained, felt that life had brought him to one of its turning points. He was trying to think through Adeline, to plot with her and the half of his self that now existed in her womb; doubling and redoubling in silence, oblivious to the world it was heading toward.

'Take my tag, Adeline.'

'What?'

'The tag! There's no time to argue, just do as I ask. Please, before they arrive.'

Adeline broke away but Leonard pulled her back. He kissed her, held her top lip between his teeth and bit her lightly so that she would understand what she had to do.

She pulled away.

'Please, Adeline, we don't have any time, just do it!'

Leonard felt her tongue run underneath his lip and over the square ridge there. She held the tag between her teeth and waited. He shook her shoulders and she bit through and twisted her head away.

Intense pain flared out around Leonard's jaw and up to the top of his head. Adeline's face became ill-defined and blurred. Leonard had forgotten how red blood was; there was now a thick smear across her face. He felt his mouth start to fill with the stuff; he swallowed and felt for the damage with his own tongue. A ragged cut, mostly on the inside of his mouth. He wanted this, it seemed a fair price, the right price. It was an end to putting himself first, a letting go of one in favour of the other.

Leonard managed to gag his moans. He focused on soaking up the blood with his coat-sleeve.

The soldiers had reached the car and were shouting.

'Get out!'

Adeline held on to Leonard's arm.

'Leonard?'

'Just do as they say.'

They yanked the doors open and pulled them both out. Adeline fell to the floor, then was dragged away and scanned.

Leonard was ordered to sit on the ground and keep his hands on his head.

'OK, she's tagged.'

The soldier with the scanner paced over to Leonard. He passed the machine over Leonard's face.

'Negative here, Sarge!'

The sergeant turned away and spoke into his radio.

'Zone thirty four reporting one live pick-up, over.'

Adeline looked completely terrified and for the moment, Leonard didn't have a clue what to do. The sergeant listened to his instruction and shook his head.

'No, the male isn't tagged. Affirmative, just one female pick-up, out!'

The sergeant turned to Adeline.

'OK, you're coming with us. Load yourself up into our vehicle. Say goodbye to lover boy.'

'But we can't leave him here!'

'Shut up and do as you're told. He's not tagged, so he stays exactly where we found him, those are my orders.'

'I'm not going without him.'

The sergeant raised his eyebrows.

'It's simple: one tag, two people. You've got five minutes to say your farewells. Get on with it.'

They led Adeline around the front of the Land Rover. She pleaded with the sergeant.

'But he had a tag.'

'You're not going to be difficult, are you?'

She stood next to Leonard who was still down on the ground. He reached up for her hand, he couldn't remember if he had ever held her like this. Her nerve endings were raw because she flinched when they made contact; this was perhaps their most intimate moment.

The soldiers moved in, pulled her away and marched her downhill. Her face, when she looked back over her shoulder, was loaded with guilt. Yet the logic of what had happened was sound, the conspiracy between them had become strong.

Leonard braced himself against the side of the Land Rover and got to his feet. He wanted to keep his composure, to at least be upright for her last glance. Two thoughts vied for importance: they'd taken Adeline by force, yet he couldn't believe they hadn't killed him. He was in pain but he felt kind of OK, he didn't feel the need to tell anyone he'd been heroic. That he had done it was enough.

He opened the door and climbed into the seat. He ripped a rag in two and pressed one half against his lip to staunch the blood-flow. He wrapped the other half around his hand and smashed what was left of the windscreen out onto the road.

CHAPTER TWENTY-SEVEN

Tony unfolded the letter. This was the last correspondence from Adeline's mother and these were her last instructions. Tony held the sheet out in front and tried to focus his tired eyes. He read out loud, to himself.

'Now stand back and take a good look. All human intelligence, whether we like it or not, is brought to bear on the single goal of survival, of food, shelter and reproduction. We are low-life on the long road to revelation.

'All the ways and means, all the evaluations of science, the reluctances of art and philosophy, pale beside this sole purpose: that we must continue.

'You may be praying for survival but remember this, you are alone, no one, no thing can help you now. Do not, in the final hours, give yourself to legend, to manmade belief: nothing is preordained. This world is an accident; it pieced itself together, invented itself out of what was lying around. As for gods and guidance, don't hold your breath. I'm sorry to disappoint, but it's not the word of the Lord that you will hear when the time comes, it is your own voice coming back off the wall. Chose your words carefully, certain formulae may well save you.'

Tony went through it a few times but he still had no idea what the mad old bag was on about. The note was supposed to be a morale booster for when the shelter was finished. For when all that was left to do was to put himself inside and wait it out. Maybe he was missing something, maybe if she'd given him more to go on... And what was that about the right formulae?

Anyway, he'd lifted all the supplies up into the structure and he was pleased with himself. The construction was sound, an egg-like oval locked into the branches of the big ash, positioned twenty feet above the ground. It was comfortable inside; the spiral mesh of willow branches was pleasing to the eye, and one thing more: he had to admit that he felt safe inside.

CHAPTER TWENTY-EIGHT

Leonard had driven for a hundred miles or so, into the small hours, and he'd only taken a couple of rest stops. He was dehydrated, his eye sockets were sore, his mouth dry. But as long as he still had diesel in the tank, he'd keep on going. He didn't have much of a plan, just to get there and chance his arm.

He still had the metallic taste of blood in his mouth. The lip had swollen up; it had been throbbing like mad, ever since it happened. The pain had brought on one long headache, which was messing with his vision. If he forgot and made the wrong facial gesture, his lip cracked open and bled again. He hadn't tried to speak, there wasn't much point anyway, there being no one there to listen. He tried humming a tune to keep himself company, but any extension of the jaw was just too painful.

The landscape was featureless outside the range of the headlights. His field of vision consisted of a white line, the worn tarmac and the roadside bushes.

He picked up a flask and sucked some cool water in through a narrow gap in his lips. He swallowed repeatedly and the pain eased.

He turned uphill and after a short climb he crossed over the ridge and began the descent down into the next valley. The valley floor though was lit up like a county fare and buzzing with activity.

This was it: he'd found them and he'd been lucky because they'd moved the final, impact-ready position. Hundreds of survival pods were lying along the valley floor; it looked like they were being overlaid with steel cabling.

They strapped Beryl into her survival pod and she took a last look out at the starry night. She could see Lena moving along the queue for her turn. She wasn't far, but she was on her own. She looked too small to be out there by herself, too vulnerable. Beryl waved and when she had her attention, she blew her a kiss.

The ground crew were taking people out one by one. Adeline held her arms across her chest as she walked, her limb movements restricted by the network of climate control tubes sewn into her nylon flight-suit.

Every couple of minutes, a series of what sounded like rifle shots echoed around the valley. These were the explosive bolts, forty of them, detonating around the circumference of a pod as the two halves of titanium were sealed.

Adeline was ready now, now that she was being ushered forward. She had convinced herself that she was doing the right thing and that she had a good chance of making it into the future.

A crewmember helped her climb into her pod, checked her into the harness and was reassuring about how well designed the machine was. He explained how to check the carbon dioxide levels by monitoring the toxicity indicator. If it crept over a certain mark she would have to replace the lithium hydroxide canisters manually.

He gave her the thumbs up and Adeline reached up for the locking mechanism. She pulled it towards her and that was that: the bolts fired and she was safe inside. She looked up at the instrument readings and waited for the levels to settle.

The world was now hanging, as predicted, by a thread. All around the perimeter of the valley, a restraining net of steel cables had been bolted into the bedrock. It was like a huge envelope, designed to hold the survival pods in the same area.

Inside, Adeline was exhausted with the twin urges - to hate herself for taking Leonard's place and to reconcile the events and say that there was nothing else she could do.

She tightened the restraining harness and tried to stop thinking. She tried to lose herself in checking and rechecking the instruments. The only saving grace was the faint acknowledgment that the new life in her was Leonard's, too.

She pulled in the thick foam pads that had been designed to cradle her skull, and would stop her from being jarred and broken. She had to lie still now, like some fragile thing in its precious case, like a bulb made of glass, containing a precious, fluorescent element.

Leonard left the Land Rover higher up-slope; he was on foot now, with his boots digging into the mud. He felt self-conscious, felt like James Bond arriving for the final scene, with the set laid out below and the world hanging in the balance.

He heard something off to his right, a snap or a crack, a dry piece of wood or maybe a knee joint settling. He lay flat out and didn't budge. There was movement ahead; he couldn't believe it, a group of people were stealing, very quietly down-slope just ahead. When the moonlight brightened Leonard could make out that they were a band of lightly armed men and women, wearing a kind of ragged civilian camouflage. They reached the fence, which was a four-metre high perimeter of barbed wire. They paused there and cut their way through.

The dogs sounded the alarm; as soon as they began howling the shooting started. The security teams on the ground figured out what was happening and returned fire.

Leonard had his diversion; he moved down behind the wave of intruders and lined himself up in their wake. A mortar fired and smoke canisters detonated, then a van drove through the fence at high speed. It accelerated before security fired, then it veered out of control and crashed into the nearest line of survival pods.

The intruders were overrunning the area. When they reached the ground crews, they shot on sight and started to haul people out of the pods and take their places.

All the security teams could do was retreat and keep at least one part of the loading area secured.

Leonard hugged the terrain; he stayed low and used the smoke screen to cover his movements as he ran into the chaos. The pods that were already sealed were locked off, they were out of the game. The intruders knew this and didn't waste time, but ran on to the loading. Leonard broke away from the main thrust of the attack, made his way to the fence and tried to get ahead of the main exchanges of fire. Hand to hand fighting allowed him to pass, so he ran on and that was when he saw Lena. A technician was trying to help her into her seat, but as he strapped her in, he was shot in the back. The intruder turned his firearm on her and Lena closed her eyes.

Leonard hit him with his full force, which knocked the man forward into the hinge space in between the two halves of the survival pod.

The man turned and aimed his pistol but before he could shoot, Leonard threw the switch, which fired the door closing mechanism. The explosive bolts detonated, smashing the man's spine.

Lena screamed out and Leonard took her in his arms.

'It's alright, you'll be alright now. There's no time but don't worry, we'll see each other again, OK?'

She smiled and nodded that it was OK. He closed the pod and Lena fired the locking bolts.

Leonard took stock of the situation. With the last pods sealed, the fighting had dropped to sporadic gunfire. A few intruders, evicted survivors and wounded security men dragged themselves off to find solace.

Leonard had seen some fuel cans stacked near the gate, so he headed off in that direction. There was nothing more to do but retreat and take his chances on the long road South.

Adeline activated the onboard camera, which gave her a video image of the exterior. The picture was noisy and green for night vision, but she could see all too well what had happened outside. She panned the camera across a battlefield, the kind of periodical carnage that has always punctuated the history of the human race. She avoided an urge to count the bodies lying on the ground outside. They looked so similar like this, the innocent and the guilty, holding the same, lifeless gestures.

Survival is of the highest importance, yes, it is. But not at all costs, not like this. Adeline eased the restraining straps and took the weight of her head in her hands. It was not everything to survive and survival at all costs cursed the ones who lived to a haunted future. It's the way you protect your life and whether you care enough about the lives of anybody else, that matters.

Adeline kept panning; she swept the perimeter and then further afield to where a man carried something, maybe it was a fuel container. She knew this movement, this body. She could see that it was Leonard and he was climbing out of the valley away from her. Adeline felt sure then that his was the one life that mattered even more than her own.

Leonard unscrewed the fuel tank and started to pour diesel into the reserve. A mechanical clatter below sent an echo around the hills. Back on the valley floor a survival pod had been cracked open and bright light now spilled from it. He couldn't quite believe his eyes: Adeline was climbing out of her pod. She looked in his direction and waved, she shouted his name and started to run from the site. Fighting resumed behind her as several people bludgeoned one another over the rights to the abandoned pod.

Leonard jumped in, fired up the engine and took off downhill.

When he reached her he could not believe the beauty of the scene: her outline in the predawn and the valley floor smouldering behind her. She was suited up for space-flight and she seemed so much larger than life. She was a mythical, archetypal woman, a divine creature.

She jumped into the Land Rover and they held on to each other. She had not committed a foolhardy act; she was not the suicidal type. She asked him a straightforward question about the state of play.

'How much time do we have?'

'Just a few hours before we're smashed to bits.'

'D'you think we can make it to the shelter?'

'Of course we can. And when we get there I'll scream down the ventilation stack and they'll open up for us! I know they will, I can see Barry's face now, full of panic and triumph. They'll drag us inside and make a huge fuss!'

The eastern horizon lit up and Leonard stamped on the accelerator. The first rays of daylight shone in, low and hard through the trees. High winds swept debris across the road. Strobed lightning coloured in the northern skyline and rolling thunder discharged overhead.

CHAPTER TWENTY-NINE

Warden still had plenty of hate left in him and he hated looking out at the action through the limited angle of the narrow basement window. It was the same as when you looked in at the television set and couldn't see past the edge of the screen. On his last legs then, he scrambled up the stairs to street level and out of the basement, to watch the fireworks. He wasn't disappointed because the horizon was rolling in like a huge, black, tidal wave. He managed to resist the urge to curl up into a foetal mass. Instead, he lifted up his arms in a gesture of welcome and screamed at the top of his voice, wild as a warmonger riding the nose of a missile.

The air whistling through the gaps in the wickerwork carried with it a smell like hammered flint. Tony's nostrils were burning and his ears hurt too; he had a needling pain in his eardrums because the air pressure was fluctuating. He stayed low, curled up in the corner of the nest, and tried to conjure up the strongest prayer he could think of.

He felt charged with electricity, a tangible magnetic field was pressing against his temples. The enormous mass of the Ice Moon was tumbling ever closer now, in vacuum charged free-fall, at great speed, towards an attractive object.

Tony knelt up and looked to the East. Ahead of the approaching pressure wave, micrometeoroids whipped through the air. Tony's skin felt like it was being sandblasted with diamond dust.

A high-pitched thunder discharged overhead, then the roof of the shelter disappeared. Tony trembled as he lay on his back, he looked up at the sky and it unzipped from its zenith in a vertical line. He felt a vibrating sensation in the centre of his stomach, in that place called the pit. That place where pain is absorbed and where joy is felt. The last thing in the world that his mind recorded was the azimuth leaking flames and the sky splitting open like a smashed focus-finder.

The Land Rover howled as Leonard gunned the engine. He looked down at the oil temperature gauge and said a quiet prayer. He had to push it; there was no way of knowing how long they had before the first shockwaves would hit them. Leonard looked out at the lovely, undulating line of the hills. All these landscapes would go, in one fell swoop, all the contours, all the lanes and rivers would be screwed up into raw clay again and all the maps would be wiped clean.

Adeline couldn't do much in the passenger seat, her hands were clasped across her stomach and she looked straight ahead. She tried not to look to the eastern horizon, but she knew the skies were darker than they should be. She knew the winds were gusting gale force and that the flickering bursts of lightening were more and more frequent. She tried to relax, to breathe evenly; it wasn't good for the baby, none of this was any good for the baby. Their baby.

Leonard felt the ground tremors as they rumbled up through the steering column. It wasn't just the Land Rover's bone-shaking suspension; it was the earth beginning to move, for all the wrong reasons. For a moment the vibration became so intense he could barely see the road ahead, the fields and trees would not stay still enough. His eyes in their sockets could not believe what they were seeing. Debris, rolling in, house-sized rocks flying through the sky and clouds of dust drawing a cloak over the sun.

'Leonard!'

Adeline dug her fingers into Leonard's arm.

Leonard turned off into a gully, where they were in the lee of the airborne debris. Day had become night and the road had become a soot-covered track. It had begun to rain hard and the only glimmer of hope was a slight brightness low in the southern sky. The engine kept running and the wheels kept turning.

The tremor eased off and they willed their way out from under the cloak of darkness. They picked up speed going downhill, until they were hurtling along an exposed stretch of 'B' road. Leonard breathed evenly; in his mind's-eye he could see the flatlands, the reeds and marshes.

Acknowledgements

So many thanks are due to:

My lovely agent Brie Burkeman, for her lateral thinking and tenacity.
Franc Roddam, for picking me up out of the pile.
Sven Hughes.
Francis Delaney.
John A. V. Caldas.

Sogyal Rinpoche: 'Meditation'
Published by Harper Collins Canada.
ISBN 0062511149

'Development of Religion and Thought in Ancient Egypt'
Akhneten's Hymn to the Aten.
Abridged translation Prof James H. Breasted
Published by University of Pennsylvania Press (November 1, 1999)
ISBN: 081221045X

'The Structure and Dynamics of the Psyche'
(Collected Works of C.G. Jung, Volume 8)
Published by Bollingen; 2nd edition (January 1, 1970)
ISBN: 0691097747